Nicola Cornick will whisk you back to
Regency England – where you can
escape into a world of passion and
privilege...deceit and desire!

Deceived was the runner-up for the
Romantic Novelists Association's prestigious
Elizabeth Goudge Trophy 2005,
where it was judged to be:

"A masterclass... A vivid range
of emotions and sensations..."

NICOLA CORNICK

Deceived

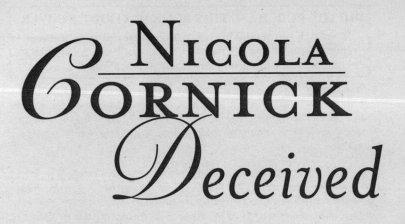

M&B™ and M&B™ with the Rose Device
are trademarks of the publisher.

First published in Great Britain 2007
Harlequin Mills & Boon Limited, Eton House, 18-24 Paradise Road, Richmond, Surrey, TW9 1SR

© Nicola Cornick 2006

ISBN: 978 0 263 85827 3

11-0307

Printed in Great Britain
by Clays Ltd, St Ives plc

Dear Reader,

When I was a child we used to go to the seaside every summer and stay in an old cottage with a wild garden. There were bent old trees to hide in, and stone statues, and the long golden curve of the sand to play on. It was this old house and garden that I remembered when I was writing *Deceived*. I wanted my heroine, Isabella, to have a place that she loved and could run away to. The old house at Salterton became the place of Isabella's childhood memories – and the place where she first met Marcus and fell in love. In the story, when Marcus, in his quest for revenge, threatens to take everything from Isabella, Salterton is the one place she is determined to fight for.

I love old-flame stories. I love reading them and I love writing them. There is something exciting about unfinished business and something poignant about what might have been. Can Isabella and Marcus overcome all the barriers and misunderstandings that fate has put between them and rekindle the love that they found in the house by the sea all those years ago? I hope that you enjoy reading *Deceived* and finding out!

With love,

Nicola

To the Cornick family with my thanks
and all my love.

Deceived

I recognize the marks of the old flame of love.
—*Dante*

Part 1–Revenge

London, June 1816

This newspaper is pleased to record the return to these shores of a certain notorious princess, whose arrival will be greeted with great glee by the gentlemen of the *Ton*. Rumor has it that the Princess IDC has not a feather to fly and is looking for a gentleman to ease her financial worries. Though whether the infamous lady will take him as lover or husband remains to be seen....
—*The Gentlemen's Athenian Mercury,* June 12, 1816

CHAPTER ONE

IT WAS A HELL OF A PLACE to look for a husband.

Most discerning females, given a choice of marriage mart, would prefer the genteel familiarity of Almack's any day to the rather more dubious qualifications of the Fleet Prison.

Princess Isabella Di Cassilis did not have that luxury. Princess Isabella was desperate.

She had explained to the jailer that her requirements were very specific. She needed to marry a man who owed so much money that to take on her twenty-thousand-pound liability would be a mere drop in the ocean of his debt. She needed a pauper—a strong one, since she did not want him dying on her and leaving her heir to his debts as well as her own—and she needed him now.

It was of no consequence to Isabella that she would be ruined if this escapade ever came to light. She was beyond ruin already. The more fastidious members of the Ton closed their doors to her, so what harm could a little more scandal do? She might even accomplish the remarkable success of being ruined twice over in one lifetime. It would be a considerable achievement for a lady of only nine and twenty.

Isabella Standish had not been born to be the princess of a European country, not even an insignificant one such as Cassilis. Her father had been a minor member of the Ton who'd aspired to be important but had never quite achieved his ambitions. Her grandfather had been fishmonger to King

George III, ennobled by the monarch in one of his bouts of madness after he had partaken of a particularly tasty piece of rainbow trout. The family title was therefore not only newly created but also the butt of some hilarity, to the great mortification of the second Lord Standish, Isabella's father.

It had been Isabella's misfortune that at the age of seventeen she had been walking down Bond Street the day before her wedding and had caught the roving eye of the jaded Prince Ernest Rudolph Christian Ludwig Di Cassilis, who had been charmed by her prettiness and her unspoiled manners. Prince Ernest had immediately made a counteroffer for her hand in marriage. It was an offer that her father was not minded to refuse, as he was about to be bankrupted by his extravagance. Prince Ernest's arrival was most timely, for Lord Standish if not for his daughter. The wedding that took place a few days later was not the one that Isabella had intended.

It was also entirely Prince Ernest's fault that a widowed Princess Isabella, some twelve years later, was following a turnkey down the narrow stone corridor into the depths of the Fleet Prison. Ernest had died most inconveniently in the arms of his mistress, leaving his widow nothing but debts and a tarnished name. When she'd returned home to England, Isabella had discovered that her late husband's infidelity had been financial as well as physical. He had run up debts in her name. He had used her to fund his debauches and she had been so happy to be on a different continent from him that she had not even noticed. So now she was driven to desperate measures of her own to extract herself from the disaster Ernest had brought on her.

Isabella shrank within her black cloak and pulled the hood more closely about her face. All her senses were under assault. It was almost as dark as night inside the prison. The air was thick with heat and the smoke of tobacco, but the scent did nothing to mask the deeper, more noxious smell of hundreds of fetid bodies pressed close. Raucous voices were raised in endless uproar, mingling with the scrape of iron fetters on stone and the wailing of babies and children in forlorn chorus. The floor was greasy and the walls ran with damp, even in the summer heat. Hands grasped blindly at the folds of Isabella's cloak as she passed. She could feel the despair of the place like a living thing. It seeped from the walls and wrapped her about with misery. Shock and compassion thickened her throat until the hairs rose on the back of her neck and she shivered with horror. Before she had entered this hellhole she had thought that she was in desperate straits. She had not even known what desperation was. And yet the distance between her situation and this was perilously short. A man—or woman—could slip once from their comfortable path and end up forgotten and unlamented in this pit.

She paused at the corner of the corridor and fumbled in her reticule for her small collection of coins. She could not really afford to part with them, but there were some whose need was greater than hers. She thrust the money toward the jailer.

"Here… Take these for the mothers and their babies."

The jailer shook his head. He did not take the money, for he still had a tiny shred of decency left. In the faint light his face betrayed pity but Isabella could not tell if it was for his charges or for her naiveté.

"With all due respect, ma'am, it would do no good. The mothers would spend it on gin and the babes would starve anyway."

Isabella hesitated, instinct prompting her to scatter the coins in the darkness and pray that some good would come of it. Then she saw the eyes watching her greedily from out of the shadows—insatiable eyes, full of hate and cupidity. The strong would trample the weak in their attempts to get to the money first and it would all be for nothing.

The turnkey took her arm, drawing her on. "Not far now."

Then, with a rough attempt at comfort as he felt her shiver, he added, "We keep a better class of prisoner in the Warden's House, madam. Nothing to fear."

Nothing to fear.

The words repeated over and over in her head as she shivered.

She had but three alternatives, Mr. Churchward had said with bluntness unusual in a lawyer. Marriage, or exile, or the debtor's prison. None of these options had been in any way appealing.

They had been sitting in the drawing room of her house in Brunswick Gardens when Churchward had broken the news of Ernest's debts. For all his frankness, the lawyer had spoken to her with compassion, as though such delicate matters were unfit for a lady's ears. Isabella had appreciated his thoughtfulness, and when she had neither fainted nor indulged in a fit of the vapors, Churchward had looked infinitely relieved.

A torch flared at the end of the passageway. The jailer opened a heavy door and it scraped across the floor with a protesting creak, as though there was seldom cause to use it. He stood back to allow Isabella to precede him. The air was fresher here, though it still carried the smells of tobacco, sweat and stale food.

The jailer stopped in front of a cell door, spat on the ground, then hastily wiped the back of his hand across his mouth as a concession to the fact that he was addressing a lady. "Here we are, madam. I have just the man for you. John Ellis. A gentleman by birth, healthy, very poor, so I'm told."

Somewhere in the depths of the jail, someone screamed. It was a sound unearthly and terrifying. Isabella shuddered and forced herself to concentrate. She knew that there were questions she should ask. If only she did not feel so callous and calculating. This was a man's life she was purchasing with the remains of her money. She bought her liberty at the price of his incarceration.

The plan had seemed quite neat in theory. Tidy, albeit ruthless. She would pay a prisoner to take on her debts. He would be behind bars. She would be free. Now that it suddenly involved a real person, the plan seemed grotesque. Nevertheless, it was his life or hers....

"Does he...have any family or friends?" She asked.

The jailer smirked. He understood what she needed to know. "No, madam. There is no one to buy him out of here and I am sure he could be persuaded to take your debts on into the bargain. He has nothing to lose by it."

"How long has he been here?" Now that she was on the point of committing herself, Isabella found that she was hesitating, looking for opportunities to put off the moment.

"Three months, near enough, and set fair to be here for the rest of his time, so I understand." The jailer cocked his head as he looked at her. "You'd not be wanting it any other way, ma'am?"

"No, thank you," Isabella said. "A permanently absent husband is precisely what I require."

The jailer touched the crisp banknotes that were nestling in his pocket. He had seen a number of ladies come to the Fleet in search of husbands. Some were looking for a father, no matter how belatedly, for an infant that was about to make its appearance in the world. Others were looking to escape a repugnant match. A few, like this lady, were trying to evade a crushing debt by marrying a man who was already in jail and could take on his wife's obligations as well as his own without it making a ha'porth of difference to him. There were plenty of men in the Fleet who would have been willing to take her on for the price of a bottle of gin, but the lady's requirements were precise. She was Quality, and she needed a man who was a gentleman by birth, but desperate enough not to be too scrupulous. Fortunately he knew plenty who fit the bill.

There was quality and then there was Quality with a capital

Q, the jailer mused. No amount of clothing borrowed from a maid could conceal the fact that this was a lady, possibly even a countess. She vibrated with a kind of despair that he had seen many times before when a person was about to make a pact with the devil. The jailer had little pity left in him. Sentiment was dangerous in his job. He fingered the money once again. Countess, duchess, it mattered nothing to him. He would find a match for the queen herself if she paid him enough. And he would ask no questions.

The door of the cell crashed open and another turnkey tumbled out, slipping on the greasy floor and spilling the contents of the tray he carried. He was swearing under his breath. The thin stew slid off the plate and splattered Isabella's cloak.

"And don't come back until you have something edible to offer me," a masculine voice said from within the cell. It was a pleasant voice but it was edged with a distinct undertone of menace.

"Is that your Mr. Ellis?" Isabella said dryly, as something thudded against the cell door as though to emphasize the words further. "It sounds as though he has the devil's own temper."

"Aye, a surly fellow is John Ellis," the jailer confirmed. "Not that you need trouble yourself over that, ma'am."

"I imagine that I would be bad tempered were I incarcerated in here," Isabella said. She looked about her and shivered. "Best to get it over with, then."

The cell was dark, lit only by one small barred window high in the wall. The first thing that shocked Isabella was that this better class of gentleman did not even possess the means to purchase a room of his own. He must be poor indeed. Her second thought was that this was not the more spacious and airy accommodation of the higher reaches of the Warden's House, but a dim chamber where the air was almost as fetid as in the stews. She felt sick with nerves and disgust.

Three men were crouching on the floor playing a game with dice and counters. They barely looked up as the door opened, so intense was their concentration. Only pennies were being wagered but the world could have ended and they would not have broken up the game.

Another man squatted in a far corner where the water ran down the walls and soaked his shirt. He appeared not to notice it. He was rocking on his heels and crooning softly to himself, and he looked at Isabella with incurious eyes. She looked back with grief and pity, remembering the times when she had been in a position actually to aid such poor unfortunates rather than look at them with such helplessness.

The thought recollected her to her current situation and she looked around for Mr. John Ellis, her unlikely savior.

At first she could not discern him at all, other than as a shadowed figure seated at the rough table with his back to the light. Then he moved, and she saw that he had been reading, for he still had a book in his hand.

Despite the jailer's description of him as surly, Isabella saw humor and vitality in his expression before it was quenched like a blown candle, leaving nothing but a grim austerity. In the dim light his face was hard, all clear-cut planes and angles beneath a dark tan that spoke of much time spent in hotter climates. His jaw was strong and square, and the uncompromising lines of his face were too harsh to be described as conventionally handsome. That seemed too soft a word. He emanated an attraction far more primitive and compelling than mere good looks. It was an attraction to take the breath away. Isabella had met many handsome men, men of charm and address. A princess tended to have such privileges. None of them, however, had driven the sense from her mind and the breath from her body in a way that made her feel slightly faint.

John Ellis placed the book on the table in front of him and

looked up at her for a very long moment. There was a stillness about him that was striking. He did not say a word.

"Stand up when a lady enters the room," the turnkey snapped at him.

The gentleman allowed his gaze to travel very slowly and insolently down Isabella's entire body, from the peak of her hood to the tips of her shoes. Then, with equal deliberation, he removed his booted feet from the table and sat up a little straighter, but still he did not stand. There was an insolent appraisal in his eyes that brought the blood to Isabella's face and her chin up in haughty defiance. His gaze fixed on her face and he did not look away for a single instant. His eyes were hard, his expression that of a man who has seen and done too much and will never again feel any emotion stronger than indifference.

Recognition, shocking and instantaneous, hit Isabella in the stomach. The world closed in around her. She felt seventeen again and a heedless debutante, barely more than a child. She remembered how her eyes had met those of this gentleman, not across some romantically crowded ballroom, but prosaically, over the teacups in her aunt's shabby drawing room at Salterton.

"Who is that young man?" she had asked her aunt, Lady Jane Southern, and Jane had smiled and replied:

"His name is Marcus Stockhaven, my dear, and he is a lieutenant in the navy." Jane had frowned a little as she'd watched Isabella's expressive face. "Do not develop a *tendre* for him, Bella, for your mama would never allow the match. He is a nobody."

She had spoken too late, of course. The *tendre* had blossomed instantly as Isabella had sat there, her gaze locked with the direct dark one of the man in the doorway. She had felt excited and faint and deliciously helpless to fight against her fate.

"He has no money and no expectations and your mama

wishes you to marry well," Jane had reminded her crisply, but her words of warning had been like an echo fading in the dark. Isabella had paid them no heed and had rushed headlong into first love. It had been a love that was going to end, quite properly, in a wedding. But then she had been obliged to marry Prince Ernest and everything had gone wrong....

Now, as her gaze met and held that of Marcus Stockhaven in much the same way as it had done in that faded drawing room twelve years before, Isabella felt a stunning sense of awareness and loss. A longing seared through her that made both the love and the heartbreak feel sharp and alive, as though all the feelings she had thought were dead had merely been sleeping and were awoken to instant life.

Then Stockhaven spoke, and the shackles of the past were broken.

"A lady," he said thoughtfully, his gaze still resting on her. "I think you mistake. What possible reason could a lady have for coming here?"

One of the gamesters looked up and made a remark so coarse that Isabella winced. She raised a hand to stop the swelling indignation of the turnkey.

"Thank you," she said crisply. "I will deal with this. Please show...Mr. Ellis...and myself to a room where we may speak alone."

Her request caused some consternation. Evidently the jailer had not anticipated that she would require a private conversation and there were few facilities to deal with such an eventuality.

Marcus Stockhaven got to his feet. "You wish to speak privately with me, madam?"

"I do," Isabella said.

Stockhaven's voice was smooth and cold and its tone was mocking. "Surely you are aware that the price of privacy is higher than rubies in a place like this, madam?"

"It is fortunate then that I have brought my emeralds with me," Isabella said, with composure. "Their price *is* higher than that of rubies."

She put her hand in her reticule and withdrew the emerald bracelet that Ernest had given her when their daughter was born. He had told her that had the child been a boy then the bracelet would have been of diamonds. The emeralds were second best, like her marriage. She had never quite measured up to Ernest's expectations, but at least his gift would come in useful at last.

In the dark light of the cell, the jewels glimmered with a deep radiance. The gamblers paused; one swore with awe and avarice.

"A private room," Isabella repeated to the jailer. "At once."

"At once, madam," the jailer repeated, adjusting his assessment of her from countess to duchess. He had not considered the possibility of a foreign princess because she sounded so English.

An empty cell was found in short order. It was bare but for a moldy mattress, one hard chair, a table and a slop bucket. It was also cold. The jailer grabbed the bracelet from Isabella's outstretched hand and it disappeared into his pocket quicker than a mouse down the throat of a snake. Marcus Stockhaven tucked his book beneath his arm and followed her from the one prison cell into the next with as little concern as though he were taking a walk in the park. Isabella admired his nerve at a time when her own feelings were in tatters. Her nerves were trembling; the conflict inside her echoed by a telltale quiver through her body.

The door scraped closed. There was a long silence, which Stockhaven did not break. He did not offer her the chair but took it himself, sitting watching her, his head at a slight slant, a quizzical look in his dark eyes. Isabella found it deeply unsettling. But then, he had always been able to disturb her with a mere glance.

"Well?"

Isabella jumped at the authoritative tone. Already it felt as though the balance of power in the interview was tilting away from her and that was all wrong. She needed to keep control of this. It was imperative that she dictate the terms. She struggled to regain the initiative.

"I—" Suddenly the words stuck in her throat. It was inconvenient to be troubled by scruples now. After she met with Churchward, she had gone straight out to the Doctors Commons to procure the special license. From there she had gone to the Fleet to purchase a husband. Desperation had kept her going and prevented her from questioning her actions too deeply. Whenever doubts had surfaced, she had fixed on the grim prospect of prison, and that had blotted out all else. But now, under the pitiless dark stare of Marcus Stockhaven, she was lost for words.

Stockhaven raised one black brow sardonically. "I have all the time in the world," he said, "but I would prefer you to state your business as soon as possible, madam. It is a surprise to see you after all this time, and not a particularly welcome one. So…" He shrugged, and said, "Say your piece and let me get back to my book."

Isabella swallowed hard. So he was not going to greet her with open arms. Of course not. How foolish of her to expect it when she had jilted him in the most painful and humiliating way imaginable. The shreds of their past passion mocked her.

"I thought that it was you," she said slowly. "I recognized your voice."

"How very flattering, after all these years," Stockhaven said dryly. He leaned his chin on his hand. "What are you doing here?"

Isabella glanced toward the door, where she imagined that the turnkey's ear was welded to the grille. There could be no names exchanged now if she wanted to preserve her anonymity, as presumably he wished to preserve his.

"I was looking for someone," she said.

"But not me, I assume." Stockhaven came to his feet with a compact grace. He was tall and broad-shouldered and his presence seemed to dominate the shabby cell. There was latent power in every line of his body—power that the stuffy confines of the room could not stifle. Isabella found that she was instinctively backing away, though he made no move toward her. She took a deep breath and forced herself to hold her ground.

"No, I was not looking for you specifically," she said, "but now that I have found you—" She paused. Could she come out with the proposal now? No, that was a little too blunt, even for her. Besides, there were things that she wished to know.

"More to the point," she said, "what are *you* doing here, sir, under the name of John Ellis?"

She saw his dark gaze narrow on her acutely, and although his expression was blank a few seconds later, she read his feelings clearly enough. This mattered to him. He did not want her to give his true identity away and he would certainly have preferred that she had not stumbled across him in the Fleet of all places.

"Forgive me, but that is none of your business." His tone was clipped.

"I think it might be." Isabella took a step farther into the cell. There were a hundred and one doubts and reasons hammering in her mind, telling her that it was the worst possible idea in the world to petition Marcus Stockhaven to marry her. She ignored them. She had been offered a chance, the possibility of a bargain, and she was going to take it.

"I have a proposition for you, sir," she said, once again careful not to address Stockhaven by name. "Help me and I will…help you. At the least, I will hold my tongue and tell no one that I have seen you."

Marcus Stockhaven did not speak. There was a quality in his silence that intimidated her. She hurried on. "I do not suppose that anyone knows that you are here?"

Still he did not reply.

"I do not suppose that you *wish* anyone to know that you are here?" Isabella pursued.

This time she saw that her words had penetrated his silence. He gave an involuntary movement. Again that hard, dark gaze raked her. "Perhaps not."

"The disgrace of the debtor's prison—"

"Quite so," he interrupted her. "Are you seeking to blackmail me, madam?" His mouth twisted in an ironic smile. "I regret I cannot pay."

"I do not want your money," Isabella said. "I need a favor."

"A favor from me?" Stockhaven's smile deepened. "You must be desperate indeed to even think of asking."

"Perhaps so. As you must be to be here in the first place."

Stockhaven acknowledged the hit with an inclination of the head. "So? In what way may we be…mutually…helpful?"

There was an element in his tone that brought color to Isabella's cheeks. There had always been something about this man that cut straight through her defenses and made them as thin as parchment. She felt astonishingly vulnerable, deeply disturbed by his presence and the memories he stirred. She sought to disguise her nervousness.

She looked around the filthy cell, from the water seeping through the walls to the bare mattress boasting a single dirty blanket.

"In return for a favor from you, I will not only hold my tongue but I am prepared to make your stay here more comfortable," she said. "A room of your own, clean linen, good food and wine—" she looked at the book he had placed on the table "—more books to read…"

Isabella saw his gaze narrow on her thoughtfully. She took

a step closer to him in silent appeal. For a moment Marcus Stockhaven was silent. She could feel herself trembling as she waited for his response.

"How generous," he said. "So what is it that you want?" His tone was even but his dark eyes were very cold.

Isabella took a deep breath. For a moment she was poised on the brink and then there was no return.

"I want you to marry me," she said.

CHAPTER TWO

IT WAS DOWNRIGHT OUTRAGEOUS.

Marcus John Ellis, seventh Earl of Stockhaven, had been waiting for an opportunity like this for twelve long years. He had not expected it to present itself in the Fleet Prison.

Marcus was accustomed to dealing with the unforeseen. Eight years spent in His Majesty's Navy before unexpectedly coming into a distant cousin's earldom had given him a wide and colorful experience of life. This, however, was something that he could never have anticipated. It was ironic, amusing, extraordinary. And it should have been out of the question, of course. But it was also remarkably tempting.

"You are twelve years too late, my love," he said sardonically, and watched the color rush into Isabella's cheeks at his casually cruel use of the endearment that had once meant so much.

"The church was booked, the bridegroom in attendance, the only thing that was missing was the bride—if you recall."

He watched her thoughtfully. She looked almost the same and yet heartbreakingly different from the debutante of seventeen who had jilted him at the altar. In the dank confines of the prison, she seemed hopelessly out of place. It made no odds that she had taken steps to disguise her appearance with a plain black cloak and practical boots. For a start, she was a great deal cleaner than anyone else who had set foot in his cell during the past three months. Then there was the fact that she smelled not of rank sweat and tobacco but innocently of jasmine. He remembered that scent on her skin and in her hair. Autumn hair, he had once told her, layered with hues of gold and copper and russet like fallen leaves. The memory sharpened an edge of hunger in him. He felt his body harden in response to images that were as potent now as they had been twelve years before. Isabella naked in his arms, his hands on her, dark against the paleness of her skin, her gasp of shocked delight as their bodies touched, famished, desperate, forgetful of everything but the shimmering desire that burned between them. He had taken her fiercely, with no consideration for her virginity, and she had responded with unguarded passion. Then, afterward, in the intimate dark of the summerhouse…

"I should not have been so wanton…." She had sounded astonished at her own behavior and the capacity for pleasure that he had unlocked within her. He had drawn her damp body close to his and kissed her with humility and a blissful disbelief that had echoed her own.

"You are lovely and I will always love you."

It had been sentimental, boyish stuff and it had been ripped apart brutally when she had left him standing at the altar and married someone else. Yet infuriatingly, no one had ever compared to Isabella in his eyes, not in all the long years since he had last seen her.

They had met as often as they could in the gardens of Salterton House. The secrecy had added an edge of excitement to their trysts that seemed well nigh unendurable. He had burned up with the need to possess her, each time more potent than the last, each caress a brand on her skin that was echoed in his heart. There, in the cool darkness of the summerhouse, he would pull her to him, his hands feverishly pushing aside the lace and silk of her clothing, kissing her with savage fervor, invading her body with his in a heated tangle of desire and need. The turbulent emotions she aroused in him had driven him to near madness.

Marcus blinked to dispel the memories and tried to rein in his galloping imagination. Such images were not conducive to clear thinking. But it was no wonder that he lusted after her even now. He had been a long time without a woman, for the whores who plied their trade in the Fleet held no interest for him. Besides, this woman would be enough to tempt a saint.

"Your love," she said, and the ragged anger in her tone quenched his desire as sharply as a bucket of cold water. "I was never that, was I, Marcus? You married India quickly enough after you lost me. One cousin or the other—it seems it mattered little to you which."

Marcus felt a violent flare of fury. He had been waiting twelve years to have this very subject laid bare between them and now she dared to put the blame on him?

"I was never so careless as to *lose* you, as you put it," he said. "You discarded me when your prince made a better offer—"

She made an instinctive gesture of protest and he broke off. His heart leaped. For a second he had been convinced that she was about to refute his claim and say something of profound importance. He waited, in hope and sharp anticipation. Then her eyes went blank and he could feel the moment slip frustratingly away.

"You are correct," she said. "That was precisely what I did. But that was a long time ago and this squabbling avails us nothing. It was foolish of me to think that you would be more inclined to help me than a stranger would. I imagine that the reverse is true."

It *was* true. To see her now brought all Marcus's feelings of anger and betrayal flaring into life again. For her to admit to being as venal as he had believed, with such barefaced lack of regret, seemed almost impossible. And yet it was all of a piece with her behavior. She had married for advantage, scorning him when a more promising offer had come along. She had cheated her cousin India out of her inheritance. And now she needed money again and she was prepared to bargain for it with the same ruthless lack of sentiment.

Only this time it appeared that he held all the cards. She needed his help. She was in his power.

"Sit down," he said abruptly. The demand came out more harshly than he had intended and he saw her jump. She was as tense as a wild animal on the edge of flight. It was implicit in the way her fingers were locked together to prevent them from shaking visibly, and in the determination and anxiety he could read in those dark blue eyes. Evidently she was in such dire straits that even she felt nervous.

She looked startled at his request, as though she had assumed he would refuse her and tell her to be gone. He could see that she was anxious to leave now but he wanted to detain her. He had been given a second chance, unexpected and startling as it was. He had been given the opportunity for revenge.

It would not be simple. He would have to lure her into trusting him, but she was desperate and so he had a good chance of success. She *must* be desperate to even think of petitioning him for marriage, with what stood between them. He could tell that she was driven to extreme measures. He could read it in her uneasiness. So it was time to take advantage.

He gestured to the chair, moderating his tone.

"I beg your pardon. Will you not take a seat, Isabella?"

Her eyes widened a little at his use of her name. It appeared that she was about to give him a setdown for his familiarity. That was revealing. Very few women rebuffed Marcus Stockhaven. Mostly they encouraged any intimacy he was prepared to grant.

"No, thank you," she said. "I prefer to stand."

He understood instinctively that she had no wish to be put at a disadvantage by sitting while he had perforce to remain on his feet, there being only one chair in the cell. She was feeling vulnerable already and did not wish to give him the upper hand. Most decidedly she was a challenge. He felt his interest quicken.

"We could both sit down together over there," he said, gesturing to the mattress in the corner.

There was a flash of disdain in her eyes. "I think not, sir. I do not seek to share your bed."

"Not this time." Marcus allowed his dark gaze to sweep over her once again. He kept all bitterness from his tone. "You merely want my name this time, or rather, my alias, since I imagine that anonymity suits your purpose as well as it suits mine. I am assuming that you wish to take advantage of my imprisonment for debt?"

He paused. A slight inclination of the head was her only reply.

"So." He thought about it. "You owe money. A considerable sum."

He saw a flicker of what looked like anger in her eyes but again she merely nodded.

"Your plan is to marry a debtor who agrees to take on your liability as well as his own. There is nothing your creditors can do to recover the money. Meanwhile your husband languishes in here for the foreseeable future and you are free to do as you wish. Do I have it aright?"

"In every detail." She matched him in coolness, although he was certain that beneath the facade she was nowhere near as dispassionate as she appeared. He gave a short laugh, incredulous. It seemed that she never changed. It had all been about money before and so it was again.

"You certainly have the effrontery to carry it off, madam."

"Thank you," Isabella said sweetly.

There was a short silence, sharp with defiance. She raised her brows.

"So? Do you accept my proposal?"

Marcus almost laughed at her audacity. He was tempted to

capitulate—she was walking straight into his trap, running even—but if he was to find out the things he wanted to know, he realized that he had to press his advantage first.

"Forgive me," he said, "but there are certain things I must know before I consider granting you the protection of my name."

She gave him a dry look. "I misjudged your situation then, sir. Are you in a position to be any more selective than I?"

Infinitely. Marcus did not say the word aloud, but he thought it. Isabella was not to know that, of course. She had assumed, not unnaturally, that he was confined in the Fleet because he was in debt. All indications suggested it, but it was in fact far from the truth. And since she had not asked him outright, Marcus was not about to tell her.

"How much do you owe?" he inquired. He pulled the chair toward him and sat astride it with his arms along the back, training his gaze on her face.

Her chin came up. She looked haughty. He read in her expression that she did not like the situation she was in and the measures she was obliged to take. She put him straight immediately.

"I owe nothing on my own account," she said. "My late husband ran up debts of twenty thousand pounds in my name. I was abroad and had no notion of it. It was only when I returned to this country that I discovered the extent of my difficulty." She stopped, biting her lip to quell the anger that was so evidently bubbling inside. Marcus smiled at the snappish tone. So she was furious with Prince Ernest Di Cassilis for landing her in such a predicament. She was proud and she hated her situation. Proud, beautiful and bankrupt. A damnable combination.

"How very annoying for you when Prince Ernest used to be such a rich man," he said affably. "Such misfortune can overset anyone's plans."

Her eyes flashed. She understood all the things that he was

implying. That she had jilted him because he was poor. That she had married Ernest for his title and his money. That everything that had come upon her was poetic justice.

"As you say." Her tone was colorless. "It is most unfortunate."

He had to admire her coolness. She had shut the door firmly in his face and denied him the pleasure of provoking her.

"If Prince Ernest had a penchant for misusing your name, you might have wished to keep him under closer scrutiny," he said.

To his surprise, he saw a flicker of amusement in her face.

"I had no wish to be anywhere near Ernest, sir," she said. "In fact, I ignored him as often as possible. No one liked him very much and I was not the exception to the rule. I even had to bribe the servants to attend his funeral and pay them double to put on a pretense of grief."

Marcus could feel his interest becoming more acute. He could not seem to help himself. When he had first met Isabella, he had been bowled over by her apparent sweetness. When she jilted him, it had been a profound shock. He had realized then that she was an adventuress. She had used that tempting body and wayward prettiness to entrap a rich and dissolute prince. Now she was using a different form of bribery to lure him into a marriage of convenience. Anger shook him. He wanted to make her admit her culpability. She was defiant and morally corrupt and ready to sell herself for gain. And he was no longer a green youth to be taken in.

He looked at her a little quizzically. "So it was not worth it in the end, then?"

Their eyes met.

It was never worth it.

Isabella did not say the words aloud, but for a disconcerting moment Marcus was sure that he had read them in her eyes.

"I cannot see the purpose of your impertinent questions," she said sharply. "I do not care to speak of my marriage."

Marcus raised his brows. "You do not think, then, that you owe me an explanation for what happened twelve years ago?"

She looked disdainful. "What can that matter now?"

He wanted to shake her. Of course it mattered. She had taken all his youthful dreams and hopes and crushed them beneath the heel of her dainty shoe. And she had done it in passing, as though it had been of no importance. She had stolen his illusions. He had been physically experienced when he had met her. He had been the seducer. He accepted that. Yet he had also been emotionally untried, with a youthful innocence and trust that had been entirely at her mercy. It was that which Isabella had ended and for that she owed him.

He thought of India. His wife. She had been Isabella's cousin. He knew that he had married her for all the wrong reasons, grasping after something that Isabella had promised that had eluded him. India too had suffered at her cousin's hands. Marcus had discovered how Isabella had set her family against one another in her quest for riches and status. She had been entirely driven by greed.

Now was the time to collect on the debt she owed him, but he had to bide his time. He could feel his anger increasing with every word and sought to control it with cool reason. It was true that cold-blooded revenge was more satisfying than a hasty reprisal. He would accept her proposal and then, although she did not know it, she would be in his power rather than the other way around.

There were still a few things that he needed to know. The more he knew of her plans, the easier it would be to thwart her.

He shrugged. "Perhaps you are right and what has passed between us no longer matters. After all, this is a matter of business. Explain to me how you envisage our agreement working."

She gave him a suspicious look, as though she could not quite believe that he had let the matter go so easily, but then she capitulated. Evidently she was so anxious to secure her future that she was prepared to make concessions.

"This so-called marriage between us would be a short-term measure to see me over a temporary financial embarrassment," she said. "Once I have sold my house and realized my inheritance, the debt will be paid off and the marriage annulled."

Marcus frowned. "In that case, can you not simply wait for your money to come through? It would surely be easier than contracting a marriage you do not want."

Isabella was shaking her head. "Matters of inheritance take time to resolve and it is time that I do not have. But in a little I shall be unencumbered by both debt and marriage."

There was a pause. Marcus found that his pride revolted at the thought of being used and discarded, no matter that he was manipulating the situation as much as she.

"I dislike the idea of being married off and then dismissed at a whim," he said slowly. "It is demeaning."

Isabella smiled with genuine warmth this time. "Well," she said sweetly, "you now know how it feels to be a woman."

Touché. He felt the clash between them like a ripple of memory along the skin. This was how it had always been with Isabella. She would challenge him rather than placate him as most women were wont to do. She had been unpredictable and exciting, and the friction between them had driven his need to take and possess her. He had been besotted with her. He had proposed marriage; she had accepted. That last spring at Salterton, before she had returned to London, they had plighted their troth secretly in the gardens and he had promised to follow her up to Town with all speed and ask her father for permission to pay his addresses to her. Marcus had not been concerned about his lack of prospects. He was a man who took his opportunities and sought out new ones. It never occurred to him that he had nothing to offer.

Lord Standish had agreed to his suit with a remarkable lack

of enthusiasm. If Marcus believed that he had prospects, his future father-in-law had not been so easy to convince. Marcus had been undeterred. He had remained undeterred up until the last moment when he had been waiting in the church of St. Mark's in the Field—the fashionable St. George's in Hanover Square having already been booked—and had noticed a suspicious lack of guests on the bride's side of the nave. Time had ticked past and Isabella had failed to arrive. Even at the last, Marcus had been unable to believe that she had jilted him. He had tried to see her, only to be turned away from her house. He had sworn that he would not believe ill of her until he heard her reject him with her own words. But she had never offered him an explanation either way.

She had never spoken to him again.

Society had been quick to judge. When the absent bride married Prince Ernest Di Cassilis in a private ceremony by special license the very next day, scandal had burst over them in a tidal wave. Ernest carried his new wife off to Cassilis and Marcus had returned precipitately to sea. He had felt a great need to be occupied. And so he had pursued the French instead of women, had gained commendations of his superior officers for his reckless bravery and had never wanted to return to shore. It was only the unexpected inheritance of the earldom from his childless cousin that had obliged him to accept a different type of responsibility. He had taken up his estate reluctantly, gone up to London and met India Southern, Isabella's cousin, at a ball…

But he would not think about that. Throughout his marriage to India, the ghost of Isabella had dogged their steps. He had never been able to forget her or dismiss the powerful feelings of recognition he had felt for her from the first. He felt the same attraction as before calling to him now, drawing him in. They looked at one another and the air between them was bright with the sparks of that old flame.

Marcus had not meant to stir up old memories. What he had meant to do was discover exactly what Isabella intended with this marriage of convenience. It was also important to know that there were no troublesome lovers hanging about who might jeopardize his plans. The fact that Isabella was here alone and unprotected in the Fleet suggested that she had no current lover, but he had to be certain.

He turned away from her, crushing down the attraction, feigning indifference.

"I do not understand why you needs must make a Fleet marriage," he said. His voice was a little rough, betraying him. "Surely there are a dozen rich and respectable men queuing up to offer for you, Isabella? Twenty thousand is not so much to a man of means, particularly if he gains a beautiful wife into the bargain."

Isabella did not appear to take this as a compliment. Marcus was interested since he thought it inevitable she must have been told many times that she was a beauty. People tended to tell princesses that even if it were not true.

"There is no one I wish to marry," Isabella said, "and more to the point, no one who would wish to marry me."

Her head was bent and she evaded his gaze. Marcus thought she seemed genuinely ruffled. He watched her, waited.

"I have…that is, my reputation—" She looked up suddenly and the expression in her eyes went straight through Marcus's defenses like an arrow into the heart.

"You may not have heard it, but my reputation is ruined," she said with a simplicity that reminded him of the girl she had once been. "No one respectable will offer me marriage now."

Marcus's eyes narrowed. He had heard all the stories. He knew her name was soiled beyond repair. Prince Ernest Di Cassilis had been known as the Profligate Prince. His debauches in all areas of his life were legendary. It was inevitable that his wife should be tarred with the same brush.

Once again he allowed his gaze to travel over Isabella, itemizing the evidence as he went. Beneath the shadow of the hood, her gaze met his directly. Her eyes, wide and blue, were very clear. Although she was no debutante now, a youthful innocence had survived in her face. It was impossible—utterly impossible—to see her as a woman with a terminally tarnished reputation.

He felt a moment's savage pleasure at what had befallen her. Call it revenge or bitterness or even justice, but an ignominious part of him wanted her to be unhappy and to suffer for her betrayal of him. Yet at the back of his mind was the smallest flicker of sympathy for her. He denounced himself as a fool. She was a witch and he cursed his susceptibility.

"Put back your hood," he said abruptly.

She paused. It was evident that she had grown more accustomed to giving than receiving orders. But then she complied and pushed back the hood of her cloak.

The impression of virtue was reinforced when he could see her properly. She had the sort of face that had been pretty in youth but had matured into beauty as she grew older. Her hair was dark gold, straight and fine, simply confined by a blue ribbon. Thick black lashes shadowed the line of her cheek. There was strength as well as beauty in the bones of her face; he looked again and amended that to resilience. Something—or someone—had made her suffer and she had learned to endure it and be strong. Marcus knew a little about how that felt. For a moment he experienced an odd mix of curiosity, protectiveness and anger at the thought of anyone hurting her. The love he had had for her had run deep and it was difficult to forget.

Damn it. Damn her. He was turning soft at the very moment he had to be ruthless.

Isabella raised one dark brow in ironic query and he realized that he had been staring. Truth to tell, it was difficult not to. He wanted to kiss her. No, he would not stop at mere kissing. He would do a great deal more. He wanted her very much.

"Well?"

It was her turn to snap the question. Marcus reflected ruefully that she might have a mouth lush and made for kissing but her tongue was as sharp as a seamstress's needle.

He shook his head.

"I cannot believe you would receive no offers," he said. "Surely you exaggerate—"

"No." She shut her lips very tightly. It was evident that no further information would be forthcoming on that topic. Their eyes met and held. He could feel the tension in her. She was desperate but she would never beg.

Marcus let out a long, careful breath. He could turn her away, in which case she would be ruined and left to molder in the debtor's prison herself. He would like to see that happen. It would be a poetic revenge.

On the other hand, he could marry her and exact a different and rather more satisfying form of retribution.

Isabella was not taking the delay well. He was pleased to see that she was barely able to control her impatience. Good. He needed her to be so on edge that she would snap up his offer when he finally made it.

She walked over to the table and picked up the book that he had been reading, holding the spine to the light so that she could see the title. *"Theoretical Naval Architecture,"* she read aloud. "It would need to be theoretical since I am told that you are likely to spend the rest of your days in here, sir."

Marcus cocked a brow.

"So?" he said. "What is your point?"

She flicked him a glance. "My point is that according to the jailer you owe a great deal of money. More than you are ever likely to be able to pay. Your family and friends are apparently unwilling to help you. Or perhaps—" she put the book down and looked up to meet his eyes "—as I suggested earlier, they do not even know that you are here? I am guessing that that is why you use the name of John Ellis. It is a sop to your pride and to keep your shame from being known in the Ton. So… you would not wish me to tell anyone your true whereabouts, or make your disgrace known…"

Her blackmail made him smile inwardly. It seemed she would stop at nothing to get what she wanted. But there was a problem. She had stumbled very close to the truth through making all the wrong inferences. It was certainly the case that no one knew he was in the Fleet and that he could not afford for the information to become public. It was not because he was ashamed of his debt, though. He was running a complicated operation and no one could know about it. Isabella could not be permitted to tell the world what she had deduced.

Even so, he would play the game by his rules, not hers.

"So you seek to persuade me to change my mind by offering to keep my presence here a secret if I agree to marry you?" He arched an eyebrow. "It seems an unequal bargain, even with some books and food and wine thrown in to sweeten the pill."

He saw her fingers clench on her reticule. She could not conceal it—she was shaking. Oddly, the sight unsettled him. He could feel her desperation and he did not want it to touch him. He did not want to feel sympathy for her.

He did not care what happened to her. He would not care. He could not.

Isabella was watching him, trying to interpret his expression.

"You are not in a strong position to strike an agreement, are you, sir?" she said steadily.

"Neither are you," Marcus countered swiftly. "How long would you survive in a hellhole like this, Isabella? For it is surely where you will end if you cannot pay your debt."

He saw her shudder but she met his eyes with defiance. "My state is not as parlous as yours," she said. "I can find another candidate for my hand."

"A candidate for your debts," Marcus corrected. "Do not dress it up as something it is not."

His anger was seething again now, whipped to a rage by her blatant determination to buy herself a husband with the last of her money and prostitute herself. He held his fury in check by the merest thread, but she could sense it.

Her eyes sparked with a fury to match his own. "Very well. If you refuse me, I shall buy myself another debtor. Is that plain enough for you?" She whirled around on him.

"And then I shall tell everyone of your disgrace, sir. A peer of the realm incarcerated in the Fleet for debt and so ashamed that he would rather hide his identity than accept the censure of the world! What would the scandalmongers make of that, I wonder? Reputation is so fragile, is it not?"

Marcus caught her wrist and pulled her around to face him. "If anyone knows the answer to that, then it is you! What would the Ton make of a disgraced princess trying to buy a debtor to save her skin?"

There was a silence heavy with challenge. Beneath his fingers Marcus could feel the racing of Isabella's pulse. Her skin was very soft. She felt warm and sweet. Temptation stirred, slicing through him like a knife. Instinctively his grip tightened, pulling her toward him. In another second she would be in his arms, her mouth crushed beneath his.

This time she was the one who stepped back, freeing herself from his grip. "I do not see why this needs must take much more time," she said. "I have made a business offer and I am awaiting your final response. If you refuse me I shall simply proceed to the next man in here who will agree."

That was direct. Marcus felt a certain admiration for her. And he knew she would have no trouble in finding a man.

They would be running a sweepstakes for the privilege of taking her on, debts notwithstanding. The thought of her proposing marriage to any of his cell mates impaled him with an intense and entirely inappropriate jealously. Damnation, he must be addled in his wits, or at the very least be led astray by some other far more basic part of his anatomy.

"You will have no difficulty in finding a man if you are not too particular," he agreed unpleasantly. "There are plenty such hopeless souls in here."

At last he had driven her to breaking point. He saw the moment when Isabella's composure snapped.

"I am desperate, too, you know!" The words burst from her and she could not erase a quiver of grief from her voice. "I am very tired of struggling—" She stopped, and Marcus saw her make a huge effort to steady herself. She was turning away, shielding her vulnerability from him. She pressed her hands together tightly. "This is nothing to the purpose." Her voice was muffled. "I think that I should leave."

Marcus put his hand on her arm. It was too late. It had been too late from the first moment she had made her outrageous proposition. He was damned if he was going to permit her to offer herself to some other debtor, and exchange a bottle of wine in return for a scrawled signature on a marriage certificate. If anyone were to wed her, it would be him, and then he would take great pleasure in turning the tables and taking settlement for everything that she owed him. She was his—at least until all debts were paid.

He looked at her. She had not moved but, despite her stillness, her heart was in her eyes. Marcus's world shivered, spun and settled on a different axis.

"I will do it," he said. "I will marry you."

CHAPTER THREE

WHEN SHE HAD BEEN SEVENTEEN, Isabella had dreamed of marrying Marcus Stockhaven. This marriage, however, was not the stuff that dreams were made of. In deference to the occasion, Marcus had paid two shillings to a fellow prisoner to borrow a clean shirt but there had been no hot water for him to shave. The chapel was gloomy, with no floral decoration to brighten the atmosphere. There were no guests and no one to dance at the wedding. It was, in short, a miserable business.

The priest had to be prized away from his brandy bottle. He glanced at the special license with vague interest and looked with a great deal more energy at the fifty guineas Isabella proffered to encourage his participation.

Marcus was also scrutinizing the special license as they stood before the altar in the Fleet chapel. His brows rose infinitesimally as he scanned the lines.

"Who is Augustus Ambridge?" he asked. "As your future husband, I feel I have the right to know."

"Oh…" Isabella felt confused. She had forgotten that she had been required to supply the name of a bridegroom in order to purchase the marriage license in the first place. Lacking any inspiration, she had chosen the first name that had come into her head, that of a gentleman who had been an admirer of hers in the two years of her widowhood, but whose intentions had never been either permanent or honorable.

"He is a…friend," she said.

Marcus's brows rose farther. "A friend? I see."

"Not that sort of friend," Isabella said. She could hear the thread of defensiveness in her tone and wondered why she felt the need to explain herself to him. She owed Marcus no information. He was to be her absentee husband only and, under the circumstances, it mattered nothing to him how she comported herself, since he could do nothing about it. Yet something in that steady dark gaze compelled her honesty.

It always had. The feeling unnerved her.

"He is merely an acquaintance," she said. "I have a great many such."

"I see," Marcus said again, and Isabella had to bite her tongue to prevent herself from pleading her innocence. That was not the way she did things. Never complain, never explain. Those were the tenets of royalty.

Looking at Marcus, at the hard, uncompromising line of his mouth and the forbidding light in his eyes, she wondered how such a man could have ended by being incarcerated in the Fleet. If such a thing had happened to Ernest, it would have been no surprise at all, but Marcus was deep where Ernest had been shallower than a muddy puddle, strong where Ernest had been weak, perceptive where Ernest had been worse than insensitive. Or, more to the point, Marcus had been all of those things when she had known him before. Twelve years could bring many changes in a man. She must remember that she knew nothing of him now.

She fidgeted with her cloak to conceal her nervousness and distract herself from the thought that she was making a very big mistake. She had wanted to meet, marry and part, remaining a stranger to her husband at all stages of the process. Yet already she had broken her own rules. She felt more deeply involved than she had ever intended to be.

"You will see that I have crossed out Augustus's name," she observed, pointing to the document and adopting a crisp attitude to mask her feelings of vulnerability.

"So that I may insert mine?" Marcus said, scowling. "I think that probably stretches the legality of the situation."

Isabella twitched the license from between his fingers and handed it to the priest. "The license is legal enough and with another hundred pounds the wedding will be recorded properly in the register. The marriage certificate will be enough to satisfy my creditors."

Marcus took the quill from the desk and wrote his name above that of Augustus Ambridge on the license. He scored out the other man's name with another thick black line, although it was already obliterated. His face was grim and Isabella's heart sank. This felt terribly wrong and suddenly she was not sure that she could go through with it. She found that she was shivering and shivering, like a dog left out in the cold. She folded her arms tightly to try to comfort herself.

"Do you have any paper?" Marcus asked the priest.

The old man looked startled, as though Marcus had requested some unacceptable privilege. After a moment, he trotted across to the dingy side chapel, returning with a sheet of rough parchment that he handed over with a look that implied another sum of money would now be in order. Isabella sighed and passed across two shillings, which disappeared into the pocket beneath the dirty surplice.

Marcus dipped the quill in the ink pot and scribbled a few lines, dusting the paper with sand to dry it. He handed it to Isabella.

"Take this. I would not wish there to be any ambiguity."

Isabella frowned as she scanned the paper. He had written a few curt lines to the effect that he was prepared to take complete responsibility for the debts incurred in his wife's name. If anything was destined to make Isabella feel even more squalid and money-grubbing than she already did, it was these few lines. They emphasized the commercial soul of the agreement in a manner that left no room for sentiment.

"Witnesses?" Marcus said. There was a clear note of impatience in his voice now.

Isabella's heart sank still further. That was the one thing she had not considered.

"I had not thought—" she began. She looked over her shoulder. The jailer was standing behind them looking hopeful. No doubt he thought there was another few pounds in it for him, both in acting as witness and in keeping quiet about it afterward. Perhaps he could even rustle up one of his colleagues to be the other signatory to the marriage lines. Hysterical laughter bubbled in Isabella's throat. Married in the Fleet, with a turnkey as witness and the priest half-drunk on the brandy she had supplied as part of the bribe...how ill-fated could a wedding be? She pressed a hand to her lips to suppress her amusement.

The jailer rubbed his palms on his dirty trousers, whistled up one of the other warders and came forward as the priest beckoned. Marcus took her hand. His touch was impersonal and yet a flicker of awareness ran through Isabella like a flame through tinder, catching in an instant and distracting her thoughts from everything but him. She almost snatched her hand away, so acute was her response to him. She knew that he would be able to feel her trembling, and felt as vulnerable as though she had been stripped naked. This was not how it was meant to be, with her emotions at the mercy of this man.

The service began. It seemed to Isabella that they were racing through it, for a Fleet wedding was never going to be a long and languorously romantic affair. There were no lingering glances of affection between bride and groom or indulgent smiles from the chaplain. There was a tense silence broken only by the mumbled words of the service, Marcus's decisive tones as he made his responses and Isabella's own, more hesitant words of commitment. At one point she faltered, engulfed by memories of her first marriage twelve years earlier, and Marcus's hand tightened on hers as he turned to look at her. She thought that she would read impatience in his eyes, but when she looked up at him, he was watching her with a strangely speculative interest. She drew on the shreds of her courage and straightened, repeating her vows in a stronger tone.

"Do you have the ring?" the priest asked.

Isabella shook her head. She had not remembered that she would need one and since she had pawned all her jewelry to meet some of her debt, she could not have provided one anyway. She heard Marcus sigh with resignation. A moment later he had taken his signet ring off and placed it on the open pages of the priest's Psalter. Isabella shot him an agonized look.

"You cannot give me your signet ring!"

Marcus looked unimpressed. "This is not the time and place to discuss it."

"But I—"

Marcus ignored her and turned back to the priest. "Proceed."

He took the ring and slid it onto her finger, clasping his hand briefly around hers in an oddly protective gesture. The ring felt warm and heavy on Isabella's hand. It was too big for her—she fidgeted with it, turning it round and round on her finger. It was inscribed very plainly with four entwined letters. *M...J...E...S...* She traced the lines in the gold.

It felt quite wrong to be taking Marcus's signet ring, wrong and too personal when she had wanted nothing more than his name on a piece of paper.

The priest folded the Book of Common Prayer away under the sleeve of his dirty surplice. He had already scribbled the marriage certificate and now he thrust it at Isabella and waited for his fee, anxious for the matter to be finished. Isabella's fingers were shaking as she folded the document carefully and stowed it in her reticule. This was her liberty, the paper that spelled her freedom. Yet when Marcus had let go of her hand at the end of the service, she had felt more alone than ever, free but not comforted.

Marcus was watching her. She thought that there was an element of mocking amusement in his eyes. No doubt he found her predicament comical, the scandalous Princess Di Cassilis obliged to marry a debtor...

"Well?" he said.

"Thank you," Isabella said, finding herself unable to look at him.

"Do not mention it." Marcus was smiling but it was not the sort of smile that comforted her. "I do believe that in return you offered me something."

Isabella met his eyes. Her errant heart skittered nervously. Her throat felt suddenly dry. Images of those long-lost evenings mingled in her mind; the tender touch of his lips against her damp skin, the dry salty scent of the sea mingled with old roses, the blazing heat of that summer...but the flames of that passion were long dead after many winters.

"Some bottles of wine, the means to purchase some proper food and a few items to make life more tolerable?" Marcus prompted when she did not speak.

"Oh, of course." Isabella could feel herself blushing at the vastly different direction her own thoughts had taken. She paused. Her purse was almost empty, but it was not that that held her back. To repeat the offer of such a crude inducement had seemed unthinkable after Marcus's angry rejection of it earlier.

"I was intending to pay you," she admitted, "but I thought you had dismissed my suggestion."

Marcus smiled again, with more genuine humor this time. "I am not so proud, I assure you. Besides, I thought that we had agreed that this is a business venture? We made a bargain."

"So we did," Isabella said. She fumbled for the coins and pressed them into his hand. He tucked them away in his waist-coat pocket.

"And you must take your ring back," she added hastily, making to draw the gold signet ring from her finger where it had rested for such a short time.

Marcus shook his head, taking her hand and holding the ring in place. "Keep it," he said. "Until we meet again."

Isabella felt a pang of disquiet. "Will that happen?"

"Assuredly."

"But not until we are safely unwed."

Marcus's smile deepened. "Of course."

They stood looking at each other for a moment. Isabella felt strangely at a loss.

"I suppose that I should go?" she said uncertainly.

Marcus's voice took a mocking edge at her obvious discomfort. "I suppose that you should. It is, however, customary to kiss the bride on the wedding day."

Isabella's nerves jumped. She took two steps backward until her skirt brushed the wooden upright of the front pew. This time when she withdrew from him, he followed her. She put out a hand to ward him off.

"As you have reminded me, this is a business arrangement, sir, and that was not part of the bargain."

Marcus smiled at her again. It was a lazy smile, full of intimate challenge. She was not sure whether he was doing this out of revenge or devilry or simply to amuse himself, but his proximity was enough to shatter her composure. She wanted to escape but she could not move.

The jailer was becoming restive and fidgeting behind them, anxious to get his man back to the cells. Marcus ignored him. He took a single stride forward, caught Isabella's arm and drew her to him, bringing the tips of her breasts up against the rough material of his jacket. He bent his head. His grip tightened on her arm. Then he was kissing her.

The pressure of his lips was no more than a whisper against hers. Even so, it was enough to cast Isabella back into the past, where the memory of his kiss had been locked away along with all the other tumbling images of passion. She had hidden those feelings from herself and from others for so long and now they were stirring, threatening to break out. So much for dust and ashes. Any tenderness there had been between them might be long gone, but the attraction still flared as hot as ever. It terrified her.

She made a small, incoherent sound and tried to put some space between them, but suddenly Marcus's arms were about her and his mouth moved over hers with an expert thoroughness that stripped away every vestige of defense. The sensual heat washed through her, burning her up, scorching her to the tips of her toes.

No one had ever kissed her the way Marcus had. Ernest had indulged in a few cursory embraces before getting down to the consummation of their marriage but his lovemaking had lacked any tenderness. In all honesty, it could hardly be dignified with the word *lovemaking*. A less appropriate description would be difficult to find.

Ernest had not courted her; he had bought her. Bought her, taken what he wanted, tried to mold her to his tastes. And when she had proved less than satisfactory, he'd claimed that she had reneged on their bargain, and they had continued in a hollow sham of a marriage until he died. No indeed, there had been precious little romance and no true passion in Isabella's life. Until now.

She trembled in Marcus's arms. The touch, taste and desire mingled as he kissed her, then released her a little only to reclaim her mouth once again. Isabella's body roused from what felt like a long sleep as she felt the hardness of him, his strength and control. Then it was all over and he let her go with an abruptness that plunged her back into darkness.

The atmosphere between them was blistering. Marcus's face was shadowed but in his eyes burned a flame that seared her.

"You should not have—" she began.

His expression was hard. "It needed to be done."

"Time to go," the jailer said from behind them. He fingered the money in his pocket suggestively. "Unless you would prefer to stay a while longer, madam? A cozy cell for the two of you to celebrate wedlock?"

Wedlock. It sounded very final.

Marcus raised an eyebrow in inquiry. Isabella wrenched her gaze away from him. "No," she said. "No, thank you."

Marcus turned away from her without a further word and fell into step before the jailer. He did not look back. Isabella listened as their footsteps faded away and the door of the chapel swung silently closed behind them. For one mad moment, she wanted to run after Marcus and drag him back, make him stay with her. But he had gone. That was it. It was all over.

The priest touched her arm.

"You will be wanting to be away from this place, ma'am. Allow me to escort you out."

Isabella followed him in something of a daze through the warren of shadowed corridors and out into the daylight. The door clanged shut, leaving her out on the street. The air was bright and the afternoon was loud with the vibrant noises of the city. She felt very odd, light-headed and confused, as though she had awoken from a vivid dream, a dream laced with sensuality and long-buried desires. Except that this had been no dream. She was legally married to Marcus Stockhaven—or perhaps illegally, given the circumstances of their wedding. The thought made her heart clench with emotion.

His signet ring felt heavy and unfamiliar on her finger. She wondered why he had not pawned it to buy himself more comfort. But a man's pride was a delicate thing and maybe selling off the family's arms was a step too far, even for a debtor in dire straits. He could scarce be said to have graced the Stockhaven name with his behavior.

He had not sold his signet ring but he had given it to her. Isabella felt a passing regret for the fact that she could not wear it. Nevertheless, she would keep it safe, and once the marriage had been annulled she would send it back to him. No matter that he had said they would meet again. She knew it would be better—safer—never to see him.

She could feel the marriage certificate stiff in the reticule beneath her arm. She was free and she was secure from arrest, and surely that had to be the most important matter. Yet as she walked quickly out of the labyrinth of alleys that snaked about the Fleet, a deep feeling of disquiet possessed her. She wondered why she was so anxious. After all, Marcus was locked up in debtor's prison and she was at liberty to carry on as though nothing had happened. She had exactly what she wanted.

For a moment she contemplated what might happen if Marcus were to regain his freedom and a shiver of apprehension shook her. With Marcus imprisoned, she felt safely in control of the situation. Marcus at liberty would be a very different matter. There was no way one could control a man like that. He was too strong, too forceful.

She turned her face up to the sunshine for comfort and told herself that it was impossible that Marcus would ever be free. Her debts would be dismissed, her inheritance would be proved and then she could pay for an annulment. She had no cause ever to see him again.

Nevertheless, she felt afraid.

MARCUS WAS LYING on the mattress in the empty cell, which was now his own, the book about naval architecture lying untouched by his elbow and a bottle of wine almost as untouched beside it. The cell looked exactly as it had when he had stepped in there in the weak light of morning. There was nothing to show that Isabella Di Cassilis had ever been there and in doing so had changed his life. There was no sign of her, yet her presence lingered in the air and wrapped itself about him so that it was impossible to think of anything else.

During the preceding twelve years he had thought about Isabella sometimes, but he would dispute that he had ever pined for her. His mouth twisted in bitter amusement. He was not a man to dwell on those things that might have been. He was not cut out to be a martyr. Bur while he had always believed that he had put the entire matter of his ill-fated, youthful love affair behind him, he now knew that was not so. Now he knew he wanted Isabella and he wanted a reckoning.

Marcus rubbed a hand across his eyes. He had tried very hard to shut Isabella out of his mind and his life, but he had not been able to ignore the tales entirely. Her husband's name had been a byword for depravity, especially in his later years when he had traveled through Europe trailing a raffish court behind him like a wayward comet and taking with him a wife whose name was inevitably ruined by association with his de-bauchery. Marcus thought of Isabella and the crippling blow that her late husband had dealt her. Twenty thousand pounds was an immense debt to burden her with, but no doubt the feckless Prince Ernest had cared as little for that as he was reputed to have cared for his wife. And one could argue that it was only just that Isabella, who had married for money, should in her widowhood be crippled by debt.

Marcus shifted, trying to achieve a more comfortable position on the hopelessly uncomfortable mattress. Isabella had chosen to marry Prince Ernest and she was now reaping the consequences of that decision. She had jilted Marcus heartlessly to marry a rich and titled man. That was the simple truth. Marcus had fallen for the charms of an adventuress.

He had not wanted to feel anything for Isabella Di Cassilis when he met her again. He had wanted to look at her and feel nothing—no love, no hatred and certainly no desire. He had failed singularly. It had taken him all of ten seconds to realize that he still wanted her and, when she had trembled under the onslaught of his kiss, he had forgotten the grim surroundings of the Fleet and ached to take her there and then on the cold stone floor of the chapel.

No indeed, indifference was the last emotion on his mind.

Marcus got to his feet and walked over to the small grille that covered the window. Tantalizing brightness flooded in, promising all the things that he had given up—light and liberty and the freedom to do whatever he wished. He had gone voluntarily into the Fleet for a most particular purpose and Isabella's assumptions about his financial state, while logical, could not have been further from the truth. He could buy up her debts three times over and not notice the difference.

He paused, staring at the small square of light. What did he want from Isabella Di Cassilis? She had chosen him for no more reason than that he was a convenient husband in the same way that she had made a calculated decision to marry Prince Ernest all those years before. Marcus had given her the freedom to escape her debts. He owed her nothing more. But she…she owed him an explanation of the past as well as a reckoning for the present. When he paid off her creditors, she would owe him a great deal more.

His work here was almost complete. He had been intending to call for his release in a week's time anyway, but that could easily be brought forward by a few days. It was probably preferable to leave now anyway. Isabella's visit, and her largesse, had made him a figure of curiosity and that he could not afford. Already there was a buzz in the air, talk of his wife's beauty and speculation about her true identity. Secrets could not be kept in a place like this.

Marcus stared up at the small blue square of sky above his head. He did not deceive himself that Isabella would be pleased to see him at liberty. If there was one thing he had learned from their interview, it was that Princess Isabella Di

Cassilis—or more accurately, the new Countess of Stock-haven—did not wish for a husband in anything more than name.

Marcus grinned. Too bad. She was about to get one. There was business unfinished between them.

He called for a pen and ink, spending one of Isabella's guineas lavishly on the privilege of having the letter delivered immediately to an address in Brook Street.

The note was very simple:

Alistair, my plans have changed. I rely on you to get me out of here with great despatch. My thanks, S.

He paused, then added a postscript.

Pray find out for me, if you would, who are the major creditors of Princess Isabella Di Cassilis.

The turnkey was waiting to take the note. Marcus knew the man would fulfill his commission. The jailers in the Fleet had a fine instinct for power and they could sniff the change in Marcus's fortunes.

This, they knew, was a man who would soon be free.

CHAPTER FOUR

MR. CHURCHWARD THE ELDER, of the renowned London firm Churchward and Churchward, lawyers to the noble and the discerning, was startled to receive a visit early the following morning from no less a personage than Princess Isabella Di Cassilis. He had seen the princess only the day before, when he had had the melancholy duty of informing her of her late husband's appalling debts. Princess Isabella had taken the news well and had promised him that she would apprise him shortly of the steps that she meant to take to clear the sum. It seemed that she had already found a solution.

Mr. Churchward came forward, hand outstretched. Had Princess Isabella not already been seated, he would certainly have dusted the chair for her. Although he professed a total impartiality toward all his clientele, it was in fact the case that Princess Isabella was one of Mr. Churchward's most favored clients. The lawyer had some very chivalrous ideas about ladies in distress and he would have liked nothing more than to see a hero on a white charger ride to the rescue of this particular courageous lady. Unfortunately he was not that man. He was only her lawyer.

"Madam!" He took her hand and shook it warmly. "There was no need for you to come to my chambers. I should have been delighted to call upon you."

"I would not dream of putting you to so much trouble, Mr. Churchward," Isabella said with a smile that made Mr. Churchward tingle down to his toes. "This is a simple matter and will take a mere moment. I have come to settle my debt and I wondered whether you would deal with Henshalls for me?"

"Of course!" The lawyer shuddered to think of a lady as delicate as the Princess setting foot in the moneylenders' offices. Not that Princess Isabella appeared fragile, precisely. A lady who had survived the rigors of marriage to the feckless Prince Ernest was to be congratulated on her hardiness. Mr. Churchward shook his head. His expression said all that was needed on the subject of profligate princes who ran through a fortune and then proceeded to accumulate debt with the gusto that others collected paintings or Grecian antiquities. *Irresponsible, foolish, selfish, callous* and *downright unpleasant* were descriptions of Prince Ernest that might have sprung to Mr. Churchward's lips had he been less discreet. His mouth compressed to a thin line as he regarded the lady who was obliged to reap the consequences of Prince Ernest's financial recklessness.

The princess gave him another of her mischievous smiles, which set his blood pressure awry and caused him to blush deeply. Delving in her reticule, Princess Isabella extracted a piece of paper.

"I believe that Henshalls will find this in order," she said sweetly. "They will not care for it much, but they cannot argue with it."

Mr. Churchward, who had expected to be holding a money order, found that he was in fact clutching a marriage certificate. Further perusal confirmed that it was for a marriage contracted in the Fleet Prison. Accompanying it was a note that stated that a certain John Ellis was prepared to take on his wife's debts in their entirety.

Mr. Churchward gasped and adjusted his spectacles, the better to confirm the news his sinking heart was telling him.

"But madam... I... You..."

"I took your advice, Mr. Churchward," Isabella said, "and arranged a marriage. You will find that it is quite legal."

Mr. Churchward was flushed with agitation. The certificate dropped from his nerveless fingers to the wooden table. He moved several files agitatedly and at random, upsetting the ordered calm of his desktop.

"My advice was to marry a gentleman of fortune, Princess, not a debtor!" he spluttered. "Upon my word, madam, I cannot believe—" He broke off and scanned the sheet of paper. "It is legal, you say?"

"Of course." Isabella looked very collected. "It is also temporary. As we agreed yesterday, Mr. Churchward, I would like you to place the house in Brunswick Gardens up for sale. I think it will fetch a goodly sum, for it is in quite a fashionable neighborhood. Once the sale is made and Aunt Jane's legacy is also proved, I will pay Henshalls what I owe them."

Mr. Churchward made a whimpering noise like a cat inadvertently trodden upon. He removed his glasses and polished them feverishly. The dent that they had left on his nose was bright red against the pallor of the rest of his face. Even his voice sounded pale.

"And the marriage, madam?"

"I will end that as well, of course." Isabella snapped her reticule shut with a decisive click. "It is a matter of convenience only. Mr. Ellis will be confined to the Fleet for the foreseeable future."

Various objections flitted through Mr. Churchward's mind. Doubtless the princess, like many other persons unacquainted with the law, thought that it was relatively simple to achieve an annulment of a marriage. Most people erroneously assumed that non-consummation was sufficient grounds. He started to rehearse the explanations in his mind, saw the decisive set of Isabella's jaw, and decided to bide his time. It was, after all, too late. Part of the skill in dealing with his noble clients lay in choosing one's moment. This was not the right time to suggest to the princess that she might in fact be wed for better or worse.

Mr. Churchward mopped his forehead with his large, practical handkerchief.

"I shall not take any more of your time, Mr. Churchward," Isabella said. She gave him a final, very sweet smile. "I shall be leaving Town for my house in Salterton in a few weeks, but I should be delighted to entertain you to tea before I go."

"Salterton... Of course... We must speak further about your inheritance...." Mr. Churchward mumbled. Another raft of objections came into his mind. He had not yet had the chance to speak to Princess Isabella in detail about her legacy from her aunt, Lady Jane Southern, for other more pressing matters had taken precedence. He wondered how much the princess knew about her inheritance of Salterton Hall and the encumbrances upon the estate.

Churchward mopped his brow again. Should he acquaint her with the difficulties now, and explain the very delicate nature of her relationship with her tenant in the dower house? He hesitated. Best not. Isabella was already on her feet in preparation for leaving. He did not wish to detain her now.

"Perhaps we might make an appointment for next week, madam," he suggested. "I would appreciate the opportunity to acquaint you with the detail of your estate."

Isabella nodded.

"Thank you, Mr. Churchward. Will Tuesday be convenient?"

She was already halfway out of the door, leaving nothing but a faint, delicious perfume shimmering in the air. Churchward heard her give an airy farewell to the staff in the outer office; there was the sound of her steps on the stairs, gathering speed as though she were rid of some tiresome encumbrance. Mr. Churchward smiled wryly. By the time she reached the street she would be almost running.

He perused the marriage lines and the promissory note for a third time. His hand stole toward the drawer of his battered cabinet, where a bottle of sherry was hidden for emergencies. This was a full-scale emergency if ever there was one. He paused. It would, however, be better to deal with Henshalls first. He did not relish giving those most ruthless of money-lenders the news that Princess Isabella Di Cassilis's debts were now impossible to claim, the responsibility of some luckless wastrel in the Fleet Prison. He reached for his hat and folded the marriage lines within the pocket of his waistcoat. Sometimes he felt he did not get paid sufficient for the trials of his work. Still, for Princess Isabella Di Cassilis he would do almost anything.

An hour later, Mr. Churchward tottered back up the stairs to his chambers. He had been pale before; now he was ashen. He went directly to the cabinet, extracted the sherry and resisted the temptation to drink it straight down from the bottle. He was shaking so much that the neck of the bottle rattled like a can-nonade against his sherry glass. He collapsed into his chair with a heartfelt sigh, raised his glass and gulped the revivifying liquid down with as little regard as though it had been water.

To his great amazement, the Henshall brothers had been very pleased to see him. Only an hour before, they had received a visit from a gentleman who had settled in full—and in cash—the debts of Princess Isabella Di Cassilis. There had been handshakes all round.

Mr. Churchward lay back in his chair as the sherry warmed his veins. He tried to make sense of the aspects of the case that puzzled him, which were practically all of them. Princess Isabella had given him to understand that her new husband was under lock and key and would remain so for the foresee-able future, yet when Churchward had arrived at the money-lenders' he had discovered that the gentleman was not only at liberty but had already paid the princess's debt.

He wondered why on earth Isabella had not told him her husband's true identity.

He wondered what on earth Marcus Stockhaven, one of the richest men in the *Ton,* had been doing in the Fleet Prison.

And he wondered what the *devil* his two most noble clients were doing contracting an apparent marriage of convenience and then expecting *him* to arrange an annulment.

"Dear oh dear oh dear," Mr. Churchward said unhappily, emptying the sherry bottle into his glass. A third glass of sherry was previously unknown in Mr. Churchward's experience, but such unsettling circumstances called for extreme measures.

"How do I look?"

Marcus Stockhaven tilted his head to one side, the better to appreciate the set of his neck cloth in the mirror above the drawing-room mantelpiece.

"Like a man who has spent three months trying to tie his cravat in a dark cellar," his friend Alistair Cantrell said brutally.

Marcus grinned. "That bad?" He surveyed his reflection thoughtfully in the mirror and rubbed a hand over the stubble shadowing his chin. "I need a barber."

"You need more than that." Alistair looked around. "Where is your valet?"

"I gave all the servants leave of absence whilst I was away," Marcus said. "Why do you think you are pouring your own brandy?"

He watched as Alistair folded his lanky length into the armchair beside the fireplace. Stockhaven House was small as London town houses went, and wholly unostentatious. The Earls of Stockhaven had never felt the need to boast their wealth and lineage through vulgar display, and Marcus was no exception. Nevertheless, a house like this required a staff to run it. The room was cold, for the June evening had turned unseasonably damp. No fire glowed in the grate. The dust sat thickly on the cherrywood furniture and the whole house felt faintly unloved.

"So," Alistair said, turning from contemplation of his brandy to study Marcus's face. "Why the change of plan?"

Marcus shrugged. "My business was all but complete," he said, "and I was starting to draw attention in a manner that I could ill afford." He took a mouthful of brandy, grimaced and put his glass down. "Either someone has been selling off my liquor whilst I was in the Fleet and replacing it with tea dregs or I have lost my taste for brandy."

Alistair looked amused. "It has an excellent flavor, Marcus."

"Then my sense of taste has definitely been ruined by the disgusting swill that passes for food inside," Marcus said, sighing. "I thought as much. A man must be desperate indeed to tolerate such appalling slops."

Alistair grinned. "Just like Harrow, as I recall. But did you discover what you wanted?" He gestured with his brandy glass. "Did you find Warwick—and his criminals? You must know that I am expiring with curiosity. Tell me all."

Marcus stretched out his long legs toward the empty fire grate. He felt as chill as the house, cold and empty. One of the reasons he had been able to spend three months in the Fleet was that there was no one to notice his absence. In the years since his wife had died, he had traveled widely. No one was in the least surprised when he disappeared for months on end, and positions in his service were eagerly sought since his servants had the longest holidays in London.

In the three days since his release from the Fleet Prison, he had noticed more than ever before the emptiness of Stockhaven House. It was odd, for previously his solitude had never disturbed him. Now, however, he felt that he wanted more— although he was not sure exactly what more was. A house full of servants did not seem the answer.

"I discovered that the prison is a fertile ground for the recruitment of men to the criminal fraternity," he said, in reply to Alistair's question. "Debtors who are desperate for their freedom will promise anything to those who buy them out of jail."

Alistair pursed his lips in a silent whistle. "Just as you thought. But surely it would be better to recruit a bunch of hardened criminals in Newgate rather than the Fleet?"

Marcus shook his head. "What is the point of recruiting a man who may well hang the next day? The debtors of the Fleet are a better class of criminal. Some may not even be criminals at all. But all are frantic for lack of money, and the man who can buy them out of prison has a hold over them for the rest of their lives."

"Is Edward Warwick one such?" Alistair asked.

Marcus nodded. Hunting Warwick, a criminal mastermind, was the reason he had gone into the Fleet in the first place. "He is certainly one of the main players," he said. "I spent three months in a cell with men who were terrified of his very name. All my cell mates were too afraid to tell me more than the merest scraps of information about him. I learned that Warwick buys a man's debts—buys their very souls—so that they dance to his tune."

Alistair narrowed his eyes thoughtfully. "It sounds as though you were wise to make your inquiries incognito. You never met the man yourself during your time in the Fleet?"

"Unfortunately not, although he regularly visits the prison to recruit his men. But perhaps it was fortunate that Warwick and I have not yet met." Marcus's mouth took on a grim line. "We will one day and I would wish to be better prepared."

Alistair Cantrell nodded. "So did you discover anything useful about the fire at Salterton? Can you tie it to Warwick for sure?"

"Yes, I can," Marcus said. His gaze turned inward, away from the cold, dusty room. It had been bad, that winter night at Salterton six months ago. It was the night that his wife's mother, Lady Jane Southern, had died. He had been up at Salterton Hall trying to restore order and bring comfort to the servants, many of whom had served the Southern family for years. Marcus had been grief struck and bone weary, and when he returned to his own house in the grounds at nigh on midnight, he had wanted nothing but the oblivion of sleep. Instead, he had caught a lad in the very act of burgling his late wife's chamber. The boy had overturned a lamp in his attempts to escape. In a matter of seconds the tapestries and curtains were ablaze and so was the boy's clothing. The lad had made a desperate leap from the window in an attempt to escape.

The evening took on a nightmarish horror.

Fire was a terrifying phenomenon. Marcus had seen it rip through a battleship more than once. Even now he could hear the crack as the arsenal exploded and feel the shock wave run through the water. The fire that had gutted the second floor of his house at Salterton had been on a much smaller scale, but it was no less devastating. He could still see the image of the young lad lying on the gravel, a small, crumpled figure barely more than eleven years old, too pitiful to think of as a criminal. When he reached the boy's side he feared him dead, but the youth was alive and delirious. His eyes were open and he kept repeating the name *Warwick* like an enchantment. When Marcus questioned him gently, he murmured, "Mr. Warwick sent me to find what is rightfully his." And then he lapsed into unconsciousness.

Marcus called the physician, who was still up at Salterton Hall, and paid for the treatment himself. He felt an obscure guilt over the boy's injuries, as though he were responsible for the lad's plight. The boy was the son of one of the Salterton villagers and they took him home to nurse him. There was puzzlement and embarrassment in their eyes as they tried to explain to Marcus that Edward was a good lad and they did not understand where it had all gone wrong. Marcus did not press charges, despite the disapproval of the constable. And then a few weeks later he heard that the lad had run away, although still dangerously weakened by his injuries. His parents shrank still further into themselves and became shadows of the people they had been. Once respected and sure of their place in the community, they became like ghosts. John Channing worked in his cobbler's shop as he had always done, but was dour and unsmiling. Mary Channing took in laundry but turned her face away from the gossip of her neighbors. And when Marcus called, he soon realized that his presence was a torment to them, not a comfort, for it reminded them of the disgrace their son had brought on their name.

It was then that Marcus determined to find out what had happened to lead Edward Channing astray. He wanted to discover the identity of the mysterious puppet master whose manipulations drove Edward to ransack Marcus's house and then burn it down. He needed to know what the lad had been searching for.

And there was another mystery. On the evening of her death, Lady Jane Southern had a visitor. No one saw him leave and, in the aftermath of her death, most people forgot him. But Marcus possessed a strange conviction that his appearance had something to do with both Lady Jane's death and the fire.

"Mr. Warwick sent me to find what is rightfully his...."

Marcus had no notion what it was that he apparently possessed. He had only the name of Warwick to give him a lead, and he trod very carefully in his investigations, making no overt inquiries, drawing as little attention as possible.

It was when he approached the home secretary, Lord Sidmouth, that he discovered the connection to the Fleet Prison. Sidmouth proved to be most interested in Warwick and his activities. The man was a master criminal, the home secretary had said, drawing his supporters from those desperate debtors who thronged the Fleet. He'd given Marcus tacit permission to continue his inquiries—inside the prison.

Alistair was waiting patiently, his gaze thoughtful on Marcus's face. His friend was the only other person who knew of Marcus's quest to find Edward Warwick.

"I had to go very cautiously to avoid suspicion," Marcus said now. "I let slip that I had heard of a fire at a big house in Salterton, and of rich pickings there, and a few agreed that Edward Warwick had said that there had been treasure there but that it had not been found."

"Treasure?" Alistair said, frowning.

"That was the word they used."

"Which could be money, or jewels…"

"Or information."

Alistair rubbed his brow. "Information in your own house of which you know nothing, Marcus?"

"Perhaps," Marcus said. "Or information that Lady Jane possessed. Curious, is it not?" He turned his empty brandy glass between his fingers. "I am no closer to discovering what it is that Warwick wants, nor to finding out any more about the man himself than I knew before. He has as many names and disguises as he has criminal interests, but he is so feared and protected that I could find out little more."

"So you asked in the Fleet and found little," Alistair said thoughtfully, "and what do you propose to do now?"

"Two things," Marcus said. He knew that he could not let the matter go now.

"I shall make further discreet inquiries into Warwick's business here in London, and if that fails to turn up new information I shall return to Salterton, where it all began, and see what else I may discover from there. The renovation of the dower house is almost complete. It will be good to see how it progresses."

"I suppose that you will have a new landlord now that Lady Jane has passed away," Alistair said thoughtfully. "To whom did she leave her estate? Freddie Standish would be her closest male relative, I assume?"

"He is," Marcus said, "but he does not inherit. The hall was not entailed." He paused. The lease on his house at Salterton, which was little more than a cottage orneé that stood in the grounds of Salterton Hall, had been granted to him when he had married Isabella's cousin, India Southern. He had plenty of houses but it had been a convenient arrangement to take Salterton Cottage for it provided India with a home of her own when she wished to visit her parents at the hall. Lady Jane had been fond of him and had allowed him to retain the lease after India's death and although he had visited Salterton less frequently, he still paid a visit there every so often. It was on one of these visits that Lady Jane had told him that she had left Salterton Hall to Isabella on her death. Marcus had already known, though he did not say so. The terms of Lady Jane's will had thrust a sharp wedge between herself and her daughter India when first they had come to light.

"Mama has always favored Isabella over me!" India had said to him once in a passionate outburst that was utterly out of character for her. "She told me that I had no need of Salterton because I was married to you, and that Isabella had always cared for the place far more than I!" India's face had contorted with distress. "My cousin has been writing to Mama and pretending to an interest and a concern that she does not feel! First she marries that disgusting old man for his money and now she cuts me out of my inheritance! I cannot believe Mama would do such a thing to me!"

Marcus had tried to soothe her but India would not be comforted, and there had been a tense atmosphere between mother and daughter ever after. Since India had predeceased her mother, the matter of the inheritance of Salterton had become almost academic, but Marcus had never forgotten the bitter betrayal that India felt. It seemed a further example of Isabella's cupidity.

A sardonic smile curved Marcus's lips at the thought of his new wife as an heiress—and his landlady. What was it that Isabella had said? Her financial embarrassment was of a temporary nature and their marriage of convenience would last only until she had sold her house and realized her inheritance. He had assumed that she had some expectation of salvaging something at least from Prince Ernest's estate, but now he wondered if it was in fact Jane Southern's legacy that Isabella was relying on. It was another link in the shadowy chain of family ties and old history that bound them to one another.

"Freddie Standish needs the money," Alistair said, breaking into Marcus's thoughts. "He will not be pleased to lose the inheritance. He survives on nothing but his pay and Miss Standish's meager allowance, so I hear. He is rather a ramshackle fellow."

Marcus had never had much to say to Freddie, Lord Standish. It was an accident of marriage that had made them cousins-in-law and their paths had seldom crossed. In fact he had once sensed a dislike of him in Freddie, all the stronger for remaining unspoken, and had steered clear of the man with an indifferent shrug.

He had a warmer regard for Isabella's sister Penelope, a fearsome bluestocking who had the misfortune to share a small house with Freddie in an unfashionable part of Town. But Pen Standish never went into society, so he did not know her well.

"I could not see Standish choosing to live at Salterton," Marcus said. "Town is his natural habitat."

"He could always have sold the house," Alistair pointed out.

"Which was no doubt one of the reasons Lady Jane chose

to leave it to another member of the family," Marcus said. "She wished it to go to someone whom she thought cared for it."

Alistair looked quizzical. "Not to you, Marcus? The old lady was monstrous fond of you."

"No," Marcus said, shaking his head a little. "She did not leave it to me."

"Then whom?"

"I believe her heir is Princess Isabella Di Cassilis," Marcus said.

Alistair pursed his lips into a silent whistle. His eyes were bright. "So *that* was why you wished me to check on the princess's debts! I had heard that she had returned to London. The papers have been full of the news."

Marcus hesitated. Despite asking Alistair to discover the information on Isabella's debt to Henshalls, he had not confided the truth of his marriage to his oldest friend. Alistair, who had been his groomsman at the ill-fated wedding twelve years ago, would be astonished to know that Marcus had offered marriage to Isabella now. No, he would be beyond astonishment. He would imagine that Marcus had lost his mind. And for Marcus to admit that his motive was a stark and ruthless revenge seemed somehow ignoble. It was not the sort of thing one man confessed to another. Nevertheless, he could not keep his friend in ignorance any longer. The whole of London would soon know of the match.

"There was another reason that I was interested in the princess's situation," he said slowly. "We were married on Tuesday."

He waited while Alistair blinked owlishly, looked at the brandy bottle and then back at him. Alistair's lips moved silently, forming the words *princess* and *married.* Marcus grinned.

"Damned if your brandy hasn't been tampered with after all, Marcus," Alistair said, after a moment. "Either that or I'm touched in the attic. I thought you said that you were married to the Princess Isabella. Must be hearing things."

"You heard aright," Marcus said. He smiled slightly. "I realize that the news of my nuptials is somewhat sudden."

"And unexpected." Alistair was frowning at him. "I had no idea that you were so attached to Salterton Hall that you were prepared to marry the heiress to gain it," he added. "Why could you not simply make Lady Jane an offer to buy the house? Or was that too easy for you?"

"It was not like that," Marcus said ruefully.

"A whirlwind courtship in the Fleet, was it?" Alistair said sarcastically. "Ah, the pure romance of it all!" He sat back in his wide armchair, looking resigned. "Damn it, Marcus, I hate the way you spring these surprises."

Marcus sighed. "In truth there is little to tell. We met, we married and now I am come to claim my bride."

"As one does," Alistair said dryly. He shifted, rubbing his brow. "I suppose you are aware that Fleet marriages were made illegal nigh on fifty years ago?"

"I am aware." Marcus stood up and dusted the sleeves of his jacket in an attempt to make the ancient evening outfit look a little less shiny and a little more acceptable for wearing in polite society. If he was to make a show of claiming Isabella, then he wanted to look his best to do it. His efforts were unsuccessful, however. He mused that perhaps he should visit his tailor as well as his barber on the morrow.

"This marriage, however, is not illegal," he continued. "It was celebrated by a proper priest and authorized by special license. It is signed and sealed. You may trust Princess Isabella to have made sure of that. She could not afford for the marriage to be overset."

Alistair nodded. "Of course. The debts."

"Precisely."

Alistair's mouth turned down at the corners with deep disapproval.

"I do believe that one of us is mad here, Marcus, and I am

not sure that it is I. How could you even countenance such an arrangement, given the history between yourself and Princess Isabella?" He caught Marcus's sleeve and compelled him to sit down. "Cease fussing over that jacket, Marcus. Nothing will make it look any better. Instead tell me what is going on."

Marcus sat back with a sigh. "It is a marriage of convenience," he said. "Princess Isabella needed a husband to keep her debtors at bay and on the strength of our brief, previous acquaintance she approached me for assistance. Which I was—" He hesitated. "Persuaded to give."

Alistair narrowed his eyes. "Of all the rum starts, Marcus! Brief, previous acquaintance indeed!"

"I appreciate that it must appear strange," Marcus said. He sat forward, feeling the constriction of the jacket across his shoulders. "Hmm. I require a new wardrobe—"

"To go with your new wife, I suppose," Alistair said. "You are not making sense, Marcus. I thought that no one but I knew of your sojourn in the Fleet. How did Princess Isabella find you?"

"By happy chance," Marcus said, a little grimly. "As I said, she needed a debtor and I was available."

"The devil you were! Does she know that you were in the Fleet by your own choice?"

"Not yet," Marcus said. "It is one of the many surprises that I have in store for her tonight. I cannot pretend that she will be pleased to see me, but that cannot be helped."

Alistair peered at him. "I always thought that weddings were supposed to be happy affairs," he said. "You do not seem very enamored of your bride, Marcus. Furthermore, this is not like you at all."

Marcus fidgeted restlessly. He felt irritable and rather suspected it was with himself.

"On the contrary it is very like me. I become bored with the conventions of society—"

"So you arrange to be locked in the Fleet and then marry a shady princess into the bargain," Alistair said.

"Exactly." Marcus paused. "The marriage is a secret for the time being, however. I should be obliged if you would keep it so, Alistair."

"Why?" his friend asked bluntly. "I mean, why is it a secret, not why should I help you keep it so, which goes without saying if you wish it of me."

"There are various reasons," Marcus said. "Firstly, my wife is unaware that I have achieved my release from prison and I wish to discuss the matter with her before our marriage becomes common knowledge. Secondly..." He hesitated. "Well, I have said that it is a match of convenience. It may be that the marriage will not endure long."

Alistair was shaking his head. "Dashed irregular. The more I hear, the worse it becomes. Hope you know what you're doing, Marcus."

"I am not certain that I do," Marcus conceded. "However, if I could ask you to keep the secret for now...?"

"Mute as an undertaker's boy, I promise you," Alistair said. He shook his head. "Lord, but I'd give a monkey to see the Dowagers' faces when they realize another earl is off the marriage mart! And caught by a lady with such a scandalous reputation—" He stopped. There was a short and very pointed silence. The bleakness in Marcus's heart was matched only by the pity in Alistair's eyes.

"Just so," Marcus said.

"My apologies," Alistair said. "You will not wish to hear your wife's name bandied about."

Marcus shut his lips in a grim line. When Alistair had spoken he had felt the kick of rage through his body like a lightning strike. God help him, if a passing reference to Isabella could do this to him...he felt a white-hot possessive fury that beat anything he had ever experienced before. By rights Isabella Di Cassilis was his, now more than ever, and he would not rest until it was true in word and deed, and the memory of all that had gone before was wiped out.

He clenched his fists in his pockets and slowly released them.

"This is a marriage of convenience, Alistair," he said, with a passable attempt at nonchalance.

"And so far the convenience appears to be all on the princess's side," Alistair pointed out. "I hesitate to appear meddlesome, Marcus, but what is the benefit to you?"

Marcus met his eyes very directly. "I want a reckoning. She owes me that."

Alistair was shaking his head. "There is nothing so bitter and empty as revenge, Marcus. Let it go."

"It is not for me," Marcus argued, knowing that he was lying in part at least. "Princess Isabella drove a wedge between India and her mother that never healed."

"And you feel guilty about India," Alistair said heavily. "So you think to make Princess Isabella suffer for your guilt."

The anger seethed within Marcus. "I would not allow many men to get away with such a remark," he said through shut teeth.

"Not many men would have the guts to tell you the truth," Alistair said with unimpaired calm.

The tension in the room simmered down a degree. Marcus gave a short laugh. "Damn you, Alistair."

"By all means, old fellow," Alistair agreed.

There was a silence.

"I do feel guilty," Marcus admitted, after a moment. "India and I led such separate lives. I was never there for her."

"She would still have died, Marcus. You were not responsible for that."

Marcus moved restlessly. "If I had been here in Town instead of at Stockhaven…"

Alistair shook his head. "Marcus, she stepped in front of a carriage. It was an accident."

Marcus did not reply. He wondered if there would ever come a time when he could think of his late wife without the mixture of paralyzing guilt and remorse that he felt now.

"I do not suppose," he said after a moment, "that you know where Princess Isabella will be this evening?"

Alistair looked at him suspiciously. "What, am I your social secretary now? She is *your* wife. That is the sort of thing that a husband should know."

Marcus sighed. "Touché, old chap. So?"

Alistair sighed, too. "You will find her at the Duchess of Fordyce's ball. The old lady is very high in the instep, but not too high to welcome royalty."

"Foreign royalty with a tarnished reputation?"

"Always welcome. It gives Her Grace's guests something to talk about."

"Hmm." Marcus found that he disliked the idea of people gaping at Isabella as though she were a freak show. He knew he should not give a rush either way, but he did, and the knowledge was not entirely welcome.

"Do you have an invitation?" he inquired.

Alistair looked wry. "Second sons do not receive invitations to the Duchess of Fordyce's events, Marcus." He frowned. "I thought that we were going to White's tonight?"

Marcus shook his head. "My plans have changed. I would like to indulge my sudden taste for society. Do you think the Duchess would welcome an itinerant earl, if not a younger son?"

"If the earl were rich and respectable enough, he would be welcomed with open arms," Alistair said dryly. "I am not certain that she approves of you, though, Marcus. You are somewhat disreputable."

Marcus looked offended. "I am not!"

"Well, at the least you are…" Alistair waved his hand about vaguely as though trying to pluck a description from the air.

"Eccentric. Different. You are not in the normal run of earls. You have odd interests."

"My interests are *not* odd."

Alistair picked a book from the table and tilted it toward the lamplight. *"Theoretical Naval Architecture,"* he read aloud. "I rest my case."

Marcus shrugged. "I am undertaking the design of a new frigate for the admiralty. They are plagued by those fast ships of the American Navy and wish to match their skill."

Alistair laughed. "I doubt that such projects, worthy as they are, will convince the Duchess of Fordyce that you are anything other than unconventional, Marcus."

"Well, if the duchess will not invite me then I must invite myself," Marcus said. "I doubt that she will go so far as to throw me from the door."

Alistair raised his brows critically. "You will attend a society ball looking like that?"

"Of course." Marcus got to his feet. "My story is that I am but recently returned from Italy. They are a great deal more casual in their dress on the continent."

"They would need to be deplorably so to pass muster looking as you do," Alistair said with a grin. "However, if we are fortunate, the evening will already be well advanced and no one will notice us."

"On the contrary," Marcus said, "I intend to make an entrance."

"To what purpose?"

Marcus's eyes gleamed. "To disconcert my wife, of course. It will be my pleasure."

He got to his feet. "An undertaker's mute, eh?" he said with a look at his friend. "How very appropriate, when I imagine that Princess Isabella will view my arrival very much as the funeral of all her plans." He clapped Alistair on the back. "Let us waste no more time. I am anxious to claim my bride."

CHAPTER FIVE

"STOCKHAVEN HAS BEEN ASKING about you, Mr. Warwick."

The room, at the top of a building in Wigmore Street, was hot and oppressive. Downstairs the expensive modiste's shop that fronted the business was closed for the night. The equally expensive brothel that operated at the back was just starting to get busy.

A dazzling peach-and-gold sunset was fading over the London rooftops, but inside the room, the dirty windowpanes seemed to block out all that was fresh and alive. A bluebottle buzzed plaintively against the glass, seeking escape. The candles hissed softly. The man behind the desk was writing. He did not pause, or look up.

"Where?" His voice was very quiet. It was one of the things about Edward Warwick that frightened people; the contrast between the smooth surface and the viciousness beneath.

"In the Fleet."

"I knew that." Warwick looked up and a slight smile touched his mouth. "I might almost feel sorry for him. Three months in that hellhole and not a thing to show for it." His expression sharpened, slate-gray eyes narrowing. "I take it that no one talked?"

"Of course not." The other man was standing in front of the desk. He had not been invited to sit. "No one would dare, sir."

Warwick stood up. He was not a tall man. Indeed, his air

of near-frailty might lead some to underestimate him. He was fair, willowy and of such indeterminate appearance that no one was likely to remember him clearly. Which was just as it suited him.

"Then why are you here, Pearce?" There was a distinct undertone of menace in Warwick's voice now. "It cannot be to tell me something I already know. I hope you are not wasting my time."

The other man was nervous. "No, sir. I'm here because Stockhaven got married. In the Fleet, three days ago. We thought you might wish to know."

Warwick froze. "Married? To whom?"

Pearce gulped. "To the Princess Isabella Di Cassilis, sir."

There was a silence. Nothing happened. Warwick was as still as though he had not heard. Nevertheless, Pearce quaked in his shoes.

"You are certain?" Warwick's voice was very soft now.

"Yes, sir. Which means that Stockhaven—"

"Owns Salterton Hall now. Yes, I realize that."

Pearce fell silent. Edward Warwick did not need him to make his deductions for him. He had a mind like a steel blade.

"I thought," Warwick said, after a long interval, "that Princess Isabella was ruined by debt and would be obliged to sell Salterton. How damnably annoying."

"Her debts were more pressing than we had been led to believe. She had no time." Pearce shook his head. "Henshalls are very discreet, sir."

Warwick sighed. Not even his intelligence was accurate every time.

"This is inconvenient."

Pearce knew that to be an understatement. He waited.

Warwick sighed again. "Very well. Leave this with me. Watch Stockhaven, and keep me informed." He opened the top drawer of the desk and took out a small bag. The contents clinked softly. Warwick pushed it across the desk to Pearce. "You have done well."

Pearce was so relieved that his body came out in a cold sweat. He brushed a droplet away from his brow. "Thank you, sir."

He took the money and went. The fresh air swirled along the corridor downstairs. He could hear the sounds of female shrieks and masculine laughter from the open windows of the brothel. He did not want to linger. He had money for drink now and he still had his job. And his life. The last man to occupy Pearce's role had disappeared and turned up six weeks later in the Thames. One could never be certain with Mr. Warwick.

ACROSS TOWN IN BRUNSWICK Gardens, Isabella was reading the evening edition of the *Gentlemen's Athenian Mercury*. That newspaper was taking a close interest in her affairs and she did not care for it.

> Members of the Ton will doubtless be disappointed to have seen so little of the lovely Princess IDC since her return from foreign shores. Can it be true that the princess has become a recluse, or is it merely that she is so short of funds that she cannot afford a new dress in which to dazzle society? Or perhaps the upright society hostesses cannot countenance such a bird of paradise upsetting their nests? One matter is for sure— the Princess will not find a rich gentleman to meet all her needs if she hides away at home….

Isabella put down the paper with a sigh. For a week now that vulgar publication had been running a series of announcements on the return of a certain royal personage whom they coyly referred to as Princess IDC. It did not take the finest minds in Europe to identify which particular princess they were referring to. Isabella sighed again. It seemed that someone was selling information about her. Most of it was presented as speculation, of course, but a couple of times the informant had been uncomfortably close to the mark. There had been a reference to her need to sell the Brunswick Gardens house, for example, and an accurate description of its tasteless opulence. Isabella found it disconcerting that someone should know so much about her life.

"Miss Penelope Standish, Your Serene Highness."

The butler's smooth tones broke into her thoughts. Belton spoke with the air of a man announcing news in somewhat dubious taste. It had been clear to Isabella from the beginning that Belton was a servant of discrimination, who felt it might be slightly beneath his dignity to work for a family where the genes of King George's fishmonger were combined with the poor reputation of a third-rate European prince. After all, he had served the most high-ranking families of the land. This could only be construed as a comedown.

The butler's tone was not lost on the young lady who entered the library, for she gave him a twinkling smile. When he responded with a faint but irresistible twitch of the lips, she went into a peal of laughter.

"Good evening, Belton. I always have the impression that you wish you had a respectable duchess to announce."

"Madam..." the butler said repressively. "It is scarcely my place to express a preference."

Pen gave him another melting smile, very like her sister's, and came forward to kiss Isabella.

"You look very doleful this evening, Your Serene Highness," she said. "Have you lost a guinea and found a groat?"

"Please drop the Serene Highness nonsense," Isabella besought. "I have asked Belton time and time again, but he insists that it is not appropriate merely to call me madam."

"I should think not," Pen said cheerfully, throwing herself down on the sofa with hoydenish abandon. "The least you can do is give your servants the gratification of addressing you properly if they have the privilege of working for a princess. There is nothing worse than a lady of consequence who will not accept her own importance, you know."

"You talk a great deal of nonsense," Isabella said. Nevertheless, she felt cheered. Until Pen had arrived she had been drinking a solitary cup of tea and staring blankly at the newspapers, wondering what the *Gentlemen's Athenian Mercury* would make of the real truth. She had importuned a former lover to marry her; she had contracted the marriage in the Fleet Prison and she intended to have it annulled as soon as she could. If the editors of the papers knew the true story, their gossip columns would likely burst into flames.

"You look tired," Pen was saying solicitously.

"I have not slept," Isabella said with a sigh. "It puts me out of countenance."

It was not in fact accurate to describe the last night as sleepless. Her bouts of wakefulness had been punctuated by broken dreams about Marcus of such astoundingly erotic content that she had been dizzy and aroused upon awakening, unable to banish him from her mind. She had been forced to dredge up her Latin declensions in order to try and bore herself to calm. It was the third night it had happened and thinking of it now was sufficient to put her out of countenance all over again.

"Are we not to attend the Duchess of Fordyce's rout?" Pen inquired, stripping off her gloves. She gestured to her rose-pink gown. "Here I am dusting down the only dress in my wardrobe worthy of the occasion and I find you sitting here with a face like a December morning." Her comical expression faded. "Oh! I forgot—you were to see Mr. Churchward this week about Ernest's debts, were you not? Was it so very bad?"

"Worse than very bad," Isabella confirmed.

Pen made a tutting sound. "Then I am surprised not to find

you at your packing," she said. "Was Mr. Churchward's advice not to return to the continent?"

"It was one of the suggestions that he made," Isabella said evasively. She did not intend to tell Pen about her marriage of convenience. This was no altruistic move designed to spare her sister the shock, but sprang from the certain knowledge that Pen would disapprove and, further, would express that disapproval in very pithy terms. And since Isabella intended to dissolve the marriage before the ink was dry on the certificate, there was no need for Pen to know anything. It would have been nice to have a confidante, but in recent years Isabella had become used to keeping her own counsel and, besides, she knew the one thing it would be dangerous to discuss was Marcus Stockhaven.

"This house is to be sold," she continued. "Not that I regret that particularly, since it was Ernest's and he furnished it in his customary deplorable taste."

Pen looked around at the ostentatious golden ornaments and flamboyant decor. "It would be appropriate for a bawdy house," she conceded, "but I cannot favor it for a residence."

"Mr. Churchward thinks that a nabob may buy it," Isabella said gloomily. "Home from home, so to speak."

"A sound idea." Pen reached over and rang the bell for another cup of tea. "And if you need additional funds," she added, "you could sell off those gaudy knickknacks Ernest bought one by one."

Isabella shook her head. "They are worthless. Just as my jewelry is mostly paste, so are the ornaments all made of gilt. The Di Cassilis treasures were pawned years ago to pay for Ernest's pleasures."

Pen sighed. "How very frustrating. You must have been tempted to go upstairs, cut up all of Ernest's English clothes and throw them into the streets out of sheer revenge."

Isabella frowned. "I cannot destroy those," she said. "I need to sell them."

The door opened to admit a footman carrying a tea tray with a fresh pot, a china cup and several floury scones.

Pen poured. "Scones at this time of the evening!" she said delightedly. "What a marvelous way to fortify oneself for a ball." She stirred honey slowly into her tea. "Where will you live when the house is sold, Bella?"

"I intend to live quietly at Salterton Hall on the money that Aunt Jane left me," Isabella said. "I rather fancy becoming a recluse."

Pen, who was about to take a mouthful of tea, almost choked.

"You have windmills in your head, Bella, if you imagine that retiring to a seaside resort will turn you into a recluse," she declared. "Surely you realize that you will always remain an object of curiosity, especially in a small society like that of Salterton?"

"After racketing around Europe in Ernest's shadow, I assure you that a little peace and quiet is what I require," Isabella said. "I am persuaded that Salterton will not find me in the least bit scandalous or even interesting."

Pen gave a disbelieving snort. "And I assure you that they will. If I had any money I would bet on it." The derisive note faded from her voice. "You will become bored, you know, Bella. It may seem appealing now to settle in a quiet backwater, but in a short while you will be looking for occupation."

"I am sure that I will find something with which to occupy myself," Isabella said comfortably. She had thought long and hard about her future and the idea of a quiet retirement was hugely attractive. "The sea cure, the circulating library, the visitors from Town... All will provide me with distraction."

Pen's face lit with a smile. "You could always write letters, I suppose. I remember that you were a prodigiously interesting correspondent during your marriage."

Isabella grimaced. "I thank you, but no." She tapped the newspaper. "It seems that some enterprising person has already chosen to profit from my activities. It is only a matter of time before my letters make it into print. It is most vexing," she added. "Such a shoddy little publication, as well!"

"Would it have been better had the gossip been printed in the *Times?*" Pen inquired.

"Certainly. One gets a better standard of scandal in those sorts of papers." Isabella sighed gustily. "It cannot be helped. My entire married life has been dogged by quizzes and gossips. But you will forgive me if I do not set pen to paper again."

Pen's brow was furrowed as she scanned the column in the paper.

"Do you know who is writing this?"

Isabella shrugged. "It could be anyone. Acquaintances, servants… Certainly it seems to be someone who has more than a little knowledge of my life."

Pen bit her lip. "Do you intend to try and find out who it is?"

Isabella raised her brows. "I shall not bother. A little more tittle-tattle can scarcely harm me."

Pen put the paper aside. "So if you are not to write letters," she said, "the seawater cure it is. Assuming that you do not expire from the excitement first!" She paused. "You do know that you will have Marcus Stockhaven as tenant at Salterton? Aunt Jane leased Salterton Cottage to him when he and cousin India were married."

Isabella, whose teacup had been balanced precariously on the arm of her chair, now jumped so much that the liquid cascaded onto the floor.

"Marcus Stockhaven? Why did you not tell me before?"

She realized that her words had come out much more stridently than she had intended. Pen was staring at her, a little flushed.

"Well, upon my word! I had no idea that the matter would be of such great import to you after all these years," she said. "Is it not Mr. Churchward's job to acquaint you with your inheritance, rather than mine?" She paused, adding more lightly, "Marcus has seldom visited Salterton since Aunt Jane died. You need have no fear of meeting him unexpectedly, if that is what concerns you."

"I beg your pardon," Isabella said, still flustered. Her pulse was thrumming and her heart beating in her throat, and it was the mere mention of Marcus's name that had done it. God forbid that she should meet him again. She would be a quivering wreck. But of course, she would not. She reminded herself that he was in prison. Perhaps the tenancy of Salterton had been a problem for him. Since he did not own the house, he would not have been able to sell it to settle his debts.

She used the opportunity provided by the spilled tea to turn away from Pen and gather up her shattered control. "I did not intend to sound so sharp, Pen. I was merely surprised." She looked up, as flushed as Pen from surprise and guilty conscience. "I do apologize."

Pen looked evasive. "Oh, it is nothing to the purpose. It must have slipped the minds of both Aunt Jane and myself to mention it in our correspondence."

Isabella hesitated. There was an odd tone in Pen's voice and an odd feeling in the room, as though something had been left unsaid. She waited but Pen merely avoided her gaze and fidgeted with her teaspoon, smearing honey over the saucer.

"I infer that Mr. Churchward did not mention the matter to you at all?" Pen added.

Isabella's shoulders slumped. She recalled that on her first meeting with Churchward after she had returned to England, the lawyer had indeed attempted to tell her something of the encumbrances upon her new estate, but she had waved the matter aside. The issue of Ernest's debts had become far more pressing than any other matter and she had forgotten all about the details of Salterton. It looked as though it would prove to be an expensive oversight. It seemed that she was tied to Marcus Stockhaven in more ways than she had anticipated, and none of them were welcome.

"No, he did not," she said. "How provoking!"

Pen raised her eyebrows. "That Churchward forgot to tell you?"

"No! Yes!" Isabella collected herself. "I do recall him mentioning something about a tenant, but I did not pursue it."

"Oh well…" Pen seemed anxious to let the subject go. "I imagine you will not be much troubled by Marcus. Salterton Cottage was damaged by fire a few months ago and is uninhabitable. Besides, Marcus chooses to live elsewhere—or to travel. One seldom sees him in society. I am not even sure where he is now."

Imprisoned in the Fleet for debt, Isabella thought.

She swallowed a variety of uncomfortable feelings and kept quiet. Her overriding emotion was a deep and heartfelt desire for Marcus to be kept under lock and key. If he were ever to be free…the very thought of it was sufficient to make her insides quake.

At the same time, she was puzzled. What had happened to render Marcus's financial state so dire? She had asked him but he had declined to explain and she had not pressed. Now she wished she had.

"I imagine you will not be much troubled by him…"

Truth to tell, she was already far more troubled by Marcus Stockhaven than Pen would ever know.

Her sister was fidgeting with her cup.

"I wish I could help you, Bella," Pen was saying. "Financially, I mean. I know this is not how you would have wished your return to England to be."

Isabella shook her head. She appreciated her sister's generosity but Pen subsisted on next to nothing as it was. Their father had left her a small allowance, enough to permit her to live quietly in an unfashionable corner of London, but there was certainly not enough to make any kind of impression on Ernest's debts.

"You are all kindness, Penelope," she said, smiling, "but my situation is not too dreadful. I have managed to stave off bankruptcy for a few months and once this house is sold, I shall be solvent again and able to afford to live in the country if I am careful. In fact my plans are falling out rather well."

Rather well if one discounted the small inconvenience of an unwanted husband, she amended silently. She made a mental note to ask Mr. Churchward for the particulars of annulment at once. She hoped that he might be able to speak of matters such as non-consummation of the marriage without too much personal embarrassment.

Pen's chatter recalled her thoughts.

"I warrant that some country gentleman will snap you up," her sister was saying. "A man of fortune and standing in Salterton society, who has great plans for the development of the place as a resort and wishes for a titled wife to add to his prestige."

"God forbid," Isabella said, shuddering. "I fear I would be too outrageous for such an upright man."

Her sister looked at her. "True," she said, after a moment. "There is something—" she hesitated "—something too sophisticated about you to sit comfortably in a small town with a small-town husband. You would always do something scandalous and shock the local worthies. I know you."

"I am not scandalous!" Isabella objected. "Ernest was scandalous. I am quite…"

"Quite?"

"Quite respectable."

"Doing it too brown, Bella," Pen said with relish. "It is true that you are not disreputable in the sense that Ernest was, but being a princess has conferred certain privileges on you that make you dismissive of society's rules."

"I insist that you give an example," Isabella said indignantly.

"Very well." Pen seemed calmly assured of the truth of her assertion. "You put your elbows on the dinner table. You address the servants directly as though they were real people. You have been known to attend a sparring match at the Fives Court. You have ridden one of those newfangled hobbyhorse wheeled contraptions, which no lady could consider genteel—"

Isabella waved a dismissive hand. "Such matters are scarcely outrageous!"

"You told the Duchess of Saint Just that she treated her niece worse than a scullery maid—"

"Well, so she did. She forced the child to starch the linen until her fingers blistered!"

"And you told Prince Bazalget that he was an old lecher to consider marrying a seventeen-year-old girl."

Isabella opened her eyes very wide. "I have strong feelings on such a subject."

"Understandably," Pen said. "But you do admit the accuracy of what I am saying?"

Isabella deflated a little. "I suppose so. Manners do not make this princess, do they?"

Pen leaned across and gave her a spontaneous hug. "You are splendid, Bella. But you will never be respectable."

A certain raucous noise from the entrance hall at that moment suggested that the remaining member of the Standish family had arrived and that Isabella was not the only one to be less than respectable. Belton threw the library door open.

"Lord Standish," he announced with dreadful calm, as though the evening could only degenerate further.

Like his sisters, Freddie Standish was very pleasing to the eye. Fair and slim, he was a general favorite with the matrons as long as he made no attempts to seek fortune by marrying one of their daughters. He shared the modest house in

Pimlico with Pen and worked—nominally, at least—for a banker who liked the prestige of having a titled gentleman to deal with the social side of his business. Despite the ignominy of his situation, Freddie always seemed good-humored and blessedly unflustered. Isabella loved him for it, though Pen maintained with dry affection that Freddie only had one mood because he was too stupid to have developed a range of them.

"Good evening, Freddie," Isabella said, tilting her face up for his kiss of greeting. "I was telling Pen that I have managed to stave off bankruptcy for a few months, until the house is sold."

"Congratulations," Freddie said, sitting down on the sofa and ungallantly obliging his sister to move up to give him more space. He looked about him. "Never liked the place myself. Far too vulgar."

"Yes, it is," Isabella said with a sigh. "I shall be retiring to Salterton instead."

Freddie looked horrified. "Salterton? In Hampshire?"

"Dorset," Pen snapped. "I told her it was a foolish idea."

"Quite right," Freddie said. He helped himself to one of the buttered scones on the dainty china tea plate. "Dorset is unspeakably dull. Why not try Kent instead, Bella?"

Isabella heard Pen give an exaggerated sigh. Not for the first time she wondered how the bookish and sharp-witted Penelope and the intellectually slow Freddie ever managed to share a house in anything approaching harmony.

"You will not wish to visit me, then," she said.

"No danger of that," Freddie said cheerfully. "I would rather work for a living than retire to Dorset."

"You are already supposed to work for a living," Pen pointed out.

"Only notionally," Freddie said with a cheerful grin.

"Unfortunately I do not have that option," Isabella said

briskly. "As a governess or a maid I would earn insufficient money in my entire life to cover Ernest's debts. And the only other alternative is to become a cyprian. I suppose one may work from home and do hours to suit—"

"Steady on, Bella!" Freddie was so scandalized that his half-eaten scone slipped off his tilting plate. Pen retrieved it.

Isabella patted his arm. "I apologize, Freddie. I was only speaking in jest."

"So I should hope," Freddie said, squaring his shoulders. "Head of the family. Couldn't approve. Sorry, Bella, but there it is."

"Of course not," Isabella said comfortingly.

"I would rather you married Augustus Ambridge than contemplate a career as a demimondaine," Freddie said. "And you won't hear me say that very often."

This time it was Pen who intervened. "I cannot agree with you, Freddie. Augustus Ambridge is the most tiresome bore."

They fell to squabbling like a pair of schoolchildren and Isabella sighed. It was fortunate that one of the alternatives she was not considering was sharing the Pimlico house with her siblings. In that event she would likely run mad within two days. They did not even notice when she slipped out of the room to find her cloak and evening slippers for the ball.

As she came down the staircase, she met Belton in full sail, like a galleon with a following wind.

"Lord Augustus Ambridge has arrived and is awaiting you in his carriage, Your Serene Highness," Belton announced, with a hint of approval in his voice at long last.

"Thank you, Belton," Isabella said. She put her head around the library door, cutting through the wrangling of her brother and sister with a crisp:

"Children! Lord Augustus is here to escort us to the ball."

"Just like the fairy godmother," Pen said. She rose to her feet. "I am looking forward to this evening, Bella. As it is your first social event in the Ton since your widowhood, you may prove to me just how inconspicuous you can be."

"I intend to," Isabella said, glaring repressively at her. "I shall be as quiet and retiring as a nun, I assure you. It will be in no way a night to remember."

CHAPTER SIX

ISABELLA HAD ALWAYS CONSIDERED royalty to be vastly over-rated. The same people who bowed and smiled this evening as she glided along the sumptuous red tartan carpet at the Duchess of Fordyce's Scottish reception would have cut her dead when she had been little Isabella Standish, without a handle to her name or a feather to fly. In fact they *had* cut her dead. She recognized plenty of faces from her season as a deb-utante twelve years before but reflected that it was more likely that she would recognize people's backs. She could still recall them turning away in disdain and those long-ago whispered conversations:

"Who is that?"

"Nobody, my dear... That jumped up fishmonger's grand-daughter, Isabella Standish..."

"Oh, oh I see.... I thought she looked well to a pass but now I realize that she is nowhere near as pretty as she would have been with a title and a fortune...."

Isabella paused patiently while Lord Augustus halted to receive the greeting of the Duchess of Fordyce herself, flanked by her three unmarried daughters and the bored-looking son and heir to the Fordyce millions. John Fordyce had brightened when he spotted Penelope following behind. Gentlemen did brighten when they saw the angelic-looking Penelope. The good impression generally lasted until she opened her mouth, when everyone else realized what Isabella and Freddie already knew—that she was a bluestocking with a tongue that could flay you alive.

"Lord Augustus!" The duchess was smiling so hard that Isabella feared her rouge would crack. She had heard that Her Grace seldom smiled for fear of the aging effect of wrinkling. Tonight, however, she had evidently granted herself a special dispensation.

"How utterly delightful to have you back with us in London, my lord," the duchess said. "And with your dazzling companion! Your Serene Highness…" A fulsome curtsy followed. "Thank you for choosing to adorn our event this evening."

Isabella heard Penelope give a snort of derision that she did not even attempt to turn into a cough. She gave her sister a quelling look.

"It is a great pleasure to be here, Duchess," Isabella said, adding with scrupulous truth, "Your Scottish exhibition is quite spectacular."

It was indeed. Ever since the Prince Regent had started a craze for all things Caledonian earlier in the year with his sudden and rather awkward nostalgic attachment to the Stuart dynasty, the Tory hostesses has adorned their houses with tartans and bagpipes and the dancing was all reels and strathspeys. Isabella could hear a fiddler tuning up in the ballroom to the right of them; when the strains of the violin where joined by the wheeze of the bagpipes, several people in the vicinity had the pained expressions of those suffering the earache.

"How marvelous," Isabella said, as the duchess winced at the sound. She turned to Augustus. "We must certainly dance the reel later, my lord."

The duchess beamed in relief and Augustus smiled, too, and gave Isabella's arm a little squeeze of approval, which irritated her with its proprietory overtones. Augustus, whom she had first met when he was a diplomat at the Swedish Court and she and Ernest were in exile there, had never been any more than a useful escort to social events. She suspected that like many men over the years, he liked to give the impression of being more than merely her friend. Her presence gave the staid diplomat a slightly risqué, man-of-the-world aura that she knew he enjoyed. Yet if it had come to marriage, she knew that matters would have been very different. There was no possibility that Augustus Ambridge would have taken on her reputation and her debts in any formal sense. He would have run from the thought like a lily-livered rabbit.

The duchess was greeting Penelope now. Her tone had cooled by at least ten degrees since she was speaking to someone with barely a title and very little fortune, whom she had identified as being an unsuitable prospect for her son. It seemed that John Fordyce had other ideas, however. Led astray by Pen's dazzling prettiness, he asked for her hand in the next Scottish dance.

"No, thank you, my lord," Pen said sweetly, "I only reel when I am drunk, and in the words of Shakespeare, drink is good only for encouraging three things, one of which is sleep and another urine. I merely quote, you understand, to illustrate my point."

One of the Fordyce sisters tittered behind her fan; the duchess's face turned still with horror and John's smile faltered as he backed away. "Some other occasion, perhaps," he sputtered.

"Oh, I do hope so," Pen said, smiling with luscious promise. "I look forward to it."

"Come along, Penelope," Freddie said hastily. "We are holding up the reception line."

Pen permitted herself to be drawn away from the group and up the sweep of stairs toward the ballroom.

"And you think that *I* am outrageous, Pen!" Isabella chided, taking her brother's arm as Augustus drew away from her with a hurried word and went off to seek the company of the duchess's more respectable guests. "We must be a sad trial to you, Freddie."

"Comes of having a fishmonger for a grandfather," Freddie said cheerfully. "Neither of you ever had any idea of how to behave. I suppose I must be the one to set the good example."

They reached the top of the staircase and he dropped their arms as abruptly as though they did not exist. A vision in pale blue had wafted across his line of sight.

"I say, there is Lady Murray!" he exclaimed with enthusiasm. "Excuse me—squiring one's sisters about is the most lamentable dead bore." And with that he dove into the crowd.

"Oh well," Pen said, linking her arm through Isabella's and drawing her into the ballroom. "So much for Freddie's manners! Lady Murray is his latest inamorata, I am afraid. It will end in tears."

"Hers?" Isabella asked.

"His," Pen said. "She dangles him on a string and there are at least three other gentlemen she dallies with."

"Now that," Isabella said, "*is* outrageous. How is it that I am tarred with scandal whilst others behave badly and no one raises an eyebrow?"

"Hypocrites," Pen said comfortingly. "Speaking of which, look at Augustus, Bella! He has eyes for no one but himself tonight."

It was true. Augustus Ambridge had stopped in front of one of the duchess's long gilt mirrors and was studying his appearance with intensity. Brown hair slicked back with Mr. Cabburn's Bear's Grease, a sovereign lotion for reviving thinning locks; buttons polished, shoulders ever so slightly padded, jacket bolstered with buckram from the Prince Regent's own tailor, calves plumped out with a little wadding to improve the shape of his leg… Indeed, Isabella reflected that he was the very image of an elegant diplomat, and barely an inch of it was real.

"Oh, Penelope," she chided. "Can you not at least try to like him?"

Penelope paused, apparently to give the matter genuine

consideration. "No," she said, at length, "why should I? Since you are not to marry him, there is no obligation on me to try. You are kinder than I am, you know, Bella. I would not even give him the time of day."

"I know." Isabella sighed.

"That is why I have never been married," Pen continued. "Nor am I likely to be. I have yet to meet a man who interests me."

"You judge too harshly," Isabella said. "Surely there must be a man who pleases you." She gestured across the ballroom. "Sir Edmund Garston, for example? He is extremely handsome."

Pen surveyed the dandified baronet as he raised a quizzing glass and ogled the gold lace on a passing lady. "No," she said. "He is too effeminate. He would teach one much about fashion and nothing about passion."

Isabella laughed. "A neat summary."

Around them the hum of the ballroom rose and fell. The orchestra was playing a strathspey with much enthusiasm and as many wrong notes. Isabella could see Augustus approaching a slender debutante in white, bow to her and ask for her hand in the dance. The girl accepted with a sketch of demure pleasure. Isabella smiled inwardly over Augustus's maneuvers. He was at the stage in his career where he required a well-connected wife with an impeccable reputation to enhance his prospects. She rather thought that this was where he and she parted company. She had served her purpose in drawing him to the attention of everyone who mattered and giving him a debonair gloss. Now he had to capitalize on that success.

People were watching her, gossiping over the perfidious behavior of her supposed lover. Isabella was accustomed to it. One of the oddest things about being an object of curiosity was that people seldom spoke to her but they always gossiped about her as though she was not there. She could hear the murmurs:

"They will tolerate any old riffraff on the continent, of

course. Her husband was a rackety fellow and her own rep-
utation is none too sweet.... Do you know, she was so indif-
ferent to scandal that she permitted her husband's mistress
to attend his funeral? She is only received because of the
title...."

Isabella sighed inwardly. Ernest's infamy was the only thing
that he had ever bestowed on her with any degree of generosity.

But the whisperer was not done yet. She had more powerful
ammunition still in her arsenal.

"Apparently they even tried to take her child away from
her.... She said she never wished for more children. An unfit
mother.... No wonder the poor little girl died."

It was like a sliver of glass in the heart. Isabella spun round
a little too quickly. Was that a real whisper or her bitter im-
aginings? Such words haunted her nightmares, even now, six
years after Emma's death...

She surveyed the nodding plumes and the eager faces
beneath the turbans. The matrons smiled and nodded back at
her, but their eyes were like ice. Then the dowager Lady
Burgoyne raised her voice a little.

"We were wondering, Your Royal Highness, whether you
are fixed in London for a while or whether your fancy will
take you elsewhere soon?"

There was a giggle and a flutter of fans. The gold-and-
white rout chairs creaked under matronly bottoms as they
wriggled with the glee of tormenting one of their own who
had stepped beyond the line. "If only you had kept to your
place," those wiggles seemed to say. "You climbed too high
and now we will punish you."

"Serene," Pen said loudly. "Princess Isabella is a Serene
Highness, not a royal one." Her face was flushed with loyal
indignation. She was as capable as Isabella at feeling the
nuances in the room.

Isabella put a gentle hand on her arm. She felt anything but serene. The hurtful jibe about Emma lodged painfully in her chest and she took several deep breaths to maintain control.

"Perhaps the princess will go wherever Lord Augustus Ambridge takes her," the voluminously padded Duchess of Plockton said, weighing into the debate. Her tortoise face surveyed the ballroom and paused at the sight of Augustus dancing with his debutante. "Oh, but it would seem that Lord Augustus's fancy has moved on." Her gaze swung back to Isabella. "Perhaps you have also found yourself a new…companion, Princess? You never allow much time to elapse, do you?"

Isabella felt Pen stiffen protectively again and open her mouth to give the duchess a blistering setdown. Pen knew no fear, but she did not deserve the disapprobation that would surely follow her outburst. On the other hand, Isabella knew that her own reputation was such that it scarce mattered what she said. Such knowledge was liberating. She dug her sister in the ribs and Pen spluttered into silence.

The music came to an end; there was a lull in the ballroom. And Isabella spoke with the clarity of a perfectly modulated bell.

"Thank you for your interest in my affairs, Duchess, Lady Burgoyne. I am sure you will be disappointed to know that my fancy seldom wanders toward any gentleman these days, and especially not whilst I am in this country. Englishmen make the very worst lovers in the entire world, as you may know."

There was a moment of silence, like the false calm before the first lightning strike, and then there was a collective intake of outraged breath. The shock broke over the ballroom like a series of intense ripples spreading out in an ever-widening circle.

Isabella smiled broadly. Let the Duchess of Plockton put that in her clay pipe and smoke on it until it choked her. Sometimes there was great satisfaction to be gained from overstepping the line, bad *ton* or not.

Across the ballroom, someone had already whispered her

words into Augustus Ambridge's ear. He straightened and looked at her with incredulous disapproval. Isabella continued to smile as she watched the outrage roll round the room like a thunderclap.

"Bella," Pen said beside her, awe in her voice, "may I behave like you when I grow up?"

Isabella was about to reply when a most peculiar sensation struck her in the midriff, depriving her of breath.

A man was standing in the doorway. His face was in shadow but there was something about his stillness that she instinctively recognized. Isabella shivered. Here was a powerful man who would be a deadly enemy but an incomparable lover. Her heart started to race. All the breath left her lungs in one gasp.

He looked magnificent. There was an uncompromising masculinity about him that seemed too rugged for the delicate air of the duchess's ballroom. It suggested that he had known every combination of risk and danger that life could offer and had invented some of his own. The dandies and the beaux suddenly looked faintly ridiculous.

Her words reached the outer edge of the ballroom and started to ripple back in toward her like an echo.

And Marcus Stockhaven stepped out of the shadows and moved toward her with a single-minded intensity, as though there were no one else in the ballroom at all.

CHAPTER SEVEN

"DAMNATION," ISABELLA SAID. She said it very quietly, so that only Pen heard, and then she watched as Marcus cut a ruthless path across the room to her side. He was not distracted by the greetings of friends and acquaintances. He looked as though he barely heard them. His attention was focused on her alone. The crowd fell back and then he was bowing before her.

"Good evening, Princess Isabella."

It was a conventional enough greeting, but there was nothing conventional about the look in Marcus's eyes. His expression was dark, dangerous and held a wickedly disturbing hint of amusement. Isabella could tell that he knew precisely how much his unexpected arrival had discomposed her and that it pleased him. Nor was the smile that played around his mouth in the least bit friendly. She drew herself up in response to the unspoken challenge in Marcus's eyes.

"Your observation on the amorous capabilities of Englishmen," Marcus added gently, "must be a provocation to any red-blooded gentleman in the room."

The question uppermost in Isabella's mind was what the devil he was doing there, but she knew that that would have to wait a little. Not by a flicker of an eyelash could she reveal the absolute mayhem rampaging inside her. She had known that twelve years of royal etiquette would come in useful one day. Now was that day.

She gave him a steely smile.

"Good evening, Lord Stockhaven," she said. "I should be sorry if you interpreted my words in the light of a challenge."

Marcus bowed slightly. "How would you like me to construe them, madam?"

"As a mere statement of fact, if you must interpret them at all." Isabella turned away from him with deliberation and drew Pen forward. "You are already acquainted with my sister, Penelope, of course."

"Of course." To Isabella's surprise, Marcus bent and kissed Pen lightly on the cheek. She had not known they were on such terms. The realization made her uneasy, for it brought him closer still into her family circle, as though she could find no refuge from him.

"How do you do, cousin Penelope?" Marcus said. "It is a pleasure to see you again."

Pen seemed genuinely pleased at the warmth of his greeting. "I am very well, thank you, my lord. Or should I say cousin Marcus?" Her bright blue gaze touched Isabella's face for a moment. "Of course my sister is also a cousin-in-law of yours, is she not? Surely she warrants the same degree of familiarity from you or she may become envious."

Isabella resisted the urge to kick Pen's ankle. Her little sister could be a dreadful troublemaker at times and just now she needed help not hindrance. Dealing with Marcus was difficult enough without Pen putting spokes in her wheel.

"I do not covet such a privilege, I assure you, Penelope," she said, giving her sister a hard stare to oblige her to keep quiet. She glanced at Marcus. "Lord Stockhaven may keep his kisses to himself—or bestow them on those ladies who appreciate them. I have no ambition for them."

Marcus looked at her. The smile still lingered on his lips and his eyes were full of a blazing light that incited a hot rush of feeling through Isabella's body. She knew he was remembering their kiss in prison. So was she. She could not help herself. The very memory of it threatened to burn her up. And Marcus was enjoying her torment, damn him. Her nerves shivered as she contemplated what he might be planning.

She turned an ostentatious shoulder, looking beyond Marcus to the gentleman behind him, who appeared vastly entertained by the whole conversation. She had no interest in him—in fact she barely saw him—but his presence there was useful because it meant that she could divert her attention away from Marcus.

"Good evening, sir," she said politely.

The gentleman bowed. He was shorter and sturdier than Marcus, with bright hazel eyes that missed very little.

"Your Serene Highness. Alistair Cantrell, entirely at your service."

"Mr. Cantrell." With a cold shock, Isabella recalled that this was one of Marcus's oldest friends, his groomsman from their canceled wedding ceremony. It was unlikely that she would receive much of a sympathetic welcome here. Marcus's friends had always struck her as being extremely loyal.

"Of course," she said. "I remember you."

"I am flattered, madam," Alistair said. His shrewd hazel gaze appraised her but she was unable to read anything of his feelings. Once again, she turned to Pen.

"Mr. Cantrell, may I introduce my sister, Miss Penelope Standish?"

Alistair Cantrell looked as dazzled as most gentlemen did when confronted with Pen's glowing prettiness. It was not at all difficult to read his feelings now. He was wondering, as did all gentlemen on first acquaintance, whether Pen could be as sweet as she looked.

"It is a pleasure to meet you, Miss Standish," he said.

"Mr. Cantrell," Pen said, inclining her head in the most perfect impersonation of a demure debutante. Isabella noted that Alistair Cantrell's lips twitched in a wry smile, and Pen actually blushed. It seemed that he was not a man to be fooled by feigned innocence.

A crush of people was pressing closer now, evidently intending to claim Marcus's acquaintance. The Duchess of Plockton clearly felt that she had been out of the limelight long enough and was pushing herself forward, dragging her pallid daughter with her, one hand clamped about the girl's wrist like a manacle. For once Isabella was glad to see her. The duchess's approach was her cue to escape. She desperately needed time to gather her thoughts and decide how to deal with her errant husband. She did not wish to give him the pleasure of provoking her in public. Yet she trembled with nervousness and anger at the thought of a private settlement of their differences.

She took a cautious step away from Marcus as the others drew near. Immediately he put his hand on the small of her back to restrain her. She could feel his warmth sear her through the thin silk of her dress. To the casual observer it would appear no more than the affectionate greeting of cousins, but to Isabella it felt like the possessive intimacy of a lover.

"Lord Stockhaven!" The duchess hailed Marcus like a long-lost friend. Isabella made another slight movement of escape and immediately Marcus's arm tightened around her.

"Oh, no, you don't," he whispered in her ear. His breath sent a quiver of sensation along the sensitive skin of Isabella's neck and she shifted with a mixture of sensuous longing and sheer nervousness. Marcus looked down at her and the heated blaze in his eyes was enough to shake her to her soul.

"How do you do, Lord Stockhaven?" The duchess was utterly insensitive to atmosphere. She shouldered her way through the group and placed herself firmly in front of them.

"Have you been on your travels again, my lord?"

"I have indeed been traveling, Your Grace," Marcus said with a slight smile. He did not appear anxious to pursue the conversation, nor to move away from Isabella's side, but the duchess was impervious to subtlety.

"Where did you visit this time?" The duchess was also nothing if not persistent.

"Italy." Marcus's brevity was matched only by his look of faint boredom. Isabella felt the arm about her waist draw her even closer. Their bodies were touching now at elbow and hip and thigh. Cold shivers of excitement were running through her blood. She could feel the color coming up into her face as though she had a fever. Any moment now, Pen, with that bluntness for which she was famed, would ask her if she was suffering from the ague.

Her Grace of Plockton was not to be dislodged by mere brevity. She dug her fan into her daughter's ribs.

"Don't stand there like a pudding, Dorinda! Ask Lord Stockhaven about his trip to Italy!"

"Did you enjoy your travels in Italy, Lord Stockhaven?" Lady Dorinda Plockton asked, as obedient as a well-trained child.

"Yes, thank you," Marcus said.

There was a short silence as it became apparent that he did not intend to elaborate. Lady Dorinda, however, did not lack the art of small talk and was anxious to prove it before her mother prompted her again.

"Whereabouts did you stay, my lord?" she asked.

"I toured Rome and Florence and Verona and traveled back through Cassilis, ma'am," Marcus said smoothly. Isabella jumped. She could feel his sideways glance like a physical touch, stroking her skin, daring her to contradict him and lay the truth bare. She kept silent.

"Cassilis is a most insignificant principality, I have always thought," the duchess said, with a quick malevolent glance in Isabella's direction. "Nothing notable has ever come out of Cassilis."

"On the contrary, Your Grace," Marcus said politely. "I

must beg to differ. There are many remarkable things that derive from Cassilis. It is a place of infinite surprise, all the more notable since most of its secrets remain well hidden."

Isabella's gaze snapped up to his face. His expression was bland as he met her eyes but she knew that amusement was not far below the surface. Once again he was trying to provoke her, damn him to hell and back. This was a game to him and he was going to play it for all it was worth.

She took a step away from his side and this time he let her go. She tilted her chin up and gave him a very straight look.

"How extraordinary that you should claim to know Cassilis so well, my lord," she said. "I had no notion that you had been there, particularly recently. I had thought you were visiting…somewhere quite different."

There was a flash of expression in Marcus's eyes. "You seem remarkably well-informed of my activities, madam," he said coolly. "Am I then of particular interest to you? I count myself flattered to think so."

"You should not," Isabella said. "My interest was not personal. I was merely going to suggest that the next time you visit Cassilis, you make a special point of seeing the Palazzo de Spinosa. It is very beautiful and houses a marvelous collection of frescoes by Piozzi. They are all based upon *fairy stories*." She paused for emphasis, adding with limpid innocence, "I imagine you would find them fascinating, given your interest in myths and fantasies."

Marcus looked at her. She looked back artlessly, brows raised. Their eyes met and held with a clash like the first crossing of swords between duelists.

"It is a tempting thought," Marcus said slowly. He looked her over thoughtfully. "Perhaps you could give me a personal view, madam. Next time I am in Cassilis."

His meaning was explicitly clear and conjured a tumble of erotic images in Isabella's mind that were far more vivid than mere painted frescoes and far too inappropriate for the duchess's ballroom. She swallowed hard, trying to banish the thought of their limbs entwined in passionate abandon, his mouth, hard and hungry, on her own.

"You may find," she said, clearing her throat, "that entry to Cassilis is barred to you, my lord. Traveling is an uncertain business, and you are—" She paused. "Not always the most welcome of visitors."

Marcus's dark eyes narrowed thoughtfully on her face. A ripple of amusement went around the group that enclosed them. Isabella jumped. She had almost forgotten that they had an audience, so tangled had she become in the strong emotions that Marcus's presence aroused.

"We shall see," Marcus said. He was still watching her. "As we have so much in common, cousin Isabella, perhaps we should step aside and discuss our mutual... passions further rather than boring these good people with our shared anecdotes?"

Isabella could feel the Duchess of Plockton bridling at her side, determined that a tin-pot princess would not upstage her, so she flashed Marcus a sweet smile.

"I would not dream of monopolizing your company, my lord," she said. "I am sure that Lady Dorinda would enjoy hearing more of your experiences whereas I, I fear, am quite exhausted by travelers' tales. So very dull."

Marcus smiled back at her. It was not a reassuring smile.

"I am devastated to think that you might find me dull, Princess Isabella," he murmured. "Give me the opportunity to persuade you to the contrary."

At last the intimacy of the exchange was beginning to have an effect on their companions. Alistair Cantrell seemed slightly embarrassed, like a man wishing he could recall another pressing engagement a long way away. Pen was looking from Isabella's face to Marcus's, her eyes bright, her gaze curious.

"We are boring our audience, Lord Stockhaven," Isabella said gently.

Marcus's gaze did not move from her face. "Then let us speak in private," he said again.

Isabella shook her head slowly. "Pray do not take offense, my lord," she said, "but I have no wish to do so. A gentleman would need to be exceptional to arouse sufficient interest in me that I would wish to spend time with him."

"As illustrated by your statement earlier, madam, about English lovers." Marcus had drawn closer to her again. His broad shoulders blocked out the rest of the ballroom. She felt isolated, cut off from the rest of the world. Her pulse was pounding, her entire body tense from the effort of matching him word for word, challenge for challenge.

Marcus spoke softly. His tone was rough, like a knife against silk.

"You should give me the chance, Your Highness. I insist upon it. You will find my tales—and my other attributes—far from dull, I assure you." He looked around and deliberately raised his voice. "To persuade you, perhaps I should reveal before all these good people that you are my—"

The word *wife* seemed to hang in the tense air between them. Isabella turned icy cold. Surely... Surely he would not call her bluff in this most public and outrageous of ways? And yet, why not? That would be so very typical of Marcus. He had no fear of scandal.

"Lord Stockhaven!" The words burst from Isabella, half in appeal and half in warning.

"—my inspiration in my travels," Marcus finished, very gently.

Isabella could hear the underlying mockery in his voice. She felt weak with a combination of relief and anger. Damn him! Damn him for doing this to her and for enjoying it. He should be safely locked up in the Fleet. It was inexcusable that he was not. Quite evidently he had tricked her, and her temper was now so frayed that she did not wish to delay telling him exactly what she thought of him. The scandalmongers wanted something to gossip over? Well, she would give it to them.

She slipped her hand through Marcus's arm. After his initial start of surprise, he kept quite still, coiled as tight as a spring and waiting to see what she would do next. She tilted her head in a provocative gesture and smiled up at him.

"I find that you inspire many feelings in me as well, Lord Stockhaven," she said sweetly, "but none of them are suitable for discussion in public." She smiled at their audience. "Excuse us, ladies and gentlemen. I simply must tell Lord Stockhaven what I think of him. In private." She arched a brow at Marcus. "Shall we, my lord?"

She knew even before he spoke that he was equal to any challenge she might throw down. The watchfulness in his eyes told her so.

"It will be my pleasure," Marcus said.

And Isabella had the disconcerting feeling that it would indeed.

MARCUS COULD FEEL THE ANGER in Isabella's body even as she placed her hand on his proffered arm. He drew her away from the knot of guests around the duchess and led her with deceptive gentleness toward the connecting door to the drawing room, where the Duchess of Fordyce had her Scottish artifacts exhibited. A huge swag of tartan draped the doorway, brushing Marcus's shoulder as they passed. The room was candlelit and very hot. The shadowy light flickered off a collection of military memorabilia including a dirk and a sword from the Battle of Sherrifmuir, a set of bagpipes that looked to Marcus's eyes to be rather moth-eaten and a chamber pot that had the dubious claim to fame of having belonged to Bonnie Prince Charlie. Neither of them was in the least bit interested in the exhibits, however. Isabella barely waited for them to achieve the privacy of a curtained alcove before she rounded on him, telling Marcus a great deal more about the tangled state of her emotions in the process than no doubt she had intended.

"What are you doing here?" she demanded.

"I should have thought that was obvious," Marcus drawled. He was enjoying her shock. "I am claiming my wife."

Isabella's blue eyes narrowed furiously. "You should be in jail—"

"Very probably," Marcus agreed. "A number of people have told me that over the years. However, the fact is that I am not."

"But *why* not?" Isabella's voice rose, but she moderated it at once. Marcus admired her self-control in a situation where most women would be having a fit of the vapors at the very least, if not resorting to a swoon. "Why are you here? You were imprisoned for debt!"

"I was in a debtor's prison," Marcus said. "Never at any point did I tell you that I had been imprisoned for debt. You made that assumption."

Isabella glared at him, eyes spitting fire. The air between them was thick with emotion. She felt trapped and she did not like it at all. He smiled gently and turned the screw still further. Leaning forward until his lips brushed her ear, he said quietly:

"I have paid off all your debts."

He felt her stiffen with fury. So now she was beholden to him as well as trapped by him, and she hated it—hated him—with a passion. He felt a dangerous rush of emotion at the power of the feeling between them. Love and hatred. The two were so close, and he wanted to wring a response—any response—from her to show that he still had the ability to do so.

"I see," she said through gritted teeth. "You are most generous, my lord."

"It was the least that I could do for my wife," he said, watching her face. "Perhaps one might call it a wedding present?"

Not by one flicker of expression did she betray her feelings at this deliberate provocation. She inclined her head with regal condescension.

"How thoughtful. Your first and last gift to me—for you may be sure that I shall sue for an annulment in the morning."

A gaggle of guests had come into the exhibition room. Marcus drew closer to Isabella, taking her elbow to draw her into a quieter corner.

"Have you any idea of how expensive and difficult an annulment can be to achieve?" he asked conversationally. "Particularly when your husband will not cooperate? You have no money to pursue it in the courts and without my promise of silence, all you will manage to do is stir up a huge scandal."

Isabella's head was bent. The candlelight picked out the strands of dark copper and chestnut in her hair. The faint scent of the jasmine perfume she always wore seemed to cloak her with all the elusive memories of their time together. An ache took Marcus then, a sudden deep desire to recapture all that they had lost. It was gone in an instant, but no less strong for all that.

He reminded himself that he had come to the ball that night to provoke her and to extract the first part of his revenge. He had wanted to make her suffer for all that she had inflicted on him by departing from his life so swiftly, only to reenter it again and imperiously demand his help without a thought for his feelings. He wished to make her feel powerless—as stripped and defenseless emotionally as her defection had made him feel all those years ago.

And he had done so, although she had concealed her feelings well in front of the crowd. He admired her for that. She was a very strong character. It made the contest between them much more enjoyable than if she had been a die-away creature with no backbone. But then, she would not have got where she was today, would not have climbed the greasy ladder to worldly riches and status, if she had not been able to trample the feelings of others on the way to her success.

However, it was not all about revenge. Two minutes in her presence had shown him that. He would have opposed an annulment anyway, simply to thwart her. Now he realized that he was going to do it not merely to make her suffer, but because he wanted her. He had never stopped wanting her.

She looked up directly into his eyes and he felt the tug of attraction so fiercely through his body that it was all he could do not to show it.

"I have no difficulty in stirring up a scandal if I have to," Isabella said coldly. "Surely you have realized that already?"

"I have noticed," Marcus said. He wondered how far she would be prepared to go. "I also care as little for the opinion of others as you appear to do, so it seems we are checkmated. Go ahead." He decided to call her bluff. "Cause a scandal. Tell the world that you married me for my money and now you wish to discard me."

Isabella frowned. Her fingers, tapping a brisk tattoo on the wooden frame of her fan, were the only indicator of her deep irritation. Marcus watched her struggles with interest.

"I do not understand why you would oppose an annulment, my lord," she said, after a moment. "Surely you cannot want this marriage any more than I do?"

Marcus smiled. "On the contrary," he said with absolute truth, "there are many aspects of the situation that appeal to me. You seem to have completely overlooked the possibility that I might wish—" He paused. "To achieve a full marriage."

He rubbed his fingers gently over the silken material of her sleeve and felt the tiniest shiver go through her. She was not indifferent to him as a man; she never had been. He felt a surge of savage triumph. He had needed that, to know that his own wanting had found an echo in hers.

"I am merely waiting," he said, a little roughly, "for you to indicate that you are ready to leave, madam. It is, to all intents and purposes, our wedding night, and after our enforced separation I find myself…eager…to be alone with you."

At last he had succeeded in shocking her. Her eyes searched his face as though trying to judge whether he was in earnest or merely playing with her, and he was certain that he saw a flicker of fear there, though when she spoke her tone was quite steady.

"I assume that you jest," she said coldly, twitching her sleeve from his fingers. "We are little more than strangers now."

Marcus shrugged. "That can be easily remedied."

She stared at him. "No!" Once again the fear flickered behind her eyes and was swiftly gone as she took a steadying breath. "It seems that I have misread you," she said. "What precisely is it that you want?"

"I have told you," Marcus said. "I want my bride."

She scrutinized him, her gaze shatteringly direct and appearing so scrupulously honest that he felt it probe his soul. It was an odd sensation and it made him feel slightly guilty. She looked so shocked, so betrayed. But that was what he had wanted. He had wanted her to feel helpless and be at his mercy.

"When I came to you in the Fleet…did you have this in mind from the very first?"

"Yes."

She blinked at his honesty.

"Why?" she asked.

"Revenge."

The stark word fell between them and into silence. In the background the pipe music skirled, a wistful backdrop to the fierce emotions between them.

"Revenge," Isabella repeated. She looked stunned. "Revenge for what?"

Marcus laughed incredulously. "Come, my love, I would think better of you if you did not pretend."

"Because I broke your heart?" There was a shade of scorn in Isabella's voice now. "I thought you were made of sterner stuff, my lord."

"I thought so, too." Marcus took her by the shoulders. He could feel her bones beneath the silk of her gown. Such a fragile creature and yet made of tempered steel. "You owe me because you are venal and corrupt and calculating and I want you to admit it," he said brutally. "I thought you all that was sweet and good, God help me. Then you dropped me to marry for money and a title. You gave me no explanation or excuse. You led the life of a whore and then you tried to buy me again when you required my help." His hands tightened mercilessly, drawing her close so that her breasts brushed his chest. She was very pale now and her gaze was blind. For a split second he wondered whether his words had hurt her, but then she tilted up her chin and defiance burned in her eyes.

"So you want to take me to prove yourself correct and to settle your debts," she said with such contempt that it burned him. "How like a man to try to make everything so simple. I tell you now—I shall not give you what you want."

Marcus let her go abruptly and stood back.

"And I will not consent to an annulment," he said stonily, "so disabuse yourself of the idea that I shall. And without my consent, my love—" he saw her instinctive, angry movement at the endearment "—you will not achieve your aim. I fear you are trapped and eventually you will come around to seeing matters from my point of view."

Isabella made a gesture that was full of repressed fury. "This is an intolerable situation!"

"It is a situation that you brought upon yourself," Marcus said.

"I require no reminder," Isabella snapped at him. "You may be certain that I shall extract myself from it one way or another as soon as I may." She took a deep breath. "I am certain for a start that our marriage must be illegal."

"And I hesitate to disappoint you but I promise it is not," Marcus drawled. "How could it be, when you went to such pains to make sure that it was lawful? And once it has been consummated, the match will be sealed as well as signed."

Two of the struts of Isabella's fan fractured under the pressure of her fingers. She rubbed the tiny splinters of wood from her gloved fingers.

"Once again, you go too far, my lord."

Marcus raised his hand and touched her cheek thoughtfully. He was hot with anger, but it could not quench the desire that drove him.

"You are my wife, Isabella," he said softly. "You have given me whatever rights I choose to take."

Her face warmed beneath his touch, but whether with fury or need he could not tell.

"Nonsense!" She sounded as though she wanted to have him flayed alive for his impudence. "I owe you nothing but the payment of my debt, Lord Stockhaven."

"Not so." Marcus's tone was hard now. "You owe me whatever I wish. You owe me a wedding night."

They stared at one another like gladiators locked in combat, captured in each other's eyes, sealed from the outside world.

One of the duchess's guests had come upon them unnoticed and now she brushed against Isabella's sleeve with a murmured apology and a more than curious glance. Isabella blinked, as though freed from a dream, and Marcus felt an almost physical tug as she pulled her gaze from him.

"We cannot discuss this here, my lord," she said. "The entire situation is—" Her voice shook a little. "It is absurd."

Marcus, too, was more shaken than he cared to admit. He cleared his throat. "Then let us adjourn somewhere more comfortable to take this…discussion…further."

"Not tonight," Isabella said. "I have no further desire for your company." Her expression dared him to insist.

Marcus hesitated. He could push the point but he had already forced her hand enough for one evening. He knew that she was on the very edge of her endurance. With infinite reluctance, he drew back.

"Then tomorrow," he said. "I shall call on you."

He took a step back, his gaze still locked with hers. Her expression was cold and unyielding but Marcus could feel what it cost her.

"Good night, my lady," he said.

Once again she inclined her head with that perfectly judged grace of royalty condescending to the lower orders. Marcus felt he had probably deserved that—he had pushed her as far from him as it was possible to go. There was dignity in her stance, but also something almost unbearably poignant and lonely. He hesitated on the verge of making some conciliatory gesture, but before he could do so she had dismissed him.

"Good night, my lord," Isabella said, and she turned from him, shutting him out as though forever.

ISABELLA WATCHED HIS TALL figure stride away across the ballroom; saw the debutantes sway like cut corn in his wake. She was willing to bet that any one of them would give their French embroidered underwear to be in her place as wife to Marcus Stockhaven.

She was no longer Princess Isabella Di Cassilis, relict of a ruinous and shipwrecked royal. She was Isabella, Countess of Stockhaven, wife to a man who apparently would not be slow to claim his marital rights unless she could prevent it. And at this moment her mind was utterly devoid of ways to circumvent him. Isabella shivered. She had miscalculated, and miscalculated badly at that. In her anxiety to escape the crushing blow of the debt, she had not thought matters through. She had trusted Marcus and that had proved a dangerous mistake. Now she was trapped. Marcus wanted something from her, and he would not let her go before he was satisfied.

You are venal and corrupt and calculating.... If she had ever cherished the least illusion that Marcus held on to some softer feeling for her, then that was now at an end.

Isabella swallowed hard. The pain was still there, an echo of the sharpness that had cut her to the bone when he had spoken. She bit her lip fiercely to repress the tears. She never cried. Early in her marriage she had discovered that Ernest had enjoyed seeing her tears, and from then she had schooled herself never to show weakness of any sort. It had become a habit but the ache was still there, wedged beneath her heart.

You led the life of a whore and then you tried to buy me again when you required my help....

Isabella clenched her jaw. Enough of that. She would think of it no more. There was bitterness in Marcus. It prompted him to seek revenge and she had to thwart him. She absentmindedly fingered the ruined struts of her fan. There was no possibility that she would reveal the truth to Marcus. She shrank from exposing all the horror and pain of the past to him and reliving it all again. She had locked all the love and the despair away in an ice-cold knot, and as long as she kept it buried there undisturbed, she would survive. A splinter of broken wood stabbed her finger and she winced.

You owe me a wedding night.

Never. She shook her head slowly. Too much had happened for her to face the prospect of being Lady Stockhaven in deed as well as in word. Twelve years ago, Marcus's touch had brought sheer bliss and the promise of future happiness. But twelve years was a long time and neither of them were the same people now.

It had broken her heart to part from Marcus when she was seventeen. Then Ernest had shown her how debased could be the other side of love, and then her daughter Emma had died, and now Isabella knew that she would risk neither love nor loss ever again. Her attraction to Marcus was dangerous—the embers of her love for him were still hot beneath the cold crust of ashes. But Marcus wanted her for all the wrong reasons. He had made his disgust of her absolutely clear and she would not give in to him, no matter the fire in her blood that she could not deny. It would be madness to give herself to him only to square the debt he thought she owed him. She would not do it.

She had bought herself some time, but now she needed to stay one step ahead of him in the game. He would come to her tomorrow and she knew she must be ready. She had to have a plan. She had to escape him.

CHAPTER EIGHT

PENELOPE STANDISH WAS DRESSED in her nightshirt, a practical, masculine, striped cotton affair with no frills. She was sitting on her bed rather than in it, and around her on the embroidered counterpane were spread sheet upon sheet of writing. Some had been discarded because they were not scandalous enough, others because they were too lurid. It was difficult to hit the correct note of suggestiveness, but Mr. Morrow, the editor of the *Gentlemen's Athenian Mercury*, thought that she was doing very well for a beginner.

Pen shuddered as she thought of what Isabella would say if she knew it was her sister who was feeding stories to the press. Isabella did not deserve such disloyalty. She had come home from her travels and taken her younger sister to her heart as though they had never been separated. Pen had been surprised and warmed by the friendship that had grown so rapidly between them. Yet now she betrayed Isabella at every turn.

The difficulty was that she was desperate. In fact, she was not simply desperate but utterly, completely and irrevocably without hope.

The house was very quiet. Freddie had escorted her home from the Duchess of Fordyce's ball and left immediately thereafter. He had not told her where he was going. These days he seldom did, and anyway, Pen required no explanation. When Freddie rolled home in the dawn smelling of drink and cheap perfume it was fairly evident where he had spent the night.

It happened more and more frequently these days. There had been a time when she and Freddie had been able to coexist in comfortable affection, sharing if not confidences, at least conversation. Nowadays they seldom saw each other and when they did, Freddie was disinclined to talk. Pen knew she hectored him and that this merely made him run from her, but she could not help herself. She worried about him. There was a hunted look in his eyes these days, as though he were trying to blot out some unpleasant truth with the drink and the women and whatever else he did in the dark reaches of the night.

The money had disappeared, too. Freddie's income had never been large, and now all of it seemed to go to support the wine-sellers and brothel-keepers of the capital. Pen's small allowance, left to her by her father, was insufficient to sustain both of them. The debts were piling up and soon, very soon, would come the creditors and then the bailiffs and the summonses and the courts. Pen remembered how her father had ended, an embittered man who had suffered half a dozen ignominious court appearances for debt and had died of bad temper at being reduced to living off the pittance of his wife's jointure. Debt stalked their family like a curse.

Which was where the information about Isabella's activities came in. Pen had tried to write fiction at first, but her work had been rejected by various publishers with the comment that it was rather too sensational for the popular taste. She had toyed with the idea of writing conduct manuals or moral fables, but her inherent irreverence always seemed to shine through at the most inappropriate moments. Then she had been tidying the study one day and her eye had fallen on an old copy of the *Mercury* that Freddie had left lying around. There had been a salacious story about the extramarital affairs of a well-known lady. And Pen had thought that she could write something at least as good if only she knew someone famous to write about….

The devil of temptation had whispered in her ear that her sister would not mind, her sister would understand, Pen needed the money and Isabella knew what it was to be poor and desperate and in debt....

Pen selected a few sheets, read the contents, then put them down with a sigh. The guilt grabbed her by the throat again. Even though she had been only fifteen when Isabella had married Ernest and gone abroad, she had been extremely attached to her elder sister. She could still remember with perfect clarity the dreadful moment when their father had told Bella, in front of the entire family, that she must marry Ernest or they would all be ruined. Pen had been too young to understand properly what was happening. She had taken Isabella's hand and said that she had been told that if her sister refused the prince they would all starve in the Fleet Prison, and surely that could not be true, and surely Isabella would not let that happen. She had seen the change in Bella's face then, a sort of crumpling beneath the surface, and had understood too late that Bella was young, too—too young to have to make such choices. And yet she had made the choice and saved them all. Ernest had been rich then, and carelessly generous to his new family. They had started over, their father investing just as poorly as before and inevitably losing it all again some years later.

Pen fidgeted with the pages. They had written to each other through the years, she and Bella. It had kept them close even when they had only met three or four times in twelve years. They had discussed, gossiped, confided. Then they had met each other again and found that they liked each other a great deal in real life as well as on paper, and Pen had felt almost as if she'd rediscovered a part of herself that had been lost.

Under the circumstances, detailing her sister's misfortunes for the press felt like the greatest deceit imaginable.

Pen tried to tell herself that her sister had not seemed

unduly disturbed by the column in the *Mercury*. It had been a relief in a way to know that Isabella did not intend to track down the author. In another sense she had felt disappointed, for now she knew that her deception could continue. Isabella would never know.

Pen bit her lip hard. She supposed that she could take the time-honored route out of trouble and find a rich husband, but she was an old maid of seven and twenty now and, although men still admired her golden prettiness, it was unlikely anyone would come to the point when she was both old and poor. Nor did she feel she had the temperament to spend her life cajoling a rich man. She would probably lose her temper with him, tell him a few pungent truths and then he would consign her to Bedlam. Besides, the only man who had interested her recently had been Alistair Cantrell and she had already discovered that he was not rich. Not in the slightest.

Thinking of Mr. Cantrell made her think of Marcus Stock-haven. Not as a potential husband—Pen did not mind admitting that the thought of marrying a man like Marcus would terrify her, for there was a physical quality about him that was quite overwhelming—but because he was the only one of her relatives who was rich enough to help her. It was a possibility, of course, but she did not know him well and she sensed that he disapproved of Freddie for some reason, and Pen loved Freddie and did not want to expose his weakness to Marcus.

Thinking of Marcus brought her thoughts firmly back to Isabella. Pen had thought—no indeed, she had *known*—there had once been something very strong and passionate between Marcus and Bella. She had been only a child that last summer in Salterton, but she had seen Isabella creeping from the house at night, and seen her return from the gardens later, a spring in her step and light in her eyes. Isabella's betrothal to Marcus had seemed the next natural step, a formal recognition of the unbreakable bond between the two of them. And yet the bond had been broken, irrevocably.

And now, curiously, both of them had returned and, judging by their behavior at the ball that evening, some pattern was re-asserting itself. Only this time they were older and the passion between them seemed darker, somehow, and more painful. Pen thought of the way that Marcus had looked at Isabella and she shivered with reaction. If a man ever looked at her in so particular a way, she thought she would probably run a mile.

There was the sound of the street door crashing open and Freddie's voice raised in drunken discord as he shouted for his valet, utterly thoughtless for the rest of the household. Pen sighed. She gathered the scattered sheets together and bundled them into the cupboard at the bottom of her nightstand. She could hear Mather, Freddie's valet, speaking softly to his master as he steered him across the landing and into his room with a minimum of damage to the furniture.

Pen got to her feet, crossed to the dresser and splashed some cold water from the ewer onto her face. She looked at her reflection in the mirror. She looked pale and tired, and behind her like a mocking ghost, the rose-colored ball gown lay discarded across the back of a chair. No husband, no prospects, no money. Miss Penelope Standish dismissed her reflection and vowed to send her next piece to the newspaper immediately, so that it would make the morning editions.

MARCUS HAD GONE STRAIGHT from the ball to the rather less salubrious surroundings of the Ratcliffe Highway in East London. Alistair, who had been cultivating the company of a Bow Street runner called Townsend, had had a tip that one of Warwick's henchmen was implicated in the recent spate of murders in that area. Marcus spent several hours and not a few guineas in a fruitless attempt to buy information. No one was talking. Everyone was too fearful.

"It is the strangest thing," Marcus said, as they took a battered hackney carriage home in the early hours, "but Warwick is nothing more than a whisper, is he? He is everywhere and nowhere. I begin to wonder if he exists at all."

"Oh, he exists," Alistair said grimly. He was sitting in a corner of the carriage, his hands thrust deep in his pockets, his chin buried in the folds of his cravat. "In one form or another, he exists. Whether it is as a legend or as a man, the effect is the same. He spreads terror with the mere mention of his name. That is what we are fighting against."

"But how to find him?" Marcus asked. "We do not even know where to look. He slips through our fingers like smoke."

Alistair turned his head and looked out of the carriage window at the strengthening daylight. Marcus thought for a moment that he would not reply. He felt cold, stiff and frustrated. There was only one benefit in such activity, and that was that it took his mind from Isabella. In a couple of hours he would have to wash and make himself presentable and go to Brunswick Gardens and confront her.

"You forget," Alistair said suddenly, "that you have something Warwick wants. Sooner or later, he will come looking for you."

A certain vivacious princess, whose return to London has been greeted with excitement by all those rakes and beaux who courted her the first time around, was last night much in evidence at the Duchess of F's Scottish Ball. The princess, never one to shirk her responsibility in providing scandal, was heard to remark that she had no intention of encouraging the amorous attentions of any gentlemen because, in her view, Englishmen are the very worst lovers in the world. Whilst we bow to the princess's superior experience in the field—she has lived much of her life abroad and therefore must have the means of contrast—we hope a gentleman may step forward to defend the reputation of his countrymen and change the princess's mind. Perhaps the Earl of S may be just the man for the job? Those with long memories will recall that the lovely princess and the gallant earl were once more than mere acquaintances....

—*The Gentlemen's Athenian Mercury,* July 3, 1816

ISABELLA SIGHED AND PLACED the newspaper carefully by the side of her plate of breakfast toast. It was scarcely unexpected to see herself mentioned in the scandal sheets again. Someone who had attended the Duchess of Fordyce's ball must have been delighted to make a swift guinea from passing on so prime a piece of gossip. In Ernest's time it had happened time and again. This piece of scandal, however, she had brought entirely on herself. Whatever had possessed her to make such an outrageous and ridiculously untrue statement about the amorous capabilities of the English male? It was not even as though she had the experience to judge. If only she had not risen to the Duchess of Plockton's barbed provocation. But the comment about her daughter, Emma, had overset her, being the one subject on which she would always be vulnerable, and as a result she had not given a damn for the proprieties.

"The ladies and gentlemen of the press," Belton said sepulchrally, from the doorway, "are encamped outside, Your Serene Highness. I have taken the liberty of removing the door knocker so that they cannot disturb you, but I fear they may attempt an entry through a window. And Miss Standish has arrived."

"I had to enter by the back door," Pen grumbled, plumping herself down on one of the rosewood chairs and slapping a pile of newspapers next to her sister's plate, making the china jump and the tea spill. "Oh, you have already seen the papers!"

"Whatever has happened to put you in such a temper?" Isabella inquired. "It is unlike you to arrive with the first post on the morning after a ball."

"I wanted to acquaint you with this." Pen gestured toward the news sheets. "But I see that I am too late. May I have some tea? I assure you that I require it."

"Please do." Isabella put down her toast and honey and wiped her sticky fingers. She drew the papers toward her. "I suppose I should have foreseen this."

"It is as I said yesterday." Pen waved the teapot around with emphasis. "You cannot even move for drawing scandal, Bella." She frowned at her sister. "Upon my word, you are very calm about this. There is a crowd outside your front door!"

"I know," Isabella said.

"The *Mercury* and the *Preceptor* are running rival columns," Pen grumbled. "It is most vexing."

"It is certainly vexing that they are two most scurrilous rags in London," Isabella agreed. She viewed her sister's flushed face with concern. "You seem to be taking this very personally, Penelope."

"I?" Pen jumped. "No… Well… Yes, I think it is a disgrace." Isabella shrugged. "The fuss will die down. It always does."

"You are evidently accustomed to this."

"Of course." Isabella fixed her sister with her amused blue gaze. "Ernest was forever attracting the attentions of the papers."

Pen leaned her elbows on the table and drank deep from her cup, her curious gaze fixed on her sister over the rim. "Yes, I see," she said. She hesitated. "Bella, that thing that you said… Is it true?"

Isabella frowned. "What thing? What did I say?"

"That Englishmen are the worst lovers in the world? I do hope not. I did not get the opportunity to quiz you about it last night since cousin Marcus seemed intent on refuting your words in the quickest possible time!"

Isabella frowned. "I am shocked that you should ask such a thing, Penelope."

Pen laughed. "My interest is purely intellectual." She made a slight gesture. "I am seven and twenty years old, Bella. Am I to pretend that I do not know such a side of life exists?"

"I suppose not," Isabella admitted. "It seems rather foolish to pretend."

Pen opened her eyes wide. "So?"

"I have no notion whether it is true or not," Isabella said. "I was merely being deliberately shocking."

Pen stared. "You do not know?"

"No." Isabella raised an amused eyebrow. "I do not have sufficient experience to judge." She stopped, thinking of Marcus. He had been her lover, but in those sweet early days of youthful indiscretion he had seemed much more. He had been her whole world.

Pen was watching her thoughtfully.

"You know full well that three quarters of my bad reputation is the result of Ernest's profligacy," Isabella added.

"And the remaining quarter?" Pen persisted.

"Ah well..." Isabella considered. "For the most part that is the fiction made up by those so-called gentlemen whose advances I rejected. Alas, they were not able to admit that I found them resistible." She sighed. "I cannot deny that there was a gentleman I turned to when I thought that there might be some affection there to sweeten my life with Ernest—" She broke off, shaking her head. It had taken years before her misery had led her to be unfaithful to her husband in the aftermath of Emma's death. She had been very lonely and had fallen disastrously in love with an Austrian soldier of fortune who had seen her unhappiness and courted her gently—and abandoned her ruthlessly only ten days later. Disillusioned, heartbroken, she soon realized everyone was discussing the affair and came to her senses. After that she had locked her heart and her unhappiness away.

"It is the greatest piece of nonsense in London that I stand accused of being a lady rakehell when in fact I am utterly uninterested in the pleasures of the bed," she said now.

Pen frowned. "How can such matters possibly be uninteresting?"

"Trust me," Isabella said, heartily munching a piece of toast. "They are."

Pen was looking dissatisfied. "Then it seems to me that it is Ernest who must bear the responsibility for being the worst lover in the world or you would not feel like that."

"Very true," Isabella concurred. She paused, elbows on the table, while she thought not of Ernest but once again of Marcus. Her first experiences of love at Marcus's hands had been undeniably dazzling. She had burned for him. Yet now it seemed a pale dream, something that had happened long ago in another life, if it had happened at all. And although he could still awaken something deep within her, she vowed he would not have the chance. When she had been seventeen, matters had seemed simple. She had loved Marcus and had given herself to him with love. Since then she had lost a great deal and she knew, with absolute certainly, that the best way to avoid future loss was not to engage with risk in the first place. Besides, Marcus held her in the lowest possible esteem now. She recalled his hostile words from the previous night. If anything proved to her that the marriage had to be ended, and quickly, it was Marcus's bitterness. She must contact Mr. Churchward immediately to arrange an annulment and the terms under which she would repay her financial debt to her husband. She could not bear to be beholden to him any longer than she must.

Pen pursed her lips. "I am disappointed that you are unable to advise me on my love affairs. I was hoping that that would be one of the benefits of having a sister with such an exciting reputation."

"I apologize for proving inadequate," Isabella said cheerfully. "My advice to you would be—do not."

"Do not indulge in love affairs?"

"Preferably not. Love is not at all as it is reputed to be in literature. It is simply not worth it."

Pen smiled faintly. "I am sorry to hear you say that." She drained her teacup and sat back. "I take it that you would apply that ruling to Marcus Stockhaven?" She added dryly, "He would not be worth the trouble of a love affair?"

Isabella could feel the bright color sting her cheeks. She wished Pen had not introduced Marcus's name again. She hated blushing. It felt naive and self-conscious.

"It would be far too perilous to consider an affair with Lord Stockhaven under any circumstances," she said, evading Pen's gaze. "There are some men that are best avoided because they are too—"

"Attractive?" Pen said.

Isabella shrugged irritably. "Too dangerous to know."

"I see," Pen said. "In which case, what was all that fascinating byplay between the two of you last night? You cannot deny it."

Isabella sighed. "You ask too many questions, Pen."

"I beg your pardon." Pen tapped the newspaper. "They are the same questions everyone else is asking."

Isabella groaned. She was expecting Marcus to walk through the door at any moment, which would only serve to fuel Pen's curiosity. But perhaps he could not gain entry because of the crowds outside. Her spirits rose to think of him struggling to persuade Belton to admit him.

Pen sighed, evidently judging that no further information would be forthcoming at this point. After a moment she acknowledged defeat and changed the subject.

"Do we go out today?" she asked.

Isabella sighed, too. "I was hoping to take some fresh air but I fear it will be impossible to escape the crowds outside."

"I supposed that you would be accustomed to fighting your way through them."

"I suppose that I am. When Ernest died in the arms of his mistress, Madame de Coulanges, I could not escape the house in Stockholm for several days, so great was the press of people outside. They all wished to know whether or not I had a view on the manner of his passing."

"And did you?"

"Certainly I did, but I was not going to share it with them." Isabella rubbed her brow ruefully. "I do so wish that I had had the same good sense last night."

"Why did you not?"

"Because that old harpy the Duchess of Plockton provoked me. She got under my skin and then I fear I was disinclined to respond with any courtesy to her following remarks." Isabella met her sister's gaze. "I can rise above most things—goodness knows, I have had sufficient practice—but when anyone makes reference to Emma and suggests that Ernest tried to take her from me because I was an unfit parent—" She broke off, swallowing hard. She had been told from the start that little Princess Emma of Cassilis must have her own household. That was the royal style. There was no possibility of the child traveling across Europe with them. Isabella had been young and inexperienced but she had also been courageous. She had dug her heels in and insisted that she keep her daughter with her. Ernest had looked down his nose and condemned her as irremediably middle class but she had not cared. Emma was the whole world to her and when she had contracted scarlet fever and died, a part of Isabella had died, too.

Pen's face had stilled into sympathy. "Yes, I do understand. That is, I cannot understand how you feel of course,

Bella, but I realize it must be intolerable for you to hear people say such foolish and malicious things."

Isabella returned the clasp of her sister's hand with a brief squeeze. "Thank you, Pen."

There was a knock at the door. "I beg your pardon for interrupting, Your Serene Highness," Belton said glumly, "but the flower cart has arrived with seventeen bouquets for you."

Pen looked astonished. "Have I forgotten that it is your birthday, Bella?"

"No," Isabella said. "My birthday was in April, as well you know."

"Then how does one explain the arrival of seventeen bunches of flowers?"

Isabella put down her napkin and rose to her feet. She gestured toward the papers again. "I rather suspect that this explains it."

Pen looked down at the newspaper column and up again, the sparkle restored to her eyes. "Oh, I say! What famous entertainment!"

The hall was overflowing with blooms. The housemaids were scurrying around trying to find sufficient receptacles in which to place them and had already pressed into service a tin hip bath, a coal scuttle and milk pail. There were many whisperings and gigglings over one particular arrangement, which Belton was attempting to usher out of the way.

"Good gracious!" Pen said. "I do believe that is shaped almost exactly like a—"

"Penelope!" Isabella said.

"I have seen plenty of sculptures of naked male bodies," Pen said irrepressibly, "and that penis looks overlarge to me."

Isabella was reading the card. "It is from Lord Forrester. He swears its dimensions are the same as his own and promises to introduce me to all the pleasures that I have been missing. He is set upon redeeming the reputation of English lovers."

Pen snatched up another card. "Oh! So is Sir Chumley Morton! And Lord Hesketh! And Mr. Styles has written you a poem, but I shall not read it for it is both rude and appallingly bad verse into the bargain."

"What on earth are these?" Isabella asked, retrieving what looked like a union flag from the center of a red-white-and-blue themed flower arrangement. "Good gracious, I do believe they are a pair of gentleman's drawers."

"Your Serene Highness!" Belton whisked them out of her hands before she could hold them up for inspection.

"Well," Isabella said, hands on hips as she surveyed the riot of flowers, "I imagine that all the bucks in London must have read the papers this morning."

One of the footmen came up to Belton and they exchanged a few urgently whispered words before he hurried off again. Belton cleared his throat.

"The Marquess of Grimstone has called, Your Serene Highness," he announced, "as have Lord Lonsdale and Mr. Carew. I have taken the liberty of suggesting that you are not at home. I hope that is appropriate."

Pen gave him an admiring look. "You are remarkably good at this, are you not, Belton? One might almost think that you are practiced in working for someone as disreputable as my sister."

Belton ignored her politely, still concentrating on addressing Isabella. "There is also a gentleman who swears that he has no connection with the popular press, Highness. He has a letter of introduction from Mr. Churchward, and has come to value the art collection."

"Thank you," Isabella said. "Please show him into the drawing room, Belton, so that he may make his inventory."

"Your Serene Highness." Belton bowed and moved away.

Isabella tiptoed over to the window and twitched the curtain so that she could peep outside. The whole street was crowded with people jostling and pointing. The one person missing was the one man who had said he would call. Marcus Stockhaven. She might have known. No doubt he was leaving her to fret over his absence, which was exactly what she was doing, damn him....

Isabella let the curtain fall back into place. "If we are to go out, then it will need to be through a rear window," she commented.

"And once we are in Bond Street we shall be plagued with gentlemen once again," Pen observed. "Drat! I have been saving for a new bonnet these three months past and was looking forward to a shopping expedition, but I do not wish to have an audience for it."

"We shall go shopping," Isabella said. "Or rather, we shall ask the shopping to come to us. Belton—" she turned to summon the hovering butler "—pray send a footman to Beaux Chapeaux in Bond Street and ask them to send a selection of their finest bonnets around for our inspection."

Pen looked enraptured. "Will they do that, Bella?"

"Oh yes," Isabella said. "I may have no money nor credit for any, but any shopkeeper worth their salt knows that when it comes to spending money on clothes, a princess will always find a way."

She threw another glance in the direction of the heaving street. She had no intention of lurking indoors for the foreseeable future. There was an opera she wished to attend that evening and she had just thought of a way in which her barrage of admirers could be used to set a false trail and lead Marcus astray. It was a most satisfying thought. And in order to be a further step ahead in the game, she would write to Churchward and instruct him to instigate an annulment forthwith. Her spirits lifted. She always felt better when she was in control of the situation.

She was about to hasten to the library and pen that very letter when Belton marched in with a final floral tribute. Penelope smiled

"Oh! Now that *is* pretty."

The bouquet was indeed beautiful; twelve tightly furled creamy pink roses in a little basket. Isabella reached for the note. Suddenly she felt nervous.

The card was written in a strong hand and Isabella needed no signature to identify it, although there was one, as strong and bold as the man himself.

Meet me at Churchward's office within the hour. Marcus Stockhaven.

Isabella felt cold. This was nothing more than a stark order.

"Who is it from, Bella?" Pen's voice broke into her thoughts and she instinctively crushed the card between her fingers.

"It is from Lord Stockhaven," she said.

"Has he written a pretty poem, too?" Pen inquired.

"Not precisely," Isabella said. "Lord Stockhaven is not the man to be subtle when bluntness will achieve his aim. I beg your pardon, Pen," she continued. "I find I have an urgent appointment. I am afraid you will have to purchase your bonnet alone." She turned to Belton, holding out the pretty little basket.

"Have that one put on the table outside my bedchamber door please, Belton," she said. "It is the closest to my bedroom that Lord Stockhaven will get."

And she tore the note into shreds.

CHAPTER NINE

MARCUS STOCKHAVEN HAD ARRIVED in Brunswick Gardens a half hour before. It had been his intention to call upon Isabella early that morning, but when he had returned from East London it was to find an urgent note from Lord Sidmouth, summoning him to the Home Office on business related to his sojourn in the Fleet. It was Sidmouth who had given him permission to run his unorthodox masquerade in the first place, and the price was that in return Marcus passed on as much information about Edward Warwick as he could, since the authorities had their eye on Warwick as a dangerous malefactor. Now there were rumors of Warwick's involvement in several political disturbances and rioting, as well as a robbery on a gunsmith's shop. Sidmouth wanted the man caught and wanted to know whether Marcus thought it likely that Warwick would take himself to Salterton again to finish whatever business he had started there.

It had been several hours before Marcus could extract himself from the meeting and he'd chafed against the delay throughout. When he finally arrived in Brunswick Gardens it was to find the place overrun with journalists and frustrated swains. The butler was informing the multitude that Princess Isabella was from home. Marcus did not believe it for an instant but he was not prepared to make a scene in front of a crowd in order to get into the house. One of Isabella's servants was mingling with the masses, selling the information that the princess intended to attend the performance of Congreve's *The Way of the World* at the Haymarket that evening. Marcus applauded Isabella's ingenuity. It was entirely possible that her servants sought to profit from her in this way, but he doubted it. He was sure that she had arranged for that rumor herself.

Marcus clenched his fists in his pockets, spoiling the elegant line of his jacket. To see so many eager bucks seeking out his wife turned his barely simmering frustrations to near madness. He was losing his head and his self-control over a woman he disliked but had to possess. He could feel the hunger and thwarted desire sharpening to a white-hot edge inside him. The longer he had to wait, the more determined he was.

He made his plans quickly. There was a flower girl on the street corner, and from her he purchased an innocent-looking bouquet of pink roses. He did not have a pen handy so he borrowed one from one of the reporters milling about the front steps. Then he went around to the tradesman's entrance, knocked at the door and delivered the bouquet into the hands of the housekeeper.

And then he waited.

It was forty-three minutes precisely before the door of the servants' quarters opened and the butler came out to procure a hack. Marcus thought that he looked distinctly unimpressed to be doing so. The carriage waited at the back door and presently Princess Isabella descended the steps and got in. She was wearing scarlet, with an outrageously fashionable hat.

As the carriage turned the corner of the street, Marcus let out a long sigh. He had not been certain that his wife would respond to the rather peremptory order enclosed in the card. In fact he had not been able to predict how she would react at all. The fact that she was on her way out did not, of course, confirm that she was heading for Churchward's chambers. She might be traveling to the other end of Town. But it was promising.

He went out onto Brunswick Avenue and hailed a hack for

himself. He was quietly confident that he was one step ahead in the game now. Even so, it would not do to be complacent. To underestimate Isabella would be the biggest mistake of all.

MR. CHURCHWARD THE ELDER was a very unhappy man.

He had reluctantly acceded to the request made by the Earl of Stockhaven to conduct a meeting between the earl and his wife at his chambers. It was the very last matter on earth in which he wished to be embroiled, and now that the two protagonists were present, he was wishing himself in Hades. The atmosphere was very tense indeed.

The Countess of Stockhaven had arrived first. She was gowned magnificently in scarlet and wore a cunning little bonnet that partially hid her expression. She greeted Mr. Churchward with cool composure and sat down to await the arrival of her husband. When Marcus Stockhaven was ushered in, she pointedly made no move whatsoever to stand up and greet him.

The earl's expression was stony and his demeanor most autocratic. Mr. Churchward reflected that it would have cowed many lesser men into silence. Isabella, however, did not appear in the least impressed.

"Perhaps we could proceed to business," she said coolly. "I am a little short of time."

Marcus looked down his nose at her in his most intimidating manner.

Isabella carelessly flicked a thread from her skirt and gave him a smile that could have frozen water.

Mr. Churchward cleared his throat.

"Madam, the earl has requested this meeting so that certain matters pertaining to your marriage may be discussed and a mutually agreeable conclusion reached."

"Cut the niceties, Churchward," Marcus said brutally. "We are here to explain to my wife the terms of this marriage." He turned to Isabella. "I have asked Mr. Churchward to be present at our meeting so that there may be no misunderstandings about the nature of our agreement, madam."

Isabella raised her blue gaze and pinned Marcus with a glare. Mr. Churchward shifted as though he was sitting on red-hot coals. Marcus appeared unmoved.

"Proceed," Isabella said. Her voice held chips of ice.

Churchward prayed for the floor of his office to open up and swallow him whole, but when that did not happen he cleared his throat again and picked up the piece of paper from the desk in front of him. His hand was shaking slightly. Marcus walked across to the window so that he was standing behind his wife. His brooding presence dominated the room.

"The Earl of Stockhaven lays down the following terms for his marriage to Princess Isabella Di Cassilis," Mr. Churchward read rapidly. "Firstly, that the marriage should be formally announced immediately. Secondly, that there will be no annulment. Thirdly, that by right of the matrimonial law, the earl claims ownership of the house known as number five, Brunswick Gardens, and instructs that it be sold." Churchward's voice picked up speed until he was almost gabbling. "Fourthly, that by the same principle the earl claims the property known as Salterton Hall, in the county of Dorset."

At last Isabella stirred. She had been sitting, head bent, utterly unmoving. Now she looked up and, although he could not read her expression clearly, Churchward knew that this hurt her. She had looked on Salterton as her own. It had been special to her. But there was nothing Churchward could do. Under the law, the countess's property belonged to her husband.

"Madam—" Churchward said unhappily.

Isabella smiled at him. Despite the situation, there was warmth in her eyes. "Please do not worry, Mr. Churchward. I know that this is none of your doing." She turned her clear, cool gaze back to her husband.

"I assume that there is more?"

"Of course," Marcus said. His expression was granite hard. "You will remove to Stockhaven House for the time that we remain in Town. You will apply to me to have any remaining debts settled and you will request my permission before you make any future purchases. You will furnish me with a note of all your social engagements—"

"And I will consult you before I speak with any of my acquaintance," Isabella snapped. "Your demands are ridiculous, sir."

Marcus thrust has hands into his pockets. "Not so, madam. My *conditions* are perfectly acceptable for a man with an errant wife."

Mr. Churchward shrank in his seat. If he made himself as inconspicuous as possible there was just a chance that he might be able to slip from the room without the earl and countess noticing. Indeed, they were so locked in their mutual antipathy that he could probably have done a dance on the desk and neither of them would have paid any heed. Mr. Churchward had negotiated on plenty of occasions between the parties in a marriage of convenience. He had seen husbands and wives whose loathing of each other was so great that they could barely tolerate being in the same room. In those cases the primary benefit of the marriage usually involved the exchange of money for a title, or the combination of two great dynasties, nothing more.

The Earl and Countess of Stockhaven did not fit such a pattern, however. Looking at them now, the earl towering over his wife, his face set and stormy, it would be easy to imagine that he hated her with a passion. Yet it was not so, Mr. Churchward could tell. Behind that chilling facade, he could sense that Marcus Stockhaven's feelings for his beautiful wife were far more complex than mere hatred. The earl had not taken his gaze once from the princess's face from the moment he had entered the room. He watched her like a hawk. And on one occasion, Churchward had caught him looking at her with such naked, angry desire that he had felt profoundly uncomfortable. Mr. Churchward the Elder was a man—although Mrs. Churchward had probably forgotten that in recent years—and so he could understand the earl lusting after his wife. But Marcus Stockhaven's expression of fury, hunger and grief was painful to witness.

"So," Isabella said, and once again her voice was cool and expressionless, "you are to take Salterton Hall from me, sir. Now that is a neat revenge."

"I do not require the property," Marcus said abruptly. "It will be sold."

Isabella tilted her head away so that the bonnet shadowed all but the curve of her cheek. Mr. Churchward was not normally an imaginative man but at the moment he felt every ounce of her grief.

"What do I get in return?" Isabella inquired, after a moment. "As this is a settlement you are proposing, my lord, what do you intend to settle upon me?"

Marcus rested both hands on the desk and leaned toward her. "Your debts have been paid, madam. *That* is the settlement you get. Was that not what you wanted?"

Isabella smoothed her gloves with small, deliberate gestures. "But what if you were to die, my lord? What arrangements are to be made for me for the future? Accidents will happen."

Mr. Churchward drew in a very sharp breath. My lady was playing a very dangerous game. He saw Marcus's hands clench against the wood of the desk.

"In the case of my death, madam," he said through his teeth, "I imagine that you would merely repeat your actions in finding another rich husband. That is your usual mode of behavior, is it not?"

"And your property and fortune?"

"Will go to my cousin. I regret that there is no benefit to you in having me murdered."

Mr. Churchward was almost whimpering now. "My lord, this is most unseemly—"

Marcus ignored him. "Unless, of course," he finished harshly, "you give me an heir, madam, in which case he will inherit."

The tortoiseshell clasp of Isabella's reticule snapped beneath her fingers, making them all jump.

"I would as lief give you the plague," she said sweetly. "You will not take me to your bed as part of this *settlement.*"

Mr. Churchward's ears were radiating the heat of embarrassment now.

"You will fulfill all the duties of a wife." Churchward saw Marcus whiten as he bit out each word with emphasis. "We will discuss that alone, madam."

Isabella inclined her head with perfect elegance. She stood up. "Then if there is no more to be said, you will excuse me, gentlemen."

Marcus took the paper from Churchward's nerveless fingers. "Not before you sign, my lady."

Isabella paused. It seemed to Churchward that an inordinate amount of time passed while she looked from the paper to her husband's set face. She looked young and defiant and very pretty indeed. Churchward could sense the tightly wound intensity of Marcus Stockhaven as he waited.

"No," she said clearly. "I shall not sign. You cannot force it upon me. Mr. Churchward, despite what has been discussed this morning, I would appreciate it if you would send me the necessary information on annulment."

Marcus straightened. "The announcement of our marriage will be in the *Times* tomorrow, with or without your consent," he said.

Isabella did not reply. She closed the door very quietly.

"My lord," Churchward said, when he had recovered his breath, "that was not well done."

Marcus appeared not to hear him. He was shaking his head abruptly as though awakening from a dream. He looked at the rejected piece of paper lying on the desk. "She will agree," he said. "She has no choice."

Churchward looked at him steadily. He wondered whether the earl knew his wife at all. Churchward's experience was small but one scarcely needed Lord Byron's encyclopedic knowledge of women to realize that Marcus had made a tactical error. He had laid down his demands. His wife had rejected them. The game was not over. In fact, it had barely begun.

SHE HAD NOWHERE TO RUN, nowhere to hide and no one to help her. Yet she was damned if she would give up the fight.

Isabella sat alone in the Di Cassilis box at Sadlers Wells Theater. She heard barely a note of *The Marriage of Figaro*. The witty tale of love, betrayal and forgiveness seemed rather too appropriate that evening. Except, for Marcus and herself, the love was gone, the betrayal complete and the forgiveness a mere dream.

She could not forget the look on Marcus's face when Mr. Churchward read out the terms of the settlement relating to Salterton. She had wondered before if Marcus was doing this out of pride and revenge, but the look of grim satisfaction on his face as he took her inheritance from her suggested that his motives ran deeper than personal reprisal. He was paying her back, not only for her betrayal of him but also for something to do with her cousin India. She was sure of it.

The promise of Salterton had been her salvation. She had not minded what else she lost as long as she could retire to the place of those happy childhood memories and recapture some of that peace. It had been naive in the extreme for her not to realize what would happen. With her marriage, all her property belonged to her husband, Salterton included. She had nothing left of her own now. It was Marcus's property and so was she.

She felt sick and cold and afraid to think of how he might assert his mastery. There were plenty of ways to humiliate her. He had already stripped her of her property and her dignity with his demands. She was fairly sure that he was not the sort of man to force her to the marriage bed—in spite of their hostility to one another, he would not use physical strength to get what he wanted. That did little to reassure her. She was worn down with the confusion of how she could dislike a man so intensely and yet at her very core feel the tug of an affinity that told her that, despite everything, they were intended to be together and always had been.

The curtains at the back of the box shifted as a figure came through the aperture and took the seat beside her. The Di Cassilis box had not only a private entrance but also a secret passageway connecting it to the dressing rooms. Prince Ernest had always enjoyed the privilege of greeting his favorite performers directly after the show, and persuading them to a different sort of performance expressly for him. Tonight Isabella had appreciated the secrecy for a different reason; it enabled her to get into the theater alone and unseen. Now, though, she did not even need to turn her head to know who was beside her.

"Congratulations, my lord," she whispered, discreetly lowering her voice so as not to distract from the performance. "I assume you are here to lay claim to the only piece of Di Cassilis property that has yet escaped you?"

Marcus laughed. "Touché, my lady. I confess I was deeply impressed when I discovered that your late husband possessed his own private box at every theater in London."

"To see and be seen," Isabella murmured.

"Naturally." Marcus stretched his long legs out and reclined comfortably in the deep velvet seat. "Which is precisely why I am here tonight."

"I imagined you must have a reason. I did not rate a love of Mozart amongst your interests."

Marcus shifted slightly. His voice hardened. "You know nothing of my interests, madam."

Isabella plied her fan. "Nor do I need to. We may be married but we do not need to bore each other with our interests—or our company. In fact—" she made to stand "—I believe that the performance has lost its charm for me. I think I shall retire."

Marcus's hand closed warm and hard over her gloved wrist, compelling her to sink back into the seat. "I think not. As the announcement of our marriage is to be in the papers tomorrow, I wish us to be seen together tonight."

"That is what you order."

"That is what I ask." There was precious little courtesy in his tone, Isabella thought. It was in no way a request.

"And if I choose not to meet your *request?*" She gave the word sarcastic emphasis. "What then?"

Marcus sighed. "My dear Isabella, you are far too intelligent not to realize that it will be more comfortable for both of us if you accede to my wishes. Why fight me? You know that I hold all the cards."

Isabella felt the anger seethe through her. "What is it that you want?" she hissed.

"I told you last night at the ball." Marcus seemed unmoved. "I want you as my wife—in every sense. I want public recognition of the fact that we are married and I want a private reckoning with you. After that, perhaps, we may consider a legal separation."

The cold callousness of it made Isabella's heart clench. The settlement that he wanted was nothing short of outright revenge.

"You want public recognition because I jilted you before," she whispered.

"Yes."

"And private reckoning—" She paused. "Because of India as well as yourself."

She felt him jump. He turned to look at her fully for the first time and his eyes were dark with some emotion she did not recognize.

"You mean that you *admit* it? You really were that calculating and corrupt?"

The knife twisted in Isabella's heart. Venal, calculating, corrupt... His opinion of her could not have been lower.

"I have no idea to what you refer," she said, keeping her tone level. "I am merely guessing that you hold something against me on India's part as well as your own and are determined to extract retribution for it."

She heard Marcus sigh in the darkness. On the stage, the aria swelled to a crescendo. Isabella kept her gaze fixed on the brightly colored figures in the light. She made sure that she was looking directly ahead as though Marcus simply did not exist.

She was as tense as a bow, yet strangely, as the opera built toward its height, she felt the power of the music sweep her away, transcending for a moment the misery inside. She felt Marcus's grip on her wrist gentle almost to a caress. His fingers entangled with hers. His touch was light now, but with a casual possessiveness that stirred a curious feeling within her. She knew she should move away and make it clear that he had no right to make this claim on her, but she could not.

Marcus held her hand for the rest of the performance and gradually her awareness of him changed from a tingling feeling in her wrist to a deep physical consciousness that seemed to suffuse her whole body. She felt hot and restless and aroused. She was sure that the telltale color stung her cheeks. She was barely able to keep still. When the music died away and the applause erupted, the sudden noise made her jump. She looked at Marcus to see that he was watching her. The hardness of his gaze had softened now and his dark eyes were full of something that looked dangerously close to tenderness. Isabella's heart fluttered. She opened her mouth to speak but then the lights came up in a harsh glare and she blinked and pulled back, dragging her hand from Marcus's.

The audience was already stirring. Boxes were designed for their occupants to be seen and plenty of people had looked up and noticed Marcus beside her now. The crowds in the stalls were making an undignified stampede for the Di Cassilis box.

Marcus turned to her. His tone was his own once more, cool and a little hard.

"We will stay here and receive them."

"No," Isabella said. The brief moment was shattered, spoiled by the pleasure she saw in Marcus's eyes at the prospect of the two of them putting on a display for the *Ton*. "You may receive whomsoever you wish, my lord. This is, after all, your theater box now. But I am leaving."

And before he could protest, she had slipped behind the curtain and taken the secret stairs to the dressing rooms. She had always known that Ernest's penchant for seducing actresses would come in useful one day.

"WHAT THE *DEVIL?*"

Marcus was standing in the Reading Room at White's, staring in blank horror at the announcement in the *Times*. He had gone there to meet with Alistair, who had left a message to say that he would be a few minutes late. In the meantime, a club servant had brought around the morning papers and Marcus had eagerly turned the pages to find the notice of his marriage to Isabella. To see a public announcement felt in some way the first step toward legitimizing the relationship and making it real in the eyes of the world. Marcus was full of anticipation.

It was there in print, staring him in the eye. First there was the declaration of the wedding: *The Earl of Stockhaven is pleased to announce his marriage to the Princess Isabella Di Cassilis....*

NICOLA CORNICK 147

All well and good. But beneath the announcement—directly beneath it—someone had inserted the following statement: *The Princess Di Cassilis wishes it to be known that she will henceforth keep the title of princess in preference to that of countess, it being the superior rank. She also wishes to make it clear that she married the Earl of Stockhaven for his money.*

There was a strange buzzing sound in Marcus's ears, as though he were seeing the rest of the world from underwater. A couple of his acquaintances passed by with a jocular remark and a slap on the back. Marcus barely noticed them as he read and reread the lines. It had to be Isabella's doing, of course. He had made the mistake of telling her about the announcement in advance and she had immediately resorted to countermeasures. His feeling of triumph withered and died.

Marcus could see Alistair Cantrell in the doorway now with a couple of other men. Lord Lonsdale and Mr. Carew had been among his wife's admirers the previous day at the melee in Brunswick Gardens. His mouth turned down grimly as they approached.

"One scarce knows whether to congratulate or commiserate with you, old fellow," Lonsdale said. "Such frankness! Very brave of you to admit she only wants you for the money."

"You provide the funds, old man, and we'll keep the princess happy in other ways," Carew began, before Marcus grabbed him by the throat and squeezed.

"Steady on, Stockhaven!" Lonsdale objected. "Marriage of convenience and all that."

"I will not give my name to another man's brats," Marcus ground out. He loosed his grip and Carew staggered back, shaking his head like a wet dog. "Stay away from my wife," Marcus said. "Stay away or I'll—"

"Marcus." Alistair caught his arm and practically dragged him away before he could plant a blow in Lonsdale's grinning face. "Leave it. They mean only to provoke you."

The simmering cauldron of fury inside Marcus seemed to settle a little. He let his hand fall to his side as Lonsdale and Carew backed off. They were still grinning maliciously, for all that Carew was fingering the bruises on his neck. Hell and the devil, he was a laughingstock. His wife had made him so. Why had he assumed that she would simply accept his strictures? Why had he not realized that she would want to settle the score?

Freddie Standish came through the door, and Alistair cursed under his breath at the appalling timing. Marcus thought for a moment that his brother-in-law was going to ignore him completely. Freddie was no hero. It was unlikely he would provoke another confrontation.

The atmosphere in the room was incredibly tense. Everyone was watching. And Freddie Standish did not walk past, but came directly up to Marcus.

"Congratulations, Stockhaven," he said. He did not offer Marcus his hand. He sounded as though the words hurt him. His gray eyes were incredibly cold. "First you marry my cousin and now you marry my sister. You are more fortunate than you deserve." He paused, and the emphasis of his words was like a hammer on metal. "I do not ever wish to hear that Isabella is unhappy or I shall call you out."

He turned on his heel and walked straight out again, followed by a whisper of shock and speculation.

"He was in earnest," Alistair said, staring after Freddie's departing back. He let his breath out sharply. "Would never have thought he had it in him."

Marcus slowly unclenched his muscles. Every one of them seemed to have been clamped tight. On previous occasions he had sensed Freddie's hostility but had thought little of it.

First you marry my cousin...

He had not thought that India and Freddie had ever been close. She had never mentioned him, but suddenly Marcus was curious. There had to be a reason for Freddie's antagonism. It preceded his marriage to Isabella, so she could not be the cause. And the reason had to be strong, for now he knew, without a shadow of a doubt, that Freddie Standish hated him.

CHAPTER TEN

"YOU COULD HAVE TOLD ME!" Pen burst into the blue saloon and flung herself down on the sofa beside her sister. "I feel a complete fool! I only discovered that you were married because Freddie saw it in the *Times!*"

Isabella looked up from her book. "Freddie reads the *Times?* Now you have surprised me."

Pen scowled. "Do not jest about this, Bella. I feel very hurt." She waved her arms about in exasperation. "What is going on? When did this happen? Where is Marcus? This is all very odd!"

"I am sorry," Isabella said. She could feel the distress beneath her sister's indignation. "It is a marriage of convenience only. We have been married a week and I have no notion where Marcus is. It could scarcely be said that we live in each other's pocket."

"You might have invited me to the wedding!" Pen said huffily. "Did anyone else know?"

"No, of course not. No one knew except Mr. Churchward and the moneylenders," Isabella said.

"Oh well, that is perfectly fine then!" Pen's face was flushed with upset. "How shabby can you be, Bella? Freddie and I are both shocked."

Isabella put out a hand. "I am sorry," she said again. "I married Marcus for his money and I planned the match to be of short duration. Alas, for a marriage of convenience it is proving excessively inconvenient."

Pen stared. "Inconvenient? You had best tell me the whole, Bella."

Isabella rubbed her forehead. "I did not know what to do, Pen," she said. "The moneylenders would advance me no further loans even though I had the expectation of Aunt Jane's inheritance. As you know, Mr. Churchward told me that I would either go to prison or be forced to flee abroad." She closed her eyes. "I did the only thing I could think of at the time."

"You went to cousin Marcus and he offered to marry you." The flawed logic of Isabella's partial explanation was not lost on her sister. She frowned. "Most people would ask for a loan, not matrimony, Bella. There was surely no need to go this far."

"I suppose not." Isabella hesitated, unwilling to divulge the full story of the Fleet wedding. "I was intending to sue for an annulment as soon as I could repay Marcus." She ran her fingers through her hair, pulling out all the pins. She could feel a headache starting. "I was not thinking, Pen. I was desperate to settle Ernest's debt."

"I comprehend that," Pen said, patting her hand, "but even so it seems a harebrained plan."

"It was. I acknowledge it." Isabella sighed. "And now it seems that annulments are extremely difficult to arrange. I had no notion I was getting myself into such a coil."

"Annulments are fiendishly difficult to achieve," Pen agreed.

"You see!" Isabella cast out a despairing hand. "Even you know it! Why did I not know?"

"I have no notion. If I had realized that you were interested, I would have told you." Pen sighed. "What of Marcus? Does he wish for an annulment?"

"No," Isabella said, blushing. "And without his agreement it is impossible."

"Yes," Pen said, "I did think that he seemed set on consummation rather than annulment when you met at the Duchess's ball."

"Pen!"

"Well?" Pen looked impatient. "It does not require the finest mind to see that he wants you in his bed. Did you not discuss this before you were married?"

"We did not talk a great deal," Isabella admitted.

"You should try it. It clarifies matters wonderfully."

"Thank you for the advice. I shall bear it in mind."

Pen smiled. "So where is Marcus? I must offer my congratulations."

"As I said, I have no notion." Isabella's shrug belied the coldness inside. No doubt Marcus would have read the piece in the paper by now and would be beating a path to her door. As would everyone else in the *Ton*. They would be anxious to get the scandalous news firsthand.

"I do not suppose that he will be pleased to read that you married him for his money," Pen said.

Isabella sighed. "Pen, you have a genius for stating the obvious."

"There is no need to be sarcastic," Pen said virtuously. "Did you do it on purpose to annoy him?"

"I fear so. He insisted on an announcement of the marriage so I decided to announce rather more than he was expecting."

"What do you think that he will say?"

"You may ask him yourself," Isabella said, with more composure than she was feeling. "I do believe I hear his voice now."

There was a quick step in the hall outside and then Belton was sailing in.

"The Earl of Stockhaven, Your Serene Highness." His tone was dark with disapproval for those members of society who had such bad *Ton* as to live apart and require introduction to their own spouse.

"Good morning, my lord," Isabella said. "We were just speaking of you."

Marcus looked at her through narrowed eyes. He had a copy of the *Times* in his hand, folded at the appropriate page, and he was tapping it impatiently against his palm. Isabella knew he was waiting for her to ask Pen to leave them. Instead she deliberately picked up the piece of half-finished needlework that lay on the sofa beside her and stitched delicately. She was no embroiderer and she never had been, but she found it useful to have a piece of work to hand. It reassured elderly ladies of the respectable nature of her household and it gave her something on which to concentrate when she wanted to avoid difficult situations. This was a prime example.

Pen jumped up to kiss Marcus.

"First a cousin and now a brother-in-law!" she said. "I am so pleased! I can borrow money from you now, Marcus!"

Marcus's grim expression eased slightly as he smiled at her, but it hardened once more as he turned back to Isabella.

"If I might have a word with you, my lady?"

"Of course," Isabella said, head bent, stitching assiduously. "Pray proceed, my lord."

Marcus again waited for her to ask Pen to leave them. Isabella was silent. After a few moments she said, "You seem strangely hesitant to speak, my lord."

Marcus looked at Pen. Pen looked back at him, eyes a limpid blue. Marcus sighed. He crossed to the door and held it open with exaggerated courtesy.

"If you would excuse us, cousin Penelope…"

"Oh, of course!" Pen turned to Isabella. "I shall be in the library perusing Plato should you need me, Bella."

"Thank you, Pen," Isabella said. She did not look up from her embroidery. There was no need to make matters easy for Marcus. Rather the contrary.

There was silence after Pen left. Isabella stitched quickly and unevenly. She hoped that Marcus could not see that her hands were trembling slightly.

She jumped when he slapped the newspaper down on the arm of the chair beside her.

"What is the meaning of this, madam?"

Isabella set her jaw. "I do not understand, my lord."

"Of course you do!" Marcus rested his hand on the arm of the sofa and leaned over her, wholly intimidating. "Married me for my money indeed! Was it necessary to tell the entire *Ton?*"

Isabella stitched a little more quickly. If he leaned any closer, she would stick her needle in him.

"It avoids misunderstanding, my lord," she said. "I always try to be truthful."

Marcus gave her an angry glare. "I wish you to send a retraction to the paper immediately. It is to be printed tomorrow."

"If you wish, my lord."

Isabella risked a quick look at his face. He looked furious, baffled and frustrated. How gratifying.

"You will do it?" he said. There was a faint note of disbelief in his voice.

"I have agreed," Isabella said composedly.

There was a moment of stillness and then Marcus straightened up. "Very well. I also wish to know when you will be removing from here to Stockhaven House."

Isabella snipped her thread carefully with her little silver embroidery scissors. "I will move to Stockhaven House when it is ready for me, my lord."

Marcus looked puzzled. "Ready? Ready in what way?"

Isabella raised her eyebrows. "Why, the house must be cleaned from top to bottom. All the chimneys must be swept. A staff must be engaged—"

Marcus snorted. "You already have a staff, madam."

"They may not wish to work for you," Isabella pointed out sweetly. "And of course the house must be provisioned—"

"Balderdash!"

"And finally there is my carriage—"

"A carriage!"

Isabella looked at him. "Of course, my lord. What will people say when they see your wife traveling by hack?"

Marcus opened his mouth and closed it again.

"You wished for a list of all my social engagements, my lord," Isabella continued. She rang the bell. "Belton, kindly pass Lord Stockhaven the list on the bureau."

Marcus glanced at the piece of paper Belton handed him. He turned it over. His brows snapped down.

"This is blank."

Isabella smiled. "Alas, I have no appointments, but if I am fortunate enough to be invited anywhere, my lord, I shall be sure to consult you."

Marcus was now looking frankly disbelieving. "This is ridiculous."

"I do so agree, my lord," Isabella said. "However, it was your wish that we should do things like this."

"I mean it is ridiculous that you tell me you do not have any social engagements, madam. Do you expect me to believe that? You must think me simple."

There was a loaded silence while Isabella looked at Marcus with brows raised slightly. "*Simple* is not the word I would use," she said.

Marcus frowned blackly. "So tell me—"

"What?"

Marcus flung himself down into a chair. "Tell me what you will be doing today."

Isabella sighed. "Well, after you have gone, I may go to Bond Street with Penelope." She saw his look of accusation and added smoothly, "I shall not be buying anything, of course, for that would necessitate asking you for money. But one may window-shop. It is not a social engagement, however, since Pen may well be immersed in Plato for the rest of the day. She is very unpredictable in that sense."

"And tonight?" Marcus pressed. "The theater? A dinner?"

Isabella shook her head. "A quiet evening at home."

"Guests? Visitors?"

"I prefer not," Isabella said. "A good book is all I require."

"Good God, madam," Marcus exclaimed, "you lead the life of a nun!"

"I have been trying to tell you so," Isabella agreed. "Unfortunately you do not believe it." She paused. "You may join me if you wish, but I cannot promise it will be very exciting."

"I have an appointment tonight," Marcus said.

Isabella felt a chill. Of course he did. Just because she was sitting blamelessly at home there was no reason to suppose he would be, too.

The satisfaction she had gained from thwarting him over the newspaper announcement vanished abruptly. She realized with a little jerk of the heart that, wrapped up in their mutual animosity and equally mutual painful attraction, she had given no thought to where Marcus spent his nights. She was too experienced to think that just because he wanted *her,* he would not take his pleasure elsewhere. Perhaps he already had a mistress. She felt as though there were a crack in her heart.

"Of course," she said, clearing her throat to cover the vulnerable quiver in her voice. "Then I wish you a pleasant day."

Marcus stood up. "When I wish you to accompany me to social events I shall give you a day's notice."

"I see." Isabella did see. Tonight, whatever the event was, he did not require her presence at his side.

"You will write the retraction for the *Times?*" Marcus added, as though he still did not quite believe her.

"Of course," Isabella said politely.

Marcus hesitated. "Very well, then. Good day, my lady."

Isabella did not move for a moment. She listened as he went out and heard him calling a cheerful word of thanks to Belton. She felt cold and stiff despite the warmth of the day.

And she felt oddly empty. What she had planned—what she had *wanted*—was to be preparing to move to Salterton by now. The social whirl of London held no attractions for her. She had spent twelve years living in a royal fishbowl and now she wanted some peace.

But that was not how matters had turned out. She was trapped in Town because her husband required it, but her days were empty. She was supposed to seek his permission for any activity she wished to indulge in and, since he held the purse strings, her options were severely curtailed. She was beginning to see that this might be how Marcus intended to punish her for what he saw as her past misdemeanors.

She stood up abruptly, spilling the needlework on the floor and leaving it there. She crossed to her escritoire. First there was the newspaper retraction to write. Then she needed to take some time to think. She had to plan very carefully, for she had no intention of letting Marcus dictate her life.

She sat down and selected a quill. Drawing the paper toward her, she started to write: *The Princess Isabella Di Cassilis would like it made clear that she did not marry the Earl of Stockhaven for his money.* There. That was a retraction. She paused, chewing the tip of the quill. *Indeed, the princess would like to point out that it is the earl who is the fortune hunter since through the match he has gained possession of Salterton Hall in Dorset, a property that he has long desired....*

She finished the paragraph, dusted it down, and reread it with a certain satisfaction. If that did not make Marcus incandescent with rage she would be extremely surprised. Well, he had asked for a retraction...but he had not said that she should not mention anything else in her statement.

"Check," she said aloud. "And you had best beware, my lord, for next time it will be mate."

The copy of the *Times* was still lying on the sofa where

Marcus had discarded it. Isabella picked it up absentmindedly, then her gaze sharpened on an article on the front page.

Return to London of the American ambassador and his wife...

She sat down slowly, still reading. When she reached the end of the article, a smile spread across her face. She had not looked for such good fortune. Since returning to England and discovering Ernest's debts, all the breaks had appeared to be against her. But now her luck had turned. She crossed once again to the escritoire, chose her best writing paper and dipped her quill in the ink.

MARCUS'S COMPANION THAT NIGHT was tall, dark and had a re-markably bushy beard. When Marcus arrived at the Golden Key Inn, Townsend, the Bow Street runner, was already seated in a quiet corner, puffing on a clay pipe that added to the general fug of the room. When he saw Marcus, he made to stand, but Marcus put a hand on his shoulder again to hold him in his seat. He did not want to be conspicuous.

"Good evening, sir," Townsend said. "Pint of ale?"

Marcus acquiesced. He had drunk far worse things when he was in the navy. He looked around. The bar, with its low ceiling and black beams was noisy and hot but no one was paying them particular attention.

"You have some news for me?"

"Aye, sir, I do." The runner drew thoughtfully on his clay pipe.

Marcus sat forward. "About Warwick?"

Townsend viewed him with his mild blue eyes. "No, sir. There's not a criminal in London would talk about Warwick. My news is about the lad you were looking for—Channing, wasn't it?"

Marcus nodded. Throughout his search for Warwick, Edward Channing had seldom been far from his mind. He re-membered the boy's delirium and the mixture of fear and respect in his tone when he had spoken of Warwick. He remembered the grief-stricken silence of Edward's parents. He had hoped against hope that one day he would be able to give them good news.

He realized that Townsend was watching him and there was a shade of pity in his eyes. "A relative of yours was he, sir?" the runner asked now.

"The son of one of my tenants," Marcus said. He focused abruptly. "You said *was?*"

Townsend nodded slowly. "Died in the poorhouse," he said simply. "In Shoreditch."

Marcus felt a huge regret, followed by a shock of anger. "Died—of what?"

"Fever, they said. He was left there a few weeks ago." Townsend cleared his throat. "Fellow who brought him in had found him on the street. He was already sickly, in a very bad way, so I'm told. Never recovered enough to tell them more than his name and his age, and that he was from the country. I think it was the lad you're looking for, sir. I found his name when I was going through the burial records. The details match."

Marcus nodded. He did not doubt it. He thought of John and Mary Channing again. All hope had been extinguished for them now. He thought of Warwick, who would use a child and discard him on the street when he became sick and useless. He felt a cold fury. Townsend was still talking.

"Might I be so bold as to inquire into your plans now, sir?"

Marcus drained his tankard. "I go to Salterton. The boy's parents must be told. And I think it is the only way to find Warwick. No one here will give him away but I have something that he wants. Sooner or later he will come for it."

The runner puffed slowly on his pipe. "You might be right at that, sir. Any ideas what it is that you have of his?"

"I am without a clue," Marcus said with a rueful smile.

"Ah, well." The runner lumbered to his feet. "I'll tell Sir

Walter the latest. He'll be glad to know you are on the case. We'll catch the bastard sooner or later." He gestured to the empty glasses. "Your shout, is it, sir?"

Marcus laughed. "Of course. Thank you for your help, Townsend. Can I press you to another?"

The runner shook his head, pulling his waistcoat down over his rotund belly. "Got a home to go to, sir. You, too, most likely. I'll say good night."

He disappeared through the fug of smoke and the crowd closed behind him. Marcus was left alone amid the bustle and noise of the public house. It was an odd feeling to be in so crowded a place and yet to be so alone. He did have a home to go to, of course, though he doubted that it would be as welcoming as Townsend's. It was more of a house than a home. He had employed only a skeleton staff the week past, knowing that there were Isabella's servants to be accommodated and also that he might be traveling to Salterton soon as well. Stockhaven House would be dark and quiet and somehow cold. It was not an encouraging thought.

He paid handsomely for the drinks and went out into the night followed by the grateful landlord's blessing. The air was thick and humid. He did not like these hot nights. The fresh heat of summer was delightful but in the city the sultry air could press down with stifling power. He thought of the slums where disease flourished and children like Edward Channing died alone and unlamented. His fury and hatred of Warwick simmered unabated.

Even though it was hot, he chose to walk home rather than take a hack. The journey was without incident, but as he turned into Mayfair he caught a glimpse of a woman hurrying around the corner. She was cloaked, little more than a flying shadow in the dark. And yet there was something about the way she moved that seemed instantly familiar…. He took an impulsive step forward.

"Isabella!"

The woman did not turn. Marcus was left in the lamplight with a watchman looking at him curiously. He felt rather foolish. Isabella had told him that she was at home that evening, and even were she not, she would hardly be walking alone in Mayfair. The simple fact was that she was beginning to haunt his thoughts. He fancied he saw her in every woman he met. Even when he was thinking of something else, her presence filled his mind.

Without realizing what he was doing, he turned into Brunswick Avenue and from there into Brunswick Gardens. The lights were still burning at the house. It was not very late. He told himself that it was a perfectly acceptable hour to make a social call. Especially on his wife.

He rang the bell.

Belton did not look impressed to see him. His lugubrious face lengthened.

"Good evening, my lord."

"Good evening, Belton." Marcus stepped inside, glancing around the hall for any sign of Isabella. He was aware of feeling a curious tension. "Is Lady Stockhaven at home?"

"Her Serene Highness," Belton said with emphasis, "has retired for the night, my lord."

A suspicion was growing in Marcus's mind; a suspicion that Isabella, far from retiring, was out on the town and that her servants were covering up for her. He had known it could not possibly be true that she had no social engagements. No doubt she was at some risqué dinner with Carew and Lonsdale dancing attendance.

"I would like to see her," he said.

Belton's mouth turned down at the corners. He was standing foursquare in front of the staircase, as though he was physically forbidding Marcus to proceed.

"I regret that Her Serene Highness gave no instructions for you to be admitted, my lord," he said.

"I am her husband," Marcus pointed out.

"That is so, sir," Belton agreed with unruffled calm. Still he did not move.

Marcus looked at Belton and Belton looked back at him, unflinching.

"Belton? Who is calling at this ungodly hour? I am trying to sleep!"

Marcus looked up abruptly.

Isabella was standing at the head of the stairs. She had a pale blue robe on and her hair was loose, tumbling about her face and down her back. Her feet were bare. It was quite obvious that she had been in bed. Marcus's heart lurched. He realized that he had not seen her like that since she was seventeen.

Isabella did not come down. She stood on the top step, one hand resting on the banister, and looked down at him. The height of the stair, its curving elegance, seemed to give her an air of untouchable authority.

Marcus looked pointedly at Belton, who in turn gazed blankly into the middle distance.

"Excuse me, Belton. I would like to talk to my wife." Marcus could barely keep the impatience from his voice.

Belton turned. "The Earl of Stockhaven would like to speak with you, Your Serene Highness."

There was a pause. "Then let him come up, Belton," Isabella said.

Marcus took the stairs two at a time and reached Isabella's side in mere seconds.

"You were in bed," he said slowly. He reached out and touched her cheek. Her skin was warm and soft beneath his fingers. Because he touched her so seldom, and wanted to touch her all the time, it felt like an intolerable temptation. He wanted to tangle his hands in her unbound hair and feel its silkiness between his fingers; that autumn hair, vivid with red and brown and gold. He saw her lashes flicker. She swallowed. Although she was unmoving beneath his touch, he sensed the same ache of longing in her blood that was in him. Her eyes were a deep blue, slumberous with a desire she could not conceal.

"It is past eleven," she said, and her tone was even although he could see the pulse beating frantically in her throat. "What did you wish to talk about, my lord?"

Marcus's mind was blank. Talking was not at the top of his priorities.

"I—" He could not begin to remember why he had come here in the first place. His hand slipped to the smooth skin of her neck, stroking down to the hollow at the base of her throat. Her fingers clenched on the robe, holding it closer to her chest.

"I wanted to see you," he said.

She looked at him briefly and then away. "I thought that you were engaged tonight?" Her tone was a little husky.

"I was. My business is concluded."

His hand was on the nape of her neck now. It's curve felt so warm and vulnerable beneath his fingers. Her hair, loose about her shoulders, brushed his sleeve. He continued to stroke her skin softly, almost absentmindedly, his gentle touch a fierce contradiction to the desire raging within him. Her mouth was so close to his. It would take very little to kiss her—as he had wanted to do since that last, incendiary embrace in the Fleet.

"I thought I saw you," he said. "Whilst I was out this evening…"

It was barely intelligible but Isabella understood enough. The light faded from her eyes and she stepped back from his touch.

"I see." Her tone was dull. "You thought you saw me, despite the fact that I had told you I should be at home. So you came to check if I had lied to you."

"No!" Marcus's objection was instinctive, even as he realized that she was in fact correct. He felt suddenly cold, as though something were slipping from him before he had truly grasped it. He fell silent, a silence that condemned him aloud.

"Well," Isabella said after a moment, "you can see that I was at home in bed. Alone. Which is where I should like to return now that you have satisfied your doubts. Belton will show you out."

Marcus hesitated. He wanted to explain that it had not simply been that he had doubted her. He had wanted to see her. He thought about her all the time. He was beginning to see that he needed her. But she had turned from him now without another word. Belton was already holding the door for him. And nothing but the hot night beckoned.

CHAPTER ELEVEN

"What the *devil...*"

"Your conversation lacks variety these days, old fellow," Alistair Cantrell complained, putting down the papers he had been reading. "Whatever can be the matter now?"

Marcus looked up from the morning copy of the *Times*. Once again they were in the reading room at White's, Alistair working on the column he wrote for the papers and Marcus reading the early-morning copies of the news. There had been a peaceful silence between them until Marcus's explosion of wrath. Now he read aloud:

"'The Princess Isabella Di Cassilis would like it made clear that she did not marry the Earl of Stockhaven for his money. Indeed, the princess would like to point out that it is the earl who is the fortune hunter, since through the match he has gained possession of Salterton Hall in Dorset, a property that he has long desired. First the earl married Miss India Southern, who at the time was heiress to the Salterton estate. Now he has married her cousin to make certain of the property—'" Marcus slapped the paper down in an explosive gesture. "Damnation! I cannot believe she has done this!"

He looked up to see Alistair trying to smother a smile. "What is the matter with you?" he demanded ungraciously. "It is not amusing!"

"Yes it is, old chap," Alistair said amiably. "Did you not ask the princess to send in a retraction?"

"Yes, but—"

"And has she not done what you asked of her?"

"Technically, but she knew that this was not what I meant!" Marcus crumpled the paper furiously in his hand. "Devil take it, I am starting to believe that she married me just to plague me!"

"Whereas she," Alistair said pointedly, "*knows* that that is the reason you married her. Revenge can work two ways, Marcus, and I hesitate to mention that you were the one who started this."

Marcus grunted. He knew Alistair was right, although he did not wish to admit it. He had provoked Isabella with his high-handed behavior and she had responded by challenging him every step of the way. There were plenty who would say that he had only himself to blame.

"You should see the *Gentlemen's Athenian Mercury,*" Alistair said, picking up his work again. "They have printed a far more scurrilous story."

Marcus grabbed the other paper. "What? Where?" He rummaged through the pages, almost tearing them in his haste.

"The Society column," Alistair said.

Marcus finally found the right page.

"'Hot on the heels of the startling news of a certain princess's less than flattering opinion of English lovers comes the even more extraordinary news that she has taken one of these gentlemen to her heart. We are assured on the highest authority, that of the august newspaper, the Times, that a marriage has been contracted between Her Serene Highness and the Earl of S. We await with bated breath the new countess's opinion on the amatory capabilities of her husband. Given the lady's outspokenness we feel it will not be long before the whole of London is aware of her judgment on the subject....'"

Marcus gritted his teeth. "Hell and the devil! Do you think that Isabella wrote that, too?"

"I doubt it," Alistair said calmly. "Have you not noticed that someone is selling stories about your wife to the papers, Marcus? The *Mercury* has been printing them for ten days or more."

"I never read this rag," Marcus said, tossing the *Mercury* aside. "It is full of nothing but scandal and slander."

"Steady on." Alistair looked offended. "I write for the *Mercury* myself. What about my advice column for young gentlemen?"

In reply, Marcus twitched the paper from his friend's hand.

"'Gentlemen, I pray that you will help me,'" he read aloud. "'My father is determined that I should marry a very old widow woman of thirty with a fortune of two hundred pounds a year and an inclination for young men and gambling. I cannot bear to make such a match. Pray assist me with your advice.'"

Alistair looked at him. "What would you tell the young gentleman to do, Marcus?"

"I would tell him to obey his father and cease writing ridiculous letters to newspaper columnists," Marcus said, putting his feet up on the table and passing the letter back to his friend.

"Hmm." Alistair bit the end of his pencil. "I do not believe you have the sympathetic nature required to advise the young, Marcus."

"Of course not," Marcus said. "I do not have the patience. Why does the father not marry the woman himself, if he is so anxious to attach her fortune?"

"I expect that the lady is more enthusiastic for a young bedfellow than an older one," Alistair said with a grin. "And who could blame her?"

Marcus shifted in his chair. He had little sympathy for the sexual frustrations of others that morning, being too preoccupied with his own.

"I cannot conceive why you bother dishing out advice to importunate young men," he said.

"Because, my friend," Alistair said, without rancor, "I am

not as rich as you. I can make a tolerable if not excessive living from my writing and occasionally the letters from youths are interspersed with something more interesting."

"Since you write for the same paper," Marcus said, struck by an idea, "you may be able to identify the mysterious gossip who writes about Isabella."

"I might," Alistair said. He smiled slightly. "I already have my suspicions."

"You do?" Marcus stared at him.

"Leave it with me," Alistair said.

"Very well." Marcus stood up and stretched. "In the meantime I shall deal with my errant wife."

"Are you going to attempt to persuade her to print yet another retraction?"

"No," Marcus said. "Clearly that did not work."

"Clearly."

"So I shall have to do something else."

"Any ideas?" Alistair inquired.

"Something will come to me," Marcus said.

Alistair looked at him over the top of his reading glasses. "You do realize, Marcus, that if you push Princess Isabella hard enough, she may well tell everyone that she married you in the Fleet—where you were masquerading as a debtor? If that story came out, you would have even less chance of finding Warwick."

Marcus's expression hardened. "Isabella and I have an agreement that if she speaks on that, I will tell everyone that she married a debtor to save her own skin."

"I have said before that your marriage is outrageously romantic," Alistair said. "I did not know the half of it!" He sighed. "Take heed of one who makes a living from giving advice, and do not try to tell Princess Isabella what to do. I have noticed that it has a detrimental effect on the feminine sex."

Marcus scowled. "India was always very biddable."

Alistair swiftly turned a snort into a cough. "Well, you know best, old man. I have never had the pleasure of being married, of course, so what do I know? I wish you the best of luck."

But as Marcus stalked out of the room, Alistair was shaking his head ruefully and mentally placing a very large bet on Princess Isabella emerging the victor in this particular contest.

I require you to accompany me to a dinner this evening with Mr. and Mrs. Henry Belsyre. I regret the short notice. Please dress appropriately. Stockhaven.

ISABELLA WAS DRUMMING her fingers on the black-and-white checkered top of the games table. Ernest had used it for cards but at one time it had had matching black and white marble chess pieces as well. Ernest had sold the set years before because chess was not a game he could gamble on.

Isabella, on the other hand, had always enjoyed chess. It was a game of skill and strategy. An old Austrian general she once played against had told her that she would have made a brilliant soldier, for she had a tactician's mind. And now her strategy was working out rather well.

Her eye fell on Marcus's note again. That was all there was. He had made no mention of the piece in the *Times* but no doubt this was his peremptory response, to curb the rein and remind her that she was his to command. Tonight he was demanding her presence at his side. She was expected to jump when he called.

The one thing Marcus had not banked upon, of course, was that she already knew Mr. and Mrs. Belsyre rather well. During the course of a long career in the diplomatic service, the American ambassador and his wife had been posted to Sweden while Isabella was also living there. They had become the greatest of friends. So much so, in fact, that when Isabella had written hastily the previous day to welcome them back to London and invite herself and Marcus to dinner, they had not minded expanding their impressive guest list to include the Earl and Countess of Stockhaven.

Marcus was not to know that, of course. Isabella had asked Mrs. Belsyre to address the invitation to her husband and to make no mention of the fact that they were previously acquainted.

She smiled. This was one order Marcus had issued that would be her pleasure to comply with. And with any luck, it would also be the last.

MATTERS WENT AWRY FOR MARCUS at a very early stage that evening. When he arrived in Brunswick Gardens to collect his wife, he found her swathed from head to foot in a black cloak and so was quite unable to tell whether she had dressed appropriately for the dinner or not. He was not in the mood to take any risks, however. He did not trust her not to have chosen some outrageous outfit simply to embarrass him.

"Take your cloak off," he said.

Isabella stared at him for an unnervingly long time before she obeyed. Her expression was quite blank. Then she permitted the cloak to slip from her shoulders and fall to the floor.

Her gown was quite simply the most sinfully beautiful creation he had ever seen. Marcus realized that he was gaping and shut his mouth with a snap. Of deep cherry-red silk, it swathed every inch of her from her neck to her ankles, wrapping her in a sinuous sheath of material. The color suited her to perfection. It made her skin radiant and her eyes glow a deep, forget-me-not-blue. She took his breath away.

There was absolutely nothing about the outfit that he could object to—and it was absolutely not the type of gown he wanted other men to see his wife wearing. Not when he was unable to strip the clothes from her and make love to her with all the pent-up fury and feeling that possessed him. The thwarted desire that he had managed to repress since the previous night came back with a potent rush. Damn it, she would drive him insane at this rate.

"That is very—" He paused. It was not too tight, yet he could see every curve, every line of her body defined in exquisite and tantalizing detail. The surge of sexual frustration that shook him then silenced him for a moment.

"Very nice," he finished lamely.

Isabella looked disdainful. "Did you think that I would dress like a whore to humiliate you? I assure you, my lord, that I have plenty of self-respect even if I have no respect for you."

Marcus winced at her accurate assessment of his thoughts. He knew respect was not a God-given right. His years in the navy had shown him that it had to be earned and he could not deny that he had done precious little to earn Isabella's in the time that they had been married. And yet he reminded himself that this was the woman who the *Ton* reviled as an adventuress, the woman who had taken India Southern's inheritance from her and ruined her relationship with her mother. He would do well to remember that whatever hand Isabella was dealt, she deserved.

He bent down and picked her cloak up for her, remembering that he had something to give her.

"I want you to wear these." He withdrew a small, velvet bag from his pocket. "They are the Stockhaven jewels."

The necklace was of diamonds, not the huge, ostentatious type, but a web of tiny, sparkling, delicate drops of light strung on a golden thread. He held them out to her but she did not take them. She shook her head slightly.

"It is not right for me to have these. I have plenty of paste jewelry."

Marcus frowned. "It is appropriate for my wife to wear the Stockhaven jewels."

Isabella pushed his hand away gently, and with it the bag and the necklace. "Appropriate. How you like that word,

Marcus. I do not think it appropriate for your estranged wife to wear this. It is so exquisite that it should be worn with love."

Estranged. It was a very lonely word.

Marcus struggled. "India never wore them. She did not care for them."

He had not meant to tell Isabella that; had not meant the words to come out at all. He owed India his loyalty, even if it was the only thing he could now give her.

He thought Isabella would look pleased that her cousin and rival had not worn the jewels. He was already proffering the necklace to her again when she turned aside from him.

"That was not what I meant." She swung round so suddenly that Marcus was startled. "Give them to someone you care for, Marcus. They are too good for anything else."

She took the cloak from him. It swirled about her as she crossed the marble floor to the door, her evening slippers clicking sharply on the stone. She did not even pause to see if he was following her.

"Are you acquainted with Mr. Henry Belsyre?" he asked as they seated themselves in the carriage.

Isabella did not look at him. "The ambassador of the United States of America? Yes, I have met him before. I did not know that the Belsyres had returned to London, though. They served a term of office here before, did they not?"

"They returned just this week, so I understand," Marcus said, "hence the short notice for tonight." He looked at her. "If you know the Belsyres, you will know that they are very influential. They move in the first political circles."

Isabella stifled a yawn. "Politics! How boring!"

Marcus cast her another look. "Tonight is important to me, Isabella. I have been doing some work for the Admiralty and the Home Office, and I may wish to pursue a political career in the future. The contacts I make this evening—" He broke off, wishing that he had not said anything. It felt as though he was exposing a weakness to her and he had already learned the hard way that Isabella would exploit any opportunity he gave her. His nerves tightened with a curious mixture of anticipation and enjoyment. He was actually *relishing* this battle with his wife. The challenge of it was addictive.

"I understand," she said neutrally. "This evening must go smoothly for you."

"It sounds as though you know Henry Belsyre well," Marcus said. "Did you meet him and his wife abroad?"

Isabella was looking out at the darkening streets. A flambeau flared on a corner as a link boy guided a couple along the pavement. A laughing group of young men jostled one another as they crossed the road. Isabella allowed the curtain to fall back into place, enclosing them in darkness.

"I have known the Belsyres for many years," she said. "Mr. Belsyre was my—" She broke off. Marcus waited but she offered no further information. He felt frustrated. He had the numbing feeling that he could never discover her deepest secrets. He was feeling none of the satisfaction he had expected to feel when he wrested her life away from her and imposed his own rules on her.

"One of your former lovers, I suppose," he said.

Her blue gaze pinned him like a shard of ice. "You suppose incorrectly," she said coldly. She did not speak again until the carriage arrived at their destination.

One glance was sufficient to tell Marcus that the rooms were packed with the luminaries of the political and diplomatic worlds. Henry Belsyre, American ambassador to the Court of St. James, was as influential a diplomat as one could find—statesmen, soldiers and politicians flocked to his soirees. Marcus's hand tightened on Isabella's arm as they approached their hosts. Belsyre was chatting to Lord Sidmouth and Princess Esterhazy, but broke off with a word of apology as he saw them and strode forward, beaming.

"Isabella! We had no notion you had returned to London! What a splendid surprise!" Under Marcus's bewildered gaze, he kissed her soundly on both cheeks, then held her at arm's length. "Rose, Isabella has arrived!"

"Good evening, sir," Isabella said, smiling. "This is wonderful! I thought you still in Washington."

"No need for the formality," Belsyre grumbled. "There was a time you called me *Uncle Henry* rather than *sir,* if you recall."

Isabella laughed. "I was about six years old then, sir, and you were not an ambassador."

Uncle Henry? Marcus stared. It was not the type of previous relationship that he had imagined between them. Rose Belsyre was actually *hugging* Isabella. Marcus was left standing unnoticed, like the plain debutante whom no one asks to dance.

"You look enchanting, my dear," Mrs. Belsyre said, smiling. She turned to Princess Esterhazy. "Maria, you have met Princess Isabella Di Cassilis, have you not?"

"Of course," Princess Esterhazy said. Her smile was warm. "My dear Isabella, I heard a rumor that you were back in Town. Why did you not call?"

"She was too busy getting married," Belsyre said, smiling broadly.

Isabella turned slowly to look at Marcus. For one dreadful moment he thought she was going to announce the entire story of their marriage to the assembled company. He looked at her and she looked steadily back at him. He knew she could read his mind. He waited for the ax to fall, and all his future plans along with it.

"I beg your pardon, Marcus." Isabella spoke with perfectly judged charm. "I was so delighted to see Mr. and Mrs. Belsyre again that I quite forgot to perform the introductions. Ladies and gentlemen—" she turned at the surrounding company "—this is my husband, Marcus Stockhaven."

It was a perfect put-down because it could not be faulted for courtesy. Marcus had a sudden and extraordinary insight into what it might be like always to be a wife in her husband's shadow, greeted second, of lesser importance. He remembered telling Isabella in the Fleet that he disliked the idea of being married for his money and then discarded, and she had told him sweetly that now he knew what it was like to be a woman....

"Stockhaven!" Henry Belsyre gripped Marcus's hand in a firm handshake. "Delighted to see that Isabella has made such a sound choice for her second match. Many congratulations."

Suddenly everyone was looking at him. It had never previously troubled Marcus when he had been an outsider. He had experienced something similar when he had joined the navy with no man's patronage to support him, and again when he had gone to Lord Standish to ask for Isabella's hand in marriage and had been received with such disparaging lack of interest. He had never cared before. It had amused him. He had made his own luck and his own prospects. Now, however, he felt as though someone had pulled the carpet out from beneath him. He looked at Isabella as she stood with Mr. and Mrs. Belsyre on each side of her, Princess Esterhazy looking down her nose at him in that way she had of examining something not quite pleasant on her shoe, the Prince de Lieven and Lord Sidmouth on the sidelines. Here was a group of people whose view of his wife was very different from the spiteful tittle-tattle of the *Ton*. Here was a group who could make or break his ambitions and at their center was Isabella. The balance between them had shifted dramatically.

He cleared his throat. "I had not realized that you were all so well acquainted," he managed to say.

Isabella smiled faintly. "Mr. Belsyre was an old friend of my father."

Oh, hell. Marcus remembered her words in the carriage, the way she had fallen silent and the way in which he had leaped to a fairly large conclusion, driven onward by his anger and possessiveness.

He caught her arm, drawing her toward him. "Why did you not tell me?" He kept his voice very low.

Her eyes were cold. She shook him off, but gently so that no one could see the repressed anger in her. "Why should I tell you anything, my lord? You never had that right. Just be grateful that unlike you, I do not stoop to shoddy revenge."

Marcus could not believe her. He remembered the way that she had bartered with him in the Fleet. "There must be something you want. What is your price? Money?"

She whitened. "You should learn that not everything can be bought, Stockhaven."

"That is rich, coming from you, madam."

They stared at one another for what seemed forever, locked in each other's eyes.

"Dinner," Belsyre said, making them both jump. "If you could escort Lady Sidmouth, Stockhaven…"

The event was stuffed with high-ranking nobility and it had not occurred to Marcus that since Isabella was retaining her title of princess, she would be seated considerably farther up the table than he would. He was obliged to watch the Prince de Condé lavish attention on his wife in what Marcus considered to be an insufferably familiar manner. And yet the rational man who was still somewhere within him was obliged to admit that Isabella dealt with the prince's offensive overtures very neatly. Since he was watching her all the time, Marcus saw the exact moment when Condé bent close to her, as though merely emphasizing a point in the conversation, and brushed his lips against her bare shoulder. Isabella said one word—a word that made Condé bite his lip—and turned away to talk to the Duke of Hamilton on her other side.

Marcus found that he was already halfway out of his seat, ready to ram the man's roast pheasant down his throat.

"Sit down, Stockhaven," Belsyre urged, catching his sleeve. He gestured for some more wine to be served, smoothing over the awkward moment. "Isabella can deal with Condé," he added under his breath. "She has had plenty of experience dealing with churlish foreign princelings." His tone softened. "Not that I blame you, man. Isabella has had a difficult time of it. Don't mind admitting that if dueling had not been outlawed, I would have taken a shot at Di Cassilis myself. Surprised the man survived as long as he did."

"Did you know him, sir?" Marcus asked, surprised at the ambassador's frankness.

"Unfortunately I did," Belsyre said. "Shocking match to make for Isabella. I was her father's oldest friend. Could barely bring myself to speak to him afterward." His blue eyes appraised Marcus shrewdly. "Still, I imagine you know all this, Stockhaven. Old history. Glad you and Isabella were able to put it all aside. She once told me that she would rather have been the wife of a sea captain than Princess of Cassilis."

He turned back to Lady Cowper on his right, and Marcus was left staring at his congealing pheasant with a certain degree of perplexity. What was it about Isabella Di Cassilis that seemed to inspire such loyalty in family, friends and servants alike? She had Pen, to whom she was clearly devoted, and Freddie, who would overcome his natural diffidence to stand up for her. She had Churchward, who would do what a lawyer should never do and actually rebuke Marcus for his behavior because he felt so strongly. And then there were these eminent people whom she had met during her years abroad, people who evidently held her in high regard.

She once told me that she would rather have been the wife of a sea captain than Princess of Cassilis....

The message was not difficult to read. There had been a time when he had been a sea captain and Isabella had accepted his proposal of marriage. It could merely have been a figure of speech on her part when she was speaking to Belsyre, but suddenly, Marcus wondered.

Isabella was tired. Reentering the sophisticated political world, so very different from the fashionable *Ton* ballrooms, had been an ordeal of another sort. Even though they had spent much of the time apart, she had been achingly conscious of Marcus throughout the evening. She knew that he had been watching her.

She had lulled him into a false sense of security, of course, by her vague references to the Belsyres and to the fact that political dinners bored her. She had seen the horror on Marcus's face when he had finally realized that these were people with whom she was closely acquainted. He had been wondering what she might do to extract her revenge. And she could not deny that the moment had been sweet. She had seen his shock and the way he had braced himself for whatever she was going to say. Turning the tables on him, feeling that power, had been heady.

Even so, she would not use it. That was not her way. If she could not have Marcus's good opinion—if she could not have Marcus's *love*—then she wanted nothing else from him other than that he would leave her alone. That was what she would bargain for.

By the time the ladies withdrew, Isabella would happily have kicked off her evening slippers, curled up on the sofa and gone to sleep, were it not for the fact that Princesses de Lieven and Esterhazy were intent upon discovering the reasons behind her hasty marriage to Marcus. Parrying their questions, she mentioned a past attachment and tried to turn the conversation. The Belsyres were such old family friends that they knew that she had been set to marry Marcus before Ernest had upset her plans. Isabella knew it was only a matter of time before the story of her original engagement to Marcus circulated, and then everyone would assume, as Rose Belsyre had already done, that this was a highly romantic reunion. They would think it a love match. How very ironic.

As soon as Marcus came into the room, she knew that he wanted to talk to her. She could read it in his face. She delighted in frustrating his efforts by engaging in animated conversation with everyone else and keeping her shoulder firmly turned toward him.

But she knew it was only a matter of time. Marcus was hardly a patient man. And then Princess de Lieven sabotaged her by patting the seat beside her and summoning Marcus over with a gesture that could not be ignored. Isabella thought that he complied with alacrity.

"We have been asking Lady Stockhaven what it was that prompted this whirlwind wedding, my lord," Princess de Lieven said. "It sounds remarkably romantic. A past attachment…old flames…"

Marcus looked at Isabella. His smoky dark eyes held a gleam she mistrusted. "Oh, it has been most romantic, ma'am," he agreed smoothly.

Isabella shifted. "Unimaginably so," she said.

The ladies sighed in unison at such a vision of loving bliss.

"And you have been wed for…" The princess paused, her gaze inquisitive.

"Ten days, ma'am," Marcus supplied.

"Each day more special than the last," Isabella said.

Marcus gave her a dark, direct look. "I am happy you should think so, my love."

"But then," Isabella said gently, "I do not have much to compare it with, do I?"

There was a slightly awkward silence while the princesses sensed that something was not quite as romantic as they had thought it.

"It said in the papers that it was a marriage of convenience," Princess Esterhazy put in, "but one can see from merely looking at you that such a notion is fair and far out."

"It could not be further from the truth, ma'am," Isabella

agreed. "No marriage has ever been less convenient. Pray excuse me. I am sure that Lord Stockhaven will be happy to give you his own version of the match."

She had wanted to have a little time on her own in the peace of the ladies' withdrawing room, but she knew it was unlikely Marcus would give her that opportunity. She was quite right. He caught up with her before she was halfway across the room.

"A moment, madam."

He caught her wrist in a grip that was not tight but that she could not have broken without an undignified tussle.

"I do not care for this game of cat and mouse," he said softly. "Tell me what you intend."

Isabella tilted her chin up. "I shall tell you nothing. I suggest that you accept the situation you are in—as others have been obliged to do before you."

"I accept nothing."

"You have no choice."

Marcus smiled at her. "Oh, I have a choice, Isabella. My one aim now is to get us both out of here and have this matter out with you once and for all."

Isabella moistened her lips. "I refuse to leave at your behest, my lord."

"Then I shall have to take extreme measures."

With a jump of the heart Isabella saw that Marcus's gaze, very dark and very intense was focused on her lips. The concentrated desire in his eyes shocked her even more deeply than the fact that he was about to kiss her in public.

"You would not dare." It came out woefully lacking in conviction. Of course he would dare. He would not even hesitate.

"Tell me to stop, then." His lazy tone held a wealth of challenge. He was calling her bluff and God help her, she could not resist him.

Slowly, very slowly, he bent his head and captured her lips with his.

His mouth incited a heated response that she felt all the way down to her toes and then she was incapable of stopping him, incandescent with the passion that ripped through her as uncontrollably as fire. Time ceased to exist. Isabella was aware of nothing except the sensation of the kiss. Her lips trembled and then parted to the thrust of his tongue. Her head spun. When he released her, the room was still spinning.

"I was about to ask Isabella what had determined her upon becoming Lady Stockhaven," Princess de Lieven said, very dryly, from her place on the sofa. "The question seems somewhat superfluous now."

Marcus's touch on her arm was triumphantly possessive. Isabella could feel it in every fiber of her being. He smiled at the room in general. "My apologies, ladies and gentlemen. Please excuse us. We have not been married very long."

There was some indulgent laughter at this.

"Do not let us keep you, Stockhaven," Henry Belsyre said. "Politics can wait, whereas some things cannot. We must arrange a meeting to discuss business soon."

"Thank you, sir," Marcus said.

Keeping Isabella pressed close to his side, he bent and spoke for her ears only. And his words sent a shiver of chill through her that she could not repress.

"It is time that you and I came to terms, my lady. I am coming home with you. Now."

CHAPTER TWELVE

IT WAS NOT LATE BUT THE HOUSE in Brunswick Gardens was silent. Two lamps shone in the hall. The footman who held the front door for them was not as accomplished as Belton at hiding his feelings; his eyebrows shot up toward his hair before he diverted his incredulous gaze away from Marcus Stockhaven and fixed it on the highly polished marble floor. Under other circumstances, Isabella might have laughed. Her servants were not accustomed to her bringing gentlemen home.

It had been a hot night and they had traveled under a summer moon. It should have been romantic but Isabella had merely felt shaken and wary, and suddenly very afraid. Across from her, Marcus looked expressionless. He had already shrugged himself out of his jacket and waistcoat, and undone his neck cloth. Isabella had hoped profoundly that the heat was the reason for his state of undress rather than an imminent intention to ravish her in the carriage. She could not be sure. In the moonlight he'd looked both elegant and ruggedly virile in his shirtsleeves and she'd turned her face away from the sight.

"Why did you not turn to your friends when you were in debt?" Marcus had asked her suddenly. "They would have been willing to help you."

Isabella had sat up a little straighter. "I do not borrow money from my friends," she said.

"Pride is an expensive commodity," Marcus had said.

"It is not pride, Stockhaven," Isabella said quietly. "It is self-respect."

They did not speak again until the carriage had drawn up in Brunswick Gardens and Marcus had helped her inside.

As Belton came forward to greet them his step did not falter nor did his discreet facade waiver at the sight of the Princess Isabella Di Cassilis arriving home on the arm of her husband. He merely bowed.

"Good evening, Your Serene Highness, my lord…" His nod was stiff and proper. "I trust that you enjoyed the dinner? May I fetch you any refreshment?"

"Thank you, Belton," Isabella said, stripping off her gloves. "I shall take a glass of port in the study." She flicked a glance at Marcus. "No, better make that a bottle. Lord Stockhaven?"

Marcus had come forward to help her remove her cloak, cutting out the butler whose expression became, if anything, even more wooden. Isabella felt Marcus's hands on her shoulders, slipping the garment from her. It felt extraordinarily intimate and she moved from under his touch as quickly as she could.

"Brandy, if you please," Marcus said.

"Certainly, my lord," Belton said starchily and withdrew.

The footman threw open the doors of the study and closed them softly behind them, leaving the pair in silence.

Isabella crossed to the window and pulled back the long curtains, welcoming the cool draft on her hot face. She felt tense and edgy. Neither of them seemed anxious to be the first to speak.

Marcus was standing with his back to the fire, hands in pockets, looking both relaxed and fully in command of himself and the situation, and suddenly Isabella was tired. Tired of the pretence and the struggle and the sheer misery of estrangement. She turned to Marcus and held his gaze very directly.

"You are trying to break me, Stockhaven," she said, "but you will not succeed."

Marcus came across to her and took her by the shoulders. He stared down into her defiant eyes.

"No," he said, and a slight smile curled the corner of his mouth. "I do not believe that I shall."

"Then…" Isabella made a slight gesture. "What do you want from me?"

"I want to come to terms," Marcus said again. "I want an explanation. I want a reckoning, and I want a wedding night. What do *you* want?"

Isabella took a deep breath. "I want you to let me go."

Marcus's gaze flared. "Then it is a bargain. If you give me what I want, I shall fulfill my side of the agreement."

Isabella stared at him, frozen. The room was shadowed and warm, a place for intimacies and confidences. Except that she did not feel like confiding in Marcus Stockhaven. She felt cold and betrayed and unhappy. Before she had understood the extent of his mistrust of her she might have given him the explanation that he craved. Now it felt like a hopeless waste of time. She would lay the past bare and still face his scorn and she was not sure that she could stand that.

As for the wedding night…

The thought made her whole body tremble. A part of her wanted it passionately, desperately, but she knew she could not give herself to a man who hated her. She was hopelessly drawn to Marcus. She always had been. A stubborn part of her told her that it was not too late, they could be lovers again. But cold reality made it impossible.

Marcus came across to her and took her arm in a light grip that nevertheless held her still. The icy cold was seeping through her whole body.

"I do not pay my debts in that way," Isabella said. She lifted her chin and looked at him in the eye. "Make no mistake of it, Stockhaven. I do not want to have to explain myself to you. That is bad enough. I cannot see what good it will do now,

after all this time, and I believe I owe you nothing. But—"
she gave a tiny shrug "—if you insist, then talking to you is
the lesser of two evils, is it not?"

Marcus stared down into her eyes for a long moment and
she was afraid that he would see everything that she was
keeping so tightly locked within—all the misery and the long-
held secrets and the love and the fear. After a moment his grip
on her arm loosened and he stepped back, but his face did not
soften.

"It is all or nothing."

All or nothing. The reckoning. The wedding night. And in
return, freedom…

The future seemed to spread before Isabella like a tantalizing web. The peace and freedom to live as she wanted, not
as someone else dictated. She had waited such a long time for
that opportunity. Her father had denied it to her by forcing her
to marry Ernest. Ernest had denied it to her by dictating her
every royal move and Marcus, unbearably, had also sought to
make her live as he wanted.

She ached to be free. Liberty was so close and yet so tan-
talizingly beyond her grasp.

"I want Salterton," she said.

"It will be yours."

"And the means to keep it."

"Of course."

"I want…"

An annulment would be out of the question if the marriage
were consummated. Isabella took a deep breath, willing
herself not to think about that, not yet.

"I want a legal separation."

She thought for a moment that Marcus was going to refuse.
A muscle tightened in his jaw.

"Very well," he said. His tone was rough.

"I do not trust you," Isabella whispered.

Marcus shrugged. "I am not a man who breaks his word. And if I did break it, you could swallow that pride of yours and go to the Belsyres and tell them whatever you liked about me. You know you could ruin my ambitions for the future ten times over if you chose."

There was an ache of tears in Isabella's throat. "I do not want it to be like this."

"This is how it is." Marcus's face was as hard as stone.

There was not a great deal of choice. Isabella knew she could either live this half life, an estranged wife in love with her husband and with no hope for the future, or she could buy her freedom and escape an intolerable situation.

Marcus was watching her.

"Very well." She cleared her throat. "I agree."

"OH DEAR, OH DEAR," Penelope Standish said unhappily. She was sitting with Alistair Cantrell in the Lime Street Coffee House. It was scarcely appropriate for a spinster to be taking coffee late at night with a gentleman alone, but Pen was not concerned that she was in any danger from Alistair Cantrell. She had seldom felt safer with anyone. They had met in the doorway of the offices of the editor of the *Gentlemen's Athenian Mercury*. Pen had been mortified. She had spent the evening working on a scandalous piece about Isabella that drew on old gossip as well as current speculation and, once it was written, she had hurried to deliver it to the newspaper, as though getting it off her hands quickly would somehow lessen her guilt. Morrow, the editor, had been delighted with it. Pen's blood money, a sovereign, was even now weighing down her reticule. She had already started to think of all the things she would spend the money on. And then she had collided with Alistair in the doorway and he had looked at her in the perceptive way of his and the wretched coin felt as though it was bursting into flames in her bag, a sign of her treachery. She had stuttered some greeting—goodness knows what—and tried to scuttle past, and then Alistair had put his hand on her arm, obliging her to stop.

"Miss Standish, might I have a word?"

And Pen had known that she was lost.

They sat in a quiet corner of the coffeehouse while the raffish nightlife of the city spun unnoticed around them.

"Miss Standish," Alistair Cantrell repeated. "You may tell me to mind my own business, of course, but I do wonder what you can be doing at the offices of the most scurrilous newspaper in Town."

"Oh dear," Pen said again. In her agitation she put another spoonful of sugar in her coffee and stirred it with quick, spiky gestures.

Alistair looked at her very directly. "You seem very fond of your sister," he said. "It makes me curious as to why you would then sell stories about her to the press."

Pen's shoulders slumped. She could lie, of course, but somehow the necessity of lying to Alistair seemed impossible.

"How did you know?" she asked in a very small voice.

Alistair smiled. "By logical deduction. The person selling the information had the kind of knowledge of Princess Isabella's life that only a confidante would know. It had to be someone very close to her. And then I met you coming out of the editor's office—" He shrugged. "Well, it seemed fairly conclusive."

"Yes," Pen said. "Yes, it was me. I feel very ashamed."

There was a pause.

"Forgive me, Miss Standish, but you do care for Princess Isabella, don't you?"

Pen's face twisted. "Yes. Oh, yes of course! Bella is the dearest creature and I love her very much." She sat forward. Would it be possible to make Alistair understand? He seemed a very loyal man and not one to condone this sort of deception. Pen found that she wanted his good opinion.

"You see, Mr. Cantrell—" she gave him an appealing look "—I have absolutely no money and I have to do something in order to survive." She hesitated, anticipating his next question. "The reason why is not important. But when I thought about it, selling scandal about Bella was the only thing that I could do. At least," she amended as she caught sight of a painted courtesan leaving the coffeeshop on the arm of a gentleman, "it was the only thing I wanted to sell."

Alistair's lips twitched as he followed her gaze. "I understand you, Miss Standish. It is a melancholy thing for a lady to be in such reduced circumstances and be obliged to look about her for other means of support, but even so…"

"I know," Pen said. "You cannot despise me any more than I do myself, Mr. Cantrell. I kept telling myself that I would stop, but I could not. It was too tempting. And Bella did not seem to mind very much when she read the reports—" She broke off. "I know it is no excuse."

Alistair touched her hand briefly. Pen was shocked and more than a little intrigued.

"I worry about Bella," she said, to cover her surprised reaction. "I know that may sound absurd under the circumstances, but I do care for her."

Alistair nodded. "I understand."

Pen found the urge to confess further was all too strong.

"Despite the fact that Bella is my elder sister and so…" She groped for words. "So experienced—oh no, I do not mean in that way, more that she has seen a great deal of the world—" her blue eyes met Alistair's hazel ones briefly "—despite all that, I sometimes have the most disturbing feeling that she does not entirely know what she is doing."

Alistair did not speak. He covered her hand again in a most comforting gesture, and this time he did not let her go immediately.

"Bella only married Ernest Di Cassilis in the first place

because our father faced financial ruin," Pen continued, "and she was unhappy for all those years, and when she came back it was to find that Ernest had left her bankrupt, but as to why she married cousin Marcus—" She broke off as she ran out of breath. Alistair was still holding her hand and it felt warm and very pleasant.

"I know that they were once very fond of each other," Pen finished. "I was barely more than a child at the time, but children notice things, don't they? I am almost certain that they were madly in love. It was going to be the perfect wedding. But something went awry and Bella married Ernest and Marcus married India, and now—" She shook her head.

Alistair's grip tightened. She felt comforted but she freed her hand to take a sip of her coffee—and almost choked on the cloying sweetness.

"Oh!" Her eyes were streaming but through them she could see that Alistair was laughing at her.

"Another cup, as you appear to have ruined that one?"

"I do not think so," Pen said, "but a dish of chocolate would be very pleasant, thank you."

The drink arrived. Pen had noticed that Alistair was most adept at organizing things with a minimum of fuss. She started to feel a little more relaxed. Alistair was watching her across the table. His hazel eyes were very shrewd.

"Miss Standish, will you promise not to sell any further stories to the press?"

Pen slumped a little more. She knew she could never do it again, but she was terrified at the thought of having no money.

"Of course. I could not…" Her voice wavered. "Oh dear…"

"It is your brother, I suppose," Alistair said. A shade of steel had come into his voice.

Pen looked defensive. "Please, I cannot discuss it. Freddie does his best, but he has never been very good with money."

Pen knew Alistair wanted to say something else, something

scathing, and only his courtesy held him silent. After a moment he said, "If you are in urgent financial need then I am sure we could come to an agreement."

"Mr. Cantrell!" Pen was so startled that she upset the dregs of her chocolate.

"I meant," Alistair said, his eyes twinkling, "a loan. Naturally."

"Oh, naturally." Pen wrenched her gaze away from a couple seated in the bow window who were entwined in each other's arms, oblivious of the crowd about them. No doubt it was the louche air of the place and the unusual excitement engendered by being out at night with a gentleman that was leading her thoughts astray.

"That is very kind of you," she added.

Alistair got to his feet. "I think that I should escort you home now, Miss Standish," he said. "I will procure us a hack. The streets are becoming a little rough but I assure you, you will be perfectly safe with me."

"I imagine so," Pen said with a sigh.

She watched as Alistair paid the bill, went to the doorway and summoned a hackney carriage with his customary orderly precision. She watched the line of his shoulders and the turn of his head and the way that his body moved beneath his neat and unostentatious garb. She had always been more struck by the written word than the visual image but now she felt hot and immodest and astounded at herself. How very frustrating. Here was Mr. Cantrell offering her his protection in the most innocent way imaginable and here she was, suddenly realizing that security was the last thing that she wanted from him.

"Shall we go?" Alistair offered her his arm.

"Thank you," Pen said, casting her gaze down like the demure spinster she no longer resembled, "you are all that is gentlemanly, Mr. Cantrell."

"At your service, Miss Standish." There was nothing but sincerity in Alistair's tone.

Pen sighed. She knew she was pretty and she knew Alistair Cantrell thought her so and she also knew that he would do nothing about it whatsoever. She could travel in a closed carriage with him from London to Canterbury and he would likely do no more than point out places of interest along the way and order refreshments up ahead. He would not pounce on her or try to ravish her or even press a chaste kiss on her hand. She felt ridiculously safe, entirely dissatisfied and utterly frustrated in a way she had never felt before, a way her mother had told her no lady ever should.

HOW ABSOLUTELY FRUSTRATING. Alistair Cantrell stood outside the small house in Pimlico and looked up at the lit window on the first floor where he was certain Miss Penelope Standish was even now unfastening her dress, loosening her golden hair from its pins and unlacing her chemise in preparation for going to bed. He could not see any of these intriguing probabilities, for the curtains were tightly drawn and of thick material, but he did not need to see in order to imagine. He could visualize Penelope's thick, tumbling fair hair, her small but perfectly formed breasts and the slenderness of her body beneath the enticing transparent shroud of her chemise. Of course, for all he knew he could be staring at the window where Freddie Standish was no doubt snoring with a bottle of brandy clasped in his arms, but really it made no difference. Pen was in the house and he wanted her and he was so close but in truth ineffably far.

She trusted him. She was a lady in need and she had confided in him and he should be honored to have that trust rather than thinking of breaking it in the most shocking way imaginable. He could not—*could not*—encourage her to rely upon him and then use that closeness to lead her astray. But oh, he wanted to. He ached to. He was exploding to do so.

He knew Miss Standish had a reputation as a bluestocking with a tongue like a dose of vinegar. He was certain she would not hold back from administering a setdown to anyone whom she regarded as a fool, and there were plenty who would fit that description. Yet he had seen her softness and vulnerability, the way she cared for her sister and the guilt that riddled her when she thought of betraying Isabella's trust. He knew how difficult it was for a gentleman in dire financial straits to make his own way, so he could imagine the frightening prospects that faced a woman in such a predicament. And he was pledged to help her, not seduce her.

Under the circumstances, it was fortunate that it had started to rain. It dampened his ardor slightly and his clothing a great deal. If he did not wish to contract the ague, he knew he should return home and cease staring up at Penelope's window like a lovestruck youth. Nevertheless a part of him wished there was a balcony and a sturdy climbing rose, while another mocked him with the thought that if there were, he would fall off it and require medical assistance. Should Miss Standish require practical help—the summoning of a hackney carriage, the procurement of a cup of chocolate—then he was the very man for the job, but should he be called upon to perform some romantic endeavor then he would only fall flat on his face.

Even so, he continued to stare at the bright square of window until the light was doused.

CHAPTER THIRTEEN

"WHERE SHOULD I START?" Isabella asked politely.

"The beginning is always a good place," Marcus said. "Why did you jilt me?"

Isabella huddled deeper within the leather embrace of the armchair. She wanted its capacious interior to swallow her up. She wanted to sleep. She wanted to feel safe. Instead she had to talk and try to make Marcus understand. Her heart quaked at the prospect.

"You left me standing at the altar," Marcus said. His tone was very controlled. "You refused to see me when I tried to find you. You did not even write. You never told me what happened." His voice kindled into feeling. "The first I knew of what was happening was reading the report of your marriage in the papers and then you sent back my ring—" He broke off. Isabella saw the shutters come down in his face. Once again the fire was banked down.

"Explain," he said now, expressionless. It was not an invitation.

"There is not much to tell," Isabella said. She kept her gaze fixed on the embers of the fire so that she did not have to look at him. That hurt too much.

"It was for my family, Stockhaven. Or perhaps it was for money. You will decide for yourself, I am sure."

She looked up briefly. Marcus's face was very still, but there was about him a controlled intensity, an anger that she suspected burned very deep. Now that the moment of truth had come, she merely wanted it all to be over and Marcus to leave her alone. She would make this as quick as possible.

"I was not aware when I was young that Papa was in serious financial difficulty," she said. She shrugged a little. "Children are often unaware of these things. They think that matters will always be the same, always safe." She sighed. "When I grew older, I discovered that Papa was forever in and out of debt, making a small fortune, losing it again, gambling, investing in dreams, unable to be prudent.... When he died, he had lost all his money, which is why Freddie is obliged to work and Pen has such a pittance on which to live."

Marcus had not moved an inch since she'd started speaking. He was sitting across from her in the leather armchair and he was very still, but with a watchful stillness that was reflected in his eyes as he studied her. His expression was cold and remote. Isabella felt chilled to see it and curled herself deeper in her own chair for comfort.

"At the time that Ernest offered for me, Papa was within an ace of ruin. Ernest was a rich man then, of course. He offered to save Papa from the debtor's prison." She laughed a little bitterly. "I was part of the arrangement. In order to save my family from ruin, I was obliged to accept Ernest's suit. It mattered nothing that I was about to marry you. Their security was dependent on my acceptance." She broke off, staring into the heart of the fire, where the embers glowed bright.

She would say nothing of how it had felt. Nothing of her father, exposed as a weak man who could not protect her, blustering and ordering her to accept Ernest's hand in marriage; her mother, ripping her little embroidered handkerchiefs to shreds in her restless fingers; Freddie, his face blank but the expression in his eyes so desperate; Pen, catching her hand and asking her if it was true, and would she let them all starve.

She had been too young to make those agonizing decisions but she had made them anyway.

"So you agreed," Marcus said tonelessly.

Isabella felt the anger rip through her. That he could sit there unmoved, condemning, when after twelve years she could still feel the despair and the hopelessness that had possessed her...but Marcus did not know any of that. For all he knew, she might have seen Ernest as the goose laying the golden eggs.

"It was not an easy choice," she said quietly. "I was in love with you. I was completely besotted." Emotion crept into her voice. "We were to be married the next day! It was a... shock...to be obliged to see matters differently."

"You could have refused," Marcus said. His mouth was a hard line. "You could have insisted on marrying me and told your father to go hang."

Isabella thought about it. She could have run to Marcus but she had been young and alone and terrifyingly uncertain of what to do. She had wanted Marcus—ached for him to be there to protect her—and yet she had known with finality that in choosing him she would be condemning her entire family to ruin. She had been torn apart.

I needed you so much...

She bit back the words. She would not tell him that now, not when he had sufficient bitterness for them both. Once it had been so very different. She felt a sharp pain at the bright simplicity of their time together. She had given herself to him because she was in love and had been heedless of the consequences. At seventeen she had been rash, reckless and unmindful of all the tenets of behavior that she had been brought up to believe in. But then the consequences had followed—her parents, Freddie, Pen—and her daughter, Emma. Their futures all depended on her making the right decision. So she had chosen their well-being over her happiness with Marcus and learned the hard way that unfettered passion and careless disregard might feel blissful at the time but that there was always a price to pay. She had paid every day in memories and regrets.

And now Marcus would blame her for her choice. He was looking at her broodingly. She knew there was no sympathy or understanding there for her. She swallowed hard.

"I suppose," he said, "that it was too dangerous for you to take a risk on me even though I might have been able to help you all. I had no money and no prospects then, and Prince Ernest was a rich man—"

"Don't you dare to suggest that I married him for his fortune!" The words broke from Isabella before she had chance to stop them. It was instinctive, straight from the heart. She had not wanted to rehearse all the anguish in front of Marcus but she could not help herself from letting this much emotion show. She saw his eyes widen at the irrefutable sincerity in her voice.

"But you did," he said slowly. "You *did* marry him for his fortune, albeit to save your family."

Isabella turned away. What had she expected—that he would hear her explanations and draw her to him with all the strength and the lost love and the warmth that she had cherished in him before? That that was exactly what she had wanted, secretly, not even admitting it to herself. But life was never so simple as that.

"Yes," she said. "I married him for his money because my family needed it. He bought me." She looked at Marcus defiantly and spoke with deliberate hardness. "Even had you and I married, Marcus, there is no guarantee that we would have been happy. We were young and so wrapped up in our feelings and so thoughtless of the future."

"True," Marcus said. He smiled faintly. "I do believe we were quite swept away in discovering such a consuming desire for each other."

Isabella had been. It had been new and exciting and utterly overwhelming. She had had no thought for tomorrow and no shame for today. Just the memory of it made her ache with a poignant mixture of longing and regret.

"Such strong desires have a habit of burning themselves out," she said, "leaving little behind. They are best left in the past where they belong."

Marcus did not reply. He looked at her as he had done in the prison, from the paste diamond pins in her hair to the silver slippers peeping from beneath the hem of her skirt, and she knew he was thinking of the wedding night she had agreed to give him. She shivered with raw emotion.

Marcus shifted a little. "You could at least have offered me an explanation," he said. "You could have written to me via the Admiralty." His mouth twisted with grim humor. "It would have been polite to explain the circumstances to me, especially given what we had been to one another."

Isabella gave a half shrug. "I could not begin to think how to tell you," she said, and that was the truth.

Marcus's gaze branded her. "I was your *lover,* Isabella! You were once able tell me anything. I thought—"

Once again, there was a taut silence. Isabella felt the tension between them stretch so tightly it would snap with the least provocation. There was no point in waiting for absolution. Marcus would never give her that. Suddenly all she wanted was for him to be gone so that she could sleep.

"So," she said. "You have your explanation. I know it is too little and too late but—" She shrugged her shoulders. That was all she was prepared to give. She felt empty.

Still Marcus did not reply. Isabella fidgeted.

"And now," she said, as the silence lengthened, "I want you to let me go."

Marcus did not answer at once. It was frighteningly plausible. All the assumptions that he had made about Isabella's desire for a title and a fortune could be turned on their head. Isabella at seventeen, alone, obliged to make the kind of choices that one hoped never to make in a lifetime…she must have felt desperately lonely and afraid.

Everything had happened so quickly between them, from the first secret, incendiary look they had shared to the raw passion that had driven them together, to the final cold fate that had pulled them apart. Time enough, and yet no time at all…

His certainties wavered. Isabella was looking very pale and tired, but he could discern no emotion on her face. She had spoken with such composure, almost as though she had rehearsed what she was going to say. And yet he could not discount the sincerity in her voice when she had protested the charge of marrying for a fortune.

There was another allegation to lay at her door, however, and he would do well to remember it. She was not exonerated. Not yet.

"What about India?" he said harshly. "I can see why you might have made the choices you did with regard to me, but she…" He shook his head. "What did she ever do to incur your dislike?"

Isabella had been waiting for his answer, tension in every line of her body. Now he saw the puzzlement creep into her eyes and a tiny frown crease between her brows.

"India?" The bewilderment was clear in her voice. "I do not understand what you mean."

Once again he felt the force of her sincerity. His interpretation of the facts told him one thing but his instincts told him quite another. He wanted to believe her false and yet her honesty seemed to thwart him at every step.

"Turning her mother against her." Marcus cleared his throat. He had never overcome the guilt that he felt toward his late wife. He had married her for all the wrong reasons and they had never been able to make each other happy, which made him all the more determined to see justice meted out. It was too late for India, perhaps, but he could lay Isabella's sins at her door and make her admit her culpability. He got to his feet and paced across the room with a caged anger.

"Throughout your visits to Salterton and your letters to Jane Southern you deliberately undermined your cousin's position." He turned to look at her. "India told me that her mother frequently goaded her with the fact that she wished she had a daughter like you. You set out to take Salterton from India. She and Lady Jane had a monstrous disagreement about it. Jane disinherited her as a result."

Isabella's eyes had widened in horror and disbelief. She was sitting stiffly in the chair now, upright, her hands clenched on the arms. She shook her head slightly. "But I knew nothing of this! I swear I never said or did anything to damage India's relationship with her mother, least of all to see her disinherited!"

Marcus thrust his fists into the pockets of his jacket. "Then why would India swear that you did? She had no reason to lie to me."

He saw Isabella's expression change and before she could turn away he caught her to him, pulling her to her feet. He held her hard and close.

"It is true, isn't it? There was something you did."

Isabella had whitened. "It is true that I made no secret of my love for Salterton," she said stiffly. "I did write, and I did tell Aunt Jane how much I missed the place. If that is a sin— if that was what led Aunt Jane to disinherit India—then I must plead guilty. But none of it was deliberate. I could no more hide my love for Salterton than I could have—" She stopped.

Than I could have hidden my love for you.

Marcus heard the words as though she had spoken them aloud. For him too the memories and feelings he had for Salterton were inextricably tied to the time he had spent with

Isabella there. Once again he felt a wave of disloyalty to India, followed by shame.

"You were the daughter that Jane really wanted," he said. "How do you think India could live with that?"

Isabella shook her head. "I cannot be held responsible for that, Stockhaven."

"You can be held responsible for all the insidious little ways in which you reminded Lady Jane of her preference for you," Marcus said sharply.

"I did no such thing. If India told you that, she was lying."

Marcus's hands tightened. "Why should she lie? You think that she was jealous? Of you?"

Isabella looked disdainful. Her face was very close to his and he could see the telltale beat of the pulse at her throat giving away her agitation, but on the surface she looked as though she could not care any the less.

"Why should she be jealous of me?" she said. "She was married to you."

"She married the man that you rejected," Marcus said sharply.

Isabella's lashes flickered down, veiling her expression. Her mouth was drawn tight; that luscious mouth that was always his undoing. He wanted to kiss her. The need rampaged through him. He wanted to kiss a woman he disliked intensely and it was very disturbing.

"I doubt that India was ever jealous of me," Isabella said, "but in truth I have no notion of what India thought about anything." Her eyes were dark, shadowed. "We did not confide. We were not close."

"Despite being of an age?"

Isabella had heard the reproach in his tone and the color flared in her cheeks. "Oh, do not try to lay that one at my door, Stockhaven! I wanted to be a friend to India but she did not seem to need me. She was—" Isabella hesitated. "A very self-contained person. Well, you knew her better than I." She moved away from him and he let her go. "So no, I told her nothing of my feelings for you either at the time or later, and even if I had—"

"She would have had no reason for jealousy, being the one that I had married," Marcus finished grimly.

"If she knew that you cared for her then she had nothing to envy," Isabella agreed. She was pale now, as though something was hurting her. She lifted her chin. "I know nothing of this, as I told you. For all I know, you could be making this entire matter up as another stick to beat me with."

Marcus made an abrupt movement. "I do not lie," he said through his teeth, "and neither did India."

"And neither do I!" Isabella's blue eyes, so like those of his late wife, flashed defiance. Marcus felt suddenly bitter. He had never doubted India's accusation because he had understood all too clearly how Lady Jane Southern might have felt. Isabella had fire and courage and spirit where India had meekness and timidity. For some mothers she would have been the ideal daughter, but not for Jane, who had had a restless spirit herself. She and India had been as dissimilar as chalk and cheese and they had never been able to live comfortably with their differences. Yet somehow it felt like a double betrayal of India for him to be able to enter into her mother's feelings and see how perfect a daughter Isabella would have been for her.

"Despite your denials, it is part of a pattern, is it not?" he said roughly, as though Isabella had not spoken. "You married Ernest Di Cassilis for his money and I am sure that the others, the men you had along the way, had to give you something you needed or be discarded." His possessive anger was fanned white hot at the thought as he continued. "You made sure that Jane Southern disinherited her daughter in favor of you. You married me to save yourself from ruin. And now you bargain to buy your freedom. There is little you will not do, little you will not stoop to, to ensure your own fortune."

Isabella had turned very white at his words. "That," she said, "is blatantly untrue."

"The facts speak for themselves."

"The facts are as I related them to you," Isabella said. "I married Ernest because at the time it was what I thought was best to save my family. As for the others…" She swallowed hard.

Marcus held himself tight with rage. "Yes?"

"There were not so many of them as you imply," Isabella said, "and all I wanted from them was affection." There was stark despair in her voice. "I know that you and others have branded me a whore on the strength of it but you know nothing. Nothing at all."

"So tell me."

Isabella looked at him and there was a faint smile in her eyes. "Oh no, Stockhaven. You did not ask that. I am not going to expose any more of my soul to you. All you wanted was the truth of what happened when I jilted you. That I have given you, whether you choose to believe it or not."

Marcus felt his frustration tighten further. "And the rest? The inheritance?"

"I have told you. I knew nothing of Lady Jane's plan to disinherit India and I deny that I encouraged her to do so. And I married you—" She paused.

"Yes?" Marcus said again.

Her eyelashes flickered, once again hiding her expression from him, but her tone was bleak. "Very well. I confess it. I married you to save myself from the debtors' prison. It was a bad mistake but I was—"

She broke off and closed her lips tightly.

I was desperate. He remembered her saying it when she had threatened to marry whichever of his fellow prisoners would have her.

He shrugged. The anger drove him on and it left no room for sympathy. "So. I have paid off your debts and you are safe.

You have told me why you jilted me and now—" He paused. In the firelight she looked fragile and apprehensive. He wondered how on earth she could look like that when she was the most brass-faced creature on earth.

"And now," he said, deliberately, "I do believe it is our wedding night."

Isabella had her hand against his chest, warding him off. "I cannot give myself to a man who does not care for me, does not trust me and I dare say does not even like me very much."

Marcus laughed. There was a wildness inside him and it demanded recompense. He wanted to slake his anger and his bitterness in her body. He wondered how she thought that any man could look on her and not feel the same desire.

"You underestimate my feelings for you, my love," he said. "I admire you and I want you."

Isabella's clear blue eyes challenged him to examine those truths he wanted to ignore. "Yet you despise me," she said.

Marcus's gaze did not falter. "A part of me does, perhaps. We need not regard it." He touched a finger to her lips. If he did not have her soon, he thought he would burn up with the wanting.

"I need you very much," he continued, the rough under-tone edging his voice. "You are not indifferent to me, either. Look me in the eye and tell me that you do not want me."

Isabella was biting her lip. She did not look up. "I want to be indifferent to you," she said.

"Ah." Marcus leaned forward and touched his lips lightly to the curve of her neck. "That is a vastly different matter, as even you will allow."

He felt a shudder run through her but then she moved from beneath his touch and deliberately put a distance between them. "You cannot have me," she said. She turned her shoulder. "Go! Go and find a harlot to satisfy your lust!"

There was a moment's stillness. Marcus did not move. He put one hand on her arm and felt the conflict in her. She was wound as tight as a spindle.

"You do not mean that," he said softly.

Isabella's shoulders slumped.

"I do not mean it," she admitted. "But you must go, Stockhaven. I told you the truth and you have chosen not to believe me. I cannot give myself, married or not, to a man who has no respect for me."

Marcus's expression was implacable.

"You can and you will. It is the bargain you made, my love."

"No," Isabella said. "I will not give myself to you when you think so little of me." She threw out a hand in desperate appeal. "You knew me before, Marcus! Was your own judgment of me so faulty then that you can believe this of me now?"

Marcus gritted his teeth. The ghosts of his love for her twisted and tormented him. "I was young," he said harshly. "Perhaps I was misled in my feelings for you."

"You loved me," Isabella said, ashen now. "Are you saying it was all based upon a lie?"

Her eyes were blazing. Before he could reply she added, "Why must you make yourself believe the very worst of me?"

It was not a question that Marcus wanted to answer. Not now, possibly not ever. At the moment he could not think beyond the shocking need to have her in his bed. He did not want to confront his demons or to acknowledge that there was a chink in his defenses. Perhaps India had lied to him. Perhaps she had been jealous of his love for Isabella. And he, out of his guilt and remorse, had tried to blame Isabella for everything rather than admit the pain.

Isabella's eyes were a deep, dark blue, smudged with desire. Her cheeks were pink with arousal and when he touched her, her skin felt heated beneath his fingertips.

"You cannot deny me." He was aching to take her, afraid

that he would lose all control if she refused him. "I was your first lover. You know that you want me, too."

"You will regret this." She said it not as a threat but a simple statement of fact. "This feels wrong. It *is* wrong when there is so much unresolved between us."

Marcus understood what she meant but he tried to close his mind against the knowledge. Why make matters complicated when they could be simple? They could forget the past, the accusations and the recriminations, in the heat of the present. Afterward…but he did not want to think about afterward. Not until he had taken her and ravished her and reclaimed her, and laid all their ghosts to rest.

"I do not know what to think," he whispered.

He caught her to him and kissed her with all the pent-up passion and torment that plagued him. She did not resist but she did not respond either. A tremor shook him; he gentled the kiss, courting a response rather than demanding it. Somehow he had to make this right. She had to want him as much as he wanted her. He felt her lips tremble beneath his before they parted to his searching tongue and then her whole body went soft in his arms and the sweetness of her yielding broke something within him.

He swung her up in his arms and made for the door.

It was only when he reached the top of the stairs that Marcus realized that he had no idea where to find Isabella's bedroom. Under other circumstances he might have found it rather amusing to be striding off to take his wife to bed, only to realize that he did not know where her bed was. Now it merely frustrated him past endurance.

"Tell me where to go," he said, "or I swear I shall take you here on the stairs. I cannot help myself."

He saw the shock mirrored in her face. A part of him was as appalled as she that he was behaving with so little finesse as to treat her like a whore, but he was too far gone in lust now to care. He had gained a response from her but he had lost it again now with his anger and desperation. Her voice was dry when she replied.

"Your wooing lacks subtlety, Stockhaven," she said.

"You will not find me lacking when the time comes," Marcus said. "The room?"

There was an agonizing second while she appeared to consider the situation. To Marcus it felt like an hour.

"The third door on the left," she said.

The room was in darkness, the curtains drawn but with a rogue beam of moonlight slicing through to speckle the floor. Marcus had a brief impression of a bed with a high, carved back. He would not have cared had it been a broom cupboard. He put her gently on the bed and crossed to the door, turning the key with deliberation in the lock. The sound seemed to echo through the quiet house, signifying exactly what he was doing. He returned to her side, ripping off his neck cloth as he came toward her and discarding his shirt. He half expected her to scramble to her feet, to make some attempt to escape or to remonstrate with him. Instead she lay still, watching him, her skirts tumbled up above her thighs, her body still and open to him, wanton, abandoned. It was the most disturbing and inciting thing that he had ever seen.

He tore the gown from her shoulders in his haste, acting with an awkwardness that spoke of nerves as well as desire. He cursed his clumsiness even as she protested.

"My dress!" she exclaimed. "I cannot afford—"

Damn the dress. It was in the way.

"I will buy you another one." Marcus bent to kiss her, rough in his anxiety, his mouth claiming hers hungrily. He wanted a response from her again. He needed one. She had admitted that she wanted him. He was not taking an unwilling wife to his bed.

He forced himself to a patience that he was so far from

feeling it felt like a mockery. He had it all to do again. He had to coax that stiffness from her body, draw the passion from her. He had to go slowly. His body cried out against the thought but this time he ignored it.

When her lips parted beneath his, he felt a surge of triumph equal only to the surge of desire within him. Her tongue tangled with his. His mouth moved on hers, possessive, demanding. He cupped her face in his hands, driving his fingers into that silky dark gold hair that he had wanted to caress from the very first. She gave a little moan and moved her body accommodatingly beneath his. Marcus's lust swelled and his erection also swelled commensurately.

He could not wait much longer.

He pulled back to draw off his boots and saw her draw the tattered remains of her bodice close in an oddly innocent gesture. It only served to draw his gaze to the skin that it exposed. He sat down facing her on the edge of the bed, placed his hands about her waist and bent his head to the hollow of her throat. He could feel the heat that spread beneath her skin. His tongue flicked the curve of her neck, tasting her. Immediately her nipples hardened beneath the shreds of her chemise, and with a sound deep in his throat, he brushed the material aside, closing his lips over one of the cool, damp peaks. Isabella's body arched in an instinctive plea but he held her tight, his hands hard on her waist now as his mouth plundered the sweetness of her exposed breasts. Her soft moans and the writhing of her body pushed him perilously close to the edge but he was determined to prolong her pleasure. He was not sure how his selfish desire for satisfaction had transmuted into a determination to please her, but now their mutual need was all embracing.

He swept the material of her gown down, his hands moving over the bare planes of her stomach and hips in subtle caresses until Isabella reached blindly for him. She was shivering, though not with cold. He could sense the ripples of feeling edging along her skin and it roused a deep hunger in him. He kissed her again. Her mouth was warm and eager against his own and as his hands slid down to clasp her hips and pull her against his body, he parted her lips with his tongue and stroked deeper, exploring, curling his tongue with sensuous abandon against hers. He knew that her need was as acute as his own. It was implicit in the urgency of her hands on his body and the soft, broken-off gasps of her pleasure.

He parted her thighs with infinite gentleness. He sensed her instinctive hesitation, then his fingers were stroking gently as he felt the wet warmth of her. He touched his lips to the smooth skin of her stomach, edging lower, tracing the curve of her thigh with the tip of his tongue. Very slowly, with infinite gentleness, his lips brushed the curly triangle of hair between her legs. He heard her gasp, and then he was kissing her there, holding her hips down as he touched his tongue again and again with aching tenderness to her quivering core.

Isabella cried out. Her body tensed, her back arched and Marcus raised himself above her, easing himself between her legs, his rigid shaft poised at her entrance. He could not hold back any longer. He slid within her, feeling the heat and the incredible tightness close about him.

All thoughts of revenge and bitterness and anger had been burned up by his white-hot desire for her. Even so, he was unprepared for that first shattering crash of feeling as he thrust inside her and the shock and memory of it wiped out all thought. They were young again and the wooden floor of the summerhouse was hard beneath them and the summer moon poured down its blessing on them. Her skin was smooth and silver pale beneath his caressing hands as they fused, mind, body and spirit, close, closer still... Her fingernails scored his shoulders, mixing pain and pleasure. He drove into her, the hard hot thrust of his body searing brighter with every driving stroke. His body was racked with blissful pleasure, so sudden and so irresistible that he cried out in both surprise and ecstasy.

I love you...

Was that then, or was it now? He no longer knew. Nor did he care. He had wanted to think her avaricious and amoral but now he realized that he had been fighting himself at every step in an effort to make her fit that image.

It had never worked.

He knew she was finer than that and that she always had been.

His hatred was vanquished and relief flowed in its place.

His bitterness burned out.

He drew Isabella close to his spent body in love and profound gratitude, and fell asleep.

IT WAS THE SWISH of the curtains that woke him. Marcus stirred. He could not remember ever sleeping so long or so well. It felt as though all his demons had finally been laid to rest. The light hovered behind his closed eyelids. He did not want to open his eyes or confront the day. He wanted to tell Isabella that he regretted the things that he had said and the suspicions he had harbored of her. He wanted to tell her that he understood how painful it must have been for her to have to make that impossible choice between her family and his love.

He reached out instinctively.

The space beside him was empty.

"Hot water, my lord."

Marcus opened his eyes. Belton was standing at the foot of his bed, an ewer in his hand and a towel over his arm. His expression was politely blank.

Marcus shot up in bed. "Isabella...where is she?"

Belton's eyebrows twitched infinitesimally. "Her ladyship has gone, my lord."

"Gone?"

Marcus looked around desperately, as though he were expecting—hoping, he realized—to see Isabella hiding behind the bed hangings.

"Gone away, my lord," Belton said lugubriously. "Her ladyship was insistent that we should not wake you."

Hell and damnation. Lost in his own bliss, Marcus thought that he had taken Isabella with him. He had wanted her to feel the same deep pleasure that had possessed him but perhaps…perhaps in his selfish enjoyment he had totally failed to notice her lack of response…or perhaps he had taken her body but her spirit had once again eluded him. He felt sick and cold and suddenly afraid.

Belton had turned away and was pouring the water into the bowl on the sideboard. Through the buzz in his ears, Marcus heard the splash of the water and saw Belton mop up a spilled drop with absolute precision. He leaped from the bed and grabbed the butler's arm.

"Where has Princess Isabella gone?"

Belton turned slowly. His expression was still impassive. "Her ladyship has left Town, my lord."

Marcus shook his arm. "When? When did she go?"

"At daybreak, my lord." The butler anticipated Marcus's next question before it was half-formed in his mind. "It is now ten o'clock, my lord."

Ten o'clock. The numbers swam through Marcus's head like fish. Daybreak was half-past four in the summer, five at the latest. Five hours' start. Isabella could be anywhere by now, running away from him, putting as much distance between them as she could.

Belton was standing upright like a soldier on duty. Marcus looked down, realized that he was stark naked, and released the butler's arm.

"Thank you, Belton," he said.

"A pleasure, my lord," the butler said. He paused. "There is a note, my lord."

A note. Ridiculous hope surged through Marcus's heart. "Where?"

Belton pointed to the little table beside the bed.

Marcus picked it up and unfolded it. He noticed dispassionately that his hands were shaking.

Stockhaven,
I have gone to Salterton. You have had your wedding night. Now I trust you to give me my freedom.
I.S.

That was all. Marcus turned the paper over to make sure. The distance between them, physical and emotional, squeezed his heart. He had fallen asleep feeling closer to her than he had ever done in his life. She had merely been waiting for the dawn so that she could leave him.

He thought now of the relentless barrage of accusations that he had thrown at her and the way he had tried to conquer her spirit. The downright cruelty of it made him shudder. He put his head in his hands.

"Do you require a shave, my lord?" Belton asked, above his head.

"No, thank you," Marcus said automatically.

"Clothes, my lord?" The butler's voice held the tiniest shade of disapproval now.

"Thank you," Marcus said automatically.

"A horse, my lord?" Now the butler's voice held a definite message. Marcus looked up.

"A horse?"

Belton almost glared. "A *horse,* my lord."

A light leaped into Marcus's eyes at the same moment that hope surged in his heart. Why not? He had to try.

"Yes, I will have a horse made ready to travel, please, Belton," he said. "A fast one."

Belton's lips twitched into the faintest of satisfied smiles. Marcus recognized this as a sign of approval. "At once, my lord," the butler said.

Part 2—Seduction

Salterton, July 1816

CHAPTER FOURTEEN

THE DEBT WAS PAID and if Marcus kept his word, she was free.

If Isabella Stockhaven had been the type of woman to confide in a bosom-bow, which she emphatically was not, she might have vouchsafed the fact that her experience of love at the hands of her husband the previous night had been outstanding. It was true that she did not have a great deal of experience with which to compare Marcus's lovemaking. Sleeping with Ernest had been like being squashed by a wardrobe that still had the key in the door. But Marcus... Well, anyone who could make her tingle and quiver and melt with such absolute pleasure and longing had to be a master of the art. It had been a perfect wedding night in all respects but one.

Her husband did not love her.

Isabella was running away as fast as she could. It was not Marcus that she was running from. She was trying to outrun her own emotions. Yet she knew that no matter how she denied it, she carried those feelings with her every step of the way. There was no escape.

She was in love with Marcus Stockhaven.

She had never stopped loving him.

She had told Marcus almost the entire truth the previous night, leaving out only the closest and most painful secret, her doubts over Emma's parentage. She had hesitated over this, too, wanting a clean sheet, but in the end she had not spoken because what good would it do? Emma was dead now and the anguish put behind her. Isabella never wanted to face the devastation of losing a child ever again. She did not want to love and she did not dare to pray for children. Once again she locked the thoughts and the feelings away.

Even without exposing that deepest of secrets, though, the disclosures had been exhausting and costly. She had opened her heart to Marcus and it had hurt when he had rejected her explanations. Today she was tired and her feelings were rubbed raw. The journey gave her plenty of time to think. To think about the matters that she had talked about with Marcus and to think about her seduction.

For she had been seduced, swept up in a maelstrom of sensation that had left no room for rational thought, as much by her own desires as by Marcus's. Her need for him had been as strong as his for her. She faced the thought squarely. She had wanted him. She wanted him still.

Marcus's rough anxiety as he made love to her had lit something in her, a longing that was irresistible. A part of her had never wanted to resist him anyway. Isabella trembled with the memory. It was so long since she had felt like that. She had almost forgotten. She had *wanted* to forget. It was a lifetime; she had been a different person then.

To be held in Marcus's arms, to kiss him, touch him, hold him to her, was like coming home. She had been swamped by the profundity of her love for him. She had felt him inside her and her body had leaped in response but even as he'd taken her with him down that swirling, painful, blissful spiral of passion, her heart had been torn with a mixture of love and fear, for this was what she wanted but it still felt all wrong and until Marcus loved her again it could never be right.

Afterward he had held her close and had fallen asleep at once. In the faint light he had looked young and his face was rubbed clean of all anger and bitterness and hatred. Her stomach had lurched with a combination of love and misery as she had looked on him and she had entwined herself in his arms, trying to block out the painful thoughts that battered her tired mind.

It had not worked.

They had achieved physical intimacy but she felt further from Marcus than ever. He did not love her. She had told him the truth in the hope that it would ease the mistrust between them. Instead she was left with an emptier feeling than before. It was as though she had gambled all on a single throw of the dice and it had not turned up the result that she desired. There was honesty between them, there was a physical closeness now that both tormented and pleasured her, but it had brought no love with it. It had never occurred to her in all the tangle of her feelings for Marcus that she had a rival for his love. Now she wondered how she could have been so blind.

What about India? Marcus had said, and for a second she had wondered at the irrelevance of his question. That was before she had seen the anger and the loyalty and the passion in his eyes and had felt her heart sink through her velvet slippers. India. Of course. India was the one that Marcus had married. India had held his love and his loyalty then and she still had it now. Isabella knew that Marcus might want her, with that desperate, aching need that she felt, too, but that was a vastly different matter from the feelings he had had for his first wife.

It hurt to think of Marcus loving India. It had hurt her the previous night and it hurt now. It had been a shock when he had sprung it on her. Now it was a dull ache inside. She felt so foolish not to have thought of it. Her pride was humbled that she had believed his passion had only ever been for her.

Sleep had been impossible. As soon as it was light she had called for the carriage and taken the road south through the sleeping city. She had packed in haste and had left orders for the servants to follow her to Salterton with due speed. Then she had taken a last look at Marcus's sleeping form and had walked away.

Beyond Richmond, the countryside unrolled into a patchwork of fields, hedges, woods and villages on every side. The road was good. It was another glorious sunny day. Isabella tried to doze but it was no use; her thoughts spun like a top.

The carriage rumbled over cobbles and came to rest in an inn yard, rousing her from her torpor. Another stop. Change the horses, gulp down scalding coffee…

"Where are we?" Isabella asked.

"The Golden Farmer Inn at Bagshot, my lady."

Late in the afternoon they passed the junction where the road to Exeter turned west and they took the southern route to Winchester. Isabella had a very specific place in mind to stay the night. The town's hostelries and hotels were not for her, but on the outskirts, under the ancient walls, was an even more ancient inn called the Ostrich. It had once been a hospice run by the monks and although it had passed into secular hands after the dissolution of the monasteries, it had been bought by a private religious order some fifty years before. The monks of St. Jerome brewed their own mead, made their own medicine and offered hospitality to travelers. The Standishes had stayed there many times when traveling to Salterton. Lady Standish had considered a monastic establishment to have the appropriate *ton* for one of her genteel standing. Now Isabella was choosing it for a different reason, for what could be more suitable for a lady journeying alone? One would always find safe haven in a monastery.

The town was busy, for it was the week of the old summer horse fair and market, and St. Jerome's was almost full of visitors. One of the brothers greeted her with a refreshingly cool tankard of mead—the road had been dusty and the weather increasingly hot as the day progressed. Isabella had a strong thirst and as few inhibitions about ladies drinking alcoholic beverages as she had of them traveling alone. Her single port-manteau, thrown together in such a hurry, was taken to a room on the first floor that overlooked the orchard. There was an ewer of cool water for washing and crisp linen on the narrow bed. Having made certain that her coachman and groom had suitable accommodation, Isabella retired to her room, lay down and closed her eyes. After a little while, the scent of roasting meat began to creep into the room and she opened her eyes, realizing that she felt sharp set. A little while after that, there was a knock at the door and an inn servant appeared bearing a tray groaning under the weight of food. Isabella began to remember what a gem of a place The Ostrich was.

In the evening she read by the light of a candle while the hum of the busy streets echoed around her and eventually, despite the noise and the light night, she fell asleep over her book.

It was dark when she awoke and she knew instantly that something had disturbed her. Someone was turning the doorknob very gently. It made a tiny click and then a sliver of light appeared at the bottom of the door. Isabella tensed.

The door opened wider and Isabella groped silently over the side of the bed to find the chamber pot. Her fingers closed over its cold porcelain edge and she clung on for dear life. She had traveled widely and knew what to do in situations like this. It was a question of strike first and ask questions later. She could scream, of course, but strangely she found that she had inhibitions about doing that in a monastery.

A dark figure slipped through the doorway, closing the door gently behind him. He approached the bed softly. Isabella swung the chamber pot around in an arc, rolling over and bringing her arm round so that the pot made contact against the side of the intruder's head with a reverberating crack. He groaned and staggered sideways.

"And let that be a lesson to you not to go creeping into ladies' bedrooms in the night!" Isabella snapped.

"The message is duly received and understood," the man said wryly, rubbing his head. "I swear never to do it again—at least not without your permission."

Isabella sat bolt upright, her heart thumping not from surprise now but from fear. "*Marcus?* What on earth are you doing here?"

She grasped the tinderbox and struck a light. The candle flared. Isabella's hand shook slightly. This was most unexpected and disturbing. She had thought that she would have plenty of time before she was obliged to see Marcus again—if she were to see him at all. A legal separation could have been achieved working through Mr. Churchward. So could the formal deed of gift giving her Salterton. There would have been no need for them to meet one another ever again.

Marcus sat down heavily on the end of the narrow bed. "Not a particularly warm welcome," he said ruefully.

"What are you doing here?" Isabella demanded. "How did you know where to find me? I told no one where I was staying, so that you…"

A smile curled Marcus's lips. It made her feel prickly with sensual heat. It conjured the memories of the previous night. His hands against her skin, his lips at her breast, the friction of his body against hers… Isabella fidgeted and looked away.

"You told no one so that I would not know where to find you?" Marcus queried.

"Precisely," Isabella said.

Marcus laughed. "I followed you along the road," he said. "You are not exactly inconspicuous, Isabella."

"Why bother to follow me at all?" Isabella argued. Her nervousness was intensifying now. "There was no need. You had your wedding night. Now it is your turn to keep your word."

Marcus was silent for a moment. His face was dark and expressionless in the candlelight.

"I could not let you go like that," he said at length.

Isabella's heart thumped. "What do you mean?"

Marcus shifted. He looked uncomfortable. "I had to talk to you." A shadow touched his face. "Isabella, I am sorry. I wanted you last night and I thought that you wanted me, too. It was never my intention to force myself on you." He paused, then added with scrupulous honesty, "At least…at the start, perhaps I did not care. But I would never take you against your will." He shifted uncomfortably. "I am sorry that I drove you away."

He had misunderstood her reasons for running away, Isabella realized. She had been intent on putting the distance between them because she could not have borne to awaken in the morning and hear the stark words that he was leaving her. But he had assumed that she had run away because she had been repelled by their lovemaking. He was looking unbearably contrite and, to her surprise, she felt the hot color flood her face. She felt tongue-tied. "Let us not speak of it."

"Why not? We are husband and wife."

Isabella's throat dried. Never in her life had she discussed intimate matters with anyone, least of all her husband. She examined her feelings and realized that she was embarrassed.

Marcus put a hand under her chin and turned it to the light.

"You are shy," he said, a note of surprise in his voice.

Isabella slapped his hand away. "No, I am not!"

"Yes, you are. I can see it in your eyes."

Isabella looked at him fleetingly and then away. "I am not accustomed to speaking on such subjects," she said with a little difficulty.

She expected Marcus to make some mocking remark, but he was silent, rubbing his head absentmindedly where she had hit him. She put out a tentative hand.

"Did I hurt you?"

He captured her hand and held it. "Yes. But as I said, it was no more than I deserved. Isabella—" His voice changed. "Why did you run away? Was it because of what happened between us?"

Isabella swallowed hard. She felt a wrench of mingled hope and despair.

"Marcus," she said. "I would not wish you to think…" She stopped. This was very difficult but honesty compelled her to tell the truth. "I wanted you, too," she said at last, very simply. "I wanted you so much that I almost forgot all that lay between us. But then I remembered and—" she shrugged tiredly "—I realized it was too late for us. It did not feel right. It can never be right again."

Marcus looked at her. His eyes were very clear. "I am glad," he said. "Not glad that you think it too late for us, but glad that I was not pressing my attentions on an unwilling lady."

Isabella freed her hand. This was becoming too difficult and too dangerous. The intimacy that she had wanted the previous night was creeping into the candlelit room, but it was too late. He had not said one word about believing her explanation of what had happened all those years ago. He had not asked for forgiveness of his suspicions or for his behavior. He had not said that he loved her and for her the restoration of trust was more important than any physical intimacy.

"It must surely have been clear to you that I was not exactly unwilling," she said.

Marcus smiled. "I thought not at the time, but when I woke and found you gone…" He shook his head.

"I left because that was what we had agreed," Isabella said starkly. "You had what you wanted and in return you agreed to give me Salterton—and a legal separation. We made a bargain, you and I. I expect you to keep it."

Marcus's gaze was searching, examining her face in minute

detail. Isabella was very afraid that he would read the truth in her heart.

"Did you make love with me merely to keep your half of the bargain?" There was an odd tone in his voice.

"No," Isabella said reluctantly, "but that is not the point, Marcus. The things I want from you—" She stopped. Love. Trust. They carried with them their own risks and she had been hurt so much she was not sure she could face that pain again.

"We agreed," she said finally.

"Do you really want a legal separation, Isabella?" Marcus was quiet but very determined.

Isabella refused to meet his eyes. "It is what we agreed."

"That is not what I asked."

Isabella let go a painful breath. "It is the only way." She threw out one hand in a gesture of despair. "What else can we do, Marcus? We cannot go back. We cannot change the past. It will always lie between us."

Marcus was silent for a moment. "We will not go back," he said at last, "but we can go on." His tone softened. "I do not want to leave you, Isabella, and I do not want you to leave me. I cannot allow that—not now."

Isabella felt trapped and frustrated. "Twice now you have broken your word to me."

"You might be carrying my child."

The words fell into silence. Isabella closed her eyes briefly. In the heat of the moment she had not really considered it. It was a very long time since she had had to think of such matters. Now she thought of Emma and her heart was wrenched with so much pain that she gasped.

"No! Oh, no."

She saw something change in Marcus's expression and knew he was hurt at the implication of her words. He did not understand. He could not.

She waited for his bitter rejoinder but instead he touched

her hand where it was clenched on the bedclothes. "I am sorry, Isabella. I know it would not be what you wanted. But I assume it must be a possibility, and until we know…"

When she did not reply, he sighed.

"We will talk on this again in the morning. Now is not the right time. You look exhausted and so am I, for I have ridden hard to find you." He bent to pull his boots off.

Isabella nervously drew the bedclothes up to her chin, a more pressing concern taking the place of the anguish inside her.

"What are you doing?"

Marcus smiled at her, a warm and wicked smile that lit his dark eyes. "I am coming to bed, of course."

Isabella gulped. "But… Have you not heard what I have been saying? There is no going back for us, Marcus, and that begins now. Surely the brothers have some alternative accommodation for you?"

Marcus looked at her. His expression was unreadable in the candlelight. He was still rubbing his head and the dark hair stood up in rather endearing spikes. Isabella ignored the urge to reach out and smooth it down.

"There is no room at the inn, Isabella," he said. "When Brother Jerome heard that I was your husband, the monks suggested that we share this chamber."

"They are very trusting," Isabella said. "Anyone might have made that claim. Are they to usher them all into my chamber?"

"I imagine that they did not think I would lie to a man of God," Marcus said virtuously, pulling his shirt over his head.

"Pshaw!" Isabella pulled the covers tighter. "The room is scarcely big enough for one, let alone two," she said. The thought of sharing so enclosed a space with Marcus made her throat close with nervousness. "You will have to sleep in the carriage."

Marcus grinned. The candlelight slid over the firm contours of his chest and shoulders turning his skin to bronze. Isabella knew she was staring. She could not seem to help herself.

"Have a heart, Isabella," Marcus said. "I am worn out with riding and it would be damned uncomfortable. There is nowhere else to go. All the inns are full since it is the Festival of St. Columba."

"I do not care if it is Christmas!" Isabella argued, thoroughly rattled now. "You cannot stay here!"

Marcus put out a hand and touched her cheek. It was a thoroughly disarming gesture. Isabella blinked, suddenly feeling vulnerable.

"You look like a shy schoolgirl," he said. "I had no notion that you would be so nervous of me." The amusement fled his voice. "I did hear what you said, Isabella. You have no need to be afraid of me."

"I am not," Isabella argued valiantly. "But this bed is tiny."

"We may sleep in each other's arms. That saves space." Marcus spoke reasonably and without emotion. Isabella gulped. She had never slept in a man's arms. Last night Marcus had held her close but she had been too upset to relax into his warmth. Now she could feel the temptation curl within her. To be held and comforted and not to be afraid…

Marcus bent again to pull off his boots as though the decision was made. Isabella watched him disrobe in the candlelight, feeling mightily relieved and equally mightily disappointed that he did not remove his breeches. She lay back against the pillows and closed her eyes, tensing as Marcus slid into the narrow space beside her. She tried to move as far away as possible from him, which was not very far given the confines of the bed. Rolling over, she almost fell out and was only saved by Marcus grabbing a fold of her voluminous nightgown.

"Did you ask one of the monks to lend you a habit in which to sleep?" Marcus inquired. "You need have no fears of ravishment, Isabella. I doubt I could find you in there even if I had not given you my word."

Isabella could feel him, even through all the layers of material. It made her feel oddly tense.

"Relax. You are like a trap about to spring," Marcus said.

"I have never—"

"What?"

"Never slept in a man's arms before," Isabella said in a rush.

"But what about Ernest?"

"We had separate palaces, let alone bedrooms."

Marcus laughed. "How very extravagant. But surely he must have stayed with you sometimes?"

"Only if he was too drunk to get out of bed," Isabella said truthfully, "and then I would be the one to leave with all despatch."

The memories of her previous marriage were making her feel anxious again. She had been trapped; forced into a role that had bent her out of shape. She could not permit that to happen again.

She sat up against the bolster and drew her knees up to her chin.

"Must you do that?" Marcus inquired. "You have pulled all the covers off me."

With a sigh, Isabella slipped beneath the sheets again.

"Your married life is full of surprises for me," Marcus said. He slid an arm about her and drew her head down to rest against his shoulder. "There now." He sounded as though he were talking to a child. "Relax."

It was amazingly comfortable. Isabella breathed in the scent of his skin and found herself nuzzling closer. His throat was warm and strong against her lips and she could hear the steady beat of his heart beneath her ear. From outside in the street came the sound of voices and the chink of harness, but for a little while, she was wrapped in peace.

"Bella?" Marcus's voice was sleepy. "Was it very important for you to claim Salterton Hall?"

Isabella sighed. "Yes."

"Because by rights it belongs to you?"

It was frightening how well he understood her.

"Because it *did* belong to me before I was foolish enough to give it to you through this hasty marriage." Isabella shifted slightly. She thought again of Ernest, and tried to explain. "I consider myself to be Isabella Standish as well as the Countess of Stockhaven, Marcus. I do not wish all that is me and mine to be subsumed into someone else's personality."

"Is that what happened before?"

"Yes." Isabella thought of Ernest and the pattern-card princess that he had required.

"I am not sure," Marcus said slowly, "that I would wish you to be like that."

"Most men would," Isabella said.

"Then," Marcus said, "perhaps I am not like most men."

That was undoubtedly true. Isabella smiled a little wryly. "Perhaps you are not, Marcus." She rubbed her cheek softly against his shoulder. She knew she should not but it was there and it was tempting and just for once....

"Go to sleep." Marcus kissed her hair.

Isabella could feel herself already beginning to drift in a warm cocoon of contentment. The real danger, she recognized, came not from any physical intimacy with Marcus but from this seductive closeness. It lulled her into believing that everything could be good between them, as good as it had once been. She closed her mind to the doubts and conflicts and allowed herself to dream. And as she was falling asleep she thought she heard Marcus say again:

"Go to sleep. I will never let you go."

FREDDIE STANDISH WAS PARTAKING of breakfast when the message arrived. He was still rather cast adrift from the previous night's drinking and so was picking at a piece of toast and trying to disguise from Pen the fact that he felt distinctly liverish. It was this that he later blamed for his inattention when the maid brought in the note. The girl had only been with them two weeks and was quite hopeless, but the woman at the employment agency had indicated that that was all they could expect for the wages they were paying. Instead of handing the message directly to him, she put it into Pen's imperiously outstretched hand. Freddie suspected that she could not read the direction on it.

The crackle of the paper unfolding mingled with the crunching of Pen indulging her hearty appetite on her third piece of toast and honey. Freddie felt vaguely sick.

"Mmm," Pen said on a vague note of surprise, through the crumbs. "There is a rather odd note here for you, Freddie." Her gaze dropped to the bottom of the page. "From a gentleman called Warwick."

The shock galvanized Freddie into action. He dropped his mangled toast, leaped to his feet and grabbed the paper from Pen's hand.

"Freddie!" Pen exclaimed, as his sleeve overturned her teacup.

Freddie did not pause to apologize. He took the stairs two at a time, reading as he went.

"Dear Lord Standish…require to see you immediately… Wigmore Street… This morning… Brook no delay…"

When he came back downstairs, having dragged on his coat without the aid of his valet, Pen was standing in the hall, a determined expression on her face.

"Are you in trouble, Freddie?"

Freddie looked at her. If only she knew. Trouble was too mild a word for it.

"Devil a bit," he mumbled. "Nothing to worry about. Fellow I owe some money to."

"Gambling debts?" Pen asked. She sounded resigned.

"Something of the sort." Freddie gave her a peck on the cheek and dashed past before she could ask him anything more difficult.

"When will you be back?" Pen called after him. Freddie turned his head slightly but did not reply, picking up his pace toward town. He did not call a hack. He could not afford it.

The fresh morning air cleared his mind but brought with it a sick dread in the pit of his stomach. Edward Warwick. How had he ever come to this? The whole matter had begun so long ago now that it was difficult to remember. He had been very distressed after his cousin India Southern had refused his marriage proposal. He had been young and unaccustomed to failure, and he had turned to the family vice of drink and debt. From there the downward slide had been imperceptible but inevitable, until that dreadful moment when he had been obliged to tell his father that he was so deep in hock that he was likely to end up in the Fleet. He could still see the late Lord Standish's face twisted with disgust and disapproval as he berated his only son for the weaknesses that he had instilled in him.

There had been nothing that his father could do to help him, of course, since by then he was losing all the money that Prince Ernest of Cassilis had so casually bestowed on him. The Fleet incident had been hushed up and then Warwick had appeared like the answer to all their prayers, offering money to father and son in return for a few words here, a favor there. There was no difficulty. It was influence that Warwick wanted—a piece in the papers, a word in the ear of an MP, a decision going his way in court… The Standish father and son obliged where they could. It would have been different had Warwick wanted social acceptance, of course. That would have been quite out of the question.

Freddie crossed Piccadilly, narrowly missing being run down by a dray cart. Lord Standish had not had huge influence himself and had therefore been of limited use to Edward

Warwick. Freddie had sensed almost from the start that Warwick was disappointed in them. He kept them short of cash and on tenterhooks. Then Lord Standish had died and Warwick had helped Freddie to find the right sort of work at Asher's Bank, where he was useful to both his employer and to Warwick himself. He was a dunce with money, of course, but neither of them wanted him for his financial acumen. Asher wanted someone with the right social connections and Warwick wanted what he always wanted. Information. Who had what sum of money, who owed whom, who had inherited, the rich, the poor, the desperate—into which category Freddie fit very firmly himself.

He reached Wigmore Street in the end, having lost himself briefly in the maze of roads around James Street. He was out of breath as he entered the high-class gown shop and went up the stairs. He was unsurprised to be kept waiting for almost an hour. Eventually he was ushered up a back stair and into Warwick's office.

Edward Warwick extended a hand to him in an approximation of courtesy.

"Standish. How good of you to come so promptly."

There was a hint of mockery behind his words. He knew how long Freddie had been waiting. Freddie felt a hot wave of humiliation and despair sweep over him. He was in too deep now. He could not cut free of this man when he was so deeply in his power. And he sensed that at last Warwick wanted something more dangerous than the provision of a few pieces of information. It was almost as though he had been waiting for this moment for a very long time, dreading it but knowing that it would come.

"So your sister is now Countess of Stockhaven." Warwick spoke slowly, but there was a tone in his voice that Freddie recognized like an animal scenting danger. He did not reply. The office felt stifling. He could feel the sweat trickling between his shoulder blades and the tension across his back. Warwick's lips thinned.

"Stockhaven always seems to have the things that I desire," he said. "The house by the sea...the fortune...the wife..."

Freddie was so startled that he spoke without thinking. "You want Isabella?"

Warwick flashed him an inimical look from his slate-gray eyes. "Not that wife, Lord Standish, charming though your sister undoubtedly is. Stockhaven was married before, although it seems to please everyone to forget it."

Freddie's stomach gave a lurch. "You mean India," he said. He wrinkled his brow against the heat and the buzzing in his head. "You knew her?"

"Intimately," Warwick said with a ghost of a smile. "It was a very long time ago. Twelve years, in fact."

Freddie rubbed his eyes. His vision seemed to have blurred and the buzzing in his head was growing louder, like a bee trapped in a bottle. It seemed inconceivable to him that India, so mild, so sweet, could have been in any way acquainted with this man from whose pores evil seemed to seep like sweat.

"I do not understand," he said.

"You never do," Warwick said, the smile still lingering on his lips. "How do you think that I first heard of you and your father and your dangerously extravagant ways?" He shrugged. "No matter. There is something that I require from you, Standish."

Freddie straightened automatically at the authoritative tone. "Yes?"

"I require to know immediately if either the Earl or the Countess of Stockhaven decide to travel to Salterton. And by immediately I mean within the hour, not two days later. Do you understand?"

Freddie nodded, bewildered. The feeling of sinking dread that had dogged his steps receded slightly. This seemed very innocuous. Information. He could provide that.

"Is that all?" he asked, a little too eagerly.

Warwick nodded, a thread of amusement in his voice. "That is all for now, certainly. You may go."

Freddie needed no second bidding. Downstairs he could smell the perfumed air of the gown shop and hear the voices of the customers. The sun was shining. The air was fresh. Freddie was tolerably certain that he could manage to eat something now. There was nothing to worry about.

He indulged in a hearty meal and rolled home feeling positively jolly. Pen was out and he was dozing in his armchair when he heard her return.

Pen's face lit up when she saw him.

"Freddie! I did not expect you back until tonight! How was your business?"

"Fine," Freddie mumbled. Seizing the opportunity to pursue his investigations he asked casually, "How is Bella?"

Pen unpinned her hat and threw it down on the table beside the door. She frowned slightly.

"Bella has gone to Salterton," she said. "You may remember that she has been speaking of it over the last few weeks."

Had she? Freddie racked his brains. He vaguely remembered Isabella mentioning that she would like to live quietly at the seaside and his reply that retirement in Dorset was far too dull a fate. He had had no notion her departure was imminent. Pen was still speaking.

"She left this morning, apparently. She must have gone in the most monstrous hurry." Pen frowned. "We had an engagement to go to an exhibition together today but she appears to have forgotten completely."

Cold fear clutched at Freddie's heart. He set off down the stairs so fast that he almost stumbled and fell. He could hear Pen's startled exclamation:

"Freddie? Freddie!"

He paid no attention. The day, which had seemed so promising only a few hours previously, suddenly took on a much bleaker aspect. What was it that Warwick had said?

I require to know within the hour...

It was already several hours since Isabella had left Town.

This time Freddie took a hackney carriage to Wigmore Street, regardless of the expense.

"I DO APOLOGIZE FOR SENDING for you, Mr. Cantrell," Penelope Standish said, "but I fear I did not know who else to call on for assistance." She pressed a hand to her temples. "This is so very unorthodox! I hope you will forgive me—"

"Miss Standish," Alistair said, drawing her down to sit beside him on the sofa, "I assure you that nothing could alter the high esteem in which I hold you. In what manner may I be of assistance?"

Pen's expression lightened. She had sent for Alistair precisely because she knew he would deal efficiently with any matter placed before him. She could rely on him. She looked down at their clasped hands and felt an uncharacteristic desire to be cared for, protected and, preferably, swept off her feet in the process. Instead, Alistair patted her hand encouragingly before releasing her. Pen sighed.

"The most extraordinary things appear to be happening to my relatives!" she said. "I was supposed to be attending an exhibition at the Royal Academy with Bella this morning."

She waited a moment for him to comment but when he did not, she continued, "When I arrived in Brunswick Gardens, I found that Bella had left me a note telling me that she had left for Salterton yesterday. I know she has been speaking of removing to the seaside recently, but to go so abruptly! I cannot help but worry what has prompted her...." She looked at Alistair and felt her cheeks warm. "Do you know whether Lord Stockhaven has accompanied her? She implied that she was alone but I wondered..." She broke off, a small frown furrowing her brow.

"I know that Marcus intended to follow your sister to Salterton with all despatch," Alistair said tactfully. "Perhaps he may even have caught up with her on the road. You should not worry, Miss Standish. She will be perfectly fine."

Pen frowned harder. "So she went without Marcus? How strange! I do not understand those two at all, Mr. Cantrell."

She saw Alistair's lips twitch. "They certainly appear to have a most...ah...complicated relationship."

Pen looked at him, half exasperated, half resigned at this diplomatic reply. Mr. Alistair Cantrell was the perfect model of the proper gentleman and where she had conceived this idea from that she wished him to be improper, she had no notion. It was best to put it out of her head and concentrate on the problem in hand. She knitted her fingers together.

"If that was my only concern, however, I might rest easy," she continued, "but when I returned from Brunswick Gardens and acquainted my brother with the facts of Isabella's journey, he immediately disappeared and now I have received the most cock-and-bull message from him telling me that he is also gone to Salterton!" She ran a hand through her hair, scattering several pins on the carpet. "He never returned to collect any belongings and believe me, Mr. Cantrell, Freddie is not the man to travel without his valet, let alone a change of clothes. Why, I do not think he could remove his own boots unaided!"

Alistair could well believe that Lord Standish would have difficulty reaching the end of the road, let alone Dorset. He looked at the exquisite creature before him, all troubled blue eyes and tumbled fair hair, and wanted to take her in his arms and comfort her. He felt it was richly unfair that Freddie Standish, who ought to take responsibility for protecting his sister, should in fact be the one in need of constant supervision. He crossed his arms in order to prevent himself from touching Pen.

"I simply must go to Salterton myself," Pen finished.

She jumped up. "I cannot sit here waiting to find out what is happening!"

"And all impatient of dry land, agree with one consent, to rush into the sea," Alistair murmured.

Pen stared at him. "I beg your pardon, Mr. Cantrell?"

Alistair blushed. "Poetry, Miss Standish. I was quoting Cowper."

Pen's brows rose. "This is not the time to be quoting poetry, Mr. Cantrell. What am I to do?"

Alistair abandoned his flight of fancy. "It seems clear to me, Miss Standish, that you must go to Salterton and that I must escort you."

Despite this being the outcome that Pen had been angling for, she felt unaccountably disappointed. All had been accomplished without the slightest hint of romance, if one left aside Mr. Cantrell's dubious quotation, which could scarce have been considered romantic anyway.

"Thank you," she said. "I should be most grateful for your escort."

Alistair smiled. "Splendid. I shall return in one hour having arranged transport and packed a bag." He got to his feet. "Will that give you sufficient time to prepare, Miss Standish?"

"Perfectly, thank you," Pen said. "I am not one of those ladies who takes an age merely to choose a gown."

Alistair's smile deepened. Pen's pulse quickened in response. "No," he said. "I do not suppose you are." He sketched a bow and made to leave the room, but Pen put out a hand.

"Mr. Cantrell, one moment, please…"

Alistair paused.

"I do not have a chaperone," Pen said in a rush. "It is most improper for me to be alone with you in a closed carriage, Mr. Cantrell."

"I will hire a maid to accompany us, Miss Standish,"

Alistair said promptly. "There is no difficulty. I am sure you will be more comfortable with some female company."

"Yes," Pen said glumly, "I am sure I shall. I hesitate to admit it but I cannot afford to pay a maidservant."

"Neither can I," Alistair said. "We shall engage one in advance and then apply to Stockhaven once we arrive in Salterton. Have no concern, Miss Standish. You may rely on me to behave as a gentleman should."

"Yes," Pen said, sighing with annoyance and thwarted desire. "I am sure that I may."

CHAPTER FIFTEEN

MARCUS SAT IN THE CARRIAGE and admired his wife's profile beneath the brim of her black straw bonnet. He had had plenty of opportunity to admire it—her face had been turned away from him for the best part of the journey so far. Her fingers drummed an impatient tattoo on the clasp of her reticule.

Marcus had woken that morning to a deep contentment. Isabella was still clasped in his arms—there was nowhere else for her to go—and she was asleep in a warm, soft tumble against his side. He had looked at her and felt a complex mixture of hope and loss. Yesterday, when she had run from him, he had known nothing other than he had to reclaim her. It had been an instinct that had kept him going, searching from inn to inn along the road, stopping, inquiring, hurrying on until he had caught up with her at last. He had been fearful that when he found her she would turn from him absolutely and irrevocably and that he would never have a second chance. She had not done so, but he did not make the mistake of thinking that matters would be simple from now on. She had not wanted a husband from the first. Now, with the possibility that she might have conceived his child, he had to persuade her to change her mind.

She had woken a few seconds after him and had smiled up at him for one perfect moment before reality had forced its way into her consciousness and she had struggled to put space between them. He was astounded at how modest and shy she was; not because she had given herself to him so freely the previous night—that had been a moment out of time—but because he had assumed she must be experienced with men. But then, he had assumed many things about Isabella that were not standing up to the test of reason. He was acutely aware that he had given her no reason to trust him and plenty of reasons to hate him.

They had breakfasted in silence, the monastery refectory scarcely being the appropriate place for a discussion of their marriage. It had been unfortunate though, because by the time the carriage was ready and Marcus had made it clear that he was coming to Salterton, Isabella had withdrawn behind a formidably cool facade.

"We need to talk," Marcus said abruptly.

Isabella looked at him, a quick distrustful glance from her blue eyes. "I agree. Yet—" She hesitated. "I am not quite sure that I know what I want to say."

"How about that I am a perfidious bastard who has twice made you a promise and then broken it?"

A tiny smile flickered across her lips. He was heartened to see it. It meant that he might have a chance.

"Is that what you would say if you were in my place?" she asked.

"Undoubtedly. And you would have a fair point, too."

Isabella's smile deepened irresistibly. "So?" She raised her brows.

"I fear it is true." Marcus saw her frown again. "However…"

She looked at him with a politely regal tilt to the head, and once again he was reminded of how well she must have had to school her emotions during the years of her marriage to Prince Ernest. He felt a sharp pang of loss for the spontaneous girl she had once been.

"I am prepared to concede certain things," he said.

"You are all generosity, my lord." Isabella smoothed the elegant green frogging on her traveling dress and waited.

Marcus took a deep breath. Apologizing did not come easily to him. He did not do it often.

"I am sorry," he said. "I misjudged you. When I saw you again I thought only of revenge for what you had done to me and to—" He hesitated.

"To India," Isabella said flatly.

The name seemed to hover uncomfortably in the air between them.

"I understand," Isabella said. "She was your wife."

Once again she turned her face away and Marcus had the frustrating feeling that he had not made himself understood at all.

"I cannot explain the difference in the accounts that you and she gave," he said, struggling a little. "But I do believe that you would never deliberately seek to take her inheritance from her. You are…too generous a person to do such a thing."

He thought that there was a tiny shade of warmth in Isabella's voice when she replied but it could merely have been his own wishful thinking.

"Too generous a person," she said. "This seems rather a sudden conversion, Marcus, after all that has happened between us."

He could not deny it. He knew that from the first he had been struggling against his own intuition as well as against her. He had wanted to believe her false and treacherous. At every turn he had blocked the evidence of his own eyes and the instincts of his heart and had tried to believe the worst of her. Yet that image had never really fitted and now the world had spun and shifted again and he saw the truth.

"I am sorry," he said again.

"Do you believe what I told you the night before last?" Isabella asked. "The reasons for my marriage to Ernest?"

Marcus hesitated. He believed implicitly what she had told him, yet he was not certain that he could forgive her for making the choice she had done, and for putting her family ahead of him.

"I understand what you told me," he said, choosing his words carefully. "I am sorry that you did not choose to come to me for help but I understand your reasons."

Isabella caught her lip between her teeth. "So you do not forgive me."

Marcus felt torn between the truth and sparing Isabella further hurt. "I have not said that, Bella. It is not really a matter for my forgiveness. I wish you had come to me but I understand why you did not."

"We all have hard choices to make," Isabella said, so softly Marcus had to lean closer to hear her. "I put the future of my family ahead of our happiness." She looked at him suddenly and his heart contracted at the anguish in her eyes. "This is very painful, Marcus."

"It is." Marcus knew that there was no way in which such matters could be ignored or swept aside. On that confessional night he had thought that they could be, but now he knew better. There was a painful lack of trust between them and it would take much to repair it. And there was no guarantee that she would give them that chance. He wanted to touch her, to offer physical reassurance, but he knew that it was too soon.

"I still want you to have Salterton," he said suddenly. "It is yours by rights and I know how much it means to you. I will give it to you—and the means to keep it."

The light leaped in Isabella's face. "Truly? You will keep your word?"

"I swear it." Marcus smiled ruefully. "On that matter I will keep my word."

The light went out of her face. "But the legal separation?"

He shook his head. "No, Bella. I cannot grant that."

Isabella's head was bent. She smoothed the seams of her gloves. Marcus watched her struggle with her temper. He understood her doubts and misgivings. He knew that he had given her much to doubt with his accusations and suspicions of her. But trust could be rebuilt, given the will to do so. He had never been able to make Isabella fit his desired image of the fortune-hunting adventuress. Now he had no wish to do so anymore, not merely because of any child she might bear him, but because he wanted to know the real Isabella once again, the wild spirit that he had known as a girl; the woman who could match him passion for passion.

Yet it seemed that Isabella did not want the same thing. She was resisting the affinity between them and he needed to understand why. It was not simply because he had hurt her. He sensed that she was afraid of something. He reminded himself that he must court her—as gently as possible.

It was difficult, however, when he wanted to ravish her as ungently as possible.

"A marriage between us will never work." She looked so adorably obstinate that he wanted to kiss her. Inconveniently, his erection stirred. He knew that this was likely to be the most difficult part of the courtship for him. He was not a patient man and having once made love to her it would be the devil's own job not to touch her again.

He tried to ignore his bodily discomfort and concentrate on her words.

"Our marriage will not work because you will not allow it to?" he asked softly.

"It will not work because the past will always come between us." Isabella made a slight gesture. "There is India, and Ernest…"

And her nameless lovers whom Marcus always tried very hard and very unsuccessfully to forget. Jealousy ripped at him so violently that he caught his breath. The obstacles were indeed great but so was his determination. He was not going to let her go.

Isabella had knotted her gloved fingers together tightly. She looked up from her clasped hands and met his gaze.

"Do you love me, Marcus?"

Her words caught him on the edge, still feeling raw. So he had not spoken aloud the night they had made love. That was a relief. He did not wish to reveal so much to her so soon. He was not certain of his deepest feelings. He knew without a doubt that he had loved her once. Now, he was not so sure. He wanted her. He needed her. That had to be enough.

Her voice had held a tone of sorrow, as though she already knew the answer. And when he did not reply, she shook her head gently.

"Having once had your love, Marcus, how do you think I could ever settle for less? It would be a second-best marriage."

Marcus took a deep breath and tried to speak calmly. He felt more vulnerable than he had in a very long time. Isabella's honesty was devastating and it made him feel as though what he was offering her simply was not good enough.

He cleared his throat. "Bella, we are married. There can be no annulment. Love is for…"

"Fools?" There was a note of bitterness in her voice.

"I was going to say that love is for the young," Marcus said. "As one grows older, matters grow more complicated."

"How very pompous you sound," Isabella said, "not to mention as old as Methuselah." She turned her shoulder to him.

"I have already lost one wife," Marcus said, a little bitterly. "I do not intend to lose a second."

He felt the intense blue of Isabella's gaze on him and thought for a moment that she was going to ask him about India. He wanted her to do so—he knew it was a barrier between them. He had neglected India and had always felt damnably guilty. He was convinced that she would not have had the carriage accident and died if only he had not been apart from her at the time. It was the guilt that held him silent. He carried it with him always.

But Isabella did not ask and he sensed the slight withdrawal in her.

"I cannot force an annulment or a legal separation, of course," she said. "I accept that. But I cannot see the point of us remaining wed when you do not love me."

Marcus leaned forward urgently. "Bella, give me a chance. I want us to stay married."

"Because there may be a child?" It sounded as though the words pained her. "We shall know that soon enough."

Marcus took her gloved hand in his. "And if there is we shall raise him or her together."

"And if there is not—" her eyes were defiant but full of fear as well "—we may go our separate ways."

Marcus shook his head. "What is it that you are afraid of, Bella?"

Isabella's face clouded. He thought for a moment that she would not reply but then she said quietly, "I am afraid of being hurt all over again."

Marcus's grip tightened on her hand. He drew her resisting body closer to his along the velvet seat of the coach. "I swear," he said, his voice rough with emotion, "that I will never hurt you deliberately, Bella. Never again."

Her face was tilted up to his, close enough to kiss. There was sweetness in her eyes but a deep sorrow as well.

"Give me a chance," Marcus said again. "A chance to court you."

He saw her mistrust and hesitation. His hand tightened on hers. "I will protect you and care for you, Bella. We may rekindle the trust between us. Let me prove it to you." He did not understand why it was so blindingly important to him but he knew that it was.

Isabella gave a tiny nod. "For the sake of the child—should there be one—I will wait a little before I make a final decision. That is all I can promise."

Marcus's heart leaped. He did not argue. Now was not the moment to insist that he would never let her go. He had gained himself some time and the chance he craved. Now he had to convince her of his steadfastness.

"Then as you are prepared to trust me," he said, "and as I trust you, there is something that I must tell you."

"YOU MAY REMEMBER," Marcus said, "that when we first met at the Duchess of Fordyce's ball, you asked me why I had been in the Fleet. I never told you the reason."

Isabella waited. She had not been expecting this. Her mind was still spinning with the implications of their previous conversation. When Marcus had told her that he believed her account of why she had jilted him, her sore heart had eased a little. It was a small concession, smaller than she might have wanted, but it was something. And he had apologized for his behavior to her. She knew that must have been difficult for him. He was not a man who could admit his fault easily.

It meant that when they came to part she would know there was no longer any animosity between them. If they did part... She shivered. How long would it be before she knew if she was with child? When Emma had been conceived she had been very slow to realize. Too slow. She might read the signs more quickly now, but the dilemma would be no easier. To stay or to go. Marcus had promised to care for and protect her, but he had not promised her his love. And without that she would always feel she was living a hollow reflection of what might have been.

She put the thought of the child from her mind. Soon enough to think of that when she had some peace and time alone. And there was the shadow of India, hovering at her shoulder as always.

I have already lost one wife...

Isabella needed no reminder of that.

But for now Marcus wanted to tell her about the Fleet. She remembered demanding to know why he had been there and

the way he had deflected her questions. She had been so in-
furiated by his presence that she had soon forgotten all about
the reasons.

"I was investigating a crime," Marcus said.

Isabella looked up sharply. "By pretending to be a
criminal yourself?"

"Exactly so." Marcus sighed. "It is sometimes the easiest
way to get close to those you are hunting."

Isabella let out a long breath. "I see. Did you succeed?"

"No," Marcus said. "I am hunting a man named Warwick.
Edward Warwick." He looked at her. "Does the name mean
anything to you?"

Isabella shook her head. "I do not think so. Should it?"

"You have a wide acquaintance. He might be a family connection." Marcus's gaze dwelled thoughtfully on her face.
"Warwick is the man whom I am convinced was responsible
for both a robbery and fire at my house in Salterton and the
death of your aunt. He is a criminal who has connections in
the Fleet."

Isabella stared at him, deeply shocked. She had not
imagined that Marcus's business in the Fleet, whatever it had
been, might have any link to her or to Salterton.

"Mr. Churchward told me of the fire at your house but he
intimated that it was an accident," she said slowly. "And I understood that Aunt Jane's death was from natural causes."
Her eyes searched his face. "Wasn't it?"

"That is the story we put about," Marcus said. He shifted
slightly. "In fact, the fire was arson, albeit unintentional. A
local lad set the house ablaze accidentally when he was
searching for something on behalf of Warwick."

Isabella frowned. "What was he searching for?"

Marcus shook his head. "That I do not know. I am trying
to find out. When I entered my house that night I sensed that
something was wrong. I found the intruder upstairs in the

chamber that had been India's. It was clear that he was searching for something." Isabella saw him wince, as though the memory was in some way painful.

"The place was in the most confounded mess, clothes and papers scattered across the room," Marcus continued. "The lad was so startled to see me that he overturned the candle and set the bed hangings alight. He jumped from the window. He was injured but before he lost consciousness he told me that Warwick had sent him. That was why I was searching for the man himself."

Isabella's thoughts were for her aunt.

"But Aunt Jane?" she said. "I did not think that there were any suspicious circumstances surrounding her death. Mr. Churchward told me that she was struck by a seizure in the evening. The servants found her. She had been quite alone—" Her voice was rising. She realized with a jolt that she was both nervous and upset. Marcus had also heard the note of distress in her voice, and he caught her hands in his. When he answered her, his tone was deliberately calm. It soothed her a little.

"I am sorry, Bella," he said. "A man called upon Lady Jane that night. According to the servants, he gave his name as Warwick. He spent some time in the library with your aunt, though no one knows precisely when he left. The servants were alerted by the violent ringing of the bell and when they arrived they found that your aunt had collapsed. They carried her to bed. She died a short while later."

Isabella shuddered, thinking of Jane alone and friendless at the end. "I do not understand. Are you suggesting that this man—this Warwick—murdered her?"

Marcus shook his head slightly. "No. There was no suggestion of murder. I called the physician myself. I think whatever it was that they discussed so shocked or disturbed her that she had a seizure and died," Marcus said. "It is in that sense that he was responsible for her death."

Isabella wrinkled her brow. "Was there a quarrel? Did the servants hear raised voices?"

"They heard nothing." Marcus sighed. There was a rueful note in his voice. "They could not even describe the man with any exactitude."

"And yet you think that this man Warwick holds the key to the arson and to Lady Jane's death?"

"I do."

Marcus had relaxed his grip and Isabella let her hands fall to her lap. She stared blindly out the window of the carriage.

"Poor Aunt Jane," she said softly. "I am so very sorry."

"It is a nasty business. And that is why I must go back to Salterton."

Isabella felt cold. So for all Marcus's avowals, he had quite a different motive for going to Salterton. "I see," she said bleakly.

There was a glimmer of amusement in Marcus's eyes. "No, I don't think that you do, Bella. I was going to say that I had planned for a little while to return to Salterton in the hope of picking up Warwick's trail there. The fact that you set off for Salterton so precipitately only made it more urgent that I should go there at once."

Isabella looked at him. "I see," she said again.

Marcus took her hand again, rubbing his thumb gently over the back of her glove. She could feel the warmth of his touch through the material.

"Bella," he said. "Please believe me. We will never trust one another again if we doubt every word and every action."

Isabella nodded. "So why are you telling me this now?" she asked.

Marcus smiled. "Because I did not wish there to be any more secrets between us," he said, "and because I thought that you might be able to help me."

"If I knew of this... Warwick?"

"Yes."

Isabella shook her head. "I am sorry, Marcus. I do not recall ever hearing the name in connection with either Salterton or the family. I would help if I could."

"No matter," Marcus said.

A sudden thought struck Isabella. "This man... I assume he is dangerous?"

Marcus looked at her. "Very. I do not wish you to be afraid, though, Bella. I am sure he has no quarrel with you."

"No," Isabella said, "but—" She stopped, but Marcus was too quick for her. He leaned closer.

"Bella, is it that you are afraid for me?"

Isabella avoided his gaze. "Well, I... If he is dangerous..."

"You *are* afraid for me!" Marcus said. He started to smile.

"There is no need to be so pleased with yourself," Isabella grumbled. "I am a compassionate person. It is nothing to do with you."

Marcus's smile broadened. He touched her cheek. "Of course not, sweetheart."

He drew her to him and gradually Isabella felt herself leaning closer until her head rested against his shoulder and the movement of the carriage lulled her into a doze. But her dreams were not pleasant ones. She dreamed of Jane Southern, calling for help and no one hearing her, and she dreamed of Marcus saying *I did not wish there to be any more secrets between us.* And she awoke to the thought that she was still keeping the biggest secret of all.

IT WAS AS THEY WERE approaching Salterton, in the fresh summer evening, that a problem arose. Isabella had slept for much of the journey and Marcus had found himself deriving a remarkable degree of contentment just from watching her. As they drew nearer to their destination, Isabella awoke and Marcus noted the tiny abstracted frown between her brows and the slight tension in her manner.

"I have been thinking," Isabella said, smoothing the skirts of her elegant traveling dress and avoiding his eyes, "that it would be better to put a little distance between ourselves until we can be sure what is to be done." She looked at him, then swiftly away. "I mean, until we know—" She broke off. Marcus understood all too well what she meant.

Until I know if I am expecting a child... Until I decide if I can leave you...

Every possessive instinct in his body rose up in protest. *There was precious little distance between us last night,* he thought. *Nor on the previous occasion when I held you naked in my arms.*

He knew it would avail him little to point this out. He could sense Isabella slipping out of reach once again. It was frustrating but he found that he was prepared for it. Generally he was not a patient man; this time he had to learn patience in order to gain what he wanted, which was Isabella permanently in his life and in his bed.

He kept his voice neutral.

"Until we decide what is to be done about...what?" he asked.

Isabella shot him a defiant look from those beautiful blue eyes. "Our marriage of course, Marcus. It is most convenient that you have a house on the estate, since you may live there whilst I reside at the hall—"

Marcus sighed sharply. "Isabella, I will be plain with you. I will not live at Salterton Cottage whilst you live elsewhere. Apart from anything else, my house is currently uninhabitable since work has not yet been completed after the fire. So I could not accede to your request to live at Salterton Cottage even if I wished to do so."

"Well," Isabella said, turning aside, "I hear that the standard of hotels has improved immensely since I was last at the seaside. No doubt you will find something to your taste."

"Salterton House is to my taste." Marcus put out a hand and pulled her closer to him. She came reluctantly into his arms.

He remembered his vow to court her gently and moderated his tone of voice—and stifled the rampant lust that suggested what a good idea it would be to overcome her scruples by making love to her here and now, in the carriage.

"If it pleases you," he said, "you may have your own bedroom—for now."

"Thank you," Isabella said dryly. "And you will reside down the drive as soon as your house is ready."

There was a note of finality in her voice. Marcus shrugged and his lips curved into a wicked smile. He reached inside his jacket and removed a piece of paper.

"If you are to be my landlady, you had better read this," he said.

Isabella pulled off her gloves, took the paper, glanced at it carelessly, then stiffened.

"What is this?"

"It is the terms of the tenancy of Salterton Cottage," Marcus said.

Isabella looked at him incredulously. "Tenancy? But I thought that it was a mere formality?"

Marcus shook his head. "You were mistaken. Lord John Southern merely loaned the house to his daughter for her use. The previous tenancy agreement had not lapsed. On India's death he very politely but insistently made me agree to sign it. I was happy to do so to keep my link with Salterton."

Isabella frowned hard as she scanned the lines. Marcus watched with amusement and no little satisfaction as he saw the uncertainty in her eyes.

"But surely… You own Salterton Hall now. You cannot be your own tenant!"

Marcus laughed. "Oh no, Bella, you cannot have it both ways! I have offered you Salterton—it was your inheritance, after all—and that makes you the landlord. The landlord who owes me certain…services." He twitched the sheet from between her fingers. "Allow me to explain the terms in more detail."

Isabella looked suddenly nervous. "Please do not," she said. "I do not wish to know."

"But you *must* know." Marcus's smile was mocking now. "As I said, it is your property."

"I have no desire to concern myself with estate matters," Isabella stuck her regal nose in the air. "Mr. Churchward may continue to administer the agreement."

"I am afraid that I must insist."

Marcus read aloud, giving his wife no chance to object further: "'The landlord agrees to furnish the tenant with a lifetime's supply of free brandy.'" He looked up. "Having been in the navy I am partial to the best. May I suggest that you make an arrangement with the local publican to keep me well provided for?"

"You are pleased to jest," Isabella said. "You know I cannot afford it. And since you promised me the means to keep Salterton you would only be funding yourself."

"No? Perhaps I will ask you to pay in kind instead."

He saw Isabella's mouth thin with irritation.

"'The landlord agrees to pay all the tenant's medical fees,'" he continued. "How fortunate that I am so strong and healthy."

"How did this ridiculous agreement ever come into being?" Isabella demanded. She reached across and tried to snatch the paper from his hand. He held it out of her way. "It is most unorthodox."

"Your aunt and uncle were unorthodox people," Marcus pointed out. "The agreement was created to secure the future of the previous tenant of the Cottage. Do you remember him? My mother's cousin, Captain Forbes? It was to visit him that I first came to Salterton."

Isabella turned her face away from him. "Captain Forbes was a delightful old gentleman. I remember him well. A pity—"

"A pity that I do not take after him?"

"A pity that my uncle created such an odd tenancy agreement," Isabella snapped.

"It was an act of charity on Lord John's part," Marcus said. "Uncle Forbes had no money. No one in the family did at that time. Your aunt and uncle took a liking to him and sought to take care of him by creating a rather unusual agreement."

Isabella sighed. "But why did it not lapse when your uncle died?"

"Because no one canceled it. The agreement was on the house and not specific to any person."

"So now you are the recipient of all this largesse."

"I would be," Marcus said, "if you were in a position to give it to me."

Isabella's chin tilted up at an even more acutely regal angle. Marcus could see only her profile, which was pink and flustered. He liked that. He loved being able to cut past that society calm and ruffle her royal feathers.

"Then you are most unfortunate since I have nothing to give," she said.

Marcus smiled. "I would have to dispute that. Wait until you have heard the rest of the agreement, Isabella, and then see what you think," he said softly.

"'The landlord agrees to provide the tenant with warm blankets, firewood and food in the winter,'" he continued. "'He or she will also take the tenant sea-bathing once a week.'"

"Sea-bathing!" The words burst from Isabella in a tone of utter disbelief.

Marcus nodded. "Uncle Forbes was an invalid. The sea water cure did him good but he required to be accompanied to the beach as he was not very steady on his feet."

Isabella looked pointedly at Marcus's booted feet as they rested with deplorable informality on the opposite seat.

"There is nothing wrong with *your* mobility," she said.

"Nor indeed with the rest of me either."

There was a flash of triumph in Isabella's expression. "So you require no such mollycoddling."

"I still require you to take me sea-bathing," Marcus said, "and—" he referred to the paper "—on any other outings or activities of my choice that will be beneficial to my welfare, both physical and spiritual."

Isabella gave an unladylike snort. "What nonsense!"

Marcus drew closer. "On the contrary, my love. It is in the legal agreement."

This time Isabella did snatch the paper from his hands. "Outings beneficial to your spiritual and physical welfare," she repeated. "It seems to me that you might profitably concentrate on the spiritual side of your welfare, Marcus. I believe there must be improvement to be made there, whereas you seem much too preoccupied with the physical."

Marcus pulled her along the seat until his mouth was about an inch away from hers. He saw her eyes darken as her gaze went irresistibly to his lips. Her tongue came out and nervously touched her bottom lip. He crushed down the urge to kiss her long and hard. Not now. Not yet. He wanted her to be as eager for his embrace as he was for hers.

"You concentrate on my spiritual welfare, sweetheart," he said softly, "and I will think about that closed bedroom door that will lie between us." His voice roughened. "Be sure to keep it locked," he added, "for I shall come knocking on it until it is open to me."

CHAPTER SIXTEEN

The strange tale of the princess and the ardent Earl of S continues to astound. Readers of this newspaper will recall their hasty nuptials. Now it seems that the new countess has been no less hasty in leaving her husband of one week. We understand that the countess has set off alone on her seaside honeymoon, with the earl in hot pursuit. Perhaps the countess has once again been disappointed in the amorous capabilities of Englishmen and has decided to find herself a foreign lover instead. Let us hope that the bracing sea breezes will encourage the earl's prowess and satisfy his lady....
—*The Gentlemen's Athenian Mercury*, July 6, 1816

"SCANDALOUS NONSENSE," Alistair Cantrell said crossly, discarding the newspaper with an angry sigh and looking with disfavor at his plate of congealed eggs. He was feeling decidedly out of sorts that morning. Across the breakfast table was the cause of his bad temper, Miss Penelope Standish, glowing with good health, as fresh as a daisy and eating as heartily as a horse in a hayfield. Evidently she had slept well. She had not been lying awake thinking of *him*.

They had reached Alresford very late, only to discover that the fair in nearby Winchester had led to an influx of visitors occupying all the best rooms at the inns. Eventually they had found a place in the smallest and pokiest of taverns. Pen and her maid had taken the last chamber, of course— Alistair had insisted—and then he had spent the night on the settle in the parlor. Naturally he had not slept a wink, tortured by the stale smell of smoke and ashes from the grate and the thought of Pen dreaming sweetly directly over his head.

"I swear it was not me this time," Pen said, munching through her third piece of toast. She looked at Alistair and frowned slightly. "Are you quite well this morning, Mr. Cantrell? You seem not quite in plump currant."

Alistair looked at her and his expression softened a little. It was not Miss Standish's fault that she had a delinquent brother, nor a sister who had the lack of consideration to inherit property in Dorset rather than in the more accessible regions of Kent or Essex.

"Do you think we shall reach Salterton today?" Pen asked hopefully.

Alistair shook his head. "I doubt it, Miss Standish. The roads are busy and we shall have to travel relatively slowly. I am hoping that we may stay in Three Legged Cross tonight and complete our journey to Salterton in the morning."

"I wonder where Freddie is," Pen said. Evidently her concern for her brother had not affected her appetite. "I hope he has not got lost upon the road. He has a very poor sense of direction."

"I am sure that he will have been able to find his way to an inn of some sort," Alistair said.

Pen's perfect pink bow of a mouth puckered. "Oh dear, Mr. Cantrell, you sound quite sharp! I would not have believed it of you. I thought you extremely good natured."

Alistair reddened. "I beg your pardon, Miss Standish."

"Not at all," Pen said, smiling deliciously. "There is

nothing wrong with strong passions in a man. I have quite a passionate nature myself."

Alistair almost choked. He had to stop this. Thinking of Miss Standish's passionate nature would drive him mad within the confines of a closed carriage.

"My main passions in life are reading and a little light gardening," he said repressively.

Pen shot him a limpid look from her very blue eyes. "Dear me, Mr. Cantrell, that sounds rather sedentary. I am surprised that you retain so fine a figure. One's anatomy can suffer badly from such lack of exercise."

A certain part of Alistair's anatomy stirred at the thought of the exercise he would like to indulge in with Miss Standish. He shifted and repositioned his linen napkin on his lap.

"Miss Standish…" He cleared his throat. Surely the minx was not teasing him? "If you could be ready to depart shortly, then I would appreciate it."

"Of course, Mr. Cantrell," Pen said. She got to her feet. "I shall be ready directly and then we may discuss our mutual passions all the way to Salterton. What a delightful means of passing the journey."

And with that she whisked from the parlor, leaving Alistair fidgeting with his napkin once again as he contemplated just where their mutual passions could take them.

HAD PEN AND ALISTAIR BUT KNOWN, Freddie Standish was a mere five miles away, wrapped up asleep in his coat on the floor of the taproom of the Maiden's Arms. He had traveled by stage to Winchester where he too had been confronted with the problem of no accommodation in the inn. He had solved it by getting so blind drunk that he could have slept in a hedge and not noticed. And since someone had lifted his wallet from him while he'd been in a drunken stupor, it would now be a considerable time until he reached Salterton.

ISABELLA WOKE EARLY on the second morning in her new home. On the previous day she had been too tired from traveling to stir, but now she was rested and eager to explore.

The room, which had been Lady Jane's, faced southward toward the sea and it was starting to fill with sunshine and the bright light from the water. Isabella slipped from the bed and went across to the window, opening wide the casement and letting in the fresh, salty air. It brought the memories flooding in with it. She could see the cluster of white painted cottages of the old fishing village down the hill to her left and the more elegant new buildings along the esplanade. In her stomach was the same pit-a-pat of anticipation that she had felt on visiting the seaside as a child.

But there were other memories too: the bend in the wide stair where she and Pen would peer through the banisters to watch the visitors arrive in the hall below, the old nursery with its smell of dust and wax, the tumbledown summerhouse at the bottom of the gardens where she had met Marcus...

And everywhere the paintings of India, or the little glass animals she'd collected, or a book upon a shelf with her name written inside in a childish hand... Salterton Hall was haunted for Isabella and as she stood by the window and watched the dawn creep across the bay, she knew how very difficult it was going to be to shake those ghosts. Even if she had not known how much Marcus had loved India, coming back to Salterton would have been difficult. Now it felt like a quicksand.

Suddenly impatient with herself, Isabella dressed carelessly and ran down the empty staircase. She needed a swim to clear her mind and wash those memories away.

The house was already astir, running with the smooth precision that characterized all well-organized households. They had sent a message on ahead from Winchester to announce their imminent arrival, but Isabella had been interested to find Salterton Hall in perfect order when the coach had rolled up the drive. Such calm efficiency argued a very well-run staff. It seemed that Marcus had been taking his custodial duties very seriously since Lady Jane's death. More telling still was the fact that the servants had greeted *her* with warmth and courtesy, but they had greeted Marcus with affection. It had impressed Isabella—not that she was prepared to tell Marcus that. Not yet.

She took the path that cut through the gardens down to the sandy lane that connected Salterton Hall to the village. The morning was quiet but for the call of the seabirds in the bay, and the air was scented with the soapy smell of gorse. Down in the harbor, a couple of fishing boats crossed the bay, leaving an arrowing wake in the still water. A white-painted bathing machine was standing at the edge of the sand, a sturdy pony standing patiently between the shafts. In front of the caravan sat an enormous woman, patiently untangling a fishing net.

Isabella stopped and smiled. Suddenly she felt twelve again, a small child running down to the beach to greet her favorite dipper.

"Martha! Martha Otter!"

The enormous woman looked up and a broad grin split her brown face. "Good morning, my lamb. We heard you were back."

"How are you, Martha?" Isabella inquired.

"The same," Martha Otter said comfortably, making Isabella wonder how one could possibly be the same after twelve years.

"You've grown," Mrs. Otter added.

"Outwards, I expect," Isabella said, with a small sigh. "I would like to bathe, Martha. I wonder if you would take me out, if you please?"

Martha lumbered creakily to her feet. "My pleasure, pet. You must be mad as a broom to go out so early, but then the sea cure never hurt anyone. Never cured anyone, neither," she added thoughtfully, "no matter what those quack doctors say."

Isabella climbed up onto the bathing machine as Martha kilted up her skirts and led the pony out into the water. The sand sloped gently here, which made the beach so perfect for swimming.

"I hope the sea cure can banish my blue devils," Isabella said. "I feel quite out of sorts this morning, which is no way to be on such a beautiful day."

Martha threw her a look over her brawny shoulder. "Ah, Salterton will do you good, my pet. What's troubling you? Not that new husband of yours, is it? No cause for concern, my pet. We heard he's sweet on you. Always was, always will be. We all know that," she added, using the word *we* in what Isabella suspected was the royal plural.

Isabella trailed her bare feet in the water as the bathing machine creaked deeper into the sea.

"I wish it were true," she said despondently.

Martha gave the pony an encouraging pat. "Nothing but a couple of children, you and milord were, but we reckoned it was forever." She turned her head to give Isabella a look over her shoulder. "What went wrong, Miss Bella?"

"All sorts of things," Isabella said with a sigh.

"All right again now," Mrs. Otter said comfortably.

Isabella sighed again. "My cousin India—"

"Ah," Martha Otter said again. "Little Miss India, God rest her soul."

Isabella felt irritated that India had Martha Otter's sympathy, and then felt churlish for being so intolerant. Somehow it did not seem fair. How could she compete with a ghost? The dead were untouchable and she would have to live in India's shadow, making her mistakes and comparing unfavorably with her cousin. It irked her and she disliked herself for the capricious feeling.

"India and I were never close," she said. "I did not know her well."

"You had plenty in common," Mrs. Otter opined. "Only you did not know it."

Isabella wondered whether Martha meant that they had both married Marcus, a thought that she did not want to dwell on, but then the dipper added, "They turned away her suitor."

Isabella frowned. It was the first that she had heard of India having a suitor. Her cousin had always seemed too shy to attract the gentlemen and Isabella could not remember a time when anyone had paid her particular attention.

"Who turned him away?" She said.

"Her parents, of course." Martha shook her head lugubriously. "Powerful proud, the Southerns. Not good enough for her, they said."

"I do not recall a suitor," Isabella said. "Who was he?"

"I've no notion," Martha said with massive indifference. "Good-looking boy, though. He had a wicked smile. Charmed the birds from the trees and Miss India with them."

Isabella was silent, listening to the splash of the water in the caravan wheels and trying to remember those last few summers at Salterton. India and she had been of an age but, as she had told Marcus, they had never confided. India was a quiet girl and very self-contained. Isabella, more extroverted, had tried to draw her cousin out but had been politely but firmly rejected.

"How strange," she said now. "I remember nothing of it. I thought that when she married Marcus..." She stumbled a little over his name just as she stumbled over the thought of India and Marcus married, "I thought it a love match. Her first love, I mean."

Mrs. Otter made a noise of disagreement that sounded uncannily like a seal blowing water. "Love match! Best to ask your husband about that, Miss Bella."

If only I dared, Isabella thought. She had seen a little of the loyalty and passion that India had inspired in Marcus and, although she felt a coward, she did not think she could broach that subject with him. Not yet, if ever. The blue devils returned to plague her and she felt impatient with herself.

"Are we out of sight of the beach here, Martha?" she inquired.

"Well enough," Mrs. Otter replied, drawing the horse to a stop. "I know what you're thinking, Miss Bella, but only the gentlemen swim naked. It's tradition."

"High time it was changed, then," Isabella said and, with a brisk gesture, she pulled off her gown and chemise and leaped into the sea.

MARCUS HAD ALSO RISEN EARLY that morning. He told himself that it was a coincidence that he had stirred at the precise moment Isabella had left her room and gone out into the gardens, but he knew that it was more than mere chance. He was so aware of her that it seemed his body was tuned to hers even through the frustratingly locked door that linked their rooms. He reflected sardonically that a few days of lying in bed imagining her close by, soft, fragrant and completely unobtainable, would be sufficient to have him taking an ax to the door, promises of celibacy be damned.

He watched from the window as she made her way down the sandy path through the gardens toward the beach. The sight of the dilapidated summerhouse where they had conducted their trysts roused all his most heated memories and did nothing to calm his ardor. Clearly some hard, physical exercise was required. He went down to the stables, saddled up Achilles and took the track away from the beach that led up to the top of the cliff. From here he had a magnificent view of the curve of the bay and the village of Salterton embraced within it. He also had a magnificent view of his wife, floating completely naked on the gentle swell of the waves.

In the growing light she looked as insubstantial and light as thistledown on the soft billow of the sea. Her hair spread out like a mermaid's tresses on the water, touched with gold from the setting moon. The pale light of morning cocooned her body in a silver shroud and turned it to mist and shadows.

Marcus's lips formed a silent, appreciative whistle. His hand strayed toward the telescope that he always carried in his jacket pocket but then he paused. It seemed rather prurient to spy on his own wife in such a manner. But how very typical that she should be the only person in Salterton who would be so careless of convention as to swim naked in the sea in the early morning, and a Sunday morning at that. There were no public entertainments in Salterton on a Sunday, for it was far too exclusive a resort to sink to the levels of depravity of Brighton or Margate. Isabella, however, was making up for that magnificently. Already he could see a crowd gathering on the esplanade.

Marcus watched her. She looked like a water nymph, pale and perfect, her skin white marble in the dawn. His eye traced the vulnerable line of her shoulder, her breasts exquisitely high and round, her waist a curve that tempted a man's hand with the need to slide down over the line of her hip and farther down still, to the long, slender length of her legs…

His horse side-stepped in protest as Marcus unconsciously tightened the reins. The smile still lingered about his mouth as he urged the beast forward down the narrow path toward the shore. A few more people were gathering on the esplanade. All of them were gazing out to the sea.

Marcus did not merely gaze. He urged his horse into the water.

He was within a few yards of Isabella, and the water was up to Achilles's chest, when she turned and looked at him. Only her head was visible above the water.

"Good morning, Stockhaven," she said. "Did you know

that there are fines for gentlemen who invade the privacy of the ladies when they are bathing?"

"They only apply if one is in a boat, not on a horse," Marcus said. "Besides, there is not a gentleman in Salterton who would not willingly pay that price to see you like this, my love."

"I cannot think why," Isabella said. "I am most decently clad."

Marcus blinked. Then he stared. Isabella was floating on her back now, as she had been when he had seen her earlier, but there was a vast difference. From neck to toe she was clad in a blue bathing gown that wafted modestly on the slight swell of the water.

"But I saw you—" He stopped. "You were naked."

Isabella raised a perfectly outraged eyebrow.

"Have you been *spying* on me, Stockhaven?"

"No…but I…" Marcus realized that he was stuttering like a schoolboy in his salad days. Surely his eyes had not been deceiving him? He frowned, unable to shake off the shaming thought that perhaps he had pictured Isabella as he would have liked her to be rather than how she actually had been.

"You *were* naked!" He burst out. "I saw you!"

"It is a Sunday morning," Isabella said coolly. "This interest in the physical seems somewhat inappropriate. Perhaps, as we discussed a few days ago, you should concentrate on your spiritual welfare, Stockhaven, rather than having lustful fantasies about your wife."

The door of the bathing caravan opened with sudden venom. Achilles shied and almost decanted Marcus into the water. Marcus, who had not realized that Isabella was accompanied by a dipper, looked up, startled. An enormous woman in a straw bonnet and blue flannel jacket was flapping what looked like a fishing net in his direction. Part of her responsibility in assisting the ladies to bathe was to discourage the more impertinent attentions of gentlemen, and this she was wholeheartedly embracing.

"Heathen indecency on the Sabbath!" she shrieked, assaulting Marcus simultaneously with the net and the strong smell of gin. "Back to the beach, sir, and preserve the lady's modesty!"

"My good woman," Marcus said, amused, "this lady is my wife and I am half-inclined to join her in the water."

"Oh no, you are not, my lord! There's no mixed bathing in Salterton." The dipper cracked her knuckles meaningfully, plunged into the sea and looked ready to set about him with hands the size of hams. Marcus quickly withdrew a few feet before the horse took fright altogether and they both drowned.

"Thank you, Martha," Isabella said. Only her head was visible above the water now, tendrils of damp hair curling about her forehead and trailing in the sea about her like Circe. "My husband is leaving now."

Martha put her hands on her hips. "Seems to me that your husband should learn a bit of respect for his wife."

Marcus raised his brows. He looked from Isabella to the protective figure of Martha Otter.

"I apologize," he said slowly. "I thought—" He stopped. This was not an opportune moment to acquaint the dipper with his fantasies. Isabella was watching him and he could have sworn there was a flicker of amusement in her eyes as she saw his discomfort.

Martha did not look appeased. She stood watching him pugnaciously as he turned Achilles and splashed through the shallows to the beach.

Your husband should learn a bit of respect for his wife....

Marcus's mouth turned down wryly. He was learning that lesson rather frequently at the moment.

He reached the shore to discover that the bathing carriage was so situated that Isabella was completely out of sight from the land and that in fact the gathering crowd was looking out to sea, where the sight of fresh sails indicated a ship coming in. He had caused more outrage by taking a horse into the water than Isabella had with her swimming. So much for his thoughts that she was disporting herself naked in front of the local populace. It was extraordinary, but he must have been imagining things. Further evidence, if it was needed, that he was completely besotted with his wife.

Marcus laughed ruefully as he urged a relieved Achilles onto dry land. He realized he was a possessive husband. It was a startling idea, for during his marriage to India he had never been moved by any emotion stronger than a mild pleasure in his wife's company. But then, he had married the wrong cousin and had always known it.

He had married the wrong cousin but now he had the chance to make amends to the right one. His courtship of his wife, no matter how slow, would end in a mutual regard that matched the mutual passion that burned between them. Of that he was determined.

CHAPTER SEVENTEEN

"Sir Stanley and Lady Jensen, Lady Marr, Mr. and Mrs. Latimer, Mrs. Bulstrode, Mr. and Mrs. Spence…"

Isabella was nervously reciting the names of all the eminent Salterton residents whom she could remember as she and Marcus ascended the carriage for their first evening at the Salterton Assembly.

"I wonder whether Miss Parry is still here and then there was Captain Walters—"

Marcus's hand closed firmly and reassuringly over hers as she fidgeted with the seam of her cloak.

"Bella, you are beginning to sound like a roll call onboard ship," he said. "Everything will be fine, I assure you. You are charming and beautiful, and if you remember their names then everyone will see that as an added benefit."

"Oh dear," Isabella said, suddenly feeling hideously nervous, "I have a lowering feeling that this will be the moment that Pen's prophecy comes true."

"Which was?"

"That I could not settle quietly in any town, let alone Salterton." Isabella bit her lip. "She considers me far too scandalous."

"Judging on your performance yesterday," Marcus said, "she could be correct."

"I do not know what you mean," Isabella said. "If you are referring to my bathing then I assure you that it was perfectly respectable."

Marcus turned swiftly to face her. "Bella," he said, "I *know* you were swimming naked. I saw you."

Isabella bit back a smile. This had been one of the most pleasing tricks she could play on Marcus. He had spent a large part of the previous day looking sideways at her as though he could not quite believe that he had made a mistake.

Besides, there was something rather satisfying about teasing Marcus in this way. His sudden appearance beside the bathing machine the previous morning had both startled and disturbed her. After he had gone, she had jumped out of the water and hastened to dress. The only alternative would have been to pull him from Achilles's back into the water beside her, and Martha Otter would have disapproved most heartily of mixed bathing, especially the sort that Isabella had in mind. Her mind told her keeping Marcus at arm's length was the only sensible course of action, but her wayward body whispered something quite different.

"I saw you," Marcus repeated. He smiled. "All of you. It was most arousing."

The temperature in the carriage was already warm, for it was a humid evening. Now Isabella felt even more hot and sticky. The air between them was incendiary.

"I was thinking," Marcus continued, "that as part of our…agreement…you might come swimming with me?"

Isabella's mind filled with tempting pictures. The water running from Marcus's body; its clear, cool touch against her skin and the press of Marcus's nakedness against her own; the hot sand beneath their feet and the sun on their backs…. She shifted uncomfortably on the carriage seat as warm tension coiled in the pit of her stomach. She had denied Marcus her bed and now he was doing his very best to change her mind and seduce her all over again. And, devil take it, she wanted to be seduced. Already. After only three days. Perhaps it was the memory of their long-ago love affair. Or perhaps it was that, having once tasted the pleasure they could give each other, she was now fighting a losing battle in trying to deny it.

Marcus's fingers, long and strong, were interlocked with hers. In the summer shadows his eyes were full of dark desire. He leaned closer.

"Bella…"

The carriage juddered to a halt.

"A damned nuisance that this isn't a longer journey," Marcus said, releasing her and descending first to help her down the carriage steps and usher her through the doorway into the blaze of light beyond.

The Salterton Assembly Rooms were newly built and adjoined the circulating library on the broad esplanade. Tonight they were absolutely packed with people. Isabella vaguely saw the master of ceremonies come forward, hand outstretched, to greet them, and then an elderly lady came rushing toward her and, to Isabella's astonishment, embraced her soundly.

"My dear! May I be the first to say that it is such a delight to see you in Salterton again? I heard the rumor that you were back and could not believe it was true!" She kissed Isabella on the cheek and held her at arm's length. "Oh, I quite remember you when you were a little girl! Such a dear child! I was a great friend of your aunt, you know."

"How are you, dear ma'am?" Isabella inquired as she freed herself from the voluminous embrace. She had no idea whom the lady was and threw Marcus a look of appeal but he gave a helpless shrug before he was drawn away to meet another new acquaintance. Isabella wondered whether they would see each other at all for the rest of the entire evening.

The stranger was still chattering as though they were the greatest bosom bows in the world. Fortunately Isabella's years as a prince's consort had made her adept at appearing to know a great many people even if she did not recognize them from Adam.

"It is indeed an age since we met," she said, smiling at the lady. "How are your family, ma'am?"

The lady beamed. "Oh, Mr. Goring is very well, I thank you. He is not here tonight. He is a martyr to his rheumatics, you know. And dear Cecilia wed last year and has gone to live near Oxford. Such a wrench."

There was a pause as Mrs. Goring wiped a teary eye. Isabella took a calculated risk.

"Cecilia is your only one, is she not, ma'am? It must have indeed been hard for you to have her move so far away."

Mrs. Goring was nodding vigorously. "What a splendid memory you have, Princess Isabella! Yes, Cecilia is my little ewe lamb so far from home. But Mr. Monkton, Cecilia's husband, has five thousand a year, you know, and keeps a house and carriage in Town. She met him here when he came to take the sea cure." Mrs. Goring sighed. "Poor man, he is afflicted by biliousness."

Isabella was privately sorry for the absent Cecilia rather than her husband. But then, she knew from extensive experience of society that a young lady might tolerate a certain degree of biliousness for the sake of five thousand pounds a year.

"It will be delightful to have a chatelaine of Salterton Hall who shows an interest in the place," Mrs. Goring continued. "Poor Lady Jane was enfeebled in her last years and that son-in-law of hers, Stockhaven, barely set foot in the place. Salterton Cottage sustained such neglect that it is no wonder someone wanted to burn it down! An eyesore, that was what it had become! Very irresponsible." She broke off and raised her quizzing glass. "Upon my word, I do believe that is Stockhaven over there! No one told me that he had returned to Salterton! How extraordinary that I missed such a piece of news!"

"Lord Stockhaven has but returned this week, ma'am," Isabella said, lips twitching, as she saw Marcus had overheard the rather unflattering references to his character. "In point of fact we returned at the same time. Lord Stockhaven and I are recently married."

Mrs. Goring's quizzing glass swung slowly around, giving Isabella a fearsome view of a much-magnified eye.

"Well!" she said. "Here is news indeed! Not that I am not happy for you, Princess Isabella, but I wonder that you could not have done better for yourself. A duke rather than a mere earl, perhaps? Even a royal one if there are any free?"

"I do not look so high, I assure you, ma'am," Isabella said, smiling openly now. "All I require now is to live quietly in Salterton, in the house that I have loved since I was a child."

"Very laudable," Mrs. Goring concurred, looking gratified. Her glance flicked to Marcus once again, and he looked up and caught Isabella's eye somewhat quizzically. Mrs. Goring raised her voice a little. "And perhaps you may instill some of your own sense of responsibility in your husband, Princess. If he comes to care for Salterton as much as you do then we shall be proud to have him as a resident." And with that she gave Isabella a warm smile, nodded in rather cool contrast to Marcus, and excused herself to go and whisper the news in the ear of the nearest lady.

Next in line to make Isabella's acquaintance was a friend of Mrs. Goring, the widowed Mrs. Bulstrode, with her daughter Lavinia. Mrs. Bulstrode was an anxious mama, surviving on a pittance and keen to see her daughter settled, especially now that Cecilia Goring had caught a husband. She was as fluttery as a moth around a candle. Lavinia Bulstrode, in contrast, was a placid, good-humored girl decked out in too many frills. They spoke on generalities for a while—the weather, the development of Salterton as a resort, the London Season and fashions. Lavinia had had a Season.

"But she did not *take*, Princess Isabella," Mrs. Bulstrode mourned, in the manner of one complaining of an awkward bloom that refuses to flower. "We went to all the balls and parties, we had vouchers for Almacks, Lady Etherington sponsored us! I cannot think what went wrong."

Viewing the lacy pink dress that the unfortunate Lavinia was tricked out in, Isabella could see exactly what had gone wrong. Taken together with Miss Bulstrode's practical, down-to-earth nature, her style of dress would put paid to all but the most devoted of suitors.

When Mrs. Bulstrode was distracted momentarily, Lavinia leaned forward and whispered to Isabella, "Do not listen to Mama, Princess Isabella! I should be happy if I never *take* at all, for all I met were foolish fops and fortune hunters. Besides—" she looked down disparagingly at the pink gown "—if Mama dresses me like the Christmas pudding, what can she expect?" She gave Isabella a half comical, half despairing look. "What would you do, ma'am?"

"I would take a pair of shears to it," Isabella said frankly. "It is an elegant gown under all that decoration."

Lavinia gave a little giggle. "Oh, do you think I could? What a splendid idea!"

Isabella could see Mrs. Bulstrode ending her conversation and added quickly, "Trust me, my dear Lavinia. I think I see the way to make your mama change her views of fashion."

Lavinia gave her a quick, sparkling glance and then Mrs. Bulstrode was upon them once more. Isabella lost no time.

"Miss Bulstrode and I were discussing London fashions, ma'am," she said, "and I was saying that she would look absolutely delightful in the *new* style of gown that has only last week been unveiled. It is a most simple design. I have some patterns with me. Perhaps I could share them with you?"

Mrs. Bulstrode looked suspicious. "Simple?"

"Elegant," Isabella said. "Not every lady will be able to carry off such a style but I do believe Miss Bulstrode has the figure for it."

"That sounds splendid," Lavinia said, taking her cue with such artlessness that Isabella reflected she would make a fine actress. "To be ahead of the fashions would be a wonderful thing."

Mrs. Bulstrode's expression softened as it dwelled on her daughter's eager face. "Very well, Lavinia," she said gruffly. "I confess to a certain fondness for adornment myself, but perhaps in a young gel…"

"Thank you!" Lavinia whispered to Isabella as they took their leave.

There were gentlemen hovering. Isabella summed them up with the practice of long experience. The Honorable Mr. Digby was a young sprig of a noble family and very conscious of his status in the small world of Salterton society. He did not seem pleased to be upstaged by a full-scale earl and a princess, albeit a foreign one. Mr. Casson was an unabashed fortune hunter whose openness on the subject made him far more attractive than had he pretended he was not hanging out for a rich wife. He pressed Isabella to invite her friends to Salterton. "If you could oblige me with just one heiress, Princess Isabella, I would be your devoted follower for life! Heiresses are uncommonly difficult to find."

"And to marry," Isabella said dryly.

"Perhaps you have a sister?"

"I do," Isabella said, "but she has no money."

Mr. Casson looked most downcast.

The Assembly boasted dandies, rakes, men on the make, half-pay officers, rich widows, poor widows, debutantes, wives…it was like London in miniature. Isabella talked and smiled, asked questions and danced with a few fortunate gentlemen, and all the time she was conscious of Marcus across the room. He had not requested the first dance and she felt a little sorry at the fact. An earnest young man had buttonholed him and seemed to be trying to persuade him of something.

She sat out the next dance beside an ancient sea captain who, far from boring her with his tales of maritime adventure, told her that gardening was now his passion and asked her opinion on the new strain of rose that was being developed by a local horticulturalist. And still Marcus did not come to her side and Isabella was obliged to remind herself that she was the one who had requested the marriage in name only. She was doing her duty here at the Assembly—they both were. They had appeared in public together and then gone their separate ways for the evening. It was expected. It was the tonnish thing to do. It made her miserable.

"Your servant, Lady Stockhaven." A gentleman was bowing before her, soliciting the pleasure of the next dance. She recognized him as a Mr. Owen, one of the summer visitors whom Mrs. Bulstrode had introduced earlier in the evening. Marcus was still deep in conversation and dancing appeared to be the last thing on his mind. Isabella smiled at the newcomer and gave him her hand.

"Thank you, sir. I should be glad to join the country dance."

As they took their places in the set, she found herself wondering how Mr. Owen was able to dance at all. He was evidently in Salterton for the sea cure, for there was a waxy pallor about his skin that suggested he was far from well. His gray eyes were dull and expressionless and he had a pronounced limp. She imagined that he could be little older than she was and yet he did not look as though he would make old bones. He smelled of mothballs and cordial, and there was some underlying element about him that made her shudder. It was nothing to do with his illness, but something far more unwholesome. Worse, there was something faintly and disturbingly familiar about him. She wished that she had not agreed to dance with him.

"Do you take the sea waters, sir?" she asked him, more to make conversation than out of genuine interest. Mr. Owen nodded.

"I suffer from the rheumatics, Lady Stockhaven, as well as having a nervous complaint and a touch of biliousness. Sea air and frequent dipping are the only cures."

Isabella remembered her aunt once saying that doctors and sea cures encouraged people to imagine that they were ill. She repressed a smile.

"I am sorry," she said.

Mr. Owen's glassy gaze fixed upon her. He gave her a faint, wintry smile. "I must confess that you seem rather too well for this place, Lady Stockhaven, but I feel sure that you will catch an ague in no time from the sea breezes."

"You reassure me, sir," Isabella said.

Out of the corner of her eye she could see that Marcus was at last attempting to draw away from the earnest young man and there was a small frown creasing his brow as he looked in her direction. There was hardly a healthier looking man in the room. Isabella found herself wanting to pounce on him and carry him off to celebrate their mutual rude health and shake off the scent of the sickroom in a way that would shock half the occupants of Salterton into an early grave. She met Marcus's eyes and he broke off his conversation, raising a brow in interrogation at whatever it was he saw in her face. Isabella's lips parted as she stared at him. Her breath caught in her throat. Their gazes locked with a sharp awareness and Marcus's attention focused on her in a way that made her shiver. It was intense, concentrated and wholly personal. Here, in the Assembly Rooms at Salterton, his entire stance told her that he wanted to ravish her within an inch of her life. He started to move toward her.

The music was drawing to a close. Isabella dragged her mind and her gaze away from Marcus and forced out another smile for the unwholesome Mr. Owen.

"Thank you for the dance, sir. May I assist you to a chair? You seem a little short of breath."

Owen nodded, leaning heavily on her arm. "I apologize for not being able to conduct you on the customary stroll around the room, Lady Stockhaven."

"Please do not regard it," Isabella said, depositing him on a rout chair with a certain relief. The skin on the back of her neck was prickling. She knew that Marcus was close.

"You must excuse me, sir," she said. "I believe that I am engaged to dance the next—"

"With me," a voice said at her elbow. Marcus extended a hand to her, bowing slightly. The expression in his eyes was for her alone and made her feel weak, though he still managed to cover the courtesies even as his gaze told her how much he wanted her.

"Good evening, Owen," he said, pulling Isabella close to his side. She spread one hand against his side, feeling the thunder of his heart against her palm.

Mr. Owen gave an invalid's loud sigh. "Evening, Stockhaven. I trust you are suffering no gout or seizures this evening?"

"No," Marcus said. Isabella could feel him shaking with silent laughter. "I thank you, sir. I am quite well."

He turned to Isabella as though he could wait no longer. "Come, my dear. I am sure we are both strong enough for a waltz. And then I think we should retire—before we exhaust ourselves too much."

Isabella had not realized that it was the waltz and she was a little surprised to find them playing it here, in conservative Salterton society. Only the most daring and fit of the village's inhabitants were attempting it. The others stood back with a mixture of envy and disapproval to see who had the courage to join in.

"I hope you are enjoying the evening, Marcus," Isabella said lightly, as they took their places. She was intensely aware of his presence but she was also conscious of the crowd of people about them. Somehow she had to try to get through this dance without betraying her feelings in public.

"I have found it a rather bruising experience, truth to tell," Marcus observed with a wince. He too appeared to be having difficulty in concentrating on small talk.

"I have been twitted for my lack of civic pride, considered a miser for refusing to invest in the pier, and overheard the Goring female's view that I was not good enough for my wife! Whereas you—" he turned and gave her an assessing look "—were feted by one and all. It is remarkable that you remembered Mrs. Goring after all these years. She seemed most gratified."

Isabella's mouth turned up in a little smile. "I had no notion who she was when she greeted me," she whispered, "but she seemed so pleased to see me that it would have been rude to confess I did not know her from Adam."

Marcus smiled. "One would not have known. How accomplished you are. And how kind." He hesitated. "They tell me that you sent them books and musical instruments for the school. That you wrote to people when your aunt passed on news of births, marriages and deaths. That you made welcome any visitors who ventured as far as Cassilis in their travels and that you used your influence to help those who would never normally have a chance to gain work or connections or education. You astound me, Isabella. I had no notion."

Isabella smiled inwardly. She rather liked the idea of surprising Marcus. He had made a great many assumptions about her and it was good to shake them. Shortly she hoped that she would shake him once again. But first there was the waltz to enjoy.

The music started.

Isabella had not waltzed with Marcus before and it was entirely delightful. More than that, it was sinful and sensual and seductive. She could feel the warmth of his palm against her back and the ripple of the muscle in his thigh against the silk of her dress. Her mind clouded and her body filled with a melting pleasure and she did not fight the sensation. There were no two ways about it—this dance was dangerous. It should be banned. As for vows of celibacy, of denying herself the pleasure of her husband's lovemaking, well…evidently she had not been thinking straight and the glasses of wine she had consumed that evening had certainly helped her to see sense.

"Bella." Marcus spoke softly in her ear and Isabella shivered to feel his breath against her skin.

"Mmm?"

"Who was that man?"

Isabella dragged herself from the sensual haze and tried to focus on Marcus's face. "Which man?" She cleared her throat. "I mean to whom do you refer?"

Marcus laughed. "You sound somewhat distracted. Are you not attending, Bella?"

"Not particularly." Isabella smoothed her fingers over the curve of his shoulder.

Marcus slanted her a quizzical look. "Then what were you thinking about?"

"I was thinking about making love with you."

Marcus missed his step. For a moment, Isabella wondered whether he would be taken aback by her brazen declaration, but then she saw the mixture of amusement and raw desire in his eyes.

"Generally or specifically?" His voice too had fallen to a rough whisper.

"Specifically. In about five minutes," Isabella whispered back.

She had pushed it too far. Marcus released her at once, but only to take her hand and pull her off the dance floor and toward the door. It seemed to take an interminable amount of time to make their farewells. There were Mrs. Bulstrode's concerns to deal with; that matron had thought that Isabella's hasty departure must owe something to a sudden indisposition, which was true but it was not the same condition that

Mrs. Bulstrode had in mind. Marcus swept the good lady aside with the promise that he would take care of his wife. Isabella dealt with Mrs. Goring's pressing invitation to take tea with summary thanks. All she wanted was to be alone with Marcus in the intimate dark and feel his hands on her. Eventually they were in the coach, the door clicked shut, and she fell into his arms with a little moan of relief, welcoming his hungry mouth on hers.

She parted her lips, trying to breathe, as Marcus crushed his mouth to hers, sliding his tongue deep. His hands tangled in her hair. The kiss was hard but seductive, possessing her but then allowing her tongue to dance with his, to parry and tease and subdue. She was as eager and as eloquent as he.

Marcus slipped his hand into the bodice of her gown and cupped her breast. Isabella pressed closer, arching against his questing fingers. Her mind was blurred with desire. Again, she vaguely remembered that she had wanted to wait before giving herself to Marcus once more, but then she realized that she loved him and to her dazzled mind this seemed reason enough.

In a very short time, she found herself naked from the waist up, facing Marcus, her legs sprawled over his thighs. His hands were braced on her waist and Isabella leaned her head back and sighed with pleasure while he used his mouth on her breasts. He was raking his teeth gently over the tip and circling it with his tongue and she…well, she was drowning in pure sensation and never wanted it to stop.

The carriage jerked to a halt and she almost fell off Marcus's lap.

"Damn it," Marcus said, "we really must plan to make this a longer journey in future."

He swiftly helped Isabella to rearrange her gown and provided a steadying hand as she stepped down and felt her legs buckle beneath her. She wanted him to scoop her up and carry her inside, up the stairs and to the bedchamber. But he was scrupulously careful. In the faint light of the carriage lamps, he turned to her and spoke very quietly.

"Bella, if you have changed your mind then I shall let you go in now. I must do, or I will never allow you to sleep alone."

Isabella grabbed his arm. "I do not want you to," she said urgently.

There were no more words. Marcus slid an arm about her waist and drew her up the steps to the front door, pulling her with him into the hall. The excited laughter bubbled up in Isabella's throat. She could feel the urgency in his hands and the ardent desire in his touch. In a moment they would be safe in her bedchamber and they could tear each other's clothes away and fall into the feather mattress and take each other with all the fierce passion that she could feel sweeping through her....

She stopped dead, all thoughts of racing up the staircase to bed abruptly banished.

A quantity of luggage was piled up at the bottom of the stairs and from the drawing room came the sound of upraised voices.

"Pen," Isabella said flatly. "And Freddie, too, I suspect."

"Lord Standish and Miss Penelope Standish have arrived, my lord, my lady," the housekeeper confirmed, bustling out into the hall, "and Mr. Cantrell."

Isabella exchanged a look with Marcus and saw an expression of faint surprise and something more in his eyes, almost as though he had been expecting this. He looked at her and shook his head with disbelief and a fierce frustration.

Isabella bit her lip. "How very inconvenient," she said.

"My lord?" the housekeeper said uncertainly. "I put your guests in the drawing room."

"Thank you, Mrs. Lawton," Marcus said slowly. He took a deep breath, smiled at Isabella and held out a hand.

"Come, my dear, and let us see what our unexpected guests have to say for themselves."

They could hear Pen upbraiding her brother even as Mrs. Lawton opened the door for them.

"Really, Freddie," Pen was saying, "whatever can have got into you? To leave in such a hurry and with no proper word!"

"I fancied a trip to the seaside," Isabella heard Freddie say defensively. "M'health, you know."

"Balderdash!" Pen denounced. "You hate the country."

"Yes!" Freddie seized on it. "I hate the country but not the seaside, Penelope…"

"Good evening, children," Isabella said peaceably, going across to the sofa to kiss Pen on the cheek while Marcus greeted Alistair. "We could hear you out in the courtyard! What a delightful treat to see you both!"

"I am sorry, Bella." Pen had the grace to look faintly embarrassed. She swung around on the sofa. "Good evening, cousin Marcus." She turned back. "I was just telling Freddie that he should not go dashing off without proper preparation."

"We heard that, too," Isabella agreed, very conscious that Marcus was studying Freddie's languid form with a curious speculative look. "I take it, then, that you did not travel down here together?"

"No indeed," Pen said indignantly, "since Freddie did not wait long enough for me to accompany him!"

"Devil a bit," Freddie said, flushing. "Spur of the moment impulse, y'know. Can a man not be spontaneous when he wishes to be?"

Isabella turned to Alistair Cantrell, who was waiting in his customary quiet manner.

"Good evening, Mr. Cantrell," she said. "I apologize for the fact that you have been obliged to tolerate my difficult siblings and I must thank you for escorting my sister safely here."

"Pleasure, Lady Stockhaven," Alistair said promptly.

"I see that you have been offered refreshment," Isabella

added, her gaze falling on the remnants of a tray of food that looked as though it had been set upon by wild animals, "and that Pen at least has partaken."

"I was hungry," Pen said defensively. "Traveling raises an appetite."

There was a silence. Isabella noticed that Alistair Cantrell was watching Pen, a smile lurking in his eyes. Isabella mentally raised her brows. Pen and Mr. Cantrell? She had noticed their mutual interest in London but had assumed that Alistair was just another of the poor unfortunates entranced by Pen's prettiness only to be disillusioned by her independent mind. Perhaps this time, however, things would be different.

"I was going to take a nightcap," Marcus said easily. "Alistair, Standish, would you care to join me?" He looked at Freddie and once again Isabella was aware of an element of speculative antagonism in his gaze. She had sensed it before, this animosity between Freddie and Marcus, but she was at a loss to explain it.

Freddie shifted a little uncomfortably. "Think I'll have a word with m'sister first, Stockhaven, if you will excuse me."

"Of course," Marcus said politely, ushering Alistair toward the door. "We shall be in the library should you care to join us." He glanced at Isabella, a smile lurking about his mouth. His look spoke of apology and promise, and Isabella understood it very well.

"Good night, my love," he said.

Isabella sighed unconsciously, then returned to her warring siblings as the door closed behind her husband.

"Tell you what, Pen," Freddie was saying, "Cantrell won't be so interested now he's seen what a virago you are, tearing a strip off me like that. No man likes a shrew!"

Pen blushed fiery red. "I am not attempting to attract Mr. Cantrell, Freddie."

"And a good thing, too!" her brother interrupted caustically. "Nothing gives a fellow a greater disgust than a haranguing woman!"

"Freddie, Pen," Isabella interposed. "If you could cease your squabbles for just one moment to tell me what is going on, I should be grateful."

"Have we interrupted your honeymoon by arriving unannounced, Bella?" Pen inquired, picking the crumbs from the tea tray. "If Marcus is not expecting to see you again tonight then I gather not. It seems a lukewarm affair, this marriage of yours."

"That is none of your concern," Isabella said with composure, resisting the impulse to tell Pen that had she not arrived so inconveniently, her marriage would have been white hot.

"What concerns *me* is why you both decided so precipitately that a visit to the seaside was in order." She looked interrogatively at her brother. "Freddie?"

Freddie shifted uncomfortably. "Fancied some company and sea air," he muttered. "No society in Town now that the Season is at an end. With you gone, too, Bella, things were dull."

"You flatter me," Isabella said dryly. She could tell from the stubborn expression on Freddie's face that she was unlikely to get any more information from him, though she doubted that this was even approaching the truth. She could see unhappiness as well as a bullish obstinacy in his face. She decided to let it lie for a little.

"And you, Pen?" she inquired.

"It was your fault," Pen said, firing up. "You seem to forget, Bella, that you were the one who left London in a hurry in the first place. I was worried about you. Then Freddie rushed off and I did not know what to do. So I sent for Mr. Cantrell."

"As one would," Freddie put in.

Pen ignored him. "We agreed that the best thing would be to come down here and ascertain that everything was well."

"How extraordinarily precipitate you have both been,"

Isabella commented dryly. "I hope you were accompanied by a maid, Pen."

Pen's blush deepened. "Naturally Mr. Cantrell arranged for the proprieties to be observed. We borrowed a servant from his mother's establishment." She sighed. "One would expect no less of him. He is everything that is proper."

With a flash of intuition and no little surprise, Isabella recognized that part of the reason for Pen's fidgets and bad temper was thwarted desire. She was flushed and agitated and on edge after hours in the company of a man whose behavior had been so utterly irreproachable that it would make one want to scream. Isabella prayed that Freddie's natural obtuseness would keep him from making the same deduction until she could spirit Pen from the room.

"Well," she said placatingly. "You are here now and I am very glad to see you both. You must be tired. Are you ready to go up to your rooms?"

"You may take Pen up," Freddie said. "I would prefer a nightcap of that brandy you have over there, Bella."

"As you wish," Isabella said. "You do not prefer to join Marcus and Mr. Cantrell?"

Freddie looked shifty. "Prefer to take a snifter on my own."

Once again Isabella felt that prickle of awkwardness in his manner. It was going to be a rather difficult house party if her husband and her brother were living in a state of armed neutrality. She sighed.

"Very well," she said. "Then Mrs. Lawton will show you to your room when you are ready."

She took Pen's arm and they went out of the drawing room and up the stairs. She could hear Marcus and Alistair talking together quietly in the library and, although Pen cast a glance in the direction of the door, she hurried past, her color still high. Isabella could see that she was deeply preoccupied. She made no observations about being back at Salterton Hall and no sooner had they reached the privacy of the blue bedchamber than she grabbed Isabella's hand.

"Bella, there is something that I simply must tell you, and then you may cast me from the house if you please!"

Isabella looked at her. "I am sure I shall do nothing so gothic, Penelope. What must you confess?"

Pen threw herself down into the armchair and wrung her hands together. "Mr. Cantrell tells me that I must tell all to you—"

"I see," Isabella said, suddenly quaking at the thought that she had misread the situation completely and that Alistair Cantrell had seduced her sister on the journey to Salterton.

"I was going to tell you in my own time, but I never seemed to have the appropriate opportunity. It was simply that we had no money, and I was so worried about Freddie's debts." Pen's blue eyes were anguished. "Oh, Bella, please forgive me! I never meant to betray your confidence."

"I have no idea what you are talking about," Isabella said, "although you are alarming me somewhat, Pen."

"The gossip column in the papers!" Pen said dramatically. She dragged her portmanteau into the middle of the floor and unbuckled the lid, talking all the time. "I wrote scandal for Mr. Morrow at the *Gentlemen's Athenian Mercury!* All the bits about your debts and the house in Brunswick Gardens and your sudden marriage…"

"I see," Isabella said slowly.

"I needed the money," Pen said miserably, rummaging through the case and sending her underwear flying. "I thought it would not matter, Bella, but then when we got to know one another again I liked you so much that I felt an absolute *traitor*…."

Isabella sat down heavily on the edge of the bed. "Let me understand you aright," she said. "You are the one who was feeding those stories to the press."

"Yes." Pen was flushed and unhappy. She sat back on her heels, copies of all the papers now in her hands. "I am so sorry! I felt as though I had betrayed you and Mr. Cantrell said—"

"Yes," Isabella said. "Where does Mr. Cantrell fit into all this?"

"He writes for the same newspaper. We met at Morrow's offices and Mr. Cantrell guessed that I had been the one submitting the column. He urged me to tell you the truth."

"I am glad that someone in this has some scruples," Isabella said dryly.

Pen blushed harder. "Oh, Bella, pray do not hate me! I was so desperate for the money, but then we met up again after all these years and it felt so wrong to take advantage and I have been desperately torn." She sighed. "I see now that it was very bad of me." She sighed. "I will never do it again. There must be other ways of finding the money rather than bartering with my sister's good name."

Isabella was silent. She understood rather more than Pen knew of what it felt like to be so desperate.

"You made reference to Freddie's debts," she said. "I had no notion. Is that what this is all about, Pen? Are they very bad?"

"I do not know for sure," Pen said unhappily, "but the household bills are mounting up and we cannot pay the maid and I fear there is a lot Freddie is hiding from me."

"Such as why he came dashing down here to Salterton on a whim," Isabella said thoughtfully. "Why did you tell me none of this before, Pen?"

"You had your own difficulties," Pen said, troubled. "I am sorry that I did not confide. I wish I had told you sooner."

Isabella was frowning. "I cannot believe that you would sell the story of my marriage to the gossip merchants."

Pen looked as though she was going to cry. "I am sorry! I swear I never meant to stoop so low." She sighed. "Do you hate me, Bella?"

Isabella shook her head. "I cannot hate you, Pen. I know all too well what it is like to be in dire financial straits. Besides, we do not have much family left, do we? We cannot afford to lose one another."

Pen burst into tears. "Oh damnation!" She blew her nose loudly on a pair of drawers. "I am so sorry, Bella! How can I make amends?"

Isabella sighed. "You can tell me everything you know of Freddie's situation," she said, settling back against the bed head. "And I mean *everything,* Pen." She frowned. "Have you ever known Freddie to rush off anywhere, least of all the seaside? There is something going on here."

Pen got to her feet. "Yes, that was the most extraordinary thing. Of course he had had that odd letter at breakfast, and he dashed off straight away, but he never came back! I had gone to see you," she added reproachfully. "We were supposed to be attending the exhibition at the Royal Academy."

"So we were," Isabella said, trying to sort her sister's jumbled information into order. Not for the first time, she reflected that very clever people could sometimes be extremely hard to follow. "What odd letter was this, Pen?"

"A letter about his gambling debts, apparently." Pen yawned. "I beg your pardon, Bella. I am so tired. I know this is making little sense." She rubbed her eyes. "He received the letter at breakfast and hurried out immediately. He never came back—he merely sent me some cock-and-bull message about going to Salterton. And he left without any luggage."

"He has some now," Isabella said slowly. "I saw it in the hall."

Pen frowned. "Now that is passing strange, for where could he have got it from?"

"He could have bought some essentials on the journey, I suppose," Isabella said.

Pen spread her hands. "But he has no money!"

"Gambling debts," Isabella said quietly. She thought of their father and his weakness for deep play and the anguish squeezed her heart. Please, God, Freddie had not got himself embroiled with some hideous moneylender who would bleed him dry.

"I do not suppose that Freddie told you whom the letter was from," she said without much hope.

"No," Pen said, "he did not tell me but I knew where it came from because I opened it by mistake. It was from an address in Wigmore Street and it was signed with the name Warwick."

CHAPTER EIGHTEEN

ISABELLA HAD BEEN WAITING for what seemed like a very long time. She had heard Mrs. Lawton escort Freddie to his room and the footmen lurching up the stairs with various items of luggage. Eventually there was the sound of voices in the corridor outside. Marcus and Alistair were parting with a quiet word. Isabella heard the door of Marcus's chamber close softly. Still she waited. After a while, the valet came out and the house was quiet. Isabella waited a little longer. Then, with a quick, nervous gesture, she scooped up her dressing robe and slipped out of the door onto the landing. She would have used the connecting door but at this inopportune moment she realized that she did not have a key to it and it seemed faintly ridiculous to knock on the door until Marcus answered.

Freddie. Freddie and Edward Warwick. She felt sick at heart to think of it but she could not put it from her mind. She was not entirely sure what she was going to do. Marcus had seemed implacable in his pursuit of Warwick and she did not want Freddie hounded and browbeaten and humiliated. Like Pen, she had a deep if exasperated affection for her hapless brother. It would be better to confront him herself rather than to implicate him to Marcus in Warwick's plots. But that also felt disloyal. She should tell Marcus what she knew. She was deeply torn.

She paused for a moment on the landing, knocked briefly on Marcus's door and went in. Marcus looked up with unqualified surprise to see her. He was sitting up in bed, a sheaf of papers scattered across the covers and a pencil in hand. Isabella realized that he had been sketching. The book on theoretical naval architecture lay on the nightstand beside him.

She also guessed that he was naked. Certainly his chest was bare and the sheets were slung low across his hips. Isabella found her attention veering away from Freddie somewhat abruptly. She had to remind herself to breathe.

"Work," Marcus said, gathering the papers together with an apologetic grin. "I find that it helps to distract my mind from certain problems. What may I do for you, Isabella? I did not expect to see you again tonight. Is all well?"

Isabella hesitated. She sat down on the edge of the bed, making sure that she kept a decent distance from him. This felt odd and very personal. She fiddled with the edge of the bedspread.

"It is Freddie," she said jerkily. "I think…that is, Pen said…that he is involved with Edward Warwick."

Marcus's eyes narrowed. He gave her a straight look. "Did Pen tell you this tonight?"

"Yes, of course." Isabella felt relief and guilt in equal measure. She looked up. There was something strange and speculative in Marcus's eyes. "Freddie is in debt and—" She stopped and looked at him accusingly. "Marcus! You knew this already!"

Marcus grimaced. "Please keep your voice down, Bella." He dropped his own so that Isabella was obliged to strain closer to hear him. "It is true that Alistair and I suspected Freddie of being involved in some way, but we did not know."

"That is why Mr. Cantrell is here," Isabella said. She felt cold. "That is why *Freddie* is here." She shivered convulsively. "What is going on, Marcus?"

"I do not know." Marcus threw back the covers and drew her unresistingly into the warmth. She huddled closer to him for comfort, his arm about her and her cheek against his chest. "I think Warwick is here in Salterton. But as yet I know nothing for certain. Your brother's arrival is an interesting development."

"You will not *hurt* Freddie, will you?" Isabella asked in a small voice, tilting her chin up to look at him.

She felt Marcus laugh. "Good God, Bella, do you think me medieval? I swear I shall not hurt my own brother-in-law." The amusement left his voice. "I imagine that whatever Freddie has got himself involved with, it cannot be so very bad. He is scarcely a hardened criminal."

"No," Isabella said. She moved her cheek absentmindedly against Marcus's, feeling the roughness of his stubble against her softness. "I think… I think he has become involved in something he cannot get out of. Gambling and debts…"

"And the provision of information," Marcus said, his voice hardening slightly. He turned his head and kissed her cheek where it rested against the curve of his shoulder. "Do you feel a little better now, Bella?"

"Yes," Isabella said. "I am glad that I told you."

Marcus gathered her closer and eased a line of soft kisses along her cheek.

"I am glad, too," he murmured. "I think you must have started to trust me a little."

His lips claimed hers and Isabella turned to him in desperation, seeking comfort, wanting to blot out the coldness in her soul. She sought his kisses with eagerness, pressing closer to him, wanting to banish the darkness. Yet all the time, it crept back into her mind and she could not make it go. Freddie and India and Ernest… They flitted like ghosts through her mind, distracting her from Marcus's caresses so that she could feel nothing.

Fifteen minutes later, Isabella felt as though she was suffocating with embarrassment and humiliation as she lay beneath Marcus in the wide double bed. The house was silent and dark and she could hear nothing but his breathing and the relentless creak of the mattress. Still she felt nothing. Nothing but panic, at any rate. She could not believe it. Earlier in the evening she had wanted Marcus so much. Now she was hot and sticky and her mind was dark and tormented with old images and secrets. She shifted painfully. She wanted to tell Marcus to stop but she could not and she was utterly mortified. She could not make love successfully with her husband even when she wanted to. How hopeless she was.

"Bella?" Marcus had stopped. He reached across and struck a light.

"I am sorry," Isabella said. "I was thinking too much."

"Of what?" Marcus's tone was unreadable. He pulled away from her and she could feel him slipping from her emotionally, and it sent a chill along her spine. Was it always to be like this—the ghosts of the past ruining everything between them? She did not think she could bear it.

She put her hands over her face. "About the past," she said. "I am sorry, Marcus. I thought I could do this. I wanted to do it. I wanted to seduce you."

The words fell into a rather sad silence and Isabella felt her heart shrivel with renewed mortification. Then she heard Marcus sigh.

"Bella." His voice had gentled. "Tell me what you were thinking about. Otherwise we shall never get past all of this."

"Marcus—" Isabella shuddered. The last thing that she wanted to do was to rehearse old love affairs.

"Tell me, Bella." Marcus's tone was low but insistent. "I need to understand." Then, as she still paused, he added harshly, "Did he hurt you?"

"Ernest?" Isabella said. She sat up, drawing her knees to her chin and making sure that the covers wrapped her completely about. She did not wish Marcus to see her naked. Not now, when she already felt exposed enough.

"No, he did not hurt me," she said. "Not in the sense that

you mean." She looked up and met Marcus's eyes very directly. "I made it clear to him early on in our marriage that I would not join in his sexual games. After that he troubled me very little."

"There is more than one way of hurting someone," Marcus said.

Their gazes locked. In the candlelight, Marcus's eyes were very dark. Isabella swallowed hard as she looked on his face. She loved him so much already that the thought of losing him again was like a knife in the heart. This was not how it was meant to be. She had meant to protect herself but once again she had made herself vulnerable.

"That is true," she said. "In other ways he hurt me every day, with his cruelty and his indifference and his spite."

"You took other lovers," Marcus said. His face was expressionless. "Tell me."

Isabella took a shuddering breath. She locked her arms about her knees, holding on tightly.

"I turned to Heinrich Von Trier after Emma's death," she said. "I was desperate for affection and I tumbled hopelessly in love with him. But for him the chase was everything." She pressed her fingers against her temples. Her passion for Heinrich Von Trier had burned out years before and she had soon recognized it as a pale imitation of love, but at the time his had seemed a double betrayal, coming so soon after Emma.

"Once he had what he wanted and could boast of it, he was no longer interested," she said. "A quick fumble on the backstairs was about the sum of it." She raised her hand to her cheek. "It was as sordid as it sounds."

Marcus took her hand in his and drew it down to the bedcovers, holding it firmly between both of his. She tried to withdraw it but he held on firmly. She could sense the conflict in him, as though he were angry with her and yet trying to conquer his feelings. It made her shake inside.

"Do not say that, Bella." He sounded fierce. "Do not demean yourself."

"I need not," Isabella said bitterly, "when there are so many others able to do it for me."

Marcus shook his head slightly. His expression was ferocious. His grip tightened on hers so much she winced.

"Damn the man." He spoke dispassionately and his coldness was far more frightening to Isabella than hot anger would have been. "Damn him to hell and back. I could kill him for betraying you."

Isabella's throat ached. "You need not spare him another thought. The French have saved you the trouble of despatching him."

Marcus's expression lightened slightly. "That is something, I suppose." He looked at her. "You say that you loved him?"

Isabella clung to his hand. It seemed a terrible betrayal to speak of her love for Von Trier to this man who had always been the true love of her life. Yet she could not offer Marcus anything but honesty.

"I thought that I did," she said. "I was very unhappy. I needed some comfort." She broke off before she slipped into excuses. "Marcus, I am sorry."

"Don't say that!" Marcus sounded so furious now that Isabella shrank back against the tumbled pillows. He turned to her suddenly and the fierce light blazed in his eyes. "Oh, I am angry, Bella," he said. "I cannot deny it. Angry and jealous. I cannot help myself. But I can still understand. You were desperately unhappy. You say that you loved him and I believe you."

There was an aching silence. Isabella did not know what else she could say. Marcus sighed.

"What of the rest?" he said, and his voice was tired.

For a moment Isabella did not understand, then she made a slight gesture. "There were no others. Is that not enough?"

Marcus looked at her, incredulity in his eyes. "But…there must have been! I heard…" He trailed off, staring at her.

Isabella almost laughed. First she had failed to satisfy her husband sexually, then she had discussed her old lovers with him and now he was finding it hard to believe that she was not the female rakehell that he had been led to believe. She doubted that it was possible for the situation to get any worse.

"You heard gossip, Marcus," she said. "That is all."

Marcus sat back slightly, scanning her face. "Von Trier? He was the only one? But…"

"I flirted." Isabella traced a pattern on the bedcover with her fingertips. "It passed the time."

"Then why—" Marcus's tone was warming into a white-hot anger now. "Why do you let them say such things about you, Bella?" His hands bit into her shoulders, shaking her. "Good God, it beggars belief! The lovers and the scandal and the outright perversions…is there anything that is not said of you?"

"I am not certain," Isabella said. "I try not to listen."

Marcus's eyes were almost black with fury. "Do not joke about this! Why did you encourage all the gossip by allowing your husband's mistress to attend his funeral, giving support to the scandal that you were engaged in some complaisant ménage à trois?"

Isabella suddenly felt a great deal older and wiser than he. "Dear, Marcus," she said ruefully, "my life with Ernest was so miserable that I would have done more than that for some peace. Madame de Coulanges made Ernest happy." She gave him a wry look. "She kept him out of my way and that was worth a very great deal. For that I thought she deserved the right to take a proper farewell of him."

She edged to the side of the bed. "I will leave you now. I am sorry that matters have fallen out the way they have."

"Stay." Marcus held her still when she would have slipped from beneath the covers. He pulled her down beside him.

"Lie down." He spoke softly. "You look exhausted. You have given me a great deal to think about, Bella, but I do not want you to leave me now."

He still called her Bella. That was a consolation, for it spoke of an intimacy that they had achieved that had apparently not been lost. Isabella felt a vast relief. The shadow of India still pressed close but for once Isabella felt hopeful. One day—one day soon—she would broach the subject of India with Marcus and discover the truth.

SHE LAY DOWN OBEDIENTLY and allowed him to draw her close to the warmth of his body. She tried to think about what he must be thinking and feeling but already the warm comfort of his body was soothing her and helping her slip toward sleep. She turned her face closer into his neck, breathing in the scent of his skin. As always, he smelled familiar and exactly right. It was a strange sensation but a reassuring one. Little by little, the trust between them was growing.

Marcus could tell the precise moment when Isabella fell asleep. Her breathing changed and the final remnants of tension slid from her body, leaving her soft and defenseless beside him. He shifted his body slightly to draw her closer, tucking the covers around her protectively and brushing the hair away from her face. She looked sweet and young and beautiful. He felt something close to despair.

This was not how he had envisaged the evening ending. It was the furthest possible outcome from that which he had intended when she had come into his chamber and stripped her clothes off with such wanton and delicious provocation. To be lying here cradling her so gently and yet to feel so much anger and jealousy and resentment, the least worthy of emotions, was extraordinary. What made him despair was that he was not sure if he could overcome that jealousy.

He was completely aware of how unfair this was. He had

had his share of women, taken without love and for mutual pleasure, and yet he resented Isabella giving herself to just one man in marriage and one other in love. Yet that was how he *felt*. She should have been his alone and she was not.

Marcus clenched a hand in his hair and expelled his breath in a long sigh. Isabella did not stir. She was curled against him so trustfully that it made his heart ache at the same time the jealousy stirred rancid within him.

He had always been a possessive man where Isabella was concerned. He had never felt like that about anyone else, least of all his first wife. His emotions for India were complex and laden with guilt but he had never felt for her one ounce of the white-hot need that he had for Isabella.

He made an effort to push the whole matter from his mind. Tomorrow would be soon enough to think of it. If he wanted Isabella—and he still did—he would have to live with this forever. He would have to find a way.

He got up when the dawn began to lighten the sky and the room grew imperceptibly brighter. He had not slept much. He felt exhausted. He knew that Isabella would wake and remember. She would want to talk and just at the moment he could not talk to her because in some obscure way he still resented the fact that she had taken a lover. Feeling wretched and a traitor, he slid from the warm cocoon of the bed.

The morning was bright and tempting and the blue water beckoned to him from beyond the window. On the horizon a ship flicked white sails in the breeze. He dressed haphazardly and walked down to Kinvara Cove, keeping his mind empty of all but physical sensation. The summer sun was already hot on his face. The air smelled of salt and the soapy scent of gorse and the sandy path crunched beneath his feet. He could feel the earth warm against his soles. It was refreshing.

When he reached the water, he did not pause to remove more than his shoes, but plunged into the water, feeling it close over his head with a cold shock. He swam out beyond Kinvara Point where he hauled himself up onto the hot rocks and felt the sun beat down and the clothes dry salty sticky against his skin and thought that he ought to be the happiest man in the world. He was sharp set by now and walked back along the path from the point, up through the gardens and into the quiet house. He went to his chamber, changed into riding clothes and was humming softly as he descended the stairs and entered the breakfast parlor.

Inside the door he stopped dead.

Isabella was sitting at the table looking collected in a riding gown of dark blue. Her face was very pale, her hair ruthlessly braided and her expression closed. Marcus could tell in an instant that she had withdrawn from him in the same way that he felt distant from her. She must have woken, found him gone, and assumed that he had been unable to forgive her for the disclosures of the previous night. A helplessness possessed him. He knew he should try to bridge the gap between them before it grew any wider and all that they had managed to build up slipped away. Yet he could not. A part of him did not want to. He did feel angry and he did feel possessive and resentful and all those ugly emotions that he did not want to admit.

A moment later it was too late and she was asking about his morning swim in a tone of polite uninterest.

They ate in silence, to the embarrassment of the footman serving them, who fidgeted from foot to foot and gazed pointedly out of the window. Looking at his agonized expression, Marcus reflected how much of a servant's life must be spent in such awkwardness. If the conversation was inappropriate or there was an argument between master and mistress, that would be as embarrassing as witnessing a total lack of accord between them. And this was how the rest of their life threatened to be now. His mind recoiled from the thought of spending his married life in this sort of approximation of intimacy. That was what he had had with India. It had been completely shallow. And now he was creating it all over again.

"Would you care to go riding with me this morning?" The words surprised him almost as much as they seemed to surprise Isabella. He was not sure what had prompted them, beyond a desperate urge to put matters right before anything else went wrong between them.

Isabella looked up and the color came into her face. She looked shyly pleased. Marcus felt a brute. He knew that he was punishing her for his own lack of tolerance and he struggled to find a way around it.

He forced a smile. "We could ride up the path to Kinvara cliffs. You always enjoyed the view from there."

For all his effort, the words came out stilted. Isabella did not miss it. The happy expression in her eyes faded a little as she nodded.

"I would like that. I will meet you at the stables in twenty minutes."

And that was that. Marcus drained his coffee cup and reflected bitterly on how smoothly and superficially life could run without any kind of real conversation between the two of them. No doubt he would have plenty more time to observe that in future.

Down in the stables, they were at least able to mask the atmosphere of strain between them by making a fuss of the horses. They rode straight out of the yard, up the track to the downs and out onto the top of the cliffs. Once again there was silence between them as the horses picked their way slowly across the springy turf. Marcus knew that Isabella was waiting to see if he would either broach the subject of their conversation last night, or indicate that it was to be ignored forever. He felt angry. He felt exasperated, equally with himself as with her. Yet what could he say? *I resent the fact that you married Ernest Di Cassilis and even more do I resent the fact that you slept with Heinrich Von Trier and I am even furious at the thought of you flirting with all those other men who use your name with such abandon.* His lips tightened. It should not be like this.

Isabella's face beneath the riding hat was serious and she did not look at him. The strain between them intensified until Marcus felt it snap into a mixture of frustration and rage that had to have some outlet.

"I will race you to the chapel," he said.

Her head came up, her eyes suddenly bright. She saw the angry challenge in his eyes and understood without need of words exactly what he was thinking. Without a word she dug her heels into Aster's flanks and gave the horse her head, and Marcus was left watching her flying figure galloping away.

Marcus turned Achilles to follow, urging every ounce of anger and bitterness and mistrust from his body as they thundered across the heather and turf. For a long, breathless time, there was nothing but the thud of the horses' hooves on the grass, the rush of fresh air in his face, a strange exhilaration in his heart and the blur of color that was Isabella still outrunning him.

She was only a few yards ahead of him now and the stone wall that encircled the chapel and marked the end of the race was rushing toward them. Isabella reined Aster in so hard that the horse almost reared. She came to a grinding halt a few feet from the walls of the graveyard with Marcus slowing down beside her.

"You won," he said. "I thought I would catch you—" He broke off.

Isabella was not looking at him. It seemed she had not even heard him. She was staring over the wall of the graveyard where a small procession of people straggled toward the door of the squat chapel, carrying a tiny wooden coffin. Isabella made a slight sound and pressed her hands to her mouth. She grabbed Aster's reins fiercely, turned the horse, and was away into the trees on the edge of the ridge before Marcus could even move.

Marcus stared as the door of the church closed behind the cortege. A child's funeral.

He knew nothing of children. He had wanted a family with India in the conventional sense of securing the inheritance, but his feelings had gone no deeper than that. He had no concept of loving a child and losing it and the destruction that that could wreak in a life. But he had imagination.

He thought about how Isabella might feel on seeing such a thing and it felt as though his stomach had dropped and the bottom had fallen out of his world. He kicked Achilles to a gallop. He had no idea where Isabella had gone or even if she would stop, but he had to find her.

In the end it was not difficult. He found her in a sodden heap within the ruins of the old beacon tower on the edge of the cliff. Aster was peaceably cropping the grass outside. Isabella had not tried to hide. She had simply taken refuge. Marcus had wanted to ask her how she felt but when he saw her face, he realized that there was no need to speak. Silently he gathered her into his arms and held her until the sobs that racked her had ceased and she rested her head against his shoulder. She had turned her face into his chest without thought or hesitation and it humbled him that in her grief she would entrust herself to him without question. He smoothed the hair away from her hot cheeks with gentle fingers, feeling her tears wet against his skin.

"The child," she said brokenly, and he gathered her closer, as if holding her so tightly could banish the pain inside her.

"I am sorry," he said. "I wish I could understand."

She shook her head and burrowed closer to him. "I do not

want to lose you, Marcus," she said. "I have lost so much and been so hurt. I could not bear for it to happen again."

Marcus pressed his lips to her hair. "It will not," he said.

And silently he felt the anger and the grief and the jealousy inside him melt as he realized that she was his now in all the ways that mattered—and that she always had been.

CHAPTER NINETEEN

IT WAS FORTUNATE THAT ASTER knew the way back down to the stables since Isabella refused to let Marcus lead her down the cliff path but she was equally incapable of doing more than sit on the horse like a sack of potatoes. She knew now why she never normally cried. She felt dreadful—her nose was at least two sizes larger and felt like a beacon; her cheeks radiated heat and she was certain that she looked at least as bad on the outside as she felt on the inside. It was fortunate that Marcus had not tried to kiss her, but for one tender touch of his lips to her forehead. Poor man, no doubt he would not want to do more anyway. Anyone who envisaged that a passionate physical reconciliation would follow so emotional a moment was fair and far out.

Her poor opinion of her appearance was reinforced when they entered the hall at Salterton to find Pen and Alistair already there. Pen, with her customary openness and staggering lack of tact, took one look at Isabella's face and exclaimed, "Bella, you look dreadful! What on earth can have happened?"

"Perhaps you could show me the library, Miss Standish," Alistair intervened, catching Marcus's eye. "I understand that your aunt had a remarkable collection of the work of the late seventeenth-century poets?"

"Oh, she did," Pen said, "but they are dreadful. I can never read more than a couple of cantos." She looked back over her shoulder at Isabella as Alistair steered her toward the library door.

"Are you sure that you will be all right, Bella? I hope it is not Marcus who has upset you so. He would be a brute to do that."

Isabella heard Marcus sigh, more with resignation than anything else.

"I am perfectly well, Pen," she said. "Something upset me, that is all. It has nothing to do with Marcus."

Pen gave her brother-in-law a suspicious look. "I hope not," she said darkly. "Yes, Mr. Cantrell, I am coming!" She gave in to Alistair's importuning gestures and preceded him through the library door.

"Poor Alistair," Marcus remarked. "He detests late seventeenth-century poetry."

"That is something else that he and Pen have in common, then," Isabella said. She caught sight of her appearance in the pier glass and shuddered. There were sprigs of heather caught in her hair and bracken stuck to her riding outfit. Her nose was, as suspected, red and shiny, and her eyes were piggy and tiny.

"I think I shall go up and rest," she said faintly.

"A good idea," Marcus agreed. "I will escort you."

"There is no need," Isabella said. "I can manage very well on my own."

Marcus looked at her and smiled slightly. She could have slapped him because she knew he was laughing at her appearance, but that gleam of intimate amusement in his eyes made her feel happier than she had imagined she ever could be. Something had happened between them, wordless but all the more powerful for that. It had washed away the bitterness and anger and misery of the previous night and left them able to start afresh.

"And to think," Marcus said conversationally, his eyes meeting hers in the mirror, "that I believed you could never appear ugly!"

"Marcus!"

The indignant word had barely left her lips when Marcus

swooped on her and kissed her insistently, not stopping until he had drawn a response from her. Isabella clutched the banister for support, breathing hard.

"Oh! You—"

He kissed her again, rough but tender, parting her lips to the relentless demand of his tongue. Isabella felt her legs weaken. She let go of the banister and held on to Marcus instead.

There was a clatter behind them and they pulled apart to see one of the housemaids, her cleaning irons tumbled on the floor, staring at them with excitement and mortification.

"There is no privacy in this house," Marcus grumbled. He kissed her cheek. "I think you should rest, sweetheart. Will you be quite well? There is something that I must do, but I shall be up to see you shortly."

Isabella squeezed his hand briefly. She realized that she did feel exhausted but very light of heart. Marcus kissed her lips again briefly, and she made her way slowly upstairs, falling asleep as soon as she had laid her head on the pillow.

She woke when the door opened to admit her sister, carrying a tray of tea and biscuits.

"Marcus said that you would probably require some refreshment," Pen said cheerfully. "I only just managed to stop him ordering you soup and a thin gruel."

Isabella laughed. She sat up, pushing the tangled hair back from her face, peered at her face in the mirror above the basin and then decided not to bother.

"Oh dear, I suppose I look a fright."

"You do rather," Pen agreed blithely, "although you have more color than before. What happened, Bella? Marcus said I was not to tease you with questions, but I need to know you are all right."

"I am quite well now," Isabella said.

"But you looked as though you had been crying!" Pen looked quite distressed herself. "You never cry, Bella!"

"Not normally," Isabella agreed, "but this was rather exceptional. We saw the funeral of a child whilst we were out riding."

"Oh, Bella!" Pen's face puckered. She grabbed her sister's hand.

"I am quite well," Isabella repeated, afraid that Pen was about to cry in sympathy. "It was a long time ago."

Pen looked distressed. "I know, but I have sometimes wondered…., They say you never wished for more children, Bella."

"No." Isabella rubbed her eyes. "It is true that I do not want children. The risk, the danger of losing everything again is too great." She turned away and studied the pattern on the bed hangings with fierce concentration to keep the tears at bay. What she said was true, and yet the real conflict for her arose from the fact that a part of her did want Marcus's child and she could not understand why. She felt torn.

"I fear I am making a shocking mull of things at the moment, Pen," she said despondently. "I swore I would never marry again, least of all for love, yet I find myself falling more in love with Marcus every day. I know he wants children of his own—" she gulped "—but the idea fills me with abject fear." She clutched Pen's hands tighter. "I knew it was a mistake not to insist on an annulment or a legal separation in the beginning."

"Too late now," Pen said. "You and Marcus are meant to be together, Bella. Have faith." She sighed and sat back a little. "When you arrived back looking so upset I was afraid that it had something to do with India," she confessed, adding with unwonted fierceness, "I know that Salterton was her home but the way this house is stuffed full of her belongings seems a little unhealthy to me!"

Isabella felt a little shocked. It was true that she had noticed the very same thing herself but in the week that she had been in Salterton she had had no thought of changing things. She knew that she did not wish to broach the subject with Marcus.

It would be like putting weight on a broken ankle and deliberately inducing pain. And now, when finally matters were beginning to improve between them, raising the ghost of India was the last thing she wanted to do.

"I would go through this house removing all the pictures of her and those silly little figurines that she collected," Pen was continuing. "Do you know, Bella, that Marcus never cleared her bedchamber after she died? Everything was left exactly as it had been during her life. Mrs. Lawton told me. It was only when there was the fire at Salterton Cottage that Marcus had all India's effects packed away in trunks and stored in the attic here."

"Pen," Isabella said reprovingly. "You have been gossiping."

"Well." Pen looked mulish. "It is like being haunted."

"I feel a little like that myself," Isabella admitted. "It is as though India is always present." She sighed. "But I cannot supplant her. She was Marcus's first wife, after all."

Pen stared. "If you think that Marcus had half an ounce of feeling for India compared with the way he feels about you, Bella, then you are fair and far out! Why, he never cared tuppence for her!"

"Then why keep all her possessions?" Isabella asked. "Why leave her room untouched? Why fill this house with things that must remind him of her? That argues an uncommon devotion. Besides—" her shoulders slumped "—I have spoken to Marcus of India. I know just how much he cared for her."

Pen looked cross. "Well, I did not like her much. She was sly."

"Pen!"

Pen flushed. She poured the tea, then sat down on the edge of the bed, cup in hand.

"I suppose I did not know her well, being younger than the two of you. I expect that you remember her better than I."

"I do not recall her very well," Isabella said. "All I remember is a thin slip of a girl with a pale face and huge blue eyes. We never spoke intimately. She was always quiet."

Pen was frowning. She picked up a second biscuit, completely forgetting to offer them to her sister, and bit into it absentmindedly.

"It is odd that you remember her as thin, Bella, for I have quite a different recollection of India. The second to last time we were all here for the summer—not the time before you—" Pen hesitated "—before you married Ernest, but the year before that—I remember that India was considerably fatter. The two of you must have been about sixteen then and there was nothing of the thin slip about her at all."

Isabella nodded. "Oh yes, I remember. Girlhood plumpness."

"She was thin again when we came back to Salterton without you the following year," Pen said, reaching for the biscuit plate again. "Did not Aunt Jane take her away somewhere in the intervening time? Her health was supposed to be poor, I recall, yet she came back even more thin and sad and quiet, so it cannot have done her any good."

"Was she not always rather withdrawn, though?" Isabella said.

"Oh yes, but in a different way," Pen said. "When we came down here in oh-four she was excited quiet, as though she was hugging a secret. The following year she was sad and quiet. I wondered what had happened to her."

"You were a most observant child," Isabella said. "I noticed nothing different about her."

To her surprise, Pen blushed. "I did tend to watch people," she muttered. "I knew that India had a beau that first year."

Isabella looked up sharply, remembering Martha Otter's words about India's suitor being turned away.

"Did you meet him?"

"No, I…" Pen looked awkward. "I know she used to meet him in secret, though. I saw them once in the gardens together."

For a moment, Isabella wondered whether Pen had been confused and it was in fact her trysts with Marcus that her young sister had unwittingly spied upon. Then Pen said, "He was a soldier, I think. Very goodlooking, with an arrogant smile, laughing, confident, a swagger in his step." For once, Pen sounded quite dreamy. "I wonder what happened to him."

"His suit was rejected by Uncle John," Isabella said. She dredged up a memory that had seemed quite insignificant at the time. "I remember him now. He came to the Assembly Rooms one night in my final season here, and tried to approach India. Uncle John called him a blackguard and had him ejected. It was most embarrassing."

She frowned, trying to remember more of the incident. She had not regarded it much at the time, for she had been dancing with Marcus and had been quite lost in the delicious and forbidden sensations created by his physical proximity. There had been a commotion at the other end of the ballroom, over by the door. Lord John Southern had been shouting—a remarkable departure from good manners—and the object of his ire had been a young army officer who was struggling against the restraining grip of the master of ceremonies and looking desperately through the horrified guests for a glimpse of India.

"How strange," she said slowly. "I had forgotten all about it."

"What happened?" Pen asked curiously.

"Not a great deal," Isabella said. "India burst into tears, of course, and had to come home, and the rest of us carried on as though nothing had happened."

"And the young man?" Pen asked.

"I never saw him again," Isabella said. She paused, for something was troubling her. Had she seen India's suitor again?

Something recently had struck a chord of memory… The recollection did not come back to her but the elusive thought stayed at the back of her mind and did not quite go away.

HAVING NEVER INDULGED in the amorous activities that her late husband had favored, Isabella had been completely unaware of how awkward a house party could be for romantic dalliance, at least for the host and hostess. She was aching for Marcus in a way that was both unashamed and unappeased. Every time they managed to steal a kiss or planned to be alone together, Freddie or Alistair or Pen would appear from the library or the drawing room or their bed chamber and engage them in conversation, as though completely unaware of the blistering atmosphere between their hosts, who wanted nothing more than to be permitted to enjoy their honeymoon alone. None of their houseguests had responded to Isabella's heavy hints about when they might be thinking of returning to Town, and it seemed that there was no time when she and Marcus could snatch some time to talk, let alone make love.

"Remind me never to invite any more guests whatsoever to Salterton," Isabella said to Marcus when they met in brief solitude at breakfast. "Pen and Alistair fell out yesterday and are at daggers drawn, while Freddie appears to be compiling an intimate knowledge of the Salterton alehouses, and you and I…" She paused.

"Never have any time alone," Marcus finished. He put out a hand and touched her wrist lightly. "Isabella, if we *could* gain a little time alone—"

"Yes?" Isabella looked up nervously into his dark eyes. She could see the same thwarted desire there as she felt inside. She moistened her lips. "If we could be alone?"

"I thought we could—" Marcus broke off as the door to the breakfast room opened to admit Freddie Standish, followed by a footman with a tray of eggs, toast and coffee. Isabella could have wept at the interruption.

"Good morning, Freddie," she snapped. "Do you have any plans for the day?"

Freddie looked at her out of the corner of his eye. His expression was that of a dog that knows it is out of favor without really understanding why.

"Morning, Bella," he said. "Thought I might go to the harbor for some fresh air."

"Again!" Isabella marveled. "The view from the alehouse is very fine, is it not?"

Freddie flushed and slunk into his seat. The door opened again. Pen came in, followed by Alistair. Neither of them were looking at one another or speaking to one another. Isabella sighed irritably as they took seats as far away from one another as possible.

"Good morning," she said. "You are both as cheerful as a wet Sunday."

Marcus got up very deliberately and brought her the teapot, ignoring the footman who stepped forward to help.

"I want you to come riding with me after breakfast," he whispered in her ear. "I have had enough of this. We are going down to Kinvara Cove alone and I am going to seduce you."

Isabella swallowed her toast the wrong way and almost choked. Through streaming eyes she could see Marcus sitting back down at his end of the table, looking extremely pleased with himself. She shifted in her chair.

"Are you quite well this morning, my dear?" Marcus asked innocently. "You look a little flushed."

"It is very hot in here," Isabella said, fanning herself ostentatiously. "Perhaps you could open a window."

It was a tactical error and she realized it almost at once. Once again the footman stepped forward to help, but Marcus sprang up before him. The window was at her end of the dining table and on his way back Marcus bent and spoke in her ear again.

"I will strip you naked and take you into the water with me."

Isabella jumped in her chair and spilled her tea. She felt so hot she thought she was going to explode. There was an ache in her stomach and a patter of excitement in her throat and she could not look at Marcus for fear that a fresh wave of sensual heat would burst in her chest.

"More toast, my love?" Marcus inquired, as he seated himself again.

"No, thank you," Isabella managed to say. "I think you have already done quite enough for me, my dear."

Marcus smiled. "I have barely started, my sweet."

Pen was looking curious. Alistair cleared his throat and reached for the morning paper. Isabella fixed her eyes on her plate and tried to ignore both Marcus and the sharp desire that possessed her body.

"Backley," Marcus said to the footman, "please take this note to Lady Stockhaven."

He had torn a piece from the top of the newspaper, scribbled on it and now folded it and placed it on the footman's silver tray. The servant trod ponderously around the table and proffered the tray to Isabella. She shot Marcus a look of profound suspicion.

"Take it, my love," Marcus encouraged.

Isabella took the folded piece of paper and put it in her pocket. Marcus looked disappointed.

"What do you plan to do today, Bella?" Pen asked brightly. "I thought that we could go to the circulating library."

"I have a far more exciting day planned for your sister," Marcus said, before Isabella could speak. "We are to ride about the estate together."

"Splendid idea!" Alistair said. "Mind if I come with you?"

"Yes, I do mind," Marcus said. "You do not care to ride, remember?"

Alistair looked from Marcus to Isabella. "Of course," he murmured. "I had forgotten that I did not enjoy riding."

"Well, I consider it most thoughtless of you to neglect your guests," Pen grumbled. "After all, you did invite us here."

"I do not recall that we did," Isabella said. She threw down her napkin. "Excuse me."

She looked at Marcus, who gave her a wicked smile. She met it with a challenge in her eyes. "I shall be ready directly," she said.

"I look forward to it," Marcus murmured.

Out in the hall, Isabella could not resist grabbing the note from her pocket and reading it. She unfolded it with shaking fingers.

We shall lie naked on the rocks in the sun.

Isabella gulped and almost dropped the piece of paper. The housemaid who was polishing the stairs looked at her with curious eyes. The dining-room door opened and Marcus came out. His gaze went from Isabella's flushed face to the note in her hand and he raised his brows.

"Not another word, Marcus," Isabella said softly, "or I shall make you suffer for it. I am already feeling far more excited than is appropriate for breakfast time."

She saw his eyes widen as he took her meaning and then the sensual smile curved his lips again and she sped away up the stairs with a light step to prepare for her seduction.

CHAPTER TWENTY

IN THE EVENT, IT WAS NOT at all as Isabella had imagined. By the time that they reached the seclusion of Kinvara Cove and settled the horses in the old stone shelter on the foreshore, they had been obliged to stop more than five times to speak with tenants and acquaintances. All thoughts of torrid seduction had fled from Isabella's mind to be replaced by the problems of low milk yields, poor grazing and broken fences.

"I had no notion that Salterton estate was in such a poor way," she said a little despondently, taking Marcus's hand to climb over the rocks that cradled the bay.

"It will take a deal of work to put it all to rights."

And a deal of money. She did not say it but she thought it and looked sideways at Marcus to see if he was thinking of it too. She knew that she had no right to ask him to invest in Salterton when he had his own estates to consider, but she hoped that he would do his best for the place. Perhaps he planned to put a tenant in. Her heart sank a little at the prospect. She loved Salterton and wanted to settle here, but she knew that Marcus would not necessarily feel the same way. They needed to discuss the matter.

Marcus picked up the saddlebag and jumped down onto the beach.

"I have been working this week past on the estate records," he said, "and making the rounds to see the tenants. I have been meaning to speak of it to you. Perhaps later…" He smiled at her. "For now we could merely enjoy the day."

Isabella nodded. The sky was an arc of blue above her head and she could feel the sand hot beneath her feet. The light was dazzling. She put up a hand to shade her eyes.

"We came here once that last summer at Salterton," Marcus said. "Do you remember, Bella?"

Isabella wondered how he could imagine that she would forget. Generally she and Marcus had not been much in company together, for Lady Standish had done all she could to frighten ineligible suitors away from her daughter. On that occasion, however, one of Marcus's navy colleagues had put together a boating party and because there was a young marquis among their number, Lady Standish had been pleased to agree. Both India and Isabella had attended. The party had been lively and fun, although India had sat a little apart, staring at the sea and had not allowed herself to be drawn much into conversation. Isabella remembered that it had been a hot day like this one. But perhaps the heat and excitement then had come from within her, for she had known that not by a flicker of a glance, or a word, or a gesture could she reveal her intimacy with Marcus. They had stayed apart, while watching each other the whole time. She had been supremely conscious of him and of the fact that he was aware of her, too, and she had known that later he would come to her in the darkened summerhouse and then all their pent-up passion and longing would explode between them.

Now it felt quite different. For all her advanced age and her increased experience, she felt shy, and a little awkward. To cover her nervousness she reached for the saddlebag, took the stone bottle of apple cordial from inside, unstoppered it and tilted it to her lips. Her hand was shaking slightly. She spilled some of the liquid and it ran down over her chin.

Marcus was watching her, a smile in his eyes. His hand closed over hers, taking the bottle from her and setting it down as she wiped her sleeve along her chin a little self-consciously.

"There is no need to be afraid, Bella," he said. "We need do nothing you do not want."

Isabella fixed her gaze on the stone bottle resting in the sand. She was very conscious of the warmth and strength of Marcus's hand on hers.

"It is not so much what I do or do not want, Marcus," she said, "but more that with all that has happened between us, I find I am rather anxious."

Marcus raised his hand to tilt her chin up. "I understand." He smiled wryly. "Such a complicated build-up that one wonders if we can possibly live up to the promise."

Isabella leaned into the curve of his shoulder. It felt wonderfully reassuring and safe. "Precisely," she said. She rested her head against him. "I like this, Marcus. This is how it should be."

"Yes." Marcus bent his head and pressed a soft kiss against her jaw. For a moment, Isabella was afraid that he might push too hard for what he wanted, but when his lips found hers, their touch was infinitely gentle and tender and she relaxed into the kiss.

"You taste of apples and sea air," Marcus murmured. The tip of his tongue touched hers, sliding along the inside of her lower lip, making her senses leap. She turned more fully toward him, wanting the kiss to deepen, but he was withdrawing from her and she almost groaned with frustration.

"Let's swim," he said. "It is such a beautiful day."

He stood up. He had already removed his jacket and loosened his cravat. Isabella averted her gaze as he started to pull his shirt over his head. The sun struck shafts of heat through her straw bonnet and made her cheeks feel hotter than ever.

"Bella?" Marcus sounded quizzical. "Is there a particular reason as to why you are staring so intently at that boulder that you are like to get a crick in your neck?"

Isabella looked at him. It was a mistake. She had not seen

him half-naked in the daylight for a long time, if not ever. The muscled shoulders, the broad expanse of chest, the flat abdomen... He was beautiful. She gulped, feeling hotter still, as though the sun was shining for her alone.

"I am affording you the privacy you require to change for bathing," she said.

Marcus sat down on a rock and pulled off his boots. "There is no need for that. We are married, after all. Are you not to join me?"

"I do not know," Isabella said rapidly, "this is a little... difficult."

Marcus laughed. The sunlight glistened on his skin, turning it a delicious, smooth golden color. Isabella's fingers itched to touch him. She wanted to slide her hands over his chest and feel his warmth, to explore the contrast of hard muscle and satiny skin, to feel his heart beating under her hand. She wanted to taste him and smell the salty male scent of him. She was radiating so much heat now that her clothes felt sticky and damp and her face was as bright as a beacon. The sea looked remarkably tempting and cool.

Marcus's hands went to the fastening of his trousers. Isabella made a faint protesting squeak. Marcus looked at her.

"Too much sun, Bella?"

"Too much of you displaying yourself so blatantly!" Isabella said. "Marcus—"

But it was too late. With a fluid movement, Marcus stripped off his breeches and underclothes and stood before her in all his glorious masculinity.

He was outrageous, virile and unashamed.

Isabella was not accustomed to men stripping in front of her. She stared, torn between shock and fascination.

"You look like a horrified virgin," Marcus said cheerfully. "How interesting."

Isabella blushed to the roots of her hair. Her first husband had never stood before her in such unabashed nudity and Ernest's anatomy, bereft of clothing, had not been a pretty sight. If he had stripped before her, Isabella was sure that quite a few stomachs would have turned, rather than heads.

"I assure you that I have never known anyone who comported himself in such a manner," she added faintly.

Marcus grinned. "So what do you think?" he asked boyishly

Isabella reflected that were she to tell him what she really thought, she would probably be contravening several of the Salterton bylaws.

"I think you are quite shameless," she said.

Marcus laughed and stepped closer. Isabella tried to find somewhere innocuous to look and failed completely. She was quite relieved when Marcus drew her to her feet and she was on a level with his chest rather than any other parts of him.

"Remember what I told you at breakfast," he said softly. "I am going to strip you naked and take you into the water with me."

Isabella made a faint, protesting squeak but his fingers had already moved to the buttons of her riding jacket, slipping them from their fastenings. The smaller buttons of her shirt gave him more trouble, but he did not hurry. Nor did he stop to kiss her. He worked intently and the look in his eyes was no less concentrated. Isabella found it extraordinarily arousing. She stood obediently still beneath his hands, held in a spell.

The jacket crumpled to the ground. The shirt followed it. The cool air raised goose pimples on Isabella's bare shoulders and arms. Her skin prickled for Marcus's touch. She wanted to beg him to hurry. She bit her lip hard.

There was a tug of material at her waist; something gave and the skirt slid down to pool at her feet. Suddenly impatient, she stepped out of it, kicked her boots off and practically tore off her remaining clothes. The old, wild spirit filled her and she threw Marcus one provocative glance over her shoulder before running into the sea.

The cold shock of the water made her squeal aloud. A flock of seabirds rose from the rocks and soared on the breeze, their cries echoing hers.

There was a splash as Marcus surfaced beside her, the water running from his shoulders in sun-streaked rivulets. He grabbed her about the waist with both hands and fitted her against him, hard wet muscle against her softer contours. She gasped again at the contact of their bodies and then his mouth was on hers with scorching hunger. She felt the shudder that shook him as their bodies pressed closer, demanding satisfaction. Then his hand sought her breast and she jumped in dazed surprise at the intimacy of the caress and opened her eyes.

There were tiny drops of water on Marcus's eyelashes and the skin of his face and shoulders was smooth and bronzed in the sun. Isabella ran her hands over him with something approaching awe and saw the surge of pure lust in his darkened eyes. With a groan he drew her back to him again, kissing her with an almost desperate longing. She writhed and twisted in his arms, the lap of the water about them and the friction of their bare bodies almost too much to bear, and then, when she thought he would take her there and then in the water, she broke away.

"I told you I would make you suffer," she said, and dived away from him through the aquamarine water, kicking out for the rocks and hauling herself up onto their hot surface. When she turned to look back, what she saw made her laugh aloud. Marcus was shaking his head and looking thoroughly dazed and the look he shot her was more than half-unfriendly.

"Minx!" He was pulling himself out onto the rocks beside her, reaching for her. Isabella rolled out of his grasp. The sun was hot and the air soft and it felt wonderful on her naked skin and she did not want to be caught. Not quite yet.

She scrambled to her feet. Marcus's hand snaked out and caught her ankle. He cushioned her fall with his body, then rolled her beneath him, pinning her down. His mouth swooped down, imprisoning hers. Isabella wriggled. He released one wrist but only to capture her breast and raw pleasure surged through her as he lowered his head to her nipple. The fire scorched through her body but she twisted away.

"Not here."

"Where, then?" Marcus's voice was harsh.

She stared into his eyes. "The summerhouse."

His bronzed hand still rested against the whiteness of her skin and the sight of it made her heart beat frantically. He withdrew slowly.

"We had better run then," he said.

Isabella did. She ran back down to the beach where she donned her skirt and jacket haphazardly, pushing her wet hair back from her face. It was only a short distance along the cliff path to the gardens, but if they met anyone it would appear that they had run mad. Isabella was almost certain that they had.

Marcus grabbed her hand. He had put on his breeches and it was impossible to ignore the absolutely enormous bulge in them. Isabella stared, her mind racing. He tugged on her hand.

"That is your doing and now we have to do something about it," he said. "Come on."

Like the young lovers they had once been, they ran along the sandy path from the cove to the gate that led into Salterton Hall Gardens. A spine of gorse stabbed Isabella's bare foot and when she gasped at the pain Marcus scooped her up in his arms, bundling her through the gate and up the steps to the summerhouse. The door resisted, creaking on its hinges. Inside, the air was dim, scented with dust and roses. Marcus placed her back on her feet and for a moment they stood looking at one another in the half light.

They both moved at once, colliding, drawn tight into each

other's arms. The atmosphere between them had changed now, slowed down, cooled almost into tenderness. Almost, but not quite. This time when they kissed it was with remembrance as well as passion. The poignancy made Isabella's eyes sting with tears.

"So much haste," Marcus whispered. "The buttons of your jacket are done up in the wrong holes." He was smiling at her and she raised her hand to unfasten them. The skirt followed. She was naked once more and to cover the slight return of self-consciousness, she stepped close to him, running her fingertips over his broad muscled chest and down across his abdomen to the top of his breeches. His skin was like slightly rough satin and when she bent her lips to kiss his chest she could taste the salt on his skin. She heard him draw his breath in sharply and then he had scooped her up again and laid her on the ancient chaise longue that had been pushed into a corner, covered and abandoned. He pulled the sheet off and Isabella lay back, remembering the way that the yielding cushions had embraced her body before. That had been so long ago. The laughter bubbled up inside her.

"Marcus, there are probably spiders' nests…"

"There can be mice for all I care." He had joined her on the bed and was entangling his hands in her hair, tilting her face to his. "We shall not notice them."

All consciousness of spiders, mice and anything else fled beneath the sensation of his lips and his hands. Isabella stretched out beneath him, arching in helpless surrender to the fingers that slid over her, stroking with such skillful reverence. He caressed her breasts, cupping their fullness with possessive pleasure, before lowering his mouth to tease her nipples and graze them gently with his tongue and teeth. Isabella entwined her legs with his and drew him close, smoothing her hands over his back and down over the curve of his buttocks.

She felt his body jolt and opened her eyes. In the shadows

of the summerhouse, his face was hard and dark with desire. It blazed in his eyes. Yet there was tenderness there as well and it made her heart ache.

With infinite gentleness he stroked over the curve of her hip and slid his hand between her legs. Old anxieties mixed with Isabella's desire and for a brief second she stiffened. Marcus felt it.

"Sweetheart…" He kissed her, his mouth soft against her own.

Her fears subsided, her body relaxed a little. Marcus stroked the inside of her thigh and, gradually, beneath the soothing of his caresses, Isabella felt her stiff muscles start to uncoil. Marcus's other hand slid to her bare shoulder and brushed the hair from the damp skin of her neck. Isabella moved slightly.

"Mmmn. I am sorry, Marcus."

"There is nothing to apologize for." Marcus's hand stole down over her breast and her eyes opened wide. "Slow is good."

It was. Marcus's voice was as gentle as his fingers, smooth, languorous. His hand swept across her stomach and Isabella shivered beneath his touch. He kissed the curve of her shoulder and she trembled, catching her breath. He moved the damp hair aside and stroked his tongue delicately down the line of her neck.

"You are mine," he murmured against her skin. "You were from the beginning. Nothing else matters."

He rolled over, trapping her beneath him again, and her body moved against his with instinctive need.

"Remember what it was like for us," he said in her ear, his breath sending the shivers coursing along her nerves. "Remember…"

She did remember. She remembered the heat and the urgency and the raw need and the love and the explosive passion. Her body softened. Marcus was kissing the sprinkling of freckles at the base of her throat now. His hair brushed her breast. She could feel the hard press of his arousal against her thigh and moved slightly in accommodation. He shook his head.

"No. Not yet. Remember. It was exciting for us, Isabella. Unbearably, intolerably exciting."

Isabella made a soft sound of surrender. She was quivering, melting beneath him with wild need. She felt his hand steal to part her legs again and this time she had no reluctance and opened to him with eagerness as his hand toyed amidst the springy hair, increasingly intimate, increasingly pleasurable.

"Sweetheart…"

Marcus was above her, parting her wide, sliding between her thighs, entering her with one hard, pulsing thrust. His face was hard in the shadowy light, concentrated, desire distilled.

"Oh!" Isabella arched, felt herself impaled. The heat pooled low within her. She grabbed his shoulders, scoring the muscle.

He rocked deeper inside her, moving faster now. Isabella's head spun as the pleasure built. The wild, sharp sensation burst through her, making her cry out and twist beneath him. Her whole body lit with an exquisite, aching sweetness. She knew that Marcus had deliberately put her pleasure first this time, as though in recompense for what had happened in London. She felt awed and moved and grateful. She lay still, catching her breath, reaching out to him.

"Thank you," she whispered. "But you…"

"Yes?" He kissed her lightly. He was caressing her stomach again with that deceptively gentle and soothing touch that nevertheless stirred something primitive in her. Isabella shifted, feeling astonishment and a renewed surge of desire. Then he was inside her again, slippery and warm. He thrust harder and faster until she could smell the mingled salt and sweat on him and see the glistening of it slick on his skin. He took her mouth, the plunge and retreat of his tongue echoing his movements inside her. His body jerked convulsively as he exploded into her and Isabella's mind splintered into a thousand dazzling pieces as she felt the spasms rack her again, felt the frantic beating of his heart against hers, and the tightness of his arms about her. They lay clasped close, with no sound but the raggedness of their breath.

Isabella had no concept of how long it was before Marcus shifted slightly. His breath stirred her hair.

"I have wanted you for a very long time, Isabella."

She moved within the circle of his arms so that she could look at him. His eyes were dark and grave and but a half smile was curving his lips.

"I thought," she said, teasing a little, "that you took what you wanted in London?"

His expression stilled and sobered. "No," he said. "I took something. At the time I thought it was all I wanted but it was worthless compared to what I have now." He kissed her possessively. "And now I want it all over again."

"Marcus!"

"I know. I am an old man these days but you push me to a degree I did not realize I could achieve. Allow me to prove the point." His mouth claimed hers. His hands were on her body. He slid down and touched his tongue to the aching central core of her and Isabella sighed and capitulated with pure enjoyment as he took her again.

CHAPTER TWENTY-ONE

"OF COURSE I ALWAYS CONSIDERED the Southerns to be a rather *unfortunate* family," Mrs. Goring said comfortably, reaching for the teapot. She and Isabella were sitting in the glass-fronted coffee parlor at the circulating library, which afforded a splendid view across the esplanade to the sea. They had been there for two hours and so far Mrs. Goring had summarized events in Salterton during the twelve years of Isabella's absence and was moving on to general reflections on the inhabitants of the town. Isabella was happy to sit and listen, to watch the sea and to observe the visitors going about their business. One learned a lot from watching, as Pen had mentioned only the other day. For instance, she had seen the Misses Belling hanging from an upstairs window across the street in a most unsubtle attempt to attract Mr. Casson's interest; she had observed Mr. Owen limping along the quayside toward the inn—evidently taking efficacious waters of quite a different sort—and she had just seen Pen and Alistair walk by arm in arm, toward the jetty. It appeared that they had settled their differences.

"Poor Lord John being the younger son, you know," Mrs. Goring continued, "and then they had no money, and little Miss India dying so young. And then there was the difficulty of the child, of course…" She let her voice trail away discreetly. "No one thought any the less of Lord John, of course. Such things happen, even to the nobility. Especially to the nobility, if one believes the accounts in the newspapers. But even so, it was rather a shock when one knew him."

Isabella tore her gaze away from the esplanade and looked at her hostess in consternation. "I beg your pardon, ma'am? What child?"

Mrs. Goring looked flustered. "Oh dear, you look rather shocked, my love. I thought that you *knew*." She busied herself with the teapot, giving its contents a rather unnecessary stir. "Of course, you were quite young then—merely seventeen, if I have the dates correct, but even so, young girls are nowhere near as naive as people imagine them. And then word did get around, as these things do."

Isabella raised her hand. "Mrs. Goring, are you implying that my uncle had an illegitimate child?"

Mrs. Goring shuddered delicately at such frankness. "Well yes, my dear, I suppose I am. Everyone knew of it. Except you, evidently. It was the outcome of a dalliance with one of the maids, so I'm told. I am not precisely sure which one." Her brow wrinkled with disappointment as she realized she could not supply this detail of the tale.

"The child—it was a boy..." She paused. "Or was it a girl? No, I am sure it was a boy.... He was given to the gardener and his wife to bring up. They moved to London shortly after and the matter was never spoken of. But of course, everyone knew.... And Lord John so frail at the time." Mrs. Goring shook her head. "You would not have thought he had it in him! Still, one never knows with men. I suppose it took the last of his strength."

Isabella was silent, not with outrage, as her hostess might have supposed, but from sheer puzzlement. Lord John Southern had been devoted to his wife. There had never been the slightest hint of infidelity in all the years of their marriage, at least not as far as Isabella was aware. And then, as Mrs. Goring had intimated, Lord John had been a frail man in his last years and racked by recurrent illness. Such an image sat ill with the picture of a rampant old man chasing the housemaids.

"I had no idea," Isabella said slowly.

"No, well…" Mrs. Goring looked uncomfortable. "It was not a suitable matter for discussion with Lord John's niece, or his daughter for that matter. I am sure Miss India would have been very shocked had she known."

"What happened to the child?" Isabella asked.

Mrs. Goring looked surprised. "Well, do you know, I have no notion? He was never heard of again after the move to London. I imagine that Lord John provided for him, for he was a man who took his responsibilities seriously."

"Yes," Isabella said. "He was." She was thinking it odd that Mr. Churchward had told her of no encumbrance upon the Southern estate. There were no regular payments to anyone at all, beyond the annuities given to retired servants. Nor had Churchward hinted at any bar sinister in the family tree, which he would surely have told her when she'd inherited. She was no shrinking violet of a lady to be shocked by such worldly matters. Now that she thought about it, it seemed most odd. She wondered whether Marcus knew anything of the case and if so why he, too, had not mentioned it. It was as though this illegitimate son had disappeared as thoroughly as though he had never existed.

"More tea, my love?" Mrs. Goring urged. She waved the plate of Bath biscuits in Isabella's direction. "Do you see Miss Belling waving in that vulgar way at the gentleman? That hussy will stop at nothing to catch a husband…."

Isabella smiled automatically and Mrs. Goring prattled on, but Isabella was not really listening. She was thinking about Lord John Southern and his illegitimate son. And despite all evidence to the contrary, Isabella could not shake her persistent conviction that her uncle had never fathered such a child at all.

PENELOPE STANDISH WAS MOST dissatisfied.

For the last seven days, since she had arrived in Salterton in company with Mr. Alistair Cantrell, he had seemed at best preoccupied and at worst utterly uninterested in her. He had danced with her at the Salterton Assembly, but no more than with any other young lady; he had escorted her to the circulating library and on her walks along the promenade, yet he seemed more animated when discussing with Freddie his plans for the day or taking a drink with him at the harborside tavern. In fact—perish the thought—Pen had started to wonder whether it was actually *Freddie* who had always held Alistair's interest and he had only been paying court to her in London in order to get close to the true object of his affections.

So that morning when they stopped on the esplanade to take a look at the sea, Pen was unsurprised to notice that, rather than scanning the horizon, Alistair's opera glasses were focused on the corner of Quay Street, where Freddie's figure could be glimpsed hurrying into the Ship Inn. She sighed, both at the depressing sight of her brother hastening toward his first bottle of the day but also for her lost hopes, for she was obliged to admit that she had held high hopes of Mr. Cantrell. And thinking on this, and the fool she had made of herself, lit her temper, so that she burst out, "It seems to me, Mr. Cantrell, that it is my brother rather than the beauties of nature that occupy your sights!"

She saw Alistair Cantrell jump and he straightened up, the hand holding the opera glasses falling to his side. There was a flush of color on his cheeks and he looked slightly embarrassed. In fact he looked guilty. Pen's temper soared.

"For myself," she said coldly, "I have no opinion about a man who prefers his own sex over the charms of the female. However, I do feel very strongly about a man who *deceives* others in the pursuit of his own happiness."

Alistair looked extremely startled. Well he might, Pen

thought. They were standing in the middle of the esplanade and were attracting considerable attention.

"Miss Standish, I do assure you—"

"From the start you led me to believe that *I* was the object of your affections," Pen said. "I resent being used, Mr. Cantrell, as a means for you to get close to my brother, who—"

"Miss Standish—" Alistair said with increasing urgency.

"Who," Pen pressed on, ignoring his interruption, "has not the least interest in men, being given to low female company instead. It pains me to break this piece of news to you, but in order to spare you future pain, I must ask you to desist in your attentions to Freddie."

Alistair grabbed her by the arms, yanked her to him and kissed her violently. Her parasol clattered to the ground unheeded.

"I have not the least romantic interest in your brother, you little goose," Alistair said. He kissed her again before Pen could reply and she melted into an embrace that was only slightly less urgent than the last.

"From the very first moment I saw you," Alistair said breathlessly the next time he let her go, "I thought you the most beautiful and infernally sharp-tongued creature it had ever been my pleasure to meet."

Pen was so enchanted by this accolade that it was she who drew his mouth back down to hers this time.

"But I never thought that you would have the folly to imagine that I lusted after your brother," Alistair finished. He shook her very gently. "It is you that I have been wanting from the first," he said, smiling down into her dazed blue eyes. "That night at the Royal Institution I wanted to seduce you. The night in the inn at Alresford I wanted to ravish you. And right now I would like to—"

Pen grabbed him again before he articulated his fantasies

and, regardless of the scandalized glances of the passersby, they kissed and kissed again on the promenade of what had previously been a most respectable resort.

ISABELLA WAS INTENT on confronting her ghosts. She had been at her desk in the estate office all afternoon, for Marcus had that morning presented her with the deed of gift of Salterton and had, most gratifyingly, left her to get to know her new estate, saying only that he was there if she required his help. Yet no matter how Isabella tried to concentrate on milk yield and acreage, her thoughts returned with tiresome repetition to India Southern, her cousin and nemesis. In the end, she knew that she would have to act.

India was the final ghost of the past, the last thorn in her side. If Marcus was ever to be truly hers, Isabella would have to banish the shadow of her cousin and understand just what it was India had been to Marcus.

It was a long walk up four flights of stairs to reach the attics at Salterton House. Isabella knew that the housekeeper would have arranged for India's trunks to be brought down for her if she had asked, but she wanted no one to know what she was doing. Specifically, she had not wanted Marcus to know. Guilt and uncertainty nibbled at her. In truth she was not entirely sure *what* she was doing, other than that she had certain suspicions about India, and that she had to understand her cousin and what had driven her if she was ever able to lay her memory to rest.

As Isabella climbed higher, the stairs narrowed and, on the final flight, the thick red carpet was replaced by hard-wearing jute matting. It was hot up here. A fly buzzed at the windowpane and Isabella's footsteps echoed on the treads. The sounds of the rest of the house were muted. She could have been alone in the world.

Opening the door softly, she stepped into the dim interior

of the first attic. The room was shuttered, dark and hot, smelling of dust and neglect. A shiver traced down Isabella's spine. She found the chests that Mrs. Lawton had mentioned. There were two of them, piled on top of each other in one corner, the most distant from the window. She crossed the floor and pulled the first one out.

It was like opening a window onto the past.

The trunk was full of clothes. Walking dresses, day dresses, evening gowns, shawls and gloves, all in pastel colors, stacked upon one another in a pile of lavender-scented cloth and accessories. Isabella remembered that India had always favored pale colors and modest styles. It was very strange to see her entire wardrobe stored here. It looked faded and lifeless, like the ghost of India herself. At the bottom of the trunk was a pile of improving books.

The second case yielded all the other bits and pieces that told the story of India's life. There were tumbles of silk stockings, petticoats embroidered with lace, bodices and stays. There was a scattering of sheet music, a little yellowed about the edges. There was a soft bag containing filigree necklaces in delicate silver and gold. There was an artist's box with the dried paint flaking around the edges and a tambour frame for needlework. Isabella felt her throat close unexpectedly with tears. How sad to see the remains of India's life spread out before her like this, a little worn and smelling faintly of mothballs...

There was no diary. Isabella had been hoping for a diary, for she had known that India kept one. Her cousin had forever been scribbling secretively in it when they were children. But perhaps Marcus had destroyed it when India died. Or perhaps Lady Jane had done so. The Southerns had always been so concerned of what other people thought that no doubt they would not want India's diary falling into the wrong hands.

Isabella straightened up feeling vaguely disappointed. For all the evidence of India's life that was spread before her, there was not a single truly personal item to give a clue as to what had happened.

There was a click as something rolled out of the folds of a silk handkerchief and fell with a soft clatter onto the bare floorboards. Isabella bent to pick it up. It was a silver locket. She paused. It seemed prying to open it but she wanted to see the miniature inside. A watercolour of Lady Jane, perhaps, or Lord John… Or maybe even a picture of Marcus… Her heart jerked with a mixture of emotions at the thought but now she knew she had to look, even if it confirmed her worst fears of the unbreakable bond between Marcus and India, even if it broke her heart.

Her fingers shook slightly as she released the catch. The hinge was a little stiff but the locket opened reluctantly to spill its secret.

The picture was indeed that of a young man. Furthermore, it was a young man in the striking red uniform of His Majesty's Army. A young soldier with an arrogant smile, laughing, confident, a twinkle in his eye…he would have a swagger in his step and the panache of a man who knows he can take what he wants and snap his fingers in the face of the world…

With a shiver like the brush of a cobweb across her face, Isabella recalled another memory—a handsome young army lieutenant introducing himself to her and to India in the Assembly Rooms thirteen years before.

He had spoken to Isabella as the elder cousin, but his eyes had been on India the whole time. Isabella had been intrigued; it was not often that her quiet cousin eclipsed her. She had been a little piqued, too, which was only natural. But then the young man had bowed deeply to India and asked for her hand in the dance and Isabella had smiled ruefully to see them go off together with eyes for no one else in the room.

She had only met him the once. Until this moment, she had not even remembered that he was the same man who had come to the Assembly Rooms a year later and been thrown out for his trouble. He was the man whom Pen had said used to meet India secretly, the suitor her parents had apparently sent away.

Isabella sat down heavily on the edge of one of the trunks. The call of the seabirds came to her softly here, mingling with the breeze along the roof and the distant crash of breakers in the bay. The air felt hot and oppressive. A lock of hair, caught within the locket, drifted down on the air to scatter on the floorboards. Isabella bent automatically to gather it up again. The hair was fine and baby soft. It was flaxen: blonder than India, fairer than her own had been as a child before it had darkened in the way that children's hair often did with age. It was tied with a small blue ribbon.

Isabella placed the lock of hair carefully within the locket and snapped the catch shut. Her mind was full of images of India, mingled with Pen's words and those of Mrs. Goring. India fatter and happy, then thinner and sad…a mysterious trip to Scotland by her cousin and Lady Jane…a lock of hair, and a miniature…a rumor of Lord John's by-blow that she had thought from the beginning must be impossible… A handsome young lieutenant making a scene in the Assembly Rooms and Lord John having him ejected in a rage….

She gave a violent shiver in the warm air. The locket rested in the palm of her hand and her fingers closed tightly over it. She knew India's secret now.

ISABELLA WAS NOT SURE HOW LONG she sat in the dusty attic room, the locket enclosed in her palm. When she finally stood up, the silver links of the chain had scored her hand and she winced a little. She closed the trunks and made her way wearily downstairs. She knew that she had to speak to Marcus now, and she quailed to think of it.

She pushed open the door of the study. Marcus was sitting at the desk by the window. Bright morning sunlight spilled through the panes and polished the patina of the wood to a deep shine. Marcus was reading a book about engineering, his glasses poised on the end of his nose. He was quite still and so utterly engrossed that he did not appear to hear her entry.

For a moment, Isabella watched him. His brow was furrowed with concentration and the sun picked out the tiny strands of gray in his hair. Neither of us, Isabella thought, *are young anymore.* She felt such a powerful rush of love for him then that she must have made some involuntary movement, for he looked up. After a moment, he smiled and put the book down. Isabella's heart started to race.

"Good afternoon," he said. "What may I do for you, Isabella?"

"Marcus," Isabella said. She stopped. Suddenly the thought of broaching the subject of India seemed so remote and impossible that she almost turned tail and ran. How could she do this? Marcus would be angry with her for rifling through his late wife's effects. As for the suggestions—accusations—that she was about to make…well, he could only greet those with contempt. He would be bitterly hurt and his memories despoiled. She loved him too much to do that to him. And yet she was sure she held the key to the mystery of Edward Warwick in her hand and she had to tell him. She could not keep silent any longer.

"I wanted to talk to you," she said. "It is about India. Marcus, it is important."

His smile faded. She saw the withdrawal in his eyes. It was the same expression he always assumed at any reference to India. It set her at a distance. But this time she was determined to persist.

"Please, Marcus," she said. "I realize that this must be very difficult for you."

There was a flicker of something in his eyes. "Yes," he said slowly. "It is difficult but I have been meaning to speak of her to you for some time."

Isabella paused. "Oh?"

Marcus gestured her to a seat and she sank down onto the cushions. He took off his glasses and rubbed his eyes.

"There is something that I have to tell you, Bella."

The silence spun out like a spider's web between them. Isabella waited, her heart beating in her throat.

"I never loved India," Marcus said baldly. "God knows, I tried hard enough but I could not do it. I pretended that I loved her—I pretended it to myself and to everyone else, but I always knew that it was false. Even at the point of marriage, when we made our vows, I knew it for the mistake it was. I married the wrong cousin and I knew it from the start." He looked at Isabella's white face and a faint smile touched his lips. "You seem startled, Bella. Did you not suspect?"

Isabella found her voice. "I…I am astounded. I had not the least suspicion in the world. I thought you devoted to her in life and to her memory now."

Marcus grimaced. He leaned against the edge of the desk and crossed his arms.

"Why on earth did you think that?"

"Why?" Isabella paused. She had misread him badly and caused herself considerable pain as a result, but she had only been basing her judgment on his behavior. There had been evidence enough.

"Where do I begin?" she said. "You were so hot to defend her when we spoke in London. You accused me of ruining her relationship with her mother. You believed her word over mine. At every turn you showed that she still held your love and loyalty." She stared unseeing at the pattern on the Turkey rug feeling indignant as well as upset.

"When you told me about the fire and I found out that you had left India's chamber untouched since her death, what was I to think?" she burst out. "It was like a shrine to the memory of your dead wife! And I knew that I—" She stopped and swallowed hard.

"That you…what?"

"That I could never compete with her memory, that you would never love me as you had loved her, that your heart was not free to love again." Isabella stopped and stared at him. "Why did you not tell me the truth of your feelings for her?" she demanded. "Why did you keep all the pictures and mementos of India, and leave her chamber untouched, unless it was because it was too painful for you to do aught else?"

Marcus's gaze was somber. "It *was* too painful," he said. "But that was from guilt, not love."

Isabella stared at him. She was clenching her hands tightly on the arm of the chair.

"Guilt? About what?"

Marcus came across and sat in the other chair at right angles to her. They were close enough to touch, but both of them held themselves stiffly upright. The tension in the room was palpable, like the crackling of sheet lightning.

"I felt guilty that I could never love her," Marcus said simply after a moment. "I realized that I could not make her happy. She deserved better." He looked up abruptly and Isabella flinched at what she saw in his eyes. "I married the wrong cousin," he said again, "and I tried to make her into what I wanted. I tried to make her you. She lived in your shadow for all of our marriage. She knew it and I knew it, but we never spoke of it."

Isabella was shaking her head with bewilderment. "I thought that *I* was the one living with the incomparable."

Marcus smiled wryly. "I can understand that you might think that. The room, the portraits, all her collections…"

"And more than anything your fierce protectiveness of her memory!" Isabella made a slight gesture. "Was that guilt, too, Marcus? That you had not been able to give her what she wanted in life, so you were determined to try to make recompense?"

Marcus put his head between his hands briefly then looked up again. "It was the least that I could do," he said bleakly. "I felt responsible for her death. If only I had been with her in Town... But I spent as little time with her as I could."

Isabella took his hand. She half expected him to pull away from her, but he did not. "I am very sorry," she said.

He glanced at her. "You have nothing to be sorry for."

"Maybe not." Isabella hesitated. "But I know what it is like to try to build something worthwhile and to fail. Although—" she smiled a little "—I must confess that with Ernest, I soon gave up trying. It was a lost cause."

Marcus smiled, too. He raised the back of her hand and pressed a kiss on it. "Was it so bad, Isabella?"

"Oh, shocking!" Isabella said. Her smile faded. "It was probably not as sad as for you, though, I think. You must have hoped for happiness with India, whereas I knew from the start that I had made a marriage of convenience."

Marcus shifted a little, though he did not let her go. "I quickly realized that there was a part of India I could never reach," he said. "You said yourself that she was very self-contained and it was true. I knew there was something troubling her. She was unhappy and I was very afraid that I was the cause."

Isabella trembled. This was her opportunity to tell Marcus about Edward Warwick and yet she hesitated to do so. Marcus had confided in her and there was a fragile trust between them. Would she blow it all apart before it had begun if she told him that she suspected she knew the real cause of his wife's unhappiness?

Marcus had felt the tremor that shook her and was looking at her questioningly. His dark gaze was suddenly so tender that Isabella felt a fierce pang of regret at what she had to do. But there had already been too many secrets between them for her to keep quiet about what she knew. Besides, there was Warwick to consider.

Still holding his hand, she went down on her knees beside his chair. She spoke very carefully.

"I am sure that it was a source of regret to both of you, Marcus, that your marriage was not as happy as it might have been. However, I think there may have been another cause of India's grief."

His hand tightened briefly on hers. "What can you mean, Isabella?"

Isabella took a deep breath. There was no going back now.

"I think that India was in love with someone else," she said. "I think she loved Edward Warwick, Marcus, and I think she had his child."

SHE SPARED HIM NOTHING. All the things that Pen had said, their memories and joint discoveries, the news of the illegitimate baby that was supposedly fathered by Lord John and the locket in the portmanteau... Throughout it all, Marcus sat silent, his dark gaze never wavering from her face, his expression impassive.

"I think that the tragedy of it all was that Warwick truly loved her," Isabella finished. "Why else would he come back to Salterton the following year but to find her? He wanted to marry her but Lord John refused to countenance his suit and he was powerless to act."

Marcus moved slightly. He had been so still and so silent that it had been impossible for Isabella to judge his reactions to her words. He had not shouted her down, or condemned her words or instinctively denied her suggestions. Even so, she could feel the apprehension gnawing at the pit of her stomach, and not only for India but also for herself. She did not wish to destroy Marcus's respect for his dead wife but she was honest enough to admit that she did not want to lose his good opinion either.

"I do not understand why Lord John and Lady Jane would

not allow her to marry Warwick," Marcus said slowly. "If she had borne his child, surely the necessity to keep the scandal quiet would outweigh any other consideration?" He sounded distant, as though he were trying to solve a puzzle that held no personal concerns but was a mere intellectual challenge.

"You knew the Southerns," Isabella said. "I loved Lady Jane in particular, but she was very conscious of her position and her status. She was similar to my mother in that respect. Why, I remember her reminding me that I should not form a *tendre* for you when we first met because you were so ineligible. India was their only child. All their hopes and aspirations were invested in her. They could not permit her to throw herself away on some nobody without fortune."

Marcus let go of her hand abruptly and got to his feet. He ran his fingers through his hair in an agitated gesture.

"India in love with another man... Giving up her child..."

"I cannot be certain," Isabella said quickly, "but the evidence suggests that may be so." She looked up at him, trying to gauge his feelings. "I am sorry, Marcus. I do not wish you to think ill of her."

"I do not know what to think," Marcus said, with a long, unreadable look at her. "I am going out for a while."

"Marcus—" Isabella scrambled to her feet. She was stiff from kneeling on the floor and her skirts were creased but all she could think of was the need to banish that empty expression from his face and soothe the hurt. She put out a hand to him but it was too late. He was already turning away. The door of the room closed with a soft click. She thought about running after him, but she did not move.

INDIA IN LOVE WITH ANOTHER MAN... Giving up her child...

Marcus sat by the sea for a very long time. His gaze traced the movement of white sails on the horizon but his mind was largely empty. He was oblivious of the stares of curious passersby. Someone even addressed him, but they withdrew when he did not even turn his head, let alone reply.

After a while he became aware that he was chilled from the onshore breeze. He rose stiffly to his feet, walked along the esplanade and took the steps up toward the Hall. He saw Freddie Standish emerge from the inn on the harbor and exchange a few words with someone standing in the shadow of the doorway. He did not want to talk to Standish, not now. He picked up speed.

The house was quiet.

He found Isabella in the laundry room. She looked up when he came in and her hands stilled in the folding of the sheet. She put it down slowly. Her face was open and troubled. He realized that she was working to blot out more uncomfortable thoughts. He could tell that she was deeply distressed at the thought that she had hurt him. It made him feel tender inside in a very different way from the raw hurt he had felt to think of India's lonely misery.

"I always wondered," he said, without preamble. "I wondered whether India was holding the memory of someone else. God knows, I could not blame her, for was I not doing precisely the same thing myself? We never spoke of it and somehow we muddled along together and yet it was like hobbling on one leg when previously one had run…. Poor India…." He smiled ruefully. "We did try, but in the end the odds were too great."

Isabella came toward him and raised her hand to rest it on his chest. A curl had come loose from the ridiculous lace cap she was wearing. It rested against her cheek. She was flushed from the warmth of the room and her exertions.

"You cared sufficiently about each other to try to be happy," she said softly. "That is what counts."

Marcus nodded. "I do not think any the less of her for what happened," he said. He turned his face away. "I did at first. I could not help myself."

Isabella was silent, watching his face.

"It was a shock," he said rapidly, pulling her down to sit beside him on a pile of sweet-scented bed linen. "I thought I knew her. Arrogant of me, I know, but we lived together for six years and I thought…" He scratched his head. "It was a shock to realize that I had got something so fundamentally wrong and did not really know her at all."

"India was a difficult person to know," Isabella said.

"I wish she could have confided in me," Marcus said, "but I see it would have been impossible for her." Instinctively he drew Isabella closer to his side.

"She must have been very lonely," Isabella said softly, echoing his thoughts.

Marcus looked down into her eyes. Her head was resting against his shoulder.

"You know how that feels do you not, my love?" he said gently.

Isabella sighed. "I have come to discover that India and I had more things in common than I had ever realized."

Marcus kissed her. The relief of rediscovering her and holding her close overwhelmed him. He felt grateful and humble and exalted all at the same time. He plucked the cap from her head and tossed it aside, burying his face in her hair, pulling her backward to lie in a tangle of sheets. Neither of them spoke, the urgency between them suddenly too great for words. Isabella ripped open his jacket and shirt to caress his chest. He kissed her with feverish insistence while his hand slid up her thigh beneath her skirts.

"Marcus." Isabella freed her mouth briefly. "We cannot do this here! The laundry maid will come in at any moment."

In reply, Marcus got to his feet, crossed the room and turned the key decisively in the lock.

"She won't now," he said.

Afterward he watched with languorous pleasure as she

tried with spectacular lack of success to tame her unruly hair and push it beneath that ridiculous cap. She glanced over her shoulder, caught his smile and looked exasperated.

"Marcus, if you would only help me instead of laughing at my efforts!"

"You would still look as though you have been tumbled in the laundry room," Marcus said. Nevertheless he got to his feet obligingly and came across to help her.

With his hands resting on her shoulders, he turned her to look at him.

"There was one thing that I forgot to ask you when we were talking earlier," he said.

He saw the bright light fade from her eyes and anxiety take its place. His hands tightened, trying to convey reassurance.

"Edward Warwick," he said. "I do not understand why he has returned to Salterton. India is dead and buried and the past with her. What is the secret that he believes I hold? What does he hope to achieve?"

An extraordinary expression chased across Isabella's face, part regret, part sympathy.

"I do believe that he has come back to find something," she said. "Marcus, I think he wants his child."

CHAPTER TWENTY-TWO

"WE SHALL HAVE TO TRAP HIM," Marcus said. He and Alistair were in the library. It was late. One lamp burned, casting a warm shadow. "Warwick is here in Salterton but we cannot flush him out without bait."

"We could use Standish," Alistair said. "Warwick trusts him."

Marcus hesitated, then he shook his head. "I doubt very much that he does. I doubt he trusts anyone."

Alistair tilted the brandy in his glass and studied it thoughtfully. "Your judgment may be affected, Marcus."

Marcus grimaced. There was no *maybe* about it. "It is," he said. "I will do everything in my power to keep Isabella's brother out of this."

"He is already in it to his neck," Alistair pointed out. "If you do not take him into account, he may well ruin our plans."

Marcus's mouth set in a stubborn line. "Isabella and I are but recently reconciled. I cannot—I will not—jeopardize that for anything, not even Edward Warwick."

Alistair's mouth twisted into a wry smile. "You are saying that there is nothing more important in the world than your wife."

Their eyes met. "I am saying that," Marcus agreed. "I love her, Alistair."

There was a moment's silence.

"So," Alistair said. "How do we trap him?"

Marcus picked up the silver locket from the desk. "With this," he said.

ISABELLA WAS IN BED, wrapped close in Marcus's arms, but she was not asleep. She was thinking of India, not in the way that she had previously thought of her cousin, but with sympathy and understanding, and a regret that the knowledge had come too late. In the morning, she thought sleepily, moving instinctively closer to Marcus's warmth, she would go up to the attic and choose something of India's for remembrance. Then she would arrange for the rest of India's belongings to be given away and then—she admitted it—she would feel that they had finally closed that chapter.

She was on the edge of sleep when she wondered suddenly what had happened to the child.

IT WAS A HOT MORNING, certainly too hot for physical activity. Nevertheless, Freddie Standish was running. Ordinarily he would never do such a thing and as he hastened through the rooms of Salterton Hall, he realized why. Running was unpleasant. It made him sweat and pant. But this was an emergency, so he was prepared to do it just this once.

He could not find Marcus Stockhaven anywhere. He was not in the library nor the drawing room, although the housekeeper had assured Freddie that both Lord Stockhaven and Mr. Cantrell were in the house. Normally Freddie would not have dreamed of seeking Stockhaven out. He had spent the last three weeks trying to avoid him. There was something about Stockhaven that made Freddie feel deeply inadequate. Stockhaven was tough and ruthless and strong and all the things that Freddie had always wanted to be and never quite achieved. But again, this was an emergency and he had to put aside his prejudices for the greater good.

He puffed down the garden passage and was about to fling open the outside door when someone stepped out of the gun room and grabbed his arm so tightly that he almost squeaked like a stuck pig. He managed to bite his lip and what came out was more of a gurgle.

"Quiet!" Marcus practically dragged him into the room and closed the door behind them. Alistair Cantrell was there. He had a dueling pistol in his hand. Freddie almost fainted.

"Warwick," Freddie wheezed. "He's in the house."

Marcus looked no more than irritated. "We know. Keep quiet, there's a good fellow."

Alistair, after a brief glance in Freddie's direction, bent to checking the pistol again.

"How long?" he asked.

"Three minutes," Marcus said, "then we go up."

Freddie grabbed his arm again. "You do not understand, Stockhaven. It's Bella. She's in the attics."

He was gratified to see that his words had rather more effect this time. Marcus swung round on him, his eyes narrowing. Freddie had all of his attention.

"Isabella?"

"That's what I'm trying to tell you," Freddie gabbled. "I heard Bella tell Mrs. Lawton that she was going up to the attic to fetch something and would Mrs. Lawton please arrange for the late Lady Stockhaven's trunks to be brought down later."

Marcus swore. "When did she go up there?"

"Fifteen minutes... T-t-twenty?" Freddie's teeth chattered although he was feeling extremely hot and sweaty. He ran a finger around the inside of his collar. "Warwick will think it's a trap."

"It is," Marcus said grimly. "Just not the right one."

Alistair cocked the pistol with a loud click. "Come on," he said. Neither of them looked at Freddie as they went out.

Freddie sagged against the table with relief. He extracted his large, spotted, rose-scented handkerchief from his pocket and mopped his brow. He had to get out of this room. It smelled of grease and gunpowder and made him think of dead animals. He shuddered.

He went out into the passage and walked slowly into the hall. The house was preternaturally quiet. Freddie went into the drawing room and sat down with the *Gentlemen's Magazine*. He could not concentrate. He would have to tell Stockhaven everything now and beg for his help. Freddie shifted uncomfortably. His brother-in-law could scarcely have a lower opinion of him than he already did, so it should not matter. Yet for some reason it did.

Freddie cast the magazine aside in disgust. Why was it so quiet? Had they caught Warwick yet? If he had escaped... Cold sweat formed on Freddie's upper lip. It was no good. He could not sit here meekly waiting to discover his fate. For better or worse he had to go to meet it.

ISABELLA KNEW EXACTLY WHAT she was looking for. In the night she had remembered the battered box of drawing sticks and the sketchbook and she had wondered whether India might have expressed her feelings in pictures rather than in words. She rummaged in the first trunk with its now-familiar scent of old lavender and dust and heard the crayons clink within their metal box. The drawing book was beneath. She pulled it out.

The pages were blank.

Isabella felt part disappointed, part puzzled. She had been certain that there would be something there. She sat back on her heels, riffling through the pages. Nothing. Nothing but for a faint pencil drawing on the last but one page. It was the cherubic face of a small child, but it was so pale and faded now that she almost missed it. The pencil lines had blurred and almost been rubbed away. The name beneath it read Edward John.

There was a step on the bare boards of the floor. She had

heard no one come up the stairs and now she realized with a frightened jump of her heart that this was because they had been here already, in the second attic, waiting....

A shadow fell across her. She looked up.

"Good afternoon, Lady Stockhaven," a voice said from behind her. "I see that you are ahead of me."

Mr. Owen was there, leaning on a gold-headed cane. He looked as sickly as he had done in the Assembly Rooms, but there was some other quality about him now. The slate-gray eyes were colder and harder than she remembered. She shivered.

"I do believe," Owen added gently, "that you have been ahead of me almost every step."

"I think I must have been," Isabella said, "Mr. Warwick?"

He inclined his head. "The very same. You know of me?"

"I have...heard of you."

"Stockhaven has been searching for me, I think," Warwick said. "I wondered if he would mention his business to you."

Isabella got to her feet a little stiffly. Warwick made no attempt to stop her. Even so, she was afraid. She could feel tension and something more in the air, something cold. And she had no means of defending herself.

"Why did you come?" she said.

Warwick smiled. He leaned against the edge of the second trunk and watched her. "I came because of the past," he said. "I came for my son."

"We have met before, just the once," Isabella said carefully. He had mentioned the past and she followed his lead. "It was in 1803, I think, at the Salterton Assembly. You danced with my cousin."

A faint smile touched Warwick's mouth. "Everyone always wanted to dance with you," he said. "You were the pretty one. But I wanted Miss Southern from the start."

He tilted his head thoughtfully. "You did not recognize me

when we met two weeks ago, did you?" he said. "It is scarce surprising. I think I have changed."

Isabella thought so, too. Gone was the dashing lieutenant with the impudent tilt of the head and the devil-may-care light in his eyes. There was nothing here of the rebellious spirit that had drawn India like a moth to the fatal flame. Everything had been doused by sickness. Isabella recognized it and felt her heart contract in surprise and pity. She had not expected to feel sympathy for Edward Warwick. She opened the book and showed him the drawing.

"There is a picture here, Mr. Warwick," she said. "I think it must be your son. He is named for you."

The pallor in Warwick's face seemed to become more pronounced. She saw his hand clench on the cane.

"There was nothing else?" He might have been discussing the weather, there was so little emotion in his voice.

"I regret not," Isabella said. She remembered the locket. She had left that on Marcus's desk. It seemed appropriate for Warwick to have it. She opened her mouth, then closed it again.

Warwick sighed. "Of course there would be no documents. I have looked everywhere, you understand, Lady Stockhaven. There is no trace." He took the locket from his jacket pocket and held it gently in the palm of his hand. Isabella caught her breath.

"You recognize it?" he said softly.

Isabella nodded silently.

"I knew it was a trap," Warwick said. "Your brother was supposed to have found it and sent it to me." He swung the locket gently by its silver chain. "Lord Standish has worked for me for six years," he added smoothly, "and during that time I have learned that he could not find a tankard in an alehouse. The likelihood of him finding a cache of Miss Southern's treasured possessions in the attic here strained credulity." He smiled at her. It chilled Isabella bone deep. "Nevertheless," he added, "I was desperate, so I came. The one thing that I did not expect to find, Lady Stockhaven, was you."

Isabella inclined her head politely. "You find me as surprised as you are yourself, Mr. Warwick."

Warwick laughed. The sound echoed around the empty spaces of the attic. "Perhaps I misjudged your brother then, Lady Stockhaven."

Isabella doubted it. She had a strong feeling that this was nothing to do with Freddie at all and that she had unwittingly stumbled into a trap herself. She wished that Marcus had told her what he planned. But he had been preoccupied that morning and she had been sick and once she had felt better again she had been so intent on banishing India's ghost forever...

"At the least, your presence is a comfort to me, Lady Stockhaven," Warwick said, "for it provides me with a way out." He looked at her. "You do not frighten easily. Not like your little cousin. Maybe that was why I always wanted to protect her."

"A pity you were not permitted to do so," Isabella said, and she meant it. Had Lord John Southern not barred this man from seeing his daughter and contemptuously dismissed his suit, how different matters might have been. But Warwick was drawing closer now, his thirst for knowledge unquenchable in the search for his son. Isabella could see it in his eyes. He would take any risk, no matter how foolhardy, dare all if he thought it would help him find the boy.

"What else do you know?" he asked.

"I know that my cousin and Lady Jane visited Scotland in the early spring of 1804," Isabella said steadily. "It was a long journey to an inhospitable place. I realize now that they had an urgent reason for doing so, though I was unaware of it at the time."

There was a silence. A beam of sunlight fell across Ned Warwick's lean cheek, emphasizing the deep lines engraved in the flesh.

"I have been to Scotland," he said quietly. "I have been everywhere and spoken to everyone I could find, and yet I cannot trace my son."

Isabella swallowed hard. She was not sure how they had come to such an implicit understanding in so short a space of time and yet she knew that for all his fearful reputation, she had compassion for Edward Warwick. She had an insight into how he felt.

"The gardener and his wife who adopted him," she said, "they lived in London."

"They are dead."

The stark words fell into the peace of the room and made the air shiver.

Isabella said, "Surely someone in Salterton must know—"

Warwick moved sharply. Again he forestalled her. "Your uncle did his business too well." There was such a wealth of bitterness in his voice that Isabella felt cold. "He was as secret as the grave. He destroyed any evidence that might sully the reputation of his daughter."

Isabella made a slight, helpless gesture. "He was doing what he thought was right."

Warwick's mouth turned down at the corners. "He was doing what would keep his fair name in the eyes of the world. He cared nothing for her feelings. He was responsible for her unhappiness."

"How so?"

"You said it yourself. By refusing me permission to pay my addresses to her." He turned toward her so suddenly that Isabella instinctively drew back before she realized that his violence was not directed toward her but toward his memories. "He would not allow his daughter—his pregnant daughter— to marry the hell-raising illegitimate son of an Irish wastrel." There was bleak amusement in his eyes. "I quote."

"Yet you came back and tried again."

"I did." His eyes touched hers briefly but Isabella knew he was not seeing her. "I came to that damned Assembly the following summer and put my fate to the touch again, and Lord John threatened to have me thrown out into the street. I lost my temper and swore I would tell everyone of his daughter's disgrace."

"But you would never have done so," Isabella said.

For a moment Warwick's gray eyes were amused as they dwelled on her. "Why not?" he asked.

"Because you loved India," Isabella said. "I'll warrant you still do. It was her father you wished to punish, not India herself."

Warwick seemed to shrink slightly. "How do you know?"

"Because whilst India lived, you made no move to cause scandal," Isabella said. "You did not seek her out or look for the child. It was only after she died that you tried to find your son."

"I tried to get her to run away with me but she would not." Warwick smiled mirthlessly. "Strange that she would give herself to me in love but would not entrust herself to me for life."

"It is not so strange," Isabella said, thinking of the cousin with whom she had more in common than she had ever guessed. "One may overcome one's scruples in the heat of the moment, but when one is confronted with the decision of a lifetime, it is easy to make the wrong choice." She looked at him. "What did you do—afterward?"

"I went back to the army." Warwick shrugged his shoulders. "It was not long before I was court-martialed for insubordination and thrown out. I went to Ireland for a while, then returned to London and fell in with bad company." He bared his teeth in a smile. "I have been in such company ever since. I run such company."

"Yet still the most important thing to you was to find your son," Isabella said. Her body was strung tight, screaming with tension. She could not keep him talking forever and she could not guess where this would end.

"It was," Warwick said. "I made inquiries in Salterton and in Scotland and in London, but drew a blank on all occasions." He was speaking conversationally now, as though the subject was of little import. "In the end, I came to Salterton myself and set a lad to search Stockhaven's house here whilst I came up to the Hall to see Lady Jane. She was the only person left who could help me."

"And once again you were refused."

The harsh lines about Warwick's mouth deepened. "Lady Jane would not compromise her daughter's memory by even acknowledging the truth."

Isabella felt no surprise. For Lady Jane, like her husband before her, protecting what she saw as India's and the family's interests was still of paramount importance, even beyond the grave.

"Lady Jane died that night," Isabella said.

Warwick's head snapped around sharply. "That was none of my doing."

"You quarreled."

"So?"

"She was a frail elderly lady. She could not stand the shock of it."

Warwick shrugged again. "As I said, that is none of my affair."

Isabella was chilled by his cold lack of concern. There was something faulty here. Where his son was concerned, he was vulnerable, but there was no chink in his armor elsewhere. The man had no pity and no emotion in him.

"So what are you to do now, Lady Stockhaven?" Warwick said softly. He moved slightly and Isabella tensed once again. "What am I to do now that you have seen me?"

"I think you should go," Isabella said steadily. "There is

nothing here for you, Mr. Warwick. Both India and her mother buried their secrets too deep to be found."

Warwick gave her a mocking smile. "You will not tell me to forget my quest?"

"What is the point?" Isabella said. She sighed. "I know you can never forget it."

Warwick straightened up. He nodded slowly. "Against all the odds, I believe that you really do understand."

"I do."

Their eyes met. Again Isabella felt that strange tug of affinity. It repelled her and yet she could not shake it off.

"Go," she said again.

Warwick straightened. His hand went to his pocket. "I will," he said. "But you are coming with me, Lady Stockhaven."

FREDDIE STANDISH WAS RUNNING again. Dimly he was aware that he simply had to stop doing this. Besides, running *up* things was a very poor idea. It winded him twice as quickly.

He had crept up the first three flights of stairs but when he realized that neither Marcus nor Alistair were anywhere near the attics and, therefore, unaccountably, unable to do anything to help Isabella, he was filled with panic. Perhaps Marcus had not understood what he was trying to say. He did not have the time to stop and find out now. He rushed up the final flight of steps, surged along the landing and threw open the attic door.

"Bella!"

Both his sister and Edward Warwick jumped at the loud intrusion. Freddie saw Warwick tense like a snake about to strike. Suddenly he had an arm about Isabella and a knife at her throat as he held her in front of him like a shield. Freddie saw the glint of steel and felt faint again, a condition not assisted by his terminal shortage of breath.

"What the devil are you up to, Standish?" Warwick snapped.

Freddie looked from Warwick's face to Isabella's and

licked his lips like a hunted fox. A bead of sweat ran down his brow. He fished out his silk handkerchief and mopped his face.

"Freddie," Isabella said. She looked sick at the knowledge of his betrayal. "I believe you already know Mr. Warwick," she said.

"Yes," Freddie said, his gaze darting to Warwick's face once again. This was no time for explanations. He spread his hands wide. "Let her go, old man. It's only me. No threat."

"You never were," Warwick sneered. He did not lower the knife. He looked around at the empty room. "Though I do wonder why you are here." His gaze snapped back to Freddie. "You saw no one enter?"

"Not a soul," Freddie said steadily. "Let her go and walk away, Warwick."

Warwick's face convulsed with fury. "You are double-crossing me, Standish."

"No idea what you mean, old chap," Freddie said. His felt gray with fear. He could feel himself shaking. He was almost wishing that he had never started this. Isabella had always been able to take care of herself. True, she did not look as though she knew what to do, but he was sure she would think of something. Whereas he had no idea what to do. "Don't have the stomach to cheat you, let alone the brains."

Isabella shifted slightly and the knife wavered at her throat, leaving a thin red line on her skin. Freddie shuddered. As a child he had always cried at the sight of blood and he was not much better these days.

"Lady Stockhaven comes with me," Warwick said.

"No," Freddie said. He took a step nearer. "No need to make a drama out of this, old man. I came to tell you that Stockhaven and Cantrell are on their way back from the dower house. Need to get away now, before any harm is done."

Warwick started to move toward the door, dragging Isabella with him like a shield.

Freddie hesitated, castigated himself for a fool—and dived for the other man's legs. Warwick let go of Isabella, joining with Freddie with a grunt and a sickening thud as their bodies connected. Freddie, who had only just regained his breath, felt as though he had been burst like a balloon.

Three things happened at once. Out of the corner of his eye, Freddie saw Isabella's arm come down and something landed with a sturdy smack against the side of Edward Warwick's head. There was the hum and a crack as a bullet winged Warwick in the shoulder and ricocheted away to take a large chip out of the plaster of the wall.

And Freddie felt the knife slice into his side. He pressed his hand to his ribs and saw the blood seeping through his fingers. Warwick was out cold but he was scarcely in better shape. What a damnable mess. He simply was not cut out to be a hero.

"Freddie!" Isabella was beside him and her tone was anguished. Freddie saw Marcus Stockhaven swing in through the window and jump down to the attic floor. The roof. Of course. If only he had thought...

Isabella was pressing an improvised bandage to his side. Freddie thought it was probably her petticoat. He wanted to tell her to stop because good linen was too expensive to waste and also because it was so damned painful.

Freddie slid down slowly against the wall and gave a groan. Isabella cushioned his head on her lap. "Help is coming, Freddie," she said. "Mr. Cantrell has gone for the doctor. You will feel better directly."

Freddie appreciated her words, though he did not for a moment believe her.

"Always wanted to help you, Bella," he said. The words seemed to take an inordinate amount of effort. "Couldn't do it when we were younger. Glad to have been of service now." He moved with a wince as Marcus pressed the bandage tighter.

"I didn't realize for years that he was the one," Freddie

whispered. "We never met. If I had known he was India's lover..." His face contorted. Isabella squeezed his hand.

"Freddie—"

"Ruined my favorite coat as well," Freddie said. And then the darkness closed in, for which he was profoundly grateful.

"HE'LL LIVE," MARCUS SAID later. He had spent the previous half hour at Freddie Standish's bedside while the unfortunate lord poured out the sorry tale of his dealings with Edward Warwick. Finally Freddie had slept, exhausted by confession and lack of blood, and Marcus had made his way to Isabella's bedroom. He had persuaded her to rest, for she had been chalk-white with strain. But he knew she was worried. Although her brother's injuries were minor—no more than a glancing scratch from Warwick's knife—he had bled profusely and the whole matter had seemed a deal worse than it actually was.

He went across to the bedside. Isabella was sitting propped up against her pillows, a dish of tea at her elbow and a book in hand. It was evident that her mind was not on the written word, since she was holding the book upside down.

Marcus took her hands reassuringly in his. "Freddie will be in a weakened state for a while yet, but he should recover quickly enough if he does not exert himself."

"I doubt we shall see much change from normal, then," Isabella said, with a flash of her old spirit. "Still, I am glad. I have lost too many people to want to lose my brother too." Her brow creased. "But what are you going to do about him, Marcus? If he was working for Warwick, that places you in a difficult situation."

Marcus smiled. "Poor Freddie. He tells me that Warwick has had him in his pocket for years, and your father before him. But he was always the smallest of cogs in Warwick's wheel. He provided information, nothing more."

He saw a mixture of relief and misery on Isabella's face.

"I had no notion," she said. "Oh, Pen said he had debts…" She rubbed her forehead tiredly.

"Do not blame him," Marcus said. "He was in desperate straits."

Isabella smiled tiredly. "I could not blame him when I know how that feels." She looked at Marcus. "Remember all the things that I have done when I was desperate and alone. My crimes were greater, I think."

Marcus took her hand and held it tightly. "They were not crimes, Bella." If he had his way, she would never blame herself for anything ever again. She was indomitable and courageous and he loved her.

He frowned to think of all that she had gone through.

"What did Freddie mean when he said that he could not help you when you were younger?" he asked.

Isabella was quiet for a moment, her face still. "I think that Freddie has always felt very keenly that he should have done something to help me when…when I was obliged to marry Ernest," she said at last. "He has never spoken of it to me directly but sometimes he has referred to it obliquely and I think he has always felt guilty."

Marcus nodded slowly. "He can have been little older than you at the time, however."

"He was eighteen," Isabella said. "He thinks that he could have stood up to our father, yet he did not."

Marcus was silent for a moment. "I suppose that he felt he had compromised his integrity by failing to stand against your father's summary decision to marry you off. Today, at least, he has regained his self-respect."

Isabella looked at him thoughtfully. "I have always had the feeling, Marcus, that you did not like Freddie. Why is that?"

Marcus hesitated. "I admit that I thought him a lightweight. But the animosity was never on my side. I always sensed that Freddie disliked me for some reason."

Isabella frowned. "He has not spoken of it to you?"

"No."

"And you do not know why?"

Marcus shook his head. "I have no notion."

There was a brief silence. Marcus could see a faint, withdrawn expression creep into Isabella's eyes as though she was thinking of something else, but when she spoke it was to change the subject.

"And what about Edward Warwick?" she asked.

Marcus sighed. "Unfortunately, he will live, too. It would have been easier had he died and saved us the difficulty of deciding what to do with him."

He saw a flicker of what looked like pain in Isabella's eyes. "You could always let him go," she said.

Marcus looked at her in astonishment. "Bella, the man tried to kill you!"

"Well, no," Isabella corrected him. "He was merely using me as a hostage to try to buy his freedom."

Marcus's lips thinned. He would never forget the way he had felt when Warwick had held the knife to Isabella's throat. He had been within an inch of shooting the man down and only Alistair, urgently grasping at his jacket, had recalled him to sanity with the whispered words that he would kill Isabella if he did not take care and wait his chance. A blinding fury had possessed him when he had seen the thin red line on Isabella's neck where the knife had grazed her. But the fury was tempered with fear; a fear greater than anything he had felt before. She might have been hurt. She might have been killed. His Isabella…

His hands tightened on hers at the thought and she winced. He let her go reluctantly. He did not want to. He wanted to clasp her to him forever through sheer terror that she might otherwise be taken from him. He did not want to lose her.

"The man is a dangerous criminal," he said, his voice rough

with emotion. "He would never have let you go, Bella. He is a murderer and a felon. He has to hang."

Isabella's eyelashes flickered. He looked at her candid blue gaze and her sweet mouth, and wanted to crush her to him.

"I do understand," she said. She shivered. He felt the tremor go through her. "Did you hear what we talked about, Marcus?"

"No," Marcus said. "We could hear nothing. I was hoping that you might tell me. And," he added, "tell me what you were doing in the attic in the first place."

He saw her shift then and set her lips as though she faced a difficult task.

"I went up into the attics to choose a memento of India," she said. Marcus realized that he must have looked astonished, for she added, "I feel for her, Marcus. We were never close and I doubt we ever could have been but still I feel for her." She was quiet for a moment. "I think we might have understood one another."

Marcus nodded. "And Warwick?"

Isabella sighed. "We talked of his son." She pressed her hands together. "I know you cannot let him go, Marcus, but the man has suffered every day. He will continue to suffer, never being able to find his child, not knowing if he is dead or alive. I understand a little of how that must feel." She broke off, head bent.

Marcus's face set hard. There was a painful compassion in her voice and it struck a chord of sympathy in him, no matter that he did not want it to do so.

"I understand some part of how you feel about that," he said slowly.

Her eyes flew to his face.

"Do you?"

"Yes. That is to say, when you told me about India's child, I had some sympathy for Warwick's plight. But for the man himself..." He shook his head.

In the candlelight, Isabella's eyes seemed very bright and blue. "Do you think we shall ever be able to find the child?"

Marcus hesitated. He did not wish her to suffer further, but he could imagine that if she did not hear the truth, she might make a crusade of trying to find and help India's lost son.

"He is already found," he said.

He saw the light leap into Isabella's eyes, then die just as swiftly as she read his expression.

"Is he…" She paused. "Is he dead, Marcus?"

Marcus nodded. His face was set. "He was never far from home at all. He was Edward Channing, the lad Warwick sent to search my house for evidence right at the beginning."

Isabella gasped. "But Warwick had looked everywhere for the boy! How was it that he did not know?"

Marcus made a slight, negative gesture. "I cannot be sure. We know that the boy was born in Scotland and subsequently adopted by the Southerns' gardener and his wife. They moved to London but on the death of his adoptive parents, Edward returned to Salterton and lived with the Channings. Channing's wife was a distant connection of Edward's parents and also worked for Lord John Southern for many years. Perhaps Lord John wished the child to be somewhere where he could watch over him."

Isabella's brow furrowed. "Yet Warwick could not discover the truth."

Marcus shook his head. "Lord John chose well with Channing. He is a taciturn man. But the boy was wild—no doubt like Edward Warwick had been wild in his youth. He fell into bad company."

"He fell in with Warwick," Isabella said slowly. "Oh, the irony of Warwick not knowing that this was the very boy he sought!"

Marcus's face was hard. "The irony is harsher than that, Bella. Edward Channing ran away to join Warwick in London but he fell sick and Warwick abandoned him. He died in the poorhouse. The reason I discovered the truth about Edward's parentage was that it came out when I went to tell the Channings the news of Edward's death."

Isabella pressed her hand to her mouth. "Warwick killed his *own son*?"

"He abandoned him to die, certainly."

Isabella made a pitiful noise of distress. "Marcus, I cannot bear it. Does Warwick know?"

"Not yet," Marcus said. He spoke slowly. "It seems fitting to tell him. Warwick will die a quick death, unlike some of the others he condemned through his criminality. To know the ultimate irony, that he had his own son within his grasp yet failed to recognize him, to know that it was his fault Edward died... That would be punishment indeed."

"That would be too cruel," Isabella whispered.

Marcus shook his head. "Life cannot always be neat and painless," he said.

Isabella closed her eyes briefly and when she opened them again her gaze clung to his. "No one knows that as well as I," she said.

Marcus took her hands in his. "It shall never again be so," he said. "I swear it."

ISABELLA WATCHED from the window as they took Ned Warwick away. He was escorted in chains down to the quay by a detachment of sailors from *HMS Sapphire*. They were to take him to London by sea for his trial. It seemed a huge amount of trouble for a man who seemed so sick he could barely walk under the weight of his restraints. Isabella remembered the dank cell in which Marcus had been incarcerated, with its walls leaching damp and the stench and sourness of imprisonment in the air. She shuddered. Day after day, without release, ending only in death... Yet that would be

Warwick's punishment anyway, regardless of whether or not he was caged. He would never find his son now. He would either die unknowing or die tortured by the truth.

Isabella watched the sad procession out of sight around the curve of the esplanade. Plenty of the residents and visitors to Salterton were treating it as a rather amusing spectacle. She felt sick at the sight. She crossed to the mirror that stood on the dressing chest. She leaned her hands on the sturdy wooden top and stared long and hard at her reflection.

Life cannot always be neat and painless, Marcus had said, and she knew it was true, for now she was faced with the greatest dilemma of all. She knew now that she was not pregnant with Marcus's child. To her confusion and shock, she had cried when she had discovered it, as though she had secretly wanted his baby after all. Now there was nothing to keep them together unless the love and trust they had been trying to build over the last few weeks was strong enough, and that she did not know. What she did know was that she respected Marcus enough to tell him the truth about Emma's parentage and after that it was up to him.

She was terrified.

CHAPTER TWENTY-THREE

IT WAS A GLORIOUS SUMMER DAY in Kinvara Cove. Pen and Isabella had taken a picnic down to the sands. They had swum from the rocks and sat in the sunshine and talked lazily. After the painful emotions of the previous day, it had been wonderful.

Pen was looking flushed and pink and very young. "Bella," she said.

"Hmm?" Isabella murmured. They were sitting in a sheltered spot. The sun was making her sleepy. She knew that she must tell Marcus the truth very soon. But she wanted to have one peaceful day before she and Marcus discussed the future.

"Being here at Salterton has reminded me of something that I should have told you long ago," Pen said. She hesitated. "I am sorry…"

Isabella opened one eye and squinted at her sister from under the brim of her straw bonnet. "More confessions, Penelope?" she said "You frighten me."

She thought that Pen was looking quite frightened herself.

"It was about the letter."

"Which letter?"

"The letter that Marcus sent you asking you to elope with him."

Isabella sat bolt upright. "Elope?"

Pen stared. "Surely he has told you? I always wondered

whether it would have made any difference…. Whether you would have run away from Ernest."

Isabella raised a hand and stopped her. "Wait, Pen. Marcus never asked me to run away with him."

"Oh, but surely… I was certain that was what it must be!" Pen bit her lip. "I found the letter under the door of the bedroom that had been yours. It was addressed to Miss I. S. I remember it particularly because it was the day after your wedding to Ernest and I wondered at someone addressing you by your maiden name. Anyway, you were no longer at Standish House, of course, because after the wedding breakfast you had stayed with Ernest in Brunswick Gardens."

"I remember," Isabella said. "It rained."

She felt strange. The day of her wedding had been hot but the following day there was a thunderstorm and the lowering clouds and constant downpour had seemed perfectly in tune with her mood. Even now the mere thought of it brought the same trapped and angry sensation to the pit of her stomach.

"It did rain," Pen agreed. "That was the problem. I put the letter in my pocket, intending to give it to you when I saw you before you left for your wedding journey. But then Miss Bentley took me out to the Academy that afternoon—I think she thought I felt neglected with all the fuss around you—and we were soaked in a downpour of rain. My dress was ruined and Molly took it away as soon as we got home and I forgot all about it and never gave the letter a second thought…." There was an edge of desperation to her voice now. "It was only later, after you had gone on your wedding trip, that Molly brought it to me. It had been washed and dried and flat ironed before they found it—" Her voice broke somewhere between laughter and tears. "I *knew* it must have been from Marcus but it was too late and I did not know what to do—"

Isabella's attention snapped up. "Why did you think that it was from Marcus? Did you read it?"

Pen shook her head. "No. It was illegible once it had been through the wash. I threw it away. But I thought…" She stopped, bit her lip. "I knew that you and Marcus had been deeply in love," she said, after a moment. "I knew that you had been lovers. I did not think that he would give you up so easily."

The sunlight dazzled Isabella momentarily and she blinked.

"I saw you slip out of Salterton House one night when we were staying with Aunt Jane," Pen added apologetically. "And although you and Marcus were always proper when you were in public together, I could tell that there was something very strong between you. I was too young to understand properly, of course, but…" She smiled. "I am not certain how you managed to keep it such a secret."

"It seems," Isabella said dryly, "that we did not."

Pen looked down at her hands. "I am very sorry, Bella. I cannot rid myself of the thought that it might have made a world of difference." Her eyes were full of pleading tears. Isabella swallowed an answering lump in her throat.

"It does not matter a scrap, Pen. Do not give it another thought."

She reached out to give her sister the hug they both needed and Pen clung tight.

"Be happy, Bella," Pen said, muffled.

"I will," Isabella said. Her heart felt wrenched. Pen would be so distressed if she and Marcus separated now, but her sister would never understand just how complicated matters had become.

Looking over Pen's shoulder, she saw Alistair Cantrell coming down the cliff path toward them. He and Marcus had been over to view the progress of work on Salterton Cottage.

"Alistair is looking for you," she said, releasing Pen with a final hug. "Run along."

Pen needed no second bidding, although once she was on her feet she paused, looking down at her sister.

"You will be quite well on your own, Bella?" she asked.

"I shall be quite well," Isabella confirmed with composure. "In a little while I shall go to find Marcus."

She watched Pen speed away up the cliff path and throw herself into Alistair's arms. They waved at her enthusiastically before they turned away and started to walk, arms entwined, across the heather toward the ruined chapel. Isabella sighed and turned away. She felt suddenly frightened. She had told herself that this was the day on which she would tell Marcus that she was not pregnant—and tell him the truth about Emma. She should have known from the start that the truth, partially told, would never be enough. But now she knew that she was in danger of destroying all the fragile structure that they had started to build between them, for what she had to say might send Marcus away forever.

She interlocked her fingers and stared out across the sea. She loved Salterton and she loved living here, but without Marcus it would be empty of real meaning, for she loved him more than anything else in the world. Nevertheless, she owed it to him to be honest. If they were to part, at least it would be with no more secrets between them.

She was shot through with another pang of terror.

Nevertheless she got to her feet, dusted the sand slowly from her skirts, and started up the path toward home. She had never avoided making hard decisions, right or wrong, and now, twelve years on from the first one, she had to do it again. She prayed fervently that this time she was making the right decision in telling Marcus about Emma.

By the time she reached the house, serene and sleeping in the afternoon warmth, she was almost beside herself with nervousness. As she went into the cool shade of the hall, she could hear Marcus talking to the architect. Their business was not quite concluded. Which meant that she had time for the one other matter that preoccupied her.

She knocked softly on the door of Freddie's sickroom and pushed it open. The housekeeper was sitting quietly beside the bed. It appeared that Freddie was asleep. He still looked pale but he was breathing easily and his fever had subsided now. Isabella felt a great rush of affection on seeing him.

The housekeeper tiptoed out and Isabella took her vacated seat. She took Freddie's hand in hers and, a moment later, he opened his eyes.

"How are you, old thing?" he said with a slight effort.

"I am well, thank you," Isabella said, smiling. "You are a hero, Freddie. You saved my life."

A hint of color stole into her brother's lean cheek. "Devil a bit," he said gruffly. "Did what I could. That man was a nasty piece of work." He blinked. "Did Marcus tell you—"

"Yes," Isabella said. "I understand why you worked for him, Freddie. There is no need to explain."

"I'm sorry," Freddie said fretfully, pulling a loose thread from the blanket and avoiding her eyes. "Made a terrible mull of things."

Isabella squeezed his hand. "We shall sort them out."

"Marcus has offered to pay my debts," Freddie said in a rush. "Splendid fellow, your husband, Bella."

"There was a time when you did not think so," Isabella said, a little dryly. "Was that because of India, Freddie?"

She felt Freddie jump. His blue eyes opened wide and fixed on her face. "Dash it, Bella, what can you mean?"

Isabella smiled ruefully. "After Warwick had shot you, you told me that you were glad that you had been able to help me at last. I understood that well enough, Freddie…." Her smile deepened with affection. "But you also implied that you had done it because of India as well."

She waited. Freddie lay still, his eyes closed now, his lashes dark against his cheek. Isabella's heart wrenched. He looked like the schoolboy he had been when he had fallen in love with his cousin.

"Pen just told me," she continued softly, "about a letter she found in my bedroom at Standish House, the day after my wedding. It was addressed to Miss I.S. and she assumed that it was for me. But it wasn't, was it, Freddie? It was for India. She had been staying with us for the wedding. She shared my room the night before the wedding and she had it to herself afterward. The letter was for her." Isabella took a careful breath. "I think it was from you."

Freddie's eyes opened. His gaze was very clear and very blue but there was something still in the depths that told her more than any words of his feelings for India Southern.

"I wanted her to run away with me," Freddie said. His voice was a little hoarse. "I could not bear it any longer. She was so unhappy. She had been ever since Lord John forced her to give Warwick up and give her child away. I knew that she did not love me—she had always been in love with Warwick and no one else—but I loved her."

The muscles of his throat corded as he swallowed painfully. "She was not like you, Bella. She wasn't strong. She could not look after herself. I wanted to care for her and so I proposed marriage, but she said that her family would never agree." He moistened his lips. "Not only was I her cousin but I was penniless—almost as poor a match as Warwick himself. And I *knew*. I knew about the child. Lady Jane wanted to make sure that India married someone who never knew the truth."

"Marcus," Isabella said. "He was not in Salterton when India first met Warwick and the following year he was so wrapped up in his feelings for me...."

"And Marcus was looking to replace you," Freddie said, "whether he realized it or not. Lady Jane thought it was a match made in heaven. It was only later, when she realized that Marcus would never feel for India as he had done for you, that she told her daughter that she wished she had been your mother instead, rather than hers. India was monstrously upset."

"And told Marcus that I had driven a wedge between mother and daughter," Isabella said, remembering. "How much you have always known, Freddie!"

Freddie shrugged, then winced beneath his bandages. "I could never like Marcus," he admitted. "First I blamed him for letting you go and then I blamed him for marrying India, yet I must confess that I was at least as culpable. I could have stood up to Papa, I could have gone to Lord John and insist that he permit India to marry me…." He shook his head. "All a damned waste."

Isabella slipped an arm behind him and propped him up so that he could sip from the glass of water she proffered.

"Thank you," Freddie said, as she put the glass down. "Thank you, Bella."

Isabella smiled and, as she left him to sleep, she placed the miniature of India that she had taken from Lady Jane's chamber on the table at Freddie's bedside.

SHE FOUND MARCUS IN THE HALL, bidding farewell to the architect. Belton, who had arrived the previous week from the London house, was holding the man's coat and cane. Marcus's face lit when he saw her.

"You are in perfect time to take tea with me, my love, whilst I tell you my plans for the cottage," he said. "Belton, a pot of tea for two in the library, if you please."

"Of course, my lord," the butler murmured.

Isabella allowed Marcus to escort her into the library but once the door had closed behind them, her nerve nearly failed her. She could see the plans and drawings scattered across the table. Marcus started to speak, but she had no idea what he was talking about and after a moment he stopped, sensing her urgency. Isabella's heart leaped, battering her rib cage, and then settled to a frightened patter. Marcus came across to her.

"Bella?" he said. "Is something wrong? You look—" he paused, took her hand "—you look frightened."

She was frightened. She allowed him to draw her to sit beside him on the love seat in the window and then he waited, one brow quizzically raised, for her to explain. Isabella swallowed hard. There had been so little time; too little time to rebuild all the love and trust that had once been between them. And now she was going to put it all to the test. If it failed—if it was not strong enough—then she had made the wrong decision again.

"Marcus," she said. Her voice came out as a croak and she cleared her throat and tried again. Best just to come out with it. "I am sorry," she said. "I am not going to have a child."

She saw the flare of dread in his eyes. He made an instinctive move, as though to take her in his arms, and then he stopped, his expression tense. He took a breath; hesitated, and waited.

Isabella understood then that he was afraid. Wrapped up in her own fears, she had not thought of how Marcus might feel. Yet he had seen that there was something very wrong and now he must be afraid that she was about to extinguish the last shreds of hope for them by telling him that she was going to leave him. There was wariness in his expression now and he held himself very still.

"I am sorry, too," he said quietly. "But this need not be the end for us, Bella."

Isabella pressed her hands together so tightly that the bones cracked. "I was very afraid when I thought that I might be pregnant," she said. "It is difficult to explain. I lost my daughter before and I never wanted it to happen again."

The expression on Marcus's face eased into tenderness. He put his arms about her.

"I understand." He spoke very softly, his mouth pressed against her hair. "But I shall always be here with you,

Isabella. It will be different next time. And though you may not be *enceinte* now, there will come a time when we shall have our family."

Isabella shrank from him. She shook her head. He thought that he understood and he wanted to comfort her, and it almost broke her heart to see his gentleness. But he did not *know*. And now she had to tell him. She warded him off with one hand.

"No, Marcus. You do not understand because I have not told you. I should have done so long ago but..." She cleared her throat. "It is to do with Emma."

Marcus went very still. His eyes were on her face, dull with shock. "You are going to tell me that she was my child," he said.

"No," Isabella said. "It is worse than that." She looked at him, then swiftly away.

"I could never be absolutely sure," she said rapidly, "whether Emma was your child or not. I was young and it never even occurred to me that I might be pregnant. I missed my monthly courses but I told myself it was a result of the strain of the wedding...." She broke off. "Emma was born seven months after I married Ernest." Her voice was toneless. "She was a frail child. She could have been Ernest's daughter—she might have been born early. That was what we told everyone, of course. But I was never sure, one way or the other. It was always a torment to me."

She stood up blindly, taking a step away from him. "I wanted her to be yours!" She said. Her heart was breaking again, once and for all. "I told myself that she was! She was all that I had left of you and then, years later, I lost her." Her voice fell again. She looked up, looked Marcus in the eyes. "I failed her. I could not keep her safe and I cannot live with that. I never wanted it to happen again. That was why I never wanted another child. I lost you and then I lost the child I always thought of as yours and I do not wish to lose any more." Isabella turned away. "I tried so hard to protect her." Her shoulders slumped. "But in the end it was not enough."

There was a terrible silence. Marcus was very white. "Did Prince Ernest suspect that you thought Emma was not his?"

Isabella could not look at him for fear of what she might see in his face. She felt icy cold from the inside out.

"I do not know. We never spoke of it. As I said, Emma was small and frail when she was born. She could have been a seven-month child. Ernest never cared for her but I doubt that was a personal matter. He detested all children."

Marcus was silent, watching her. Isabella could feel the tension in all her muscles. Her body was as tight as a drum.

"After Emma died, I tried to forget the whole matter," she said. "And then of course I grew to know you again." She wanted to tell him that she loved him, that she had always loved him, that she always would. Instead she bit her lip. She had to finish this now, before she found it impossible to carry on.

"The closer we became, the more it preyed on my mind that I had kept this secret from you. I was afraid to tell you in case it destroyed what we were building between us. I could not live with this secret between us and I hope you can understand."

She turned away. Through the library window she could see the summerhouse, its edges blurring through her tears. She waited for Marcus to leave.

"Isabella," Marcus said.

Isabella turned.

He grabbed her so suddenly that she gasped for breath.

"Marcus!"

"Bella." Marcus's grip was painfully tight as he held her to him. "I understand. I wish—" He took a breath. "I only wish that I had always been there with you when you needed me. But I am here now." He held her a little away from him and her heart soared at the fierce light in his eyes. "I am here and I shall never leave you and you do not need to be afraid ever again."

Isabella gave a little sob and buried her face against his chest.

There was a knock on the door.

"Tea, my lord," Belton said lugubriously. He placed the tray on the table, fussily moving the plans aside, and completely ignoring the odd position in which he found his employers. "Do you wish for cake, my lord, my lady?"

"No, thank you," Marcus said. "We wish for champagne, but perhaps not until dinner."

He turned back to Isabella. "I love you," he said. He took a deep breath. "Do you remember when I gave you my signet ring at our marriage service?"

Isabella nodded mutely. She could not have spoken had she tried.

"I loved you even then," Marcus said. "I wanted to protect you." He took her hand and looked ruefully at the plain gold band that had replaced his signet ring. "You were mine and I wanted you to wear my ring because I could not go with you." He smiled into her eyes. "You said that you were tired of struggling. You do not need to struggle alone any longer, Bella."

Isabella smiled through her tears. "I love you, too, Marcus."

"I am sorry," Marcus said, "that it has taken me so long to understand how much I love you."

Isabella looked up to see Belton waiting stiffly to be dismissed, an expression on his face that suggested he had overheard some shocking conversations in his time, but never had he been unfortunate enough to eavesdrop on a declaration of love from his employer.

"Do you require anything else, my lady?" he asked stiffly.

"No, thank you, Belton," Isabella said. "Other than to be undisturbed."

She thought she saw a flicker of a smile on the butler's lips.

"Certainly, my lady," he said.

Isabella burrowed closer to the warmth of Marcus's body and felt his arms tighten about her and felt a violent surge of elation that they had not only survived but had also found each other again. Marcus pressed his lips to her hair and they stood, bound together tightly, for a very long time. When Marcus finally he released her, they were both slightly breathless.

"Has Belton gone?" Marcus inquired.

Isabella looked round. "I think so. I think he may even have locked the door."

"Thank goodness." Marcus was starting to undo the little row of buttons at the neck of her dress. He drew her bodice apart and started to kiss the pale, freckled skin that he was exposing. Isabella caught her breath.

"Marcus, we cannot do this here."

"Why not?" Marcus was tugging on the laces that held her chemise together.

Isabella gasped. "Because…"

The laces fluttered apart and Marcus slid a deft hand inside, palm against her breast. Isabella felt her knees weaken. She grabbed his arms.

"We should be more responsible now," Isabella said. "We have been married a whole two months."

Marcus sat down in the big armchair and pulled her down on top of him in a tumble of lace. "We can be very responsible. We can be responsible for choosing whether to do it on the table or in this chair, or on the lovely soft rug on the floor…."

Isabella gasped. "Not the table! You will crush all the architect's plans!"

"On the floor then," Marcus said. He pulled her down with him on the rug before the hearth. He pushed her bodice aside and kissed the curve of her shoulder and she trembled, catching her breath.

"I love you," he said. He moved her hair aside and stroked his tongue delicately down the line of her neck. "You are mine. You were from the beginning and now you always will be."

He rolled over, trapping her beneath him, and her body moved against his with instinctive need. His breath sent the shivers coursing along her nerves. He framed her face in his hands.

"Do you love me, Bella?"

"Yes," Isabella whispered. "I told you."

"Tell me again. I need to hear it many, many times."

Isabella grabbed his shirt and pulled him close. "Only if you tell me, too."

His mouth swooped down to take hers.

"I love you," he said when he drew away briefly for breath.

With one hand he brushed the shreds of the bodice away from her breasts.

"I love you," she said, as his mouth ravished the tender skin he had exposed.

"Always." His mouth came back to hers, courting and demanding a response at the same time. He eased away for a moment, unfastening his pantaloons with feverish haste.

The irrepressible laughter bubbled in Isabella's throat. "Marcus, making love to a lady with your boots on is not the behavior of a gentleman—"

Her words ended in a gasp as he pulled up her chemise and his hand lingered on the bare skin at the top of her silk stockings.

"Then I am no gentleman." He thrust into her. "But I do love you."

"Oh!" Isabella arched, felt him inside her, slick and hard. Her stomach muscles shivered, contracting. The shimmering heat built within her. She grabbed his shoulders, scoring her fingers on the material of his shirt.

"Marcus, the windows—"

"Yes."

"And the servants—"

"Yes."

"Anyone could see us—"

Marcus moved faster, deep inside her. Isabella's head spun. "When," she gasped, feeling the sensations build, the tantalizing ripple of desire along her skin, "when will you stop being so outrageous?"

"Never." With one final thrust, Marcus took her over the edge, to fall helplessly and blissfully together in a tumble of pure sensual pleasure. He buried his face in her damp shoulder. "But I do love you."

Later, curled up together in the chair with a cold cup of tea, Isabella told him about Pen finding the letter, and about Freddie—and India.

"The extraordinary thing," she said, "was that it was India who told Warwick about Freddie's weaknesses in the first place and gave him the lever he needed to get him in his power. I am sure she meant no harm by it, but she was his undoing." She rubbed her cheek against Marcus's shoulder and settled deeper into the curve of his arm. "Freddie told me that he had loved India since they were children. He never knew that it was Warwick who had been her lover." She paused. "Oh, he knew that India had had a lover and child, for she confided in him. He was the only one she ever told. But she never told him Warwick's name and he never asked. They worked together for years and never knew."

Marcus pressed a kiss to her brow.

"The letter that Pen found," he said. "Did you mind that the letter was *not* from me to you?" He sighed. "I wish I had pushed harder to find you, Bella, to talk to you. I loved you so much. I would have run away with you, married or free…."

Isabella smiled. "No more regrets, Marcus. We do not need them now." She touched a finger to his lips to silence him. "Nor do I need the affirmation of a letter," she said. "Not when I have you."

And she turned once more into the warmth of his embrace.

What news! A certain vivacious princess, whose lack of enthusiasm for the amorous skills of Englishmen was reported in this paper last year, has found eternal bliss with her very own Adonis in the form of the Earl of S. It is to be assumed that the earl was successful in changing the lady's mind on the subject of Englishmen being the very worst lovers in the world, for apparently the couple are expecting their first child in a few months' time. What alacrity! What enthusiasm! We wish the earl and countess a very happy and amorous future together.

—*The Gentlemen's Athenian Mercury*, May 18, 1817

Read all about it…

MORE ABOUT THIS BOOK

MORE ABOUT THE AUTHOR

WE RECOMMEND

Read all about it...

NICOLA CORNICK ON WRITING
Deceived

I love writing Regency romance. It was a period of huge contrasts with the glittering social whirl at the top of society throwing the abject poverty and depredation of the underworld into sharp relief. One of the reasons why I think the Regency period is so popular is the fascinating contrast between the outward show of manners and the intense emotions that may be hidden beneath the surface. One of the challenges for the writer is to find a way that these emotions may be expressed within the constraints of the manners and behaviour of the time.

The idea of giving *Deceived* a seaside background came to me when I was reading *Sanditon* by Jane Austen. This was the period when the seaside resort was becoming fashionable and replacing the inland spa as a place to take the waters. George III liked to visit Worthing. The Prince Regent preferred Brighton. Bathing machines – small sheds on wheels taken out into the water by horses – were in use as early as 1735. Bathers were helped down into the water by male and female dippers, many of whom were fat and frequently drunk, who wore waterproof wrappings and, in the women's case, large bonnets. The seaside town began to acquire all the trappings of the fashionable spa town with assembly rooms, a circulating library and social events to entertain the visitors.

My own love of the sea combined with my research into the history of seaside resorts to provide the background to the second half of *Deceived*. When I was a child we took seaside holidays every year, visiting Somerset and staying in an ancient cottage with little stone

"... I love writing Regency romance..."

3

monuments in the garden that were covered in moss and were totally intriguing to a child. I loved the beach, the freedom of walking for miles along the sands, and the way that the nature of the sea changed so quickly from calm to storm.

Read all about it...

4

Read all about it...

FURTHER RECOMMENDED READING

If you would like to find out more about this fascinating period in history, Nicola Cornick recommends the following books:

That Sunny Dome: A Portrait of Regency Britain by Donald A Low

The Prince of Pleasure and His Regency by JB Priestley

Our Tempestuous Day: A History of Regency England by Carolly Erikson

The English: A Social History 1066 – 1945 by Christopher Hibbert

Piers of the Isle of Wight by Marian Lane

The British Seaside by John Walton

Please note that these are Nicola Cornick's recommendations. Inclusion on this list does not indicate recommendation by the publisher, or any representation as to the content of these sources. Nor does it indicate that any of these entities have endorsed *Deceived* or use of their listings here.

AUTHOR BIOGRAPHY

Nicola was born in Yorkshire and spent the first eighteen years of her life there. She credits these early years with having a formative effect on her writer's imagination in several ways. Firstly she went to school in an historic house – Gateways High School, the eighteenth century dower house that once belonged to the Earls of Harewood. In such auspicious surroundings her love of history and writing flourished, encouraged by some wonderful teachers. She also spent hours walking on the moors that inspired the Brontës and devoured a diet of costume dramas and historical novels. It was also during this time that she developed a love of choral music and sang with various choirs that toured the UK and Europe.

When she was eighteen Nicola went to London University, where she studied Medieval History and met her future husband. It was also at this time that Nicola began her first book, which, fourteen years later, was to be published as *True Colours*.

"...She also spent hours walking on the moors that inspired the Brontës..."

After graduation, Nicola returned to Yorkshire and took a post working at Leeds University organising student scholarships. Over the next fifteen years she was to develop her career in university administration, and worked in various educational institutions, organising examinations and degree ceremonies, arranging open days and managing a team of staff providing pastoral support to students. She worked for the Department for Education in the South West for three years, organising the provision of funding for short courses for adult learners. This job necessitated a move to Somerset, where her home was a seventeenth century cottage haunted by the ghost of a cavalier.

Read all about it...

It was during this time that Nicola and her husband travelled widely and her fondest memories include lying in the snow to watch the Northern Lights in Norway, taking a balloon over an African game reserve, swimming in hot spa springs in Iceland and swinging through the rainforest canopy in Costa Rica.

Nicola went back to university in 2004 to study for a Masters Degree in Public History at Ruskin College, Oxford. She is currently researching the history of the National Trust property Ashdown House, in Oxfordshire, where she works as a guide. Her other interests are wildlife and conservation – she does voluntary work for the RSPB – and training guide dog puppies for the Guide Dogs for the Blind Association.

NICOLA CORNICK ON WRITING

What do you love most about being a writer?

I feel very happy to be able to do a job that I love. I love creating characters and sharing their world. And the feeling I get when the writing is going well and I'm on a roll fills me with elation.

Where do you go for inspiration?

I go to several different places for inspiration. If I'm feeling studious I will turn to my history books for ideas and stimulation. If I need to think I will go out for a walk on the hills to clear my head. And if I want to soak up some historical inspiration I will visit a castle or ancient site and just absorb the atmosphere.

Where do your characters come from and do they ever surprise you as you write?

"... My characters surprise me all the time..."

My characters surprise me all the time because I can never predict in advance what they are going to do. As the story progresses they will take on a mind and a will of their own and react to the developments in the plot in their own way, and that's just how it should be. They become very real to me. Sometimes they spring from a story idea I have had, sometimes they are a mixture of qualities and behaviours that I have observed in real people, but mostly they are individuals whose needs and motivations develop naturally.

Do you have a favourite character that you've created and what is it that you like about that character?

Asking me to choose a favourite character is like asking me to choose between my cats! I love them all. In *Deceived* I liked Isabella's sister Pen a lot because she was so pretty on the outside but sharp as a needle underneath and I felt she had a real conflict in loyalty towards her sister whilst needing to survive.

When did you start writing?

I started to write stories when I was at school and I still have the reports praising my imagination but telling me to cut down the number of adjectives and adverbs! I started my first book, *True Colours*, when I was about eighteen and used to read passages out to my college friends over a late night coffee. I was writing the same book for fourteen years. The difficulty was fitting in my writing between the demands of my family and day job, but I never gave up on it and when it was finally accepted for publication I was over the moon. Before that I hadn't even considered a career as a writer.

What one piece of advice would you give to a writer wanting to start a career?

Believe in yourself and your writing. Believe that you will be successful even if you are trying to juggle your writing with a job, family and a hundred and one other responsibilities. Don't give up. Writers need to be determined to succeed!

What are you currently working on?

I'm working on a Regency historical set in Yorkshire in 1812. The heroine has a dark past and has reinvented herself completely, but she never feels quite safe with all the secrets she has to keep. And then the hero arrives and throws her life into disarray because she realises he is a threat to her, both in terms of exposing her past and because of the way he makes her feel. It's very dark, intense, sexy and passionate!

"... Believe in yourself and your writing..."

A DAY IN THE LIFE

The cats – Bob and Petra – wake me up at 6.00am demanding that I let them into the bedroom. I know that if I ignore them they'll rip the carpet to shreds so it's easier to stumble out of bed, still with my eyes closed, and open the door. Once we're all in the bedroom it's a four-way fight for the duvet between Bob, Petra, my husband and me. I lose. I am just drifting off to sleep again on my remaining square centimetre of bed when the alarm goes off. I push my husband several times until he gets up to make our morning tea, at which point the cats move onto his side of the bed, the dog comes up to join them and I shiver under my tiny bit of duvet.

"... I love walking on the hills whilst the sun is rising..."

If it's my turn to take the dog out for a walk I will go out early. I love walking on the hills whilst the sun is rising and the dew is still fresh on the grass. My best writing ideas come to me when I am out in the open air. Out on the Downs, walking along the Ridgeway, I can actually *feel* the layers of history beneath my feet and the presence of it all around me. There is something so refreshing and inspirational for me in being outside. Sometimes when I am in the house I feel too confined. If I am stuck on a point of plot or uncertain which direction my characters are going to take, I'll put on my walking boots and set off for the hills. Our dog gets plenty of walks! Sometimes I think he'd rather lie on the couch, fast asleep, but he never refuses to come with me.

When I get back at about 9.00am I'll make a cup of tea and settle down to my writing. My office has big windows looking out over our garden and the fields beyond. This is a problem because the view is so wonderful and frequently distracts me. In the summer I have the long windows open so that it is almost working outside.

I write directly onto the computer although I make notes longhand in lots of big notebooks. Sometimes the writing is quick and easy, flowing so smoothly that I can't bear to stop and resent any interruption or other demand on my time. At other times it feels leaden and seems to take forever just to get the words down on the page. But it's important to persist because I can improve on bad writing whereas I can't improve on a blank page. I always find a cup of tea in hand helps too! Occasionally I will look at the clock and realise that for fifteen years I worked nine to five in an office and although I miss the people I worked with, I would far rather be an author. Then I feel very fortunate.

If it's my day to work for the National Trust at Ashdown House I will go out after lunch and spend several hours there guiding visitors around the house and gardens. I love Ashdown with a deep passion and enjoy sharing it with other people and showing them what a fascinating place it is. It's a seventeenth century hunting lodge with an extremely romantic history and I am busy researching the estate at the moment in order to write a book about it one day. Working in an historic house is another huge inspiration for me. Sometimes I just stand on the stairs and inhale the fabric of history that is all around me. To me, history isn't just something that's in the past. It's tangible in the present, all around us, influencing what we do and how we think. I love to try and capture that feeling in my writing and make my historical stories come alive.

My husband usually cooks dinner for us. He enjoys cooking and is great at it so there's no point in me slaving away in the kitchen to produce a vastly inferior meal. I always do the washing up, though! In the evening I'll often go back to my writing again, re-read what I wrote

that morning, decide it isn't too bad and add a
few more pages before bedtime. If I'm not
writing then I'll be reading, either for pleasure or
for research. I love historical non-fiction but I
always have to read with a paper and pen at my
elbow so that I can jot down story ideas that
come to me. Occasionally we'll go out to the
theatre or cinema, but my husband says I am the
worst sort of person to see a film with because I
will always be analysing the plot and the
structure as I go along and will make whispered
comments that put him off the story. It's hard
not to do that as a writer. The books and films
that I admire the most are the ones that are so
good I forget to analyse and just sit back and
enjoy.

"...If I'm not writing then I'll be reading..."

At about 8.00pm I will have my final cup of tea
of the day and then I take the dog out for his
bedtime stroll around the fields behind our
house. It's very peaceful and I will take in the
view and unwind after the day. Sometimes we
will see a barn owl hunting over the fields, or
watch the moon rise over the hills and the stars
come out. I need my eight hours sleep a night so
by 10.00pm I am usually curled up in bed with a
good book – what could be better?

Read all about it...

NICOLA CORNICK'S FUTURE PROJECTS

My next book, *Lord of Scandal*, is set against the background of the Great Frost Fair of 1814. The heroine, Catherine Fenton, is heiress to a huge fortune but her family is falling apart and she is desperately trying to hold them all together. When her path crosses that of Ben Hawksmoor, celebrity and friend of the Prince Regent, the scandalous lord determines to have Catherine and her fortune for himself, but he has underestimated Catherine's determination to re-sist him. In *Lord of Scandal* I particularly enjoyed exploring the idea of celebrity in nineteenth century London and the parallels with modern life.

Lord of Scandal will be available
in February 2008.

Don't miss it!

Read all about it...

If you enjoyed *Deceived*, we know you'll love these great reads.

The Steepwood Scandals

A young woman disappears. A husband is suspected of murder. Stirring times for all the neighbourhood in *The Steepwood Scandals*... When the debauched Marquis of Sywell won Steepwood Abbey years ago at cards, it led to the death of the then Earl of Eardley. Now he's caused scandal again by marrying a girl out of his class – and young enough to be his grand-daughter! After being married only a short time, the Marchioness has disappeared, leaving no trace of her whereabouts. There is every expectation that yet more scandals will emerge, though no one yet knows just how shocking they will be. Regency drama, intrigue, mischief...and marriage.

On sale now!

The Railwayman's Daughter by Dee Yates

In 1875, a row of tiny cottages stands by the tracks of the newly built York – Doncaster railway... Railwayman Tom Swales, with his wife and five daughters, takes the end cottage. With no room to spare in the loving Swales household, eldest daughter Mary accepts a position as housemaid to the nearby stationmaster. There she battles the daily grime from the passing trains – and the stationmaster's brutal, lustful nature...

On sale from 16th March!

Smile old here
forget the art of us